Secrets of the Heart

Secrets of the Heart

by

Jannifer Hoffman

To Eliane

Wonderful to meet
you on the Princess Star
Enjoy Reading

Jannifer Hoffman

Resplendence Publishing, LLC
http://www.resplendencepublishing.com

Resplendence Publishing, LLC
P.O. Box 992
Edgewater, Florida, 32132

Secrets of the Heart
Copyright © 2008, Jannifer Hoffman
Edited by Chantal Depp
Cover art by Rika Singh
Print format ISBN: 978-1-934992-21-0
Electronic format ISBN: 978-1-934992-41-8

Electronic release: September, 2008
Trade paperback printing: December, 2008

For the children in my life

Troy, Dustin and Kyle Soderman
Jamie and Jessie LeClaire
Sarah and Rebecca Madsen
Ava and Jaymes Christie
Mikaela Gobel

Many thanks to
Bonnie Barrett and Louise Hoffman, my first readers
Alice, Sara, and Joann from the Augsburg writers group
Kelly Kirch and Terri Schultz (I love you guys)
Pinkie Paranya, terrific friend and writer
Laurie Soderman for just being there
Chantal, my fantastic editor
And last, but not least, Tony Hoffman
Always willing to drive the extra mile(s) for his mom

Chapter One

New York City

Forced to a crawling pace, Hunter took special pains to avoid looking at the crash site. However, keeping his eyes fixed on the Ford mini-van ahead of him, didn't block out the stench of burnt oil, the hiss of steaming radiators, and sobbing victims, or the oppressive memories that sent his heart rate slamming into overdrive.

The accident must have happened in the last few minutes because, though sirens screamed in the distance, neither ambulance nor police were on the scene.

Hunter's memories carried him to another time. He was nine years old, and Diana was screaming for help. They—the people who seemed to know these things—said she couldn't have screamed; she died instantly, but he still woke up in a sweat hearing her screams. Not so often anymore, but always when he least expected it.

In two weeks, on June first, Diana, with her flaming red hair, cute button nose, and ear-to-ear freckles, would have turned thirty. Because of him, Diana never reached her sixth birthday.

How many years had to pass before guilt gave you peace?

An hour later, home in his upscale Manhattan apartment, Hunter picked up his mail, downed a glass of orange juice, and headed to his spare bedroom to give himself a mind-clearing workout.

Ten minutes into his routine, the phone rang. Stifling his irritation, he dropped his weights, grabbed a towel, and headed for the nearest phone. He answered it with a curt, "Yeah, Hunter here."

"Hunter... Douglas?" The woman's hesitant question when she said his last name, prepared him for a telemarketer.

"Yeah, and I'm not buying anything."

"Sorry if I disturbed you," she said. "This is Karen Wilda from the 249th Precinct in Manhattan."

Hunter swiped the towel over his sweating brow. "What can I do for you, Ms. Wilda?"

"Well, unfortunately I have some sad news for you. A friend of yours, Brenda Casey, died this afternoon."

Friend? She'd found his business number in the phone book and hired him to locate her biological father. Afterwards, they'd had a brief affair, then parted on good terms by mutual agreement. He wasn't happy to hear she had died, but he had no idea how the police connected her to him.

"I haven't seen or heard from Brenda in over seven years," he said. "Why are you calling me?"

"She left a note with your name and phone number."

Hunter sank down in a chair, not liking where this was going. "A note? What was the cause of her death?"

Karen sighed. "There will be an autopsy but it appears to be suicide. She left several notes actually, one of them concerning her two children."

Hunter's heart kicked up a notch. "Two children?"

"Brenda left papers asking you to be the person to notify her sister in Minnesota. The sister, Nicole Anderson, signed a document agreeing to take custody of the children should anything happen to Brenda. An attached memo states that you'd know exactly how to locate Ms. Anderson and could deliver the children to her. Since Chief Connors here knows you personally, he vouched for your credibility."

Hunter would have to remember to thank his good friend, Ralph Connors.

Karen went on to explain that the department was willing to pay for his services, plus expenses, and could he please pick the children up within the hour.

* * * *

Staring at the six-year-old child asleep on his sofa, Hunter experienced a tightening in his chest. Her frayed jeans suffered from too many trips through the washing machine; her stained jacket—not enough. Dirty toes peeked through faded, pink tennis shoes long since outgrown. Her thin arms clutched protectively around her equally tattered four-year-old brother.

The sleeping girl with her unkempt, matted red hair looked like somebody's throwaway Raggedy Ann doll. She bore no resemblance to him whatsoever, but the rich, red hue of her curls, the freckles, and the button nose... identical to Diana.

He pulled a faded photograph from his wallet; the last one taken of his pixie faced little sister. The likeness was uncanny. It left no doubt in his mind. The child was his.

Pain welled inside him. Gut-wrenching pain. Damn her! Why couldn't Brenda have told him he had a daughter? He would have helped. Then again, from what he remembered of Brenda Casey, she probably didn't know whose baby she carried.

It suddenly struck him. After passing the crash on the highway earlier, he'd been recapping his life and found it seriously lacking. He just didn't know what it lacked until this very minute. He came from good family stock, a loving mother and father. Maybe raising this mistreated child, giving her a happy home, could somehow make up for the little girl who never had a chance to grow up, because of him.

But what were the chances that Nicole Anderson would turn her niece and nephew over to him? With a paternity test, he might be able to gain custody of the girl, but he didn't have a fireman's chance in hell of getting the boy. Only God knew who had fathered him. After what those two had been through, it would be cruel and unconscionable to separate them. He had to convince Ms. Anderson they'd be better off with him.

He picked up the phone and dialed the Minnesota number.

* * * *

Nicole put the finishing touches on a complicated sketch of a Renaissance costume when the phone rang. She glanced irritably at the clock. Who would be calling her at midnight? Without taking her eyes from her sketch, she reached past the sample books, spread out in front of her, for the receiver.

"Hello."

After a moment of silence, a man's husky voice came over the line. "Hello. Nicole Anderson?"

Nicole laid her drawing pencil down. "Yes."

"Ms. Anderson, this is Hunter Douglas. You don't know me, but unfortunately, it was left to me to make this call. I'm afraid I have some bad news for you."

Nicole jumped to her feet. "My God, is it Billy? Has something happened to Billy?"

"No. It's not your brother. It's your sister, Brenda. I really hate doing this over the phone, but with you living so far away, I had no choice. Your sister is… your sister died this afternoon."

Red-hot anger sliced through Nicole. "Who are you and what kind of a sick joke is this?"

"This is Nicole Anderson, isn't it? Your father was Robert C. Anderson of Anderson Design, was he not? You have a brother, William, and you live in your grandfather's house on Sunset Lake in northern Minnesota."

Nicole slumped back into her chair, her breathing laborious. "Yes, but—"

"Are you all right? Do you have anyone there with you?"

"Yes, I'm fine and no, I have no one here with me. Just who are you exactly, and who put you up to this nonsense?"

"I told you, my name is Hunter Douglas. I'm—I did some work for Brenda a few years ago, and she left my name as the person to contact in case of an emergency. Why are you snapping at me?"

"Listen, Bozo. I don't have a sister!" Nicole pressed the receiver into its cradle. Prank phone calls were an invasion of her privacy. She despised them.

Clasping her shaking hands together, she glanced about her homey little studio, trying to calm the adrenaline rush the call had given her. Her skin felt hot and clammy at the same time. How did he know her father's name and that she had a brother?

Rubbing her neck, she swiveled her head, trying to knead out the knot of tension that came from leaning over a sketchbook all day. Maybe she'd give Billy a call just to make sure he was okay.

Just as she reached for the phone, it started to ring again. She snatched her hand back as though something had bit it. It was probably that obnoxious Hunter Douglas again but maybe it was Billy.

Drawing a deep breath, she lifted the handset and put it to her ear.

"Nicole?"

It *was* Hunter Douglas.

"Nicole! Don't hang up again. Please."

Nicole gritted her teeth. "All right, you have thirty seconds to explain why you've chosen me to be on the receiving end of your little joke."

"Look, I don't know what your relationship was with your sister, but that's not the point here—"

"Will you get it through your thick skull? I don't have a sister, period."

"Lady, if it wasn't for the kids, I'd gladly hang up on you—"

"What kids?"

"Brenda's kids!"

Nicole made a frustrated growling sound. "Mister, you are testing my patience. But I'll admit you've piqued my curiosity."

"Well, thank God for small favors."

"Sarcasm will only get this phone slammed in your ear. Now kindly tell me who Brenda is and why you think she… was my sister, and what do you have to do with all this?"

An exasperated sigh came through the line. "About seven years ago, Brenda hired an investigator to find her father. All she had was a name and a city. In truth, I suspect she just wanted to know why the checks stopped coming."

"What checks?"

"The checks your father sent to Brenda's mother every month."

Nicole took a deep breath, then another one. "My father sent checks to Brenda's mother? Why?" The last word came out in a suspicious squeak.

"I think you already know the answer to that."

"Keep talking."

"Apparently your father had an affair with a woman named Yvonne Casey. Brenda must have been the result of that liaison. Look, I'm sorry. I thought you knew. She knew all about you and Billy. So I just assumed—"

"How did she know all about us?"

"As I said, she hired an investigator when the checks stopped coming."

"Let me guess, you were the private investigator?"

"Actually, I'm more of a genealogy investigator, but yes, I did the research for her."

"Then you know my father died seven years ago."

"Yes."

"Just exactly how old was Brenda when she died?"

"Around, twenty-nine, I think."

Nicole rubbed a shaking hand over her eyes wishing she could blot out this entire conversation. She was twenty-eight. Billy twenty-two. Dear God. Her parents had always seemed so loving toward each other. They rarely argued. But if he sent checks every month…

"Are you still there?" he asked.

"Yes. I'm kind of in shock here."

"Under the circumstances, that's understandable, I guess. But…like I said before, I wouldn't be calling if it weren't for the two kids, Shanna and Kyle. Brenda listed you as next of kin. She granted custody to you."

"What?"

"She granted—"

"I heard you. I'm just having a little problem believing all this. You're telling me I'm now responsible for two kids? Kids that belonged to a sister, a half-sister, I didn't even know I had?"

Nicole had to pause a moment to remind herself to breathe—and think. This whole thing was preposterous. She couldn't take on two kids. Lord, they could be toddlers. The haunting memory of a stillborn baby had long ago proved she was unfit to be a mother.

Frustration and anger, at being put on the spot, goaded her. "You may as well know, Mr. Douglas, I have zero maternal instincts. I have no desire to have kids of my own, much less, someone else's. I have a business to run and a career. Where is her husband? Why isn't he responsible for them?"

"Brenda never married."

"Fine, they must still have a father?"

"Why don't you calm down, Nicole?"

She gritted her teeth. "Don't tell me to calm down. I have a legitimate reason to be upset."

"No you don't. The kids have a good home to go to if

you don't want them. All you have to do is sign some papers and it will be taken care of. I'll contact you in a couple of days. We can handle it over the phone and with faxes, if you would like."

Nicole tried to think. He was giving her an out, but why was he suddenly being so amiable? She was getting a real uneasy feeling in her gut. "Where will they go?" she asked.

"I was under the impression you didn't care."

"Why are you being such a jerk? I'm not exactly heartless. You throw all this at me in a heartbeat, then, without even giving me a chance to think, calmly act as though it's no big deal. If I don't take them—who will?"

The long silence that followed her question increased Nicole's uneasiness by the second.

Finally, he said, "I will."

A chill shot through her that had nothing to do with room temperature. "Why? Is there possibly some insurance money involved?"

"You really are heartless, aren't you? You didn't even ask how old they are, or how they're handling the death of their mother, or who's caring for them now. Does it matter to you that their mother was likely a prostitute and they've been living in a two-room hell-hole where they were lucky if they got one meal a day?"

Nicole winced, suddenly finding it an effort to breathe. This nightmare-delivering messenger was twisting a knife in her chest. If Brenda truly was her sister, even half-sister, these children were blood relatives. She had an obligation to make sure they went to a good home.

"I'd like to see them," she whispered.

"Why? So you can decide if they're worthy of your affections?"

"That's an asinine thing to say. You don't know me. You don't know anything about me. I said I want to see them. For all I know you're a… a money-grubbing, two–bit investigator working out of a cluttered, smoke-infested, little office with a short-skirted secretary whose main goal in life is getting her nails buffed."

"Miss Anderson, you've read a few too many dime store novels."

"I want to see those kids. Now, where are they?"

"Asleep on my sofa."

"I mean what city? Where are you calling from...Minneapolis?"

"New York."

Groaning, Nicole swallowed hard at the lump in her throat while trying to think. She had twenty-five Renaissance costumes to design and make for a play opening in six weeks. That would include a full day in Minneapolis taking measurements after receiving approval for the designs.

"I want to come and see them, but I need to check my schedule. Give me a number where you can be reached."

He rattled off a number. "That's my fax. Send me directions to your place. I'll bring them to see you—along with the papers to sign." The next thing she heard was a click, then a buzz. He had hung up.

Nicole stared at the phone, swearing under her breath. *The arrogant ass.* He gave her no clue as to when he was coming. She had no way to contact him, except by fax. How old were the children anyway? Boys? Girls? One of each? He had told her their names, but she hadn't been listening at the time. *Damn him.* Did she dare swear on a fax?

Thinking about the children, brought to mind the mother—Brenda. Nicole didn't recall Hunter Douglas mentioning a last name or how Brenda died. He had said she was a prostitute. What a traumatic life they must have had. If Nicole's father really had an affair, she'd had an older sister—half sister. That thought was more than a little disturbing.

* * * *

After a restless night trying to sleep, Nicole decided

her best course of action was to be civil to Hunter Douglas, at least, until she knew a few more details. She postponed calling Billy. For all she knew, the whole thing could be a hoax. She found it impossible to comprehend her father having an affair. For the first time in six years, she was glad her mother was dead and wouldn't have to deal with any of this. God, what morbid thinking.

She wrote out the directions he wanted, along with a map simple enough for a dimwit to follow and requested that he let her know when to expect them. She also asked if he could kindly send some info regarding the ages and sex of the children. She included her own fax number, hoping he'd communicate that way rather than calling her again. She stuck the memo in the fax, punched in the number, and pressed send.

With that finished, she went back to her drawings and buried herself in her work. As a rule, just being in her cozy studio, surrounded by heavy volumes on costume design and medieval styles, did that for her. The sizeable room took up but a minor corner of the three-story Victorian mansion she'd inherited from her grandfather. The elegant old home was a community landmark and built on the shore of picturesque Sunset Lake.

Off the studio, a spacious room—a ballroom at one time—housed the shop where they did sewing and assembly, and served as a store that was open to the public by appointment only. She employed two women to help with the sewing, and one man, Chuck Martin, did the leatherwork, ordered shoes, and any necessary metal parts for the costumes. Besides being her right-hand man, Chuck was her dearest friend.

An eight-foot-wide open stairway led to the five bedrooms on the second floor. The third floor was an open attic used for storage. Her housekeeper and cook, Berta, lived in three rooms above the garage with her husband, Hank, who did the grounds work and maintained a small vegetable garden.

The house was entirely too big for Nicole and too costly to keep up, but she loved it along with all the antique furnishings that came with it. It took a lot of long hours each day to pay her expenses. Fortunately, Billy had a trust fund to pay for his college.

For what seemed the hundredth time that day, Nicole checked the fax machine beside her worktable. Nothing. Damn that man. He was ignoring her on purpose.

The next day she faxed her completed sketches to the theater director in the Twin Cities and got back an approval an hour later. Tomorrow was Saturday. In the morning, she had to make the hundred-mile drive into Minneapolis to do the measurements.

Nicole considered sending Hunter Douglas a memo telling him she'd be gone for the day but decided against it. He was really irritating her. She had a sinking feeling she might never hear from him again. That thought should have made her happy but it didn't. It was impossible to get those kids off her mind.

What would make her **happy was** to find out Douglas was really a decent guy with a nice wife who really wanted to add two kids to their family. Trying to imagine that was a stretch.

* * * *

Her Saturday in Minneapolis had been grueling but successful. Nicole turned her Chevy Blazer north onto the freeway for the hour-and-a-half drive home. She glanced at the clock on the dash—almost seven. Her back ached from all the bending and stretching she'd done; her empty stomach growled angrily for food; and she'd been unable to push aside a feeling of foreboding.

To add to her misery, the sky clouded over, and the glow of lightning on the northern horizon promised a May thunderstorm. The farther north she got, the more threatening the sky became. It looked like a torrential downpour was in store, and she seriously doubted she'd make it home before it unleashed its fury.

If that weren't enough, she'd bet a hundred dollars there wouldn't be a fax from Hunter Douglas waiting for her.

On a whim, she'd stopped at a toy store and picked up a curly-haired doll, a squishy Teddy bear, and some books for various ages ranging from two to five. She could kick herself for not remembering those names. She really wanted to kick Douglas for being so rude and not giving her a chance to ask more questions.

The man was an arrogant jerk, probably middle-aged, pudgy, balding—and short. Perfect. She'd love to be able to stare straight into his face—or better yet—look down on him from her five foot eight inch height.

Driving rain pelted her windshield when she pulled up to her house and spied a dark blue sedan parked out front.

Chapter Two

The car parked in the circular drive directly in front was still running. The house was completely dark; including the security lights outside. The storm must have knocked down some power lines.

Nicole's heart did leapfrog in her chest. She tried to still her nerves and think rational thoughts as she pulled up to the garage on the south side of the house and pushed the opener. Of course, nothing happened. Damn. The rain still came down in sheets.

She swore again as she dug in her purse, looking for her house keys. She didn't have an umbrella, and now she had to race in the rain to get to the front door. This was not at all how she envisioned meeting Hunter Douglas for the first time.

By the time she got her front door open, she was soaked. Without closing the door behind her, she hurried to the fireplace, found a match, and lit the large oil lamp on top of the mantel. When she replaced the tall glass chimney, its soft glow filled the immediate area.

"Do you have a flashlight?"

Nicole whirled around with a small gasp. A tall man, towering actually, stood in the darkened doorway.

"Sorry, didn't mean to startle you. Do you have a

flashlight?"

For a second, she held her breath, gaping open-mouthed at the shadowed figure. Even if she hadn't recognized the deep timber of his voice, the New York accent would have told her who he was. Of course, he had an umbrella—and a jacket.

She found her voice quickly. "Yes, in my studio. I'll get it." She fumbled her way to the studio and quickly lit another lamp on her worktable.

"What's with all the lamps? Is this a common occurrence here?"

Nicole gave a startled shriek.

"Woman, you sure are jumpy."

"I'm not used to having a strange man follow me around in the dark," she snapped.

"I'm Hunter Douglas. I've been called a lot of things but never strange. You must be Nicole Anderson."

Nicole stared up into deep-set Steven Seagal eyes, the kind her assistant, Carmen, called bedroom eyes. They were dark, made even darker by the pallid light. His straight Roman nose and sturdy jaw line added to his masculinity, as did his dark hair—the exact shade undistinguishable where he stood in the shadows. A wayward strand fell over his forehead in a jaunty, Clark Gable, sort of way.

His full lips were anything but smiling, making her aware that she was staring. She gave herself a sharp mental kick, determined not to allow this man to intimidate her.

"Yes, I'm Nicole. Sorry you had to wait, but since I didn't know when you were co—"

"No problem. We've only been here a few minutes. This place is the devil to find in the dark and even harder, with the rain. Does that thing work?"

She handed him the flashlight. "I'm not sure, try it. Are the kids in the car?"

"Yeah. They're both sleeping. I'll bring them in."

"I'll help you."

"No. I'll do it." He took the flashlight, tested it, then turned and walked out.

Nicole stared after him. This was not going to be pleasant.

She took the lamp back into the foyer, suddenly aware of her wet clothes and the damp chill in the air. She flicked the switch on the gas fireplace in the huge entrance hall. At least that worked without electricity.

Hunter returned with a child sleeping on his shoulder. "I think he's out for the night. Do you have a bedroom handy?"

Nicole nodded. "Upstairs. Follow me." She held the lamp high and led the way up the open staircase gracing the center of the room.

Continuous flares of lightning from the wall of windows beyond the stairway gave the huge cavity of the house a strobe-like effect. Each flash closely followed by a horrific crash of thunder.

"This place looks like something out of a Gothic novel," he said in a hushed voice. "How many people live here anyway?"

"Just me," she said over her back. "Oh, and Mr. Komodo."

"You live in this monstrous house alone? With a dragon?"

"Mr. Komodo is a cat. He belonged to my grandmother. I only mentioned him because he is rather large, and he has a habit of showing up at the oddest times. He's quite harmless though." She opened the first bedroom door, went inside, and set the lamp down. "The housekeeper and her husband live in the rooms above the garage. It is a big house, but I work here too. It doesn't look nearly as ominous with lights."

"That's encouraging. I was beginning to wonder if you even had electricity. You seem awfully comfortable with those lamps."

"I am. They put me in the proper mood when I work."

She pulled the covers back on a double bed so he could lay the sleeping child down. When he bent over, Hunter's short leather jacket squeaked of quality. Nicole moved the lamp, so the boy's perfectly round, little face showed in the light. He had a smooth, olive complexion and dark hair that seemed a bit too long. "He's beautiful," she whispered, brushing dark curls back from his angelic sleeping face.

A corner of Hunter's mouth kicked up ever so slightly as he pulled the boy's jacket and shoes off before covering him. "I guess they can just sleep in their clothes tonight. Boys don't like to be called beautiful, Nicole. Maybe handsome, even cute, but never pretty or beautiful." Not waiting for her to comment, he added, "I better get Shanna before she wakes up out there alone. You can wait here."

Nicole turned the gas fireplace in the room on low and waited at the top of the landing with the lamp. Moments later, Hunter came up the stairs with a redheaded girl in tow. She looked at Nicole with sleepy, wary eyes.

"Hello, Shanna," Nicole said softly.

Shanna turned, pressing face and thin body against Hunter's leg. He picked her up, and she put her arms around his neck and buried her face in his leather shoulder. "It's okay honey. There's nothing to be afraid of. The storm put the lights out. They'll be on tomorrow, and everything will be better then."

When Nicole started to lead the way to a second bedroom, Hunter stopped her. "They need to sleep in the same room."

"I have plenty of rooms—"

He carried Shanna into the first bedroom while speaking over his shoulder. "I'm sure you do, but they need to be together. I'll explain later." Hunter set her on the bed to take off her shoes and jacket. "Do you need to use the bathroom?" he asked. She shook her head and leaned over to whisper something in his ear.

Hunter's gaze flicked briefly to Nicole before he placed a quick kiss on Shanna's forehead, a soft chuckle rumbling from his throat. "I know sweetheart, but I'm sure it's only because she was out in the rain. To bed now. If you need anything, just call for me. Okay?"

Shanna nodded, crawled under the covers, and laid down, wiggling over until she was molded against her brother. She gathered him to her like a little mother protecting her child.

Across the bed, Nicole met Hunter's gaze in quiet understanding.

Hunter left the door ajar, and they walked down the stairs together, Nicole holding the lamp.

"What did she say?" Nicole asked.

"That you were scary." A slow grin lifted the corners of his mouth. "Before you say anything, you should look in a mirror holding that lamp in front of you like that."

Nicole opened her mouth, but nothing came out. Her hand went to her hair hanging to her shoulders like wet strings. The phrase "drowned rat" came to mind. "Good heavens, I must look like a witch."

Hunter snickered. "You said it, I didn't." He glanced at her dress. "Do you live in the dark ages here?"

Nicole looked down and groaned. She forgot she was dressed in a sixteenth century morning gown. She often wore her costumes when she worked. It added authenticity to her work and was a good form of advertising.

"I—I can explain this, but I think I better go change and dry off first."

"Okay, I have some bags to get out of the car. I hate to impose on you, but I can't leave them here alone to wake up to a complete stranger. Do you have a room I could use?"

"You can have the one next door to the kids…where I was going to put Shanna. That way you can be nearby if they need you. There's a bathroom connecting the two rooms. Real running water, even." He raised an eyebrow at that, but she left him wondering if she were being serious. "If it's chilly, you can switch the fireplace on. It'll be toasty warm in no time at all. I'll meet you back here in a few minutes. Do you want me to get a lamp for you?"

He gave her an amused, sideways glance. "I think I'll just use the flashlight if you don't mind. You have a fireplace in every room?"

Nicole managed a small smile. "Not quite, but the house was built at the turn of the century and was the only source of heat for the upstairs rooms. Most of them were converted to gas, for convenience, in the fifties. That's when the electricity was installed."

"Any ghosts?"

"Only three."

Hunter shook his head with a short laugh. "Heaven help me."

"Don't worry," she replied. "They hang out in my wing."

When Hunter disappeared out the front door, Nicole hurried toward her room. In the bathroom, she looked in the mirror. With the lamp shining eerily on her face and stringy hair, she looked like a creature from a horror movie. It's a wonder Shanna hadn't started screaming. To make matters even more embarrassing, her chilled nipples formed distinct peaks on the front of her wet cotton dress.

With a disgusted groan, she set the lamp down and peeled off her wet clothes. She started drying herself with a towel, reaching for her hair dryer simultaneously. Of course, it was dead. Wonderful! She threw the dryer down and started towel drying her thick, shoulder-length hair. She finally gave up. Who was she trying to impress anyway? Hunter Douglas?

Slipping into snug-fitting jeans and a forest-green sweater, she gave herself a quick once-over in the mirror. The sweater complimented her rich auburn hair and matched the color of her eyes. At least she had lost the witch look. She put lipstick on, then hastily grabbed a tissue and rubbed it off.

As she made her way back downstairs guided by the

lamp, her stomach growled, reminding her that she hadn't eaten since noon. Then she remembered Berta and Hank were on vacation. Chuck usually saw to the food and cooking when Berta was gone but only during the week. Today and tomorrow, she was on her own.

Hunter leaned casually against the fireplace under the glow of the lamp, one arm resting on the mantel, the other hand in the pocket of his jeans. He wore a red, pullover, polo shirt that fit snuggly over extremely wide shoulders and muscular arms. His dusky gaze followed her, studying her as she came down the stairs. The man was as beautiful as the boy up in the room. Chuck would call him a real stud muffin. The thought brought an ill-concealed grin to her lips.

"What is it you find so amusing?" he asked.

"I doubt you'd appreciate it."

"Try me."

She avoided eye contact with him. "Maybe later. Let's talk in the kitchen. I haven't eaten anything to speak of all day."

Hunter grabbed the flashlight and followed. "Neither have I. The kids had fast food, but at the time, I was more interested in staying ahead of the rain than eating. I hope you have a gas stove."

Nicole let loose with an unrefined snort. "It's gas, but unless you can cook, we're out of luck. I can't even boil water."

"Can you make coffee?"

She set the lamp on the center island counter and turned to face him with a sheepish grin. "Sure...with an electric percolator. But you'd have to be a masochist to drink it."

"How on earth do you manage?"

"I have Berta."

"Who's Berta?"

"She's the person who does the cooking, the cleaning, and all the little domestic things. She's on vacation for a week."

"Great." He shined the flashlight around the kitchen. "Interesting place you have here; Stove. Refrigerator. Dishwasher. Toaster. Wow, I'm impressed."

Nicole assessed him with a slanted glare. Carmen would take one look at his backside and call him a stud— probably to his face. He did have a way of filling out an ordinary pair of jeans. Unexpectedly, her pulse kicked up. *Stop staring at him*, she warned herself.

"Has anyone ever called you sarcastic?" she asked.

"You mean, besides you?"

Nicole laughed. She couldn't help it. The whole situation was too ridiculous. Still smiling, she perched herself on a cane-back stool at the counter and folded her hands in front of her. "I'm hungry. You did say you could cook, didn't you?"

His cryptic gaze flicked over her in the semi light. A wry grin played on his lips. "I don't recall saying that, but at least I can boil water. You mind if I look around to see what our possibilities are?"

Nicole waved her hand. "Not at all. Make yourself at home. I really am helpless in the kitchen."

He grunted, opened the refrigerator and shined the flashlight inside. "We have a dozen eggs, milk, and a block of cheddar cheese. Ooh, half a ham." He started removing the things as he called them out. "Where are the canned goods?"

She pointed to a door on his right. "In the pantry."

"Of course, I should have known this place had a pantry." He disappeared inside the tiny walk-in room and came out with a can of mushrooms, an onion, and a container of decaf coffee. He set the coffee down on the counter by the percolator. "We really are slaves to electricity, aren't we?" he murmured, fishing around for a manual can opener.

Nicole watched him work with increasing interest. His dark hair had just a hint of red, best described as mahogany. He was continuously pushing that unruly curl away from thick, finely arched, mahogany eyebrows. An inch-long scar, she hadn't noticed before, curved at the outer edge of his left eye. She wondered about the scar and about the man. One thing was certain; he knew his way around a kitchen.

She took a deep breath. "Could you tell me about the kids while you work?"

He reached over and took the lamp to light his working space, leaving her to sit in the shadows. He gave her a quizzical look and started breaking eggs into a bowl. "There's not a whole lot to tell. Shanna is six. Kyle is four. I haven't located their birth certificates yet, so I don't know when their birthdays are. They came to me with two sets of ragged clothes, looking as though they hadn't had a bath or meal in a week. I doubt that Brenda won any mother-of-the-year awards. I'd say her maternal instincts were at zero or less."

Nicole flushed. "I suppose you remember every word of our phone conversation," she said dryly.

"I have an excellent memory."

"I was angry."

"So was I, by the time I hung up." He set a pan none too gently on the stove.

Nicole wanted to say she was sorry but wasn't quite ready to do that. Moreover, if memory served her right, arguing got them nowhere fast.

An uncomfortable silence hung between them. Looking for something to do, she reached into the drawer beside her and pulled out four fat candles and matches. She lit the candles and spread them out on the counter. With the rain pattering softly on the widows and the candles licking away at the darkness, it might have been a cozy setting at any other time. Right now, she still had too many unanswered questions floating around in her head.

"Can I ask you a personal question?" she asked finally.

"How personal?"

"Very."

"Go ahead. But, I reserve the option not to answer."

"I'm trying to understand your involvement in this, but I'm not coming up with anything that makes sense to me. Shanna doesn't resemble you at all with her bright red hair, but Kyle has dark features like you. Is he, by chance, your son?"

He stopped chopping onions long enough to turn and stare at her. She couldn't tell whether he was annoyed or amused.

Finally, he grunted. "If he was my son, I'd have a legal right to custody, and I wouldn't even have had to come here." He let her absorb that for a moment before going on. "Seven years ago, Brenda hired me to locate your father. It took me two weeks to get all the information she wanted. I didn't see or hear from her again until I got a call to come and get the kids. I saw them for the first time three hours before I called you. Besides," he added, "When you see Kyle in the daylight, you'll realize he has a distinct olive complexion—possibly Middle Eastern or Indian."

"Then why you? Why did they call you?"

Hunter returned to his chopping. "I imagine because she trusted me and knew I could find you. She probably spent her last few dollars to have a lawyer draw up legal papers, giving you custody and leaving me in charge of seeing that you get them. She was quite explicit in her instructions, and I had every reason to believe you knew all about it. The papers had your signature agreeing to adopt them as next of kin. Obviously, she forged it."

Nicole drew a deep breath, releasing it slowly. "She must have cared for them if she went through all that trouble to ensure they'd be taken care of if something happened to her."

Hunter stopped what he was doing and came over to brace his hands on the counter across from her, his hard gaze unflinching. "Nicole, you may as well know, she did this all two days before she died. Two days before she took an overdose of pills, or whatever and killed herself, leaving those two kids watching television in the next room. The last thing she did was call the police, asking them to pick up Shanna and Kyle. Instructions, along with the legal papers, were lying on the table. She had their suitcase packed, for God's sake."

"My God! They were there with her?"

He turned back to the stove. "Yes." His voice was gritty. "And they haven't stopped clinging to each other since. Kyle won't speak with anyone but Shanna. She's like a little mother hen with him. She only talks when she has to. I thought I could bring them out of it, but it seems I have no parenting skills either. I haven't been able to get so much as a smile out of either one. Maybe you'll have better luck."

Nicole didn't know what to say. The rain was still pattering at the window, and the candles were still flickering. Thunder rumbled outside like far-off, muffled bombs. Their silence made everything seem more vivid. She tried to imagine a mother doing what Brenda had done, but she just couldn't grasp it.

She was so deep in thought she jumped when Hunter finally spoke.

"Look, I'm sorry I sounded off like that," he said softly. "I'm not angry with you, and I don't blame Brenda for what she did. Nobody can really know what's in another person's mind, or fully understand what makes them do the things they do. If I'm upset with anyone, it's myself. Watching those two kids is just so frustrating. They're so damn innocent in all this. I just wish... hell we both know we won't solve anything tonight, so how about we change the subject."

"I'll second that."

"Good, now do you know where the spices are kept?"

"You mean salt and pepper?"

Hunter chuckled. "I was thinking more in the line of

dill weed or cilantro. You know those little containers that cost about as much as a used car and keep falling out of the cupboard when you open it."

"I'm getting a vivid picture of your kitchen," Nicole replied, laughing. "Try the door below and to your left. Berta's short; she likes to keep things where she can reach them."

Hunter tried the door, found what he was looking for, and made an appreciative *oohing* sound. "I'd bet your Berta is underpaid."

"You can tell that by looking at spices?"

"And the fact that nothing fell out when I opened the door."

Nicole stared at his back. She enjoyed watching him, and his keen observations amazed her. Her internal response to having a man in her kitchen amazed her even more. She couldn't remember ever actually feeling sexual attraction toward any man, much less, an almost total stranger. The last time she'd allowed her thoughts to stray in that area she was sixteen, and they weren't men, they were boys. But that was all before her life fell apart.

"Food's ready," he announced, interrupting her thoughts.

He set a spectacular omelet in front of Nicole that would have done a professional chef proud. It not only looked good; it smelled heavenly. When he handed her a fork and a napkin, his fingers brushed against her hand.

She drew back with a jerk.

He took a seat on the opposite side of the island without taking his eyes off her. "Are you always so skittish, or is it just me?"

Nicole flushed. "No... I... you just startled me."

Hunter's look, as he picked up his fork, was skeptical. "Are you afraid of me, Nicole?"

Her head came up quickly. "Of course not. I'm just not used to... never mind. Let's eat. This looks delicious. I'm so hungry I could chew on tires."

"Studded or regular?"

"It would have to be regular, studs aren't allowed in Minnesota."

"Really?"

She took a taste of the omelet and then another. It proved to be just as good as it looked. Her moan of ecstasy brought an easy grin to his face. "Can you cook other things too?" she asked.

"As long as I keep it simple. I've been on my own for some time, so it was cook or go hungry. Eating out just to eat isn't to my liking—unless it's a special occasion. Would you like some wine? I think I saw a bottle of Cabernet in the pantry."

Nicole nodded. "Sounds wonderful. I've had a chill ever since I got wet." That wasn't entirely true. Watching him work had warmed her motor far more than she cared to admit.

Hunter took a bite of omelet and got up to get the wine. In less time than it took to blink, he had the cork pulled, found the glasses, set them on the counter between them, and started pouring. When he tried to hand Nicole one of the glasses, she didn't reach for it. She ignored his curious frown as he set the glass down in front of her.

She took a quick sip of the red wine. Its warm glow hit her almost instantly. It also gave her the courage to ask something she'd been wondering about.

"I guess that means you're not married then?" she asked.

"Not anymore. I was. It lasted only a couple of years. We had nothing in common. She was a party girl, and I was a stay at home stick-in-the-mud."

Nicole smiled. She had a hard time imagining someone who looked like he did, being a stick-in-the-mud. "Her words?"

Hunter's candlelit eyes sparkled with amusement. "Yes, but true. How about you?"

"I've never taken time for a relationship. I just work."

It was a subject she didn't choose to continue. "Hunter is certainly an unusual name. Is it a nickname?"

"Nope. My mother is just an unusual lady."

"Let me guess, your middle name is Orion, and you have a brother named Aries."

He stopped chewing with his mouth full and gave her a fixed stare. He glanced past her toward the sitting room, then at the candles spread out on the counter, and back to her face before he swallowed. "If you're going to tell me you have séances in this place, I'm outta here."

Nicole's musical laughter filled the room. "You actually have a brother named Aries?"

"No, but my middle name *is* Orion. Not a person outside of family has ever guessed that."

Nicole shrugged. "It doesn't take a mind reader to know astrology or astronomy."

"Probably not, it's just that nobody's ever put the two together before. Not even my ex-wife knew my middle name. I just use the initial." He drained his wine and refilled it along with hers. "So," he said after a moment, "if I had a sister, what would her name be?"

Nicole shrugged. "Most likely, Diana."

Hunter stiffened. His wineglass stopped midway to his lips, his fingers tightening around the stem.

Nicole's own eyes widened. "Please, don't tell me I'm right," she squeaked. "It was just a guess. Honest. They're all in the stars."

His facial features softened. "Okay, I won't tell you. But I'm certainly not going to ask you anymore questions like that." He went back to eating. "Tell me about your work. When you aren't gazing into crystal balls, what do you do?"

"I design and create period costumes for plays and events, sometimes even movies. Besides, Berta and her husband, Hank, I employ three people to help me in the shop. Carmen and Amanda help with the sewing, and Chuck takes care of the leather and metal work."

"I guess that explains your, Gone with the Wind, getup tonight."

"That was a sixteenth century gown. I'm working on the Renaissance era right now. Scarlet O'Hara wore crinolines and flounces," she said matter-of-factly.

"Shows you what I know on that subject. Do you always wear those clothes when you work?"

"Sometimes. It's free advertisement; plus, it helps keep me focused. I spent the day in Minneapolis taking measurements."

"I imagine you get a lot of strange looks."

"You mean, like the one you gave me when I said the name Diana?"

He laughed. "I've had a candles-eye look at this house. I'm still trying to convince myself you don't have a set of tarot cards hidden away somewhere."

"The house is really quite beautiful. It won't look nearly as sinister in the daylight. Maybe you've seen one too many horror movies."

His lips twitched into a grin. "Touché," he said, raising his wineglass. He took a sip then set the glass back down. "You don't have a problem with me staying here, do you?"

Nicole hadn't actually thought about it. The idea that he would be sleeping down the hall from her should probably have bothered her, but somehow it didn't. After all, they weren't exactly alone in the house. "There's plenty of room," she said casually. "And the kids might need you during the night. I didn't make much of a first impression."

"We'll see if we can remedy that tomorrow." He got up and started to gather the dishes. "It's been a long day, and I'm ready to turn in, if that's okay with you."

Nicole stood up to go, hesitating. "Can I ask one more question?"

"Of course."

"What did Brenda look like?"

Hunter brought the lamp from the stove. When he

made a move to hand it to her, she took a half step backward. He set it on the counter in front of her.

"It's been seven years. After my assignment was finished, I never saw her again." His gaze flicked over Nicole from her auburn hair to the long lines of her legs. "From what I recall, she was about your size and height, same coloring; except, she was blond—I suspect with the help of a little peroxide. Overall, she was beautiful, stunningly beautiful."

* * * *

When Hunter got upstairs, the first thing he did was check on Shanna and Kyle. Flashlight in hand, but switched off, he stepped into the room using the doors connected by the bathroom. The fireplace cast a muted light on the room. Halfway to the bed, he froze. Two large, glowing eyes stared back at him from Shanna's feet. Holding his breath, he raised his hand and aimed the flashlight at the eyes, then switched it on.

Mr. Komodo.

"Christ!"

He let out a *whoosh* of air. Calling that yellow monster 'a large cat' was a gross understatement. The damn thing was nearly as big as a German shepherd, and he had no face. His nose pushed into his furred head as if slammed into a brick wall. He approached the cat cautiously then held out his hand to test its friendliness. Mr. Komodo rubbed his head against Hunter's hand and started purring with the velocity of a lawnmower.

"Mr. Komodo," Hunter murmured, rubbing his ears, "you are just about the ugliest cat I've ever seen, but it looks like you're doing a good job here."

Mr. Komodo answered with an even louder purr. When Hunter withdrew his hand, the cat closed its eyes and laid its head back down on the covers over Shanna's leg. Hunter made sure the kids were covered before going back to the bathroom.

He splashed cold water on his face, towel dried it, then

went to his room and undressed. Tired to the bone, he sought out the bed, more than eager to put an end to what had been an exhausting, but interesting, day.

Instead of the sleep he was looking for, an image floated in front of him—an image of Brenda Casey walking down the stairway with a lamp in her hand. His blood started to run cold until she spoke with the voice of Nicole Anderson.

In his line of business, not too many things surprised or shocked him. In just two hours, Nicole Anderson had managed to do both. From her bizarre house, to her tenderness with the children, to her striking looks—she was an enigma. Then there was her reaction to him. She was as skittish as a chicken in a wolf den.

He'd known plenty of women. Attracting women hadn't been a problem for him since he was sixteen. In truth, women had become a nuisance in recent years. It seemed he couldn't turn around without one trying to ring his finger. It's not that he didn't want to marry again. It was just that he always seemed to attract the wrong kind of women. But never had he encountered one that cringed at his touch. Was it just him? Was it men in general? Or was there something else eating at her?

One thing he did know was he wanted to touch her—all over. More than he'd ever wanted to touch a woman in his life. He wanted, in fact, to do a lot more than touch her. But, she had a wall of ice built around her that could withstand the fires of hell. Maybe it was just as well. He was here to attend to the business of two little kids sleeping in the next room. He would do well to keep his mind focused on that. And maybe, just maybe, Nicole Anderson had already come to that same conclusion. The lady was strictly business. Shit. She was the original virgin ice queen.

Chapter Three

Nicole awoke in a cold sweat, silent screams caught in her dry throat. Hands were all over her, tearing at her clothes, at her body, at her dignity. Wide-awake now, she rolled over to check the clock on her nightstand. It was blank. The electricity was still out. She fumbled for her wristwatch in the drawer and depressed the button, lighting the dial—Four a.m. Groaning, she snuggled back into the covers and closed her eyes. Only, she already knew the dream wouldn't leave her. It was too vivid, too easily remembered. The only thing that would chase it away was work.

Methodically, she got up and dressed; putting on the same sweater and jeans that she'd taken off the night before. It was a routine all too familiar. On her way downstairs, she stopped to look in on the children. By the glow of the fireplace she could see they were sleeping peacefully, but still meshed together like Velcro.

How could she help chase away their demons when she couldn't get rid of her own?

In her studio, she lit the lamp she'd carried with her, then realized her sketches were still in the car. At least it sounded like it had quit raining. She located her car keys, unlocked the front door, and hurried through the damp early morning to her car. Grabbing the heavy portfolio and the bag of toys, she lugged everything back toward the house in one load. A light from Hunter's car stopped her. The trunk was open. He must have accidentally left it open when he brought his suitcases in. She set her bundles inside the house, then walked back to the car and pushed the trunk shut. It was a Mercedes. A little fact she'd missed in the rain. That Dick Tracy work must pay pretty well.

Moments later, she was back in her studio and unpacking her sketches. The first thing she needed to do was match each sketch with the numbers of the pattern pieces she would use. Each costume used parts from different patterns. That way she could make numerous authentic looking outfits and yet, create a different look for each one. When Carmen and Amanda got there Monday morning, they could start right in with the cutting and sewing. The hats, boots, and weapons she would leave entirely to Chuck.

* * * *

Hunter knew he was dreaming. Diana was sitting on the bed tickling his face with a feather. His sister was such an adorable little imp. She made strange noises that reverberated in his ear.

The wet coldness pressed against his cheek finally woke him up. He stared directly into the fur-impacted nose of the ugliest face he'd ever seen.

Mr. Komodo.

Hunter pushed the whiskered animal away from his nose. "Don't you have some mice to go chase or something?"

Mr. Komodo leaped off the bed and disappeared into the bathroom.

Hunter looked around the room. There was light. Daylight. The room wasn't exceptionally large, probably twelve by twelve, and furnished in Louis the XV décor with exquisite lavish adornment. The main feature was the large, silk-canopied, Chippendale, mahogany bed he slept in. It was obviously meant to be a girl's room, right down to the replica of Di Vinci's *Virgin on the Rocks* and rose-sculptured, pink marble mantel. His mother, an avid collector of antiques, had taught him just enough to appreciate the value of preserving a setting such as this. She would give her eyeteeth to sleep in this room, in this house.

He got up, pulled aside the heavy drapes, and looked out the window. Actually, he realized, it was a patio door. It led to a balcony that ran the entire length of the back of the house. He opened it and stepped outside wearing nothing but pajama bottoms. He hadn't slept in the nude since the kids had come to his house.

The view before him was like a scene in a painting. A light fog hung over the lake. A lake that was as still and smooth as glass. Pines and newly budded aspen hugged the shoreline as far as he could see. It was the first time in his life he had looked on a scene that was absolutely nothing but nature.

He breathed deeply the rich pine smell, and thought about the envelope in his briefcase addressed to Nicole Anderson. It had come inside a larger envelope addressed to him—two days after he'd picked up the kids. The note that came with it instructed him to give it to Nicole, only if she accepted custody of the kids. He really wanted to open it to find out if Brenda might have named him as Shanna's father, but his conscience wouldn't allow it. Besides, since he fully intended to take the kids back to New York with him, he wasn't about to hand the letter over to Nicole, just yet. If Brenda did name him, he wasn't ready to share that information with anyone. He was still getting used to the idea himself.

He glanced at his watch. Quarter after six. Going back inside, he peeked into the other bedroom. Shanna and Kyle were still sleeping, and Mr. Komodo was back on duty. He clicked the switch in the bathroom; rich, beautiful light blinded his eyes.

Twenty minutes later, he left the room feeling totally refreshed from a shower and shave. He was more than a little anxious to view the rest of the house in daylight.

He looked down into the front hall from a balustrade that surrounded the second floor on three sides. A total of six doors opened to the balcony. The rooms occupied by him and the kids were in the center, flanked by separate wings on either side. Each wing had two doors.

Downstairs he could see the front door straight ahead of the stairs with the doorway to the kitchen to the right. A seven-foot library table stood in the center of the hall under a heavy bronze chandelier that was straight out of a history book. It had short fat candles in it, for God's sake. He remembered Nicole's studio was on the left, opposite the kitchen. He had to move to the stairs to see that door. As he walked down the stairs, he marveled at the cherry wood walls and ornate woodwork. A great fresco, depicting fluffy clouds in blue sky, centered the two-story, paneled ceiling.

Behind the stairway, he caught a glimpse of a modern sitting room and a giant wall of glass looking upon the same scene as his bedroom upstairs. It opened onto a deck that appeared too new to be part of the original house.

He came back to the hall intending to see the kitchen in daylight. A glow from Nicole's studio altered his direction. The studio, about fourteen by sixteen, had walls covered with bookshelves, drawings, and paintings. An oil lamp burned with a low flame on a worktable where Nicole was asleep, sitting in her stool with her arms and head resting on a pile of open books. A pencil still clutched in her fingers and auburn hair spilled softly over her face.

Hunter approached her, cautiously. He didn't want to startle her if she woke suddenly. For a moment, he just watched her. She had an innocent, childlike quality to her when she slept. He turned out the lamp, picked up a knitted afghan from the settee behind her, and gently draped it over her shoulders.

As he turned to leave the room, he spotted a bag on a

chair by the door. A stuffed bear peeked from the top of the bag. A constricting knot tightened in his chest. Nicole Anderson was anything but a heartless wench.

* * * *

Nicole woke to the smell of pancakes. Pancakes! She raised her head with a start, painfully aware of the stiffness in her back. What time was it? As if in answer, the grandfather clock in the corner chimed nine bells. Unless Chuck showed up to make breakfast or Berta cancelled her vacation, Hunter was in the kitchen.

When she got up to stretch her limbs, her grandmother's afghan fell to the floor. A wistful smile tugged at her lips. The arrogant, Mr. Douglas, was full of surprises.

Thinking anxiously about the upcoming meeting with Brenda's kids, Nicole hurried through the door, connecting the workshop to her studio where there was a bathroom. She washed quickly and ran a comb through her hair, then set out to investigate the promise of pancakes.

As she suspected, Hunter was bending over the stove. Shanna and Kyle sat at the island counter facing away from her. Nicole took in the scene, hesitating. Shanna wore a lime green pullover and crisp jeans that looked too new to have yet seen a washer. She had the brightest red curls Nicole had ever seen. Kyle was smaller than she'd initially thought. He, too, wore new jeans, and a yellow and green tie-dye T-shirt. His coal-black hair was as curly as Shanna's.

Nicole took a deep breath, smoothed back her hair, and put a cheery smile on her face. "Good morning, everyone."

Hunter turned to look her up and down. "Good morning. You really know how to bury yourself in your work, don't you? It's time you met Shanna and Kyle."

They had both turned at the sound of her voice. As she came around the counter to face them, she found herself greeted by open-mouthed stares. Kyle's dark eyes were large and round. They showed—fear? Shanna reached over and grabbed his wrist, but her inquisitive green gaze never left Nicole's face.

Nicole shrank back. She had expected them to be leery of her, but not blatantly afraid. She didn't know what to do.

Kyle spoke first.

"Mama?"

Shanna gave his arm a tug. "No, Kyle, it can't be mama. Mama died."

Nicole felt faint. She couldn't find her breath. They were both looking at her as if she were a ghost. She didn't even flinch when Hunter led her to a stool.

He released her quickly. "Nicole. I'm sorry. I should have warned them."

"Warned them of what?" she croaked.

"Of your likeness to Brenda."

He reached across the counter to grab Kyle's hands. "She's not your mama, Kyle. She's your aunt; your mama's sister." He looked at Shanna. "Do you understand that sweetheart? She looks like your mother because she is her sister."

Shanna nodded without taking her eyes off Nicole.

"Your voice is different," Hunter said. "Say something so they hear it, Nicole."

Nicole opened her mouth, searching for words, any words. "You should have told me," she whispered.

"I didn't realize the extent of the likeness in the dim light last night, or I would have. I had no idea this would happen. Please say something."

Nicole worked at the lump in her throat. She knew she had to talk. She pasted a frozen smile on her face and looked to Kyle. "I'm so happy you came to visit me. I hope you like it here in Minnesota. There is a big lake out back with woods and trees to climb. You can go swimming and fishing. Have you ever gone fishing, Kyle?"

Kyle still looked at her somberly, but he slowly shook his head. She turned her attention to Shanna. "How about you, Shanna? Would you like to go fishing? I have a friend with a boat. We could even go out in the boat to fish. Would you like that?"

The expression on Shanna's face relaxed. She looked at Kyle. "It's okay, Kyle. She just looks like Mama; because, she's our aunt."

Kyle glanced at Hunter and back at Shanna. "Can we really go fishing?"

Hunter reached across the counter and ruffled his hair. "If Nicole says you can go fishing, then I'm sure you can. She's my friend, and she wouldn't lie to you."

Nicole breathed a huge sign of relief. "I think I smell pancakes burning."

Hunter let out a bark and made a dash for the stove. His mild oath brought her back to earth. She smiled at the two faces still watching her from across the counter. "I'm giving the both of you special permission to call me Aunt Nicky; I don't let anyone else call me that. Will that be okay with you?"

Kyle looked at Shanna and when she nodded, he turned back to Nicole and nodded too.

"Good, now that we have that settled, let's see if our cook salvaged any of those pancakes." She got up and went to peer over Hunter's shoulder.

"Make yourself useful and pour the coffee," he said. "The pancakes are done."

Nicole finished setting the table then took a seat across from Kyle. Hunter brought the stack of pancakes over and put one on each of the children's plates.

Shanna picked up her fork, but stopped to look at Nicole. "You need to cut Kyle's pancake, Aunt Nicky. I can do my own."

Simultaneously, Nicole and Hunter exchanged silent glances. She reached over to cut the pancake while Hunter poured syrup. He handed the syrup to Shanna so she could pour her own. An outsider, looking in, would have thought they were a family sitting down to a routine breakfast.

Watching those sullen kids eat, Nicole knew the scene was anything but normal. She remembered the happy chatter in her own family at mealtime. Billy was usually doing some mischief. Her father was always teasing her or Billy, and flirting with their mother. They'd had such a cozy, comfortable life. How could he have had an affair?

The whole time Kyle ate, he kept stealing glances at Nicole as though still trying to convince himself she wasn't his mother. The scene was entirely too serious.

Nicole laid down her napkin and stood up. "Excuse me for a moment; one of our guests is missing." She walked out of the room, went to her studio, picked up the stuffed bear, and brought it back to the kitchen. She plopped the bear on the counter between her and Hunter. Three sets of curious eyes now stared from the bear to her.

"This is my friend, Mr. Bear," she said matter-of-factly. "I've invited him to join us." She gave Hunter an imploring look that challenged him to participate.

Hunter took the bait without batting an eye. "So how does Mr. Bear like the pancakes?"

"He thinks they'd be better with blueberries," Nicole said.

Kyle looked to Hunter for an answer.

"Maybe Mr. Bear should make breakfast tomorrow morning. What do you think, Shanna?"

Shanna's lips moved to form the subtle makings of a smile. "Bears do like blueberries," she said quietly.

Without speaking, Nicole reached over and moved the bear away from Hunter and closer to her.

Hunter's brows shot up. "Now what?"

"He's afraid of you," Nicole said.

"Why, what did I do?"

Nicole tried hard to keep her face serious. "It's your name. He's a little nervous around someone named Hunter."

Kyle's eyes lit up when he looked at his sister. "It's true, Shanna, bears don't like hunters. I saw it on TV."

This time Nicole spoke directly to Kyle. "Do you think we should give Hunter a different name for Mr. Bear?"

Kyle gave a quick nod.

"Mr. Bear would like to call him, Honeypot." She ignored Hunter's mumbled protest. "What do think, Kyle? Is that a good name?" He was watching Hunter shake his head.

"Bears like Honey," he said to Shanna.

Nicole grinned. "Okay, Honeypot it is then."

Hunter's gaze narrowed playfully on Nicole. "Don't I have any say in this?"

Nicole looked at the bear then back at Hunter. "All right," she said, "he'll give you a choice. It's either Honeypot or Pumpkin Face."

Hunter looked at Kyle. "I can't decide. You choose."

Kyle looked to Shanna for a decision.

Shanna gave Hunter a disarming smile. "Honeypot," she said.

Kyle glanced back at Nicole. "It should be Honeypot," he said. A timid, little-boy grin wrinkled his features.

A lump rose in Nicole's throat. Over the bear's head, her eyes met Hunter's gaze in silent wonder. He was about to say something when a sharp *rat-a-tat-tat* sounded on the door leading from the kitchen to the deck outside.

It was Chuck's special knock. He lived in a small cottage across the lake and, weather permitting, usually came over in his sixteen-foot, Lund fishing boat. Rarely did he show up on a weekend unless they had a critical deadline in the shop.

Nicole got up to let him in and was greeted with a fierce hug.

"How are you doing, Nick? Thought I'd better come over and feed you so you don't faint on us again…" Chuck Martin's voice faded as he took in the scene around the table. "Am I interrupting something?" he asked slowly, his eyes settling on Hunter.

Nicole shook her head, amused at the piercing look on Hunter's face. The man actually looked jealous. Chuck had a great build, blonde tousled hair, and looked like he just stepped out of a magazine ad. Chuck was also gay. He wore a Green Bay Packer's cap and a smirk that was decidedly irritating.

She gave him a warning look. "Come in, I'll introduce you."

Nicole made the introductions, giving Chuck no information other than first names. She knew he had questions—lots of them. In their eight-year association, this was the first time he'd seen her within ten feet of a man that didn't include business. Let him wonder. She had a right to a private life.

Twenty minutes later, Nicole stood at the door, watching Shanna and Kyle clutching Mr. Bear, follow Chuck down to the dock for a ride in his boat. Feeling strangely light-hearted, she turned to Hunter. He was lounging back on his stool, feet hooked in the rungs, his hand covering the top of his coffee mug, and index finger tapping slowly on the rim. He was studying her with those deep-set, soul-piercing eyes. If she met that gaze, she would blush to the roots.

She picked up her coffee mug, refilled it, and took the chair Kyle had vacated, as far away from Hunter as she could get without being obvious. She expected him to comment on her interaction with Chuck, or Honeypot, or the fact that the kids had looked to her for permission to go out in the boat.

"You have fainting spells?"

Jeez, the man didn't miss anything. "You don't miss anything, do you?" she quipped dryly.

"It helps in my line of work. How often do you faint?"

"Once. I fainted once, for Pete's sake. It's no big deal. I hadn't eaten all day." She wasn't gong to tell him she was menstruating too.

"Were you—low on blood?"

Now she did blush to her roots. "What is this, a twenty question drill?"

"Was this before or after I called?"

"Before," she snapped. "In fact, now that I think of it, it was at three o'clock the same day. My ESP must have been warning me to not to answer the phone."

A crooked grin kicked up on his face.

"You left your trunk open last night," she said.

His dark brows furrowed. "I'm sure I closed it. It must have popped back open. I left a suitcase in there. I better go check if it got wet." He unfolded his lanky frame from the stool, mumbling something about rental cars.

Nicole was starting the dishwasher when he came back in. He perched on a stool, his narrow gaze, narrower than normal, leveled on her. "Nicole, did you take the suitcase out of the trunk?"

"Of course, not. Why would I want your suitcase? I didn't even look inside the trunk. I just slammed it shut so the light wouldn't run your battery dead."

"What time was that?"

"Four-thirty."

Hunter's brows shot up. "You were outside at four-thirty this morning!"

"I… I couldn't sleep. I went out to get my portfolio from the car so I could work."

"You don't sleep, you don't eat. No wonder you faint."

"I don't faint. It happened one time."

"Was it raining?"

"When I fainted?"

"No, when you went out to the car."

God, he was back to the twenty questions again. She took a deep breath. "No, it wasn't raining."

"That explains why it was dry inside the trunk, but it doesn't explain why the suitcase is missing."

"Maybe you took it up with the others last night? Why don't you check?"

"I don't need to. I didn't take the bag out of the trunk, and I didn't forget to slam it shut, either."

Obviously, Hunter Douglas never did anything wrong. "If you need anything we can go into town, and you can buy it."

"Nicole, the trunk was pried open. All the papers from Brenda were in that suitcase. I never had a chance to go through them."

An apprehensive chill began to snake its way up Nicole's spine. "What kind of papers?"

"I'm not sure. Probably birth certificates, medical records, insurance policies, and maybe tax papers. Hell, maybe nothing. They were literally dumped in a battered old file box included with her personal effects. The police gave everything to me, so I could turn it over to you. The only things I brought with me were the papers from the file box, a few pieces of costume jewelry, some pictures, and keepsakes that I thought the kids might like to have some day."

"Was there a picture of Brenda?"

"Hell, I don't know. I think there may have been a small album. With the kids there and making plane reservations, with everything else I had to do, I didn't have time to deal with it; especially, since I didn't expect to find anything of importance. From what I could tell, the most valuable thing Brenda owned was a five-dollar wristwatch. I just threw it all in the old suitcase that came with the kids and brought it along. I had my hands full last night, so I left it in the car."

Nicole dropped to a stool. She ran a hand through her hair trying to collect her thoughts. "There are a lot of seasonal homes up here that get hit by vandals. With the lights out, it might have looked like nobody was home."

"It wasn't vandals."

"How can you be so sure?"

"Because, they left a four hundred dollar stereo and a cellular phone inside the car and took a battered old suitcase that wouldn't bring thirty-five cents at a rummage sale. Unless you're telling me, Minnesotans are really as dense as they appeared in that Fargo movie."

Nicole chose to ignore that remark. "So what do we do now? Call the police?"

"So they can clutter their files with a meaningless theft? No. We go Dumpster diving."

"Dumpster diving?"

"I'll explain on the way. I don't know my way around here, so I need you with me. We'll have to take the kids along. I'd rather not have them wondering what we're doing, but I don't know what else to do."

"What about Chuck?" Nicole suggested. "I'm sure he'd look after them for a couple of hours, if you don't have a problem leaving them with him."

"You know him better than I do. If you think he's reliable, then I'm okay with it. Shanna and Kyle seemed to trust him easily enough to go out in the boat with him. But let's make sure we ask them. Can we get his attention out on the lake?"

Nicole gave him a cutesy smile. "Youbetcha." She hurried out the kitchen door and rounded the deck to the back of the house.

Hunter followed.

Chuck's red and gray Lund was free floating about five hundred yards out. Nicole reached in a large box full of patio chair cushions and pulled out a four by six US flag. She walked to the edge of the deck, leaned over, and began waving it in a figure eight. When she made the sixth revolution, an engine purred to life, and the boat headed toward them.

Hunter gave her a grin of admiration. "Nothing like having a man at your beck and call. I'll bet you folks go all out for the Fourth of July."

"Carnival, fireworks, hot dogs, and watermelon until you bust."

"Yippee." Hunter's New York drawl was less than

enthusiastic.

She called over her shoulder as she ran down the steps to meet the boat. "Don't knock it till you've tried it, city boy,"

Watching her bounce down the eight steps to the dock, Hunter realized that, other than looks, Nicole was entirely different from his memory of Brenda. Brenda was makeup, hairspray, and spiked heels. She literally dripped of external sexuality, and she made good use of it. Nicole, on the other hand, had a subtle, internal sensuality. He doubted she was even aware of it. She also had a scrubbed-clean look. She had the kind of face he wanted to kiss all over, and when he finished with her face, he would move to the rest of her sensuous parts—all of them—one at a time. He wanted to taste her. He wanted to feel her soft body beneath him.

She bent over in the boat and planted a kiss on each one of the kid's heads, and in doing so, presented him with a delicious view of her derriere. Shortly after, she was coming back up the stairs—on the run. Hell, it was going to be tough to try to get a kiss from someone he couldn't even touch.

Shit. What was he thinking? He was hard as a rock. If she had any experience with men at all, she could tell at a glance he'd been lusting after her.

She was panting by the time she reached him. "Okay, we're all set. Chuck is taking them crappie fishing. If we aren't back by noon, he'll take them to his house for lunch. Either we can put out the flag and he'll bring them home, or we can stop over and pick them up. Whose car, yours or mine? Hunter? Are you listening?"

He walked away from her quickly. "Yours, you know where your going."

"I'll get my keys."

Chapter Four

Two minutes later, they were buckling their seat belts and Nicole backed out of the driveway. "Okay, this is your game, where to?"

"The nearest business that might have a large, commercial dumpster."

"That would be Ray and Marge's Resort. They're on the next lake over, less than a mile."

By the time they reached the resort, Hunter managed to have his mind off Nicole's tight jeans and back on business. "Pull up next to it on my side. You can stay in the car."

Hunter got out, checked the blue dumpster and got back in the car.

"Where's the next one?"

"Red Oak Inn. It's a local hangout with a bar and small restaurant."

"How far?"

"Two miles along the lake." Nicole pulled out on the road, heading west. "Do you really expect to find something?"

"We can only hope."

"I don't quite understand why someone would bother throwing it in a dumpster. There are a million trees and heavy brush where a suitcase could be thrown."

"If they leave it in the bushes, it stays there until it's found. A dumpster gets picked up within a couple of days. Its contents disappear in a landfill and are never seen again. When they found out there was nothing of value in it, I'm hoping they wasted no time getting rid of the evidence. We have a small streak of luck with it being Sunday. That last dumpster was all but empty. I'd guess the local service picked up yesterday. Sometimes you have to fish through a week of smelly garbage."

"You've done this before?"

Hunter chuckled. "Many times."

"Sounds thrilling. Do you ever stop and have lunch while you're in there?"

"No, but that's not a bad idea. Let me know when you get hungry—I'll see what I can find. There it is. Pull around to the back."

Nicole stopped beside the Red Oak's dumpster, glad that no one was around to recognize her. Hunter was in and out in fifteen seconds.

"Next."

"There's a One-Stop gas station right up ahead. Does that count?"

"If they have garbage to haul, then yes."

"This sounds like a wild goose chase to me. There are probably a hundred of these things within a ten-mile radius. You want to check them all?"

"If we have to."

Nicole groaned. "I'll keep driving, but just for the record, I think you're nuts."

"Would you like to make a little wager?"

"Now, I know you're crazy." She shook her head laughing, "How much?"

"You name what you want. I'll name what I want."

She pulled up to the gas station. There were two dumpsters, one partially full. It took him a couple of minutes to get back in the car. "Where now?"

"Motel, across the freeway."

"So what's your price?" he asked.

"You take me to the Red Oak Inn for a hamburger and fries."

"Deal."

"Okay, what do you want? Your pants pressed? Beware, I don't iron any better than I cook."

"I don't see a dumpster here. Go to the next place."

She started to make a U-turn in the drive. "So what do you want?"

"A kiss."

"What?" She slammed on the brakes and stared at him. "What kind of a ridiculous thing is that to ask for?"

Hunter shrugged matter-of-factly. "You're so sure you're going to win. What does it matter?"

Her eyes narrowed on him. "All right, Honeypot. You're on. Only we call it quits after fifty dumpsters."

"Agreed. Now drive. We still have forty-seven to go."

"Forty-six."

"Motel doesn't count; they didn't have a dumpster."

"The One-Stop had two!"

"You're right. Forty-six."

Nicole shook her head. "Lord, I can't believe I'm driving around the country counting trash containers." She drove across the road to a combined bottle shop/laundromat. The trash bin was only half the size of the others. "We're counting this one," she said tenaciously.

Hunter let out a bark of laughter. "Woman, you're crazier than I am." He got out to check the bin then got back in the car. "Where to now?"

She sighed. "That's all the local ones. There are two towns nearby. Willow River is five miles to the south. Moose Lake is five miles north."

"Which one is larger?"

"Moose Lake."

"Then let's hit Willow River first."

She was backing out, when a large, stooped man

popped out of the laundromat. Short wisps of white hair covered the top of his head, and brown age spots speckled his arthritic hands. He wore faded, but clean, bib-overalls.

"Nicole? Nicole Anderson, is that you?"

"Oh, God. It's Barney."

"As in Fife?" Hunter asked.

"As in Johnson, you idiot." She rolled down her window.

Barney Johnson put his big hands on the doorframe to lean down and peer into the car. "How the heck are you, Nicole?" His words directed at Nicole, but his curious gaze settled on her companion. "Looks like you finally got yourself a feller there. About time, I'd say." He reached past Nicole to offer his hand to Hunter. "Barney Johnson's the name."

Hunter put his hand in the man's mammoth, time-weathered paw. "Hunter Douglas," he said.

"Where you from, Hunter?"

"New York."

"Holy shit! You a dumpster salesman or what?"

Nicole glanced at Hunter and back at Barney. "No," she said," he just lives out of them. Somebody stole his suitcase, and we're looking for it."

Barney's shaggy brows drew together. "I would think a fancy New York fellow like you could afford a better suitcase than that old thing."

"You found it!" Nicole shrieked.

Hunter was already getting out of the car. "Show me where it is Barney."

"Inside." Barney started walking back to the laundromat. Hunter was on his heels, followed closely by Nicole.

The suitcase was on the counter, half-full of neatly folded clothes.

"Where's the stuff that was in it?" Nicole asked.

He pointed to a tall trashcan in the corner. "Gosh, sorry, I didn't know it was somebody's things. That feller that ditched it was in such a hurry to get out of here, he spun gravel all the way to the pavement. Small wonder, if he'd stolen it."

Hunter turned with the trashcan in his hands. "You saw the man who threw it away?"

"Sure did. Won't forget him too easily, neither. He looked like one of those Middle East terrorists, black beard and all. I half expected to find a bomb in there."

"What kind of car was he driving?" Hunter asked.

Barney started taking clothes out of the suitcase. "Black."

"Two-door or four-door?"

"Four-door, I believe."

"Ford, Chevy, Oldsmobile? How old?"

Barney shrugged his wide shoulders. "Don't rightly know what kind. It was a compact though... a cheap car... not new."

"I don't suppose you got a license plate number?"

"Nope. Like I said, he peeled out of here like a cat what got his tail caught in a meat grinder."

"Or a thief on the run," Hunter muttered. He dumped the contents of the trashcan back into the suitcase. "Did you notice anything else? What he was wearing? Was he alone?"

"He was alone, alright." Barney said, nodding his head. "Wore a jacket that looked itchy. Oh, and one of them flat hats that don't keep the ears warm."

"What time was it?"

"About an hour ago."

"Shit. Nicole, give Barney your phone number in case he thinks of anything else."

"Ain't necessary," Barney said. "I know the number. You staying there?"

Hunter ignored the question. He extended his hand to the older man. "You've been a great help. Thanks Barney."

"Youbetcha, Mr. Douglas. Anytime. You take care of that little gal now."

Nicole got in the car shaking her head. "You should work for the FBI or the KGB. I've never seen anybody rattle off a string of questions like that."

Hunter grinned. "Got a lot of information though, didn't I. I'll make you another bet he calls within twenty-four hours with something else that he remembers."

Nicole started the engine. "No more bets. I'm starting to believe you. Where to now?"

"We can wait to go through the suitcase until the kids are in bed tonight. Is there a grocery store anywhere close? We need to pick up a few things. Your refrigerator looks like Old Mother Hubbard's cupboard."

"I think you need to experience the Willow River Mercantile."

"Youbetcha."

"You're such a brat," she snipped. "You do realize that the suitcase wasn't actually in a dumpster."

"Technicalities will not save you from your fate," Hunter said. He had expected her to argue, maybe even become distraught. Once again, she surprised him. She was staring straight ahead at the road—and smiling. For a man who earned his living going on hunches and character reading, he was certainly batting a zero when it came to Ms. Anderson. Damn, she had a good-looking mouth on her, even if it was a smart-ass one. The rest of her wasn't too bad either. He wanted to suckle her nipples.

Hunter, get a fucking grip.

Nicole had already decided that kissing Hunter might not be all that unpleasant, and she really had no choice. Disturbing warmth settled in her belly. It was more than warmth; it was downright heat. Actually, it was a little lower than her belly. Could she be experiencing what Carmen called the 'hots'? She glanced at the pensive, silent man beside her. The heat intensified. Yes, she decided, she definitely had the hots for Hunter Douglas. Who was she kidding? Just the thought of acting on her feelings turned her stomach inside out.

Her fingers clenched the steering wheel, and she stared out the side window so Hunter wouldn't notice the moisture building in her eyes. Her past refused to stay buried. There was little doubt in her mind she would be a failure in any man's bed. What man wanted a twenty-eight-year-old virginless virgin?

At the mercantile, Hunter did his shopping while Nicole called Chuck. She finished with the phone then waited for Hunter at the checkout counter. When she reached in her purse for money, he gave her a hard glare.

"Don't even think about it."

Nicole mumbled something under her breath about macho men and stuffed her wallet back in her purse. They were on their way out the door when the clerk called after them.

"Nicole, I almost forgot. My sister Marge wants to bring her first-grade class to your house for a little history lesson sometime this week. Would that be all right?"

Nicole stopped to answer. "Of course, Clare. Have Marge give me a call to set up a time. If I'm not there, Carmen or Amanda can give them a tour."

"She'd like Chuck to do it—in his Robin Hood costume."

"No problem, he loves doing Robin Hood."

Hunter tossed his bags in the back seat. "Does everyone in this bloody community know you?"

"Except for the summer visitors and many of them have been to an open house. I even get a lot of drive-bys. The house does sort of attract attention."

"No, shit."

Nicole met his eyes over the top of the car with an impish grin. "By this time tomorrow, five-thousand people will expect to be invited to our wedding."

"You don't date much, do you?"

He was already in the car, so he missed the startled look on her face. By the time she slipped behind the wheel, she had her emotions under control.

"What did Chuck have to say?" Hunter asked, snapping his seatbelt in place. "Are the kids okay?"

"Both Shanna and Kyle caught fish. They already had lunch. Shanna was coloring and Kyle is sleeping. He said to take our time, so I'd like to make one more stop."

"Fine with me."

Nicole pulled away from the store.

Hunter turned to look at her. "I never did get a chance to thank you for what you did for those kids this morning," he said.

The gentleness in his voice both surprised and moved her. "Their expressions were, by far, thanks enough. They seem so... sad. I suppose that's to be expected after what they've been through. I imagine they miss their mother. I wonder if they'll ever laugh and play like normal kids."

"You accomplished more in a few minutes than I did in three days." Hunter said. He turned to watch the trees speed by, "What are we going to do about them?" He turned back to look at her. "I don't want to give them up, but if you want them, I have no say in the matter. Even if I got custody, I'm starting to question my ability to raise them." His attention moved back to the trees. "What a damn mess, and with two innocent little lives slam dunked right smack in the middle of it."

"I don't think a person is born with parenting skills," Nicole said. "That's why they come as babies, so you can get used to the idea, slowly." She gave him a furtive glance. "Right now, I have no answers either." Then she asked the question she had been avoiding. "How long can you stay?"

He was looking at her again. "For as long as it takes or for as long as I'm welcomed, whichever comes first. Either way, I'm sure as hell not leaving until we know who took that suitcase out of my car—and why."

When she headed north past the turnoff to Sunset Lake, he frowned. "Where are we going?"

"To visit my grandmother. She has a room in an

assisted living home."

Hunter's dark brows shot up. "The, Mr. Komodo, grandmother? She's still alive?"

"And kicking," Nicole said laughing.

"Your mother's side or father's?"

"Father's; Besides Billy, she's my only living relative. I imagine you already know my mom died a year after my dad."

Hunter nodded. "How old is your grandmother?"

Nicole pulled into the parking lot, stopped under a tree in the corner, and got out of the car. A smile tugged at her lips. "Gram is ninety-one. You are the most inquisitive person I've ever met."

He gave her a lopsided grin. "Habit, I guess. I just like to have all the facts. Surprises are okay if they concern cake or presents. Otherwise..." He shrugged.

"If you don't want surprises, I better fill you in on the rest of Gypsy Anderson."

"Gypsy?" He opened the entry door for her, then followed her inside. "Her real name?"

"Who knows? Anyway, if Gram doesn't want to talk about something, she'll act, very successfully, addled. And she'll use the same tactic when she wants to get her opinion across. It doesn't work with me. I know her too well. Billy and I spent summers with Gram and Gramps at the lake when we were kids. I'm just giving you fair warning. If you're getting cold feet, you can stay in the lobby."

"And miss this? Are you kidding? I can't wait to see her crystal ball."

Nicole gave him a sideways grin. "Just keep in mind that she used it as a weapon to make us eat our vegetables."

"Lord. You're serious, aren't you?"

"What do you think?"

"I think you're serious."

"Damn, you're good."

Gypsy Anderson was sitting at a small card table. She had a phone pressed to her ear and solitaire cards spread out on the surface. Her sunken eyes literally sparkled when they settled on Nicole.

"DeeDee, my lovely, Sweet Pea," she said, hanging up the phone.

Nicole wrapped the small woman in a gentle hug, and then sat down in the chair on her left. "Hi, Gram. How are you?"

"Oh I'm—" her keen gaze fixed on the tall figure hesitating in the shadowed doorway. "Did you bring me a present, DeeDee, Sweet Pea?"

"No Gram. He's just a friend."

"Well, Just-A-Friend, get yourself over here in the light where I can get a look at you." Gypsy patted the chair at her right, across from Nicole.

Hunter gave Nicole an "are you going to help" look, which she ignored.

Hunter settled into the squeaky folding chair, adjacent to Gram. "Hello, Mrs. Anderson," he said, allowing her a wary smile.

"Oh, you are a pretty one, Just-A-Friend," she replied. Her grin displayed a full set of timeworn teeth. "You can call me, Gypsy."

Hunter raised a single eyebrow at Nicole.

"His name is Hunter, Gram."

Gram tested the name. "Hunter. Hunter Douglas. Any relation to those Douglas' on television?" At Hunter's blank stare, she added, "They live on that farm, Green Acres?"

Hunter's heart did a hammer dance in his chest. Nicole had not given her a last name!

Gram adjusted her wire rim glasses. "Let me see your hand, son."

Glancing at Nicole, Hunter put his hand on the table. He expected her to come to his rescue, but all he got was a less than reassuring smile.

Gypsy turned the hand, palm up and settled a grip on

his wrist with one hand. Using the other hand, she spread his fingers wide. Her knobby fingers started tracing the lines in his hand from heel to center palm and back again. She was silent for some time. "Do you have a middle name, Hunter Douglas?"

Hunter didn't answer. He was not going to give her any ammunition.

Gypsy sighed. "Very well, then I will give you one. I will call you Orion the Hunter."

Hunter stared hard at Nicole. She was picking lint from her sweater.

"You came a long way to see my DeeDee Sweet Pea. You come from a city, a big city—as big as New York even."

The hammer dance picked up velocity. Lord, he should have stayed in the lobby. He really wanted his hand back, but the woman had a grip of steel on it with her frail, knobby fingers. She continued the delicate assault on his palm, murmuring incoherently. Nicole had finished with the lint and now, appeared to be counting the little pebbled flecks in the ceiling.

Gypsy's fingers suddenly stopped moving. She became still. "You have healing powers," she said in a low raspy voice. "Are you a doctor of some sort?"

Hunter shifted in his chair. "No, Ma'am." His own voice was a bit thick.

"Ah yes, I see it over here. You're not a doctor, but you do have the power to heal. You have the power to heal my DeeDee Sweet Pea."

Nicole's spine straightened. "Gram."

Gypsy's fingers started to move again. "I see pain. Lot's of it. Hidden away, deep. Twelve years deep. Not your pain, Orion Just-a-Friend. My DeeDee Sweat Pea's pain."

Nicole jumped to her feet. "Enough, Gram, you've had your fun. Stop it right now, or I'm calling the devil to make you a reservation."

Gypsy sighed and released her grip on Hunter's wrist. She smiled at him and winked. "She always was a testy child." Gypsy turned to Nicole. "You can sit down now, DeeDee Sweet Pea. I'm finished here. What did you come to ask me?"

At that, Hunter's brows raised.

Nicole released a deep, gushing breath of air and sat down. "Gram, do you know who Brenda is?"

Gypsy's eyes darted from Nicole to Hunter then quickly glazed over. "Brenda, Brenda, good news, bad news," she murmured.

"Gram, did my father have an affair with Brenda's mother?"

Gypsy suddenly swiveled startled eyes toward Nicole. "No, no. DeeDee Sweet Pea. All planned."

"What do you mean, 'all planned'?" Nicole prodded.

Gypsy slowly shook her head. "Cappy's secret. Not mine to tell."

When Nicole looked up at him, Hunter knew she was hoping he understood what Gypsy was saying. He gave her a weak smile, raised his brows, and shrugged. His mind was still reeling from the palm reading.

She turned back to her grandmother. "Gram, Brenda died."

Gypsy became intensely still. A single tear traced a path down her aged cheek. She closed her eyes and lowered her head.

"Gram?" Nicole said quietly.

With watery eyes, haunted by sadness, Gypsy looked at Nicole. "Cappy's secrets are locked in my heart, DeeDee Sweet Pea."

"How can I unlock the secrets, Gram?"

Gypsy fingered the buttons on her blouse. "Where flames burn and flowers bloom; a gift of love in another time. Resting. Waiting. Cappy's secret, not mine." Gypsy closed her eyes. She began rocking back and forth, humming an off-key tune.

Nicole sighed. "You don't have to say anymore, Gram. If you made a promise, I won't ask you to break it. I want you to know, however, that Brenda had two children."

Gypsy stopped humming. Her head came up. "Children? Babies?"

Nicole laughed softly. "No, not babies. Shanna is six and Kyle is four. They're staying with me. Would you like to see them?"

The sparkle returned to Gypsy's eyes. "Yes, oh yes. One flower dies, two more bloom." She turned to Hunter. "That's how it should be. And when you, Orion Just-a-Friend, are no longer just a friend, then Sweet Pea will bloom. It's such a lovely flower, don't you think?"

* * * *

By the time they got back to the car, Hunter still hadn't said a word. He finally looked at Nicole. "Have I just been run over by a steam roller or is she really psychic?" he asked.

"I tried to warn you."

"How did she know my last name, and my middle name, and that I was from New York?"

When Nicole put the keys in the ignition, he reached over and plucked them out.

"We're not leaving this parking lot until I know exactly what went on in there."

Now she was grinning. "The clues are all there. Figure it out, Mr. Investigator."

His eyes narrowed on her, his mouth set in a thoughtful frown. She glanced at her wristwatch, settling back in the seat to observe him at work. The wheels were turning in his head, compiling data. It took him exactly one minute and ten seconds for his expression to change.

"Barney. She was on the phone when we walked in her room. Everybody in this community seems to know everybody else. Barney must have called her from the laundromat. She came up with Orion the same way you did."

"Damn, you are good." Nicole said with admiration. She reached for the car keys, laughing. "I didn't even tell you that Barney's been sweet on Gram for thirty years. That calculating mind of yours needs to be under lock and key. You could be downright dangerous."

"So, what was all the rest of that about?"

"Everything Gram said was a clue to something she promised not to tell." Nicole backed out of the parking lot and turned onto the road heading back toward Sunset Lake. "I should tell you what it was like living with Gram during the summers. She liked to buy us little presents, hide them around that big house, and give us clues so we could find them. Sometimes, Billy and I spent hours looking for something as small as a candy bar. She enjoyed those games even more then we did. Unfortunately, this isn't a game, and she knows it. You looked like you were in a daze back there. I hope you remember some of what she said."

"Who is Cappy?" Hunter asked.

"Gram calls everyone by his or her middle name. Cappy was my father. It's short for Capulet."

"As in Romeo and Juliet?"

Nicole laughed. "Gram was a bit theatrical. Gramps chose practical names like Robert, but he let Gram go wild on the middle names."

"Your middle name then is DeeDee."

"Actually, it's De Carlo. She shortened it. No doubt, she picked that name too."

For a time, Hunter stared out the front window. Nicole could almost hear his cerebral wheels turning again. Leaving him to his thoughts, she put her own mind on recalling Gram's words. Where flames burn and flowers bloom? Love in another time. Was she remembering it right? She should have written it down.

"What happened twelve years ago?" Hunter asked quietly.

Nicole's heart leaped. She should have known he

would ask. She should have known and yet, when he did, she was unprepared. "It was a long time ago, and it has nothing to do with all this," she said. "It's best left buried."

"Your grandmother doesn't seem to think so."

Nicole turned her face away from him, said nothing, and concentrated on her driving.

"Is it the reason you can't tolerate being touched?" Hunter persisted.

"I touch people all the time when I do measurements," Nicole responded indignantly.

"That's you touching them, not them touching you. Big difference."

"So now you're a psychiatrist?" she snapped. She shifted in her seat looking for a more comfortable position but not finding one. The fact that she didn't like people touching her, men in particular, was not open for discussion. Now or ever. "I think you're letting your imagination work overtime," she said with a tone of finality.

She didn't bother to look at him, but she could feel his eyes on her, studying her, unconvinced. At least he had the decency to be silent about it.

After a couple of minutes, she thought he had dropped the subject. She was just beginning to relax when he suddenly reached over and laid his hand on her arm.

Nicole gasped. She jerked the car toward the shoulder and slammed on the brakes. Without bothering to take the car out of gear, she jumped from the vehicle and ran into the ditch, toward the trees.

Hunter swore as he slammed the gearshift into park and charged after her.

"Nicole, stop!"

About forty feet from the road, she stopped. Grabbing on to the trunk of a large oak tree, she pressed her face into the rough bark, breathing fast and heavy. When she heard him come up behind her, she cringed.

"Go away."

"Nicole, I'm sorry. I shouldn't have done that."

She just clung to the tree, not answering.

"That was a cruel, insensitive thing to do. I swear I'll never—Nicole, please talk to me."

Her breathing slowed. Finally, she turned, but she refused to meet his gaze.

"I'm sorry," he repeated softly. "I had no right to do that."

Nicole kept her head lowered. Her back braced against the tree. "No, you didn't." she said hoarsely. "What happened to me can't be erased. Not by you or anybody else."

"How can you be so sure, if you don't let anybody close enough to you to try? Do you want to talk about it?"

"No."

"Let me help you."

Nicole flashed him an angry glare. "Four years of therapy couldn't help me. What makes you think you can?"

"If I understand you right, that was a long time ago. Besides, Gypsy said I had the power to heal you."

"And you believe her?" Nicole shrieked. She threw her hands up in the air. "Now that's certainly showing a great deal of intelligence."

"How do you know I can't help you, Nicole, if you won't give me a chance?" He reached out to her. "Just take my hand."

Nicole pressed back against the tree, edging away.

"Don't be afraid of me," Hunter said quickly. I won't touch you again without your permission."

Nicole fought the emotions welling up in her chest. "I'm—I'm not afraid. I'm just... just... I don't know what I am, Hunter. I don't know. I don't want to be this way, and you're right—that therapy was a long time ago. I wasn't ready for it."

Hunter dropped his hand. "You said you didn't have a problem touching when you took measurements."

Nicole nodded miserably.

Hunter spread his hands, palms up, at his side. "Imagine your taking my measurements then." When she hesitated, he reassured her. "Go ahead. I promise I won't make a move."

He waited, silently, not moving; giving her time to think about it.

Nicole took a deep breath. She didn't know how to tell him that she was mentally able to detach herself from her clients. Detaching herself from him was a different story entirely.

His patience won her over.

She started by touching him on the upper arms, first with one hand, then with both. His arms were firm and rippling with muscle. He was warm. She could feel the heat radiating through his clothes. Her hands moved from his arms to his chest, slowly, hesitantly. They began to move over his chest, toward the rib cage. While she touched him, she carefully avoided eye contact. This was nothing like taking measurements. Taking measurements was highly impersonal. It was a necessary part of her job that she'd never particularly enjoyed. Touching Hunter, feeling him, being aware of his heart beating rapidly beneath her fingers, was extremely pleasurable, erotic.

Standing there immobile while Nicole caressed him was the hardest thing Hunter had ever done. He worked at not sucking his breath in sharply every time she changed the position of her hands. When she splayed her soft fingers over his nipples, he nearly lost it. It was impossible to stop his body from responding. He hoped she was too concerned about what she was doing to notice. By the look on her face, she seemed to be concentrating only on touching him; totally unaware of the torture she was putting him through.

His breathing deepened. "You have to stop now," he said raggedly.

She looked up at him with questioning eyes. "Why?"

"Because I can't take any more," he snapped. He

backed away from her and started walking toward the car. She was right behind him. "Wait, Hunter, it was good for me. I was touching you and it wasn't even bothering me."

Hunter turned on her. "Well, it was bothering me," he barked louder than he'd intended.

The look on her face was crestfallen. "I'm sorry, I didn't know. You told me to—"

Guilt rode him. She was standing only inches from him. He reached out to take her in his arms and soothe away that look but stopped, remembering his promise. Besides, at this moment, soothing her was the last thing on his mind.

She was staring at him with hooded green eyes that almost looked inviting. When she nervously wet her lips, he started reaching for her again.

The slamming of the car door caught Hunter's attention even before the voice did. "Nicole Anderson, you in there? Nicole?"

"What the hell does he want?" Hunter asked with a hiss, stepping away from Nicole. "Is there anybody around here who doesn't know you?"

She looked at him, shrugging sheepishly. "Not many. That's John, the sheriff. We had better go out, or he'll come looking. He knows my Blazer."

"Next time, we use my car," he mumbled, walking back toward the road with Nicole beside him. Being aroused by Nicole was not something he'd planned, nor was it something he intended to follow up on. It put him in a sour mood.

Nicole stopped him with a soft touch on the arm. "Wait," she said, drawing back her hand quickly.

Hunter stopped and looked at her, hoping she wouldn't see the irritation on his face.

She didn't.

Nicole gave him a shy smile. "Thank you for—for what you did back there."

The irritation drained from him in an instant.

"You won't jump if I touch you anymore?" he asked.

She shook her head, smiling. "I—I don't know. Let's work up to it. Slowly."

Smiling, Hunter put a hand up to stroke her upper arm. She stood firm. He gave her a light squeeze. "Good girl, let's go see if your sheriff friend is waiting to cuff me."

They walked out of the woods together. By the look on the officer's face, Hunter was certain that one word from Nicole would put him behind bars for life.

"You okay, Nicole?" The man's eyes were trained on Hunter like a cobra preparing to strike.

"I'm fine, John. Hunter was just showing me some—some survival tricks."

Hunter could tell John wasn't buying that lame explanation, but he nodded, hesitated, and then headed back to his car. Halfway there, he stopped. "I almost forgot. My wife's sister and her husband, from Detroit Lakes, are going to be visiting this week. They're having a centennial or something back home and would like to buy some costumes. Okay if I bring them over to your shop?"

"That's fine, John, as long as they don't expect a tour. We aren't having another open house until Memorial Day."

"You take care then," he said. He started to leave again but turned back to her. "I almost forgot." He pulled a slip of paper out of his shirt pocket and approached, handing it to Nicole. "Clare at the mercantile said you dropped this in the store. I told her I would stop by your place and return it. This'll save me a trip."

She glanced at the paper, thanked him, stuffed it in her jeans, and trekked backed to her vehicle.

"Anything important?" Hunter asked, after they were in the car.

"No, just a list of phone numbers."

Hunter was watching the sheriff's car through his side mirror. It didn't move. The guy was obviously not going to go anywhere until they did. He shook his head. "Let's pick up the kids and go home. I've had all the friendly neighbors I can stand for one day."

Nicole put on her turn signal and pulled back on the road.

Fifteen minutes later, they pulled in front of Chuck's house. Shanna and Kyle were kneeling on the steps and staring into a large bucket. Chuck was sitting beside them hand-stitching a leather hat.

"We caught fish," Shanna said.

"I caught four, and Shanna got two," Kyle chimed. "Chuck said they're sunfish. They have yellow tummies."

Nicole and Hunter exchanged curious glances.

"It sounds like you two had a good time," Nicole said, smiling.

Hunter peered in the bucket. "Danged if they don't have fish in here. What are you going to do with them?"

Chuck laughed. "I was going to clean them, but they acted like I was trying to skin the family dog."

"Can we take them home with us?" Kyle asked, reaching in to nudge one of the wriggling sunfish. It scurried away, avoiding his touch.

Kyle saying the word home gave Nicole a warm feeling. Ever since Gram went to the care center, she'd thought of it as a house rather than a home. She sat down on the steps beside Kyle and looked in the bucket. "It seems to me like they're not having much fun in there. I bet they would be much happier if you let them go swimming back in the lake. Then you can catch them again next time you go fishing."

"We can go fishing again?" Kyle asked with little-boy surprise.

Something tugged at Nicole's heart. "Of course, you can, honey."

Kyle looked at Shanna. "Should we put them back, Shanna?"

Shanna thought for a moment. "I think that would be

best," she said, adding a bit sadly, "Chuck said they would die if they stay in the bucket too long." She looked at Hunter. "Will you carry them down to the lake for us?"

Nicole found herself taken back by the raw emotion on Hunter's face. He lifted the heavy pail as though it weighed no more than a feather, the muscles on his biceps bunching to attention. In contrast, he took Shanna's hand with extreme gentleness.

"Let's go set them free," he said.

Kyle hurried to catch up. "Can I let mine go by myself?"

Nicole knew Chuck watched her stare after them. "Nice kids," he said. "Really quiet. I don't think they've ever been out in a boat before, much less fishing. They sure seemed to have a good time though. Are they his?"

Nicole smiled. Chuck was truly her best friend. "Not yet," was all she said.

"And if I asked if he was somebody's husband would you say 'not yet' to that too?"

Nicole burst out laughing. "No. I would say mind your own business."

Chuck grinned. "I figured as much."

"Thanks for watching the kids," Nicole said quietly. "Give me a few days, I'll explain everything."

"That ought to be interesting. A man, with looks to die for, is staying at your house, with two kids who don't seem to belong to anybody. That story will be worth waiting for."

Hunter returned, carrying the empty bucket with Kyle riding on his broad shoulders. Shanna skipping beside him, toting Mr. Bear, reminded Nicole of the doll, still in the bag in her studio. She would give it to Shanna as soon as they got back to the house, along with the books for both of them.

Nicole turned to Chuck. "I'll see you at the shop tomorrow, brat. Don't forget, we have a deadline to meet."

Chapter Five

It was nine-thirty by the time Shanna and Kyle were tucked into bed, and Hunter brought in the suitcase. He set it on the kitchen counter where they had decided to work. Everything inside was in a disorderly mess, so he just dumped the entire contents out.

"We'll have to sift through this, one piece at a time," Hunter said, taking a seat across from Nicole.

Nicole immediately reached for the small photo album. Almost reverently, her fingers touched the faded gold lettering on the outside. It simply said 'Photos'.

The first few pages held pictures of people that must have been part of Brenda's life at one time or another. Nicole looked closely at them, trying to determine if one might be Brenda's mother. No person stood out as a clear possibility. Many of the pockets were empty.

"Some of the pictures must have fallen out," she said. "There seems to be a lot missing."

Hunter was reading and sorting the papers in piles. "I imagine we'll come across them if they're here. Barney sure made a mess of things when he tossed it all in the trashcan. I'll keep out what looks important and put the rest back in the suitcase. We won't throw anything away for now, except the dryer lint."

He grimaced when he picked up a wad of local grocery receipts. "Some of this stuff was obviously in that can before he dumped the suitcase. It's too bad I didn't go through it before it was stolen. We won't even know if something is missing. I don't think—"

When he stopped talking in mid sentence, Nicole looked up. He was staring at a document with a hardened expression. "What is it?" she whispered.

"Shanna's birth certificate."

"Does it say who her father is?"

"No. It says unknown." He handed it to her, swearing under his breath. "Her birthday is March fourteenth. She turned six two months ago."

Nicole gave him a sideways glance and took the certificate. It had a raised seal in the lower left corner. It listed only the mother, Brenda Marie Casey. "She had the same middle name as my mother," Nicole said softly. "I really wish I could have known Brenda."

"She lived a rough life. I doubt you would have had much in common."

Nicole handed the birth certificate back to Hunter and returned to the photo album. There was a close up baby picture with Brenda's name scrawled across the bottom. She took it out and handed it to Hunter. He glanced at it and handed it back.

"Here's one of Shanna," she said.

Hunter quickly stood up and came around the counter, and looked over Nicole's shoulder. "Look at those beautiful red curls," he said, leaning in close to see.

He wasn't touching her, but Nicole could feel the warmth of his body. It wasn't hard to remember earlier that day when she'd had her hands on his chest, feeling the hard muscles through the soft fabric of his shirt. The last thing on her mind was taking measurements. A warm flush settled over her, his nearness quickly turning the warmth to heat. She was relieved when Hunter returned to his seat and his paper sorting. Moments later, she spread out four more pictures of Shanna at various ages.

"Well, what the hell?"

Hunter's voice brought her head up again. He stared at a piece of paper, frowning heavily.

"What?"

"It's Brenda's birth certificate. She was twenty-nine in January."

Nichole's eyes widened. This time it was her turn to dash around the counter. "Does it look legitimate?" she asked, peering over Hunter's shoulder.

"It has a stamped seal."

She searched out the father's name. Robert C. Anderson. Tears pooled in her eyes. "I just don't understand how Dad could have done that to Mom." She turned away, wiping at her cheeks.

"Well this certainly can't be a coincidence," Hunter said. "Brenda's mother's name is Yvonne DeCarlo Casey."

Nicole's glare raced to the name. "He gave me her middle name. How could he do such a thing? He had to have had more than a casual affair with her. Mom couldn't possibly have known. She would never have allowed it." Nicole grabbed a tissue and went back to her seat.

"I'm sorry," was all Hunter said.

"It's not your fault my father was a rotten person. How could he have fooled me like that? I always trusted and believed him in every way. I wonder how Billy will take this news. I couldn't even bring myself to call him yet. He absolutely idolized Dad. But then, so did I," she added flatly. Her chest felt like a truck had parked on it.

Nicole dried her eyes and flipped through the rest of the album, then flipped the pages back again. "There are no pictures of Kyle," she said. "Not one."

"Maybe they fell out." Hunter suggested. "He lifted the mound of papers, sifting through them. "Here's a couple." He looked at the photos before handing them to her. "Not Kyle, I'm afraid. A baby picture of Brenda and another at about age one or two."

The second photo was black and white. A little girl stood in some trees holding a tiny bouquet of wild flowers. Scrawled across the bottom, in the same handwriting as the other pictures, was the name 'Brenda'.

A wave of dizziness swept over Nicole. Her throat closed, making it hard to breathe. Before Hunter could say anything, she threw the picture in front of him and ran from the kitchen. "I'll be right back," she called over her shoulder.

Nicole came back to the kitchen, handed him a picture she'd brought with her, then stood beside him waiting, breathing hard. He held the two pictures side by side. They were identical. He turned Nicole's picture over. It had a different number.

"One is a duplicate," he said quietly. "Where did you get this?"

"It's been in our family photo album since I can remember. I always believed it was a picture of me, but it was Brenda all along, wasn't it? My father had a picture of his love child in our family album, for God's sake. He flaunted her in front of us all. Then he goes and dies, so I can't even scream at him." Tears slid down her cheeks.

"Would you like a hug?" Hunter asked quietly, holding out his arms.

Nicole nodded, sniffing piteously, though she made no move toward him.

Hunter reached out and drew her between his legs into his arms. He held her while she cried softly into his shoulder. Her fingers dug into his back with fierce intensity.

"Would you like to stop with this tonight? We can go over the rest tomorrow."

Nicole shook her head. "No, let's keep going. I can't imagine finding anything that would make me feel worse than I do right now." She drew herself away from him almost reluctantly. Having a man's arms around her, comforting her, was a new experience, a feeling she liked.

She walked back to her chair, grabbing a wad of tissues on the way. "I'm sorry I'm acting like such a sap," she said. "It's just that—"

"You have a right to be upset, Nicole. But there's something about this whole thing that bothers me. When you asked your grandmother if your father had an affair with Brenda's mother, she said no. It was all planned."

"Of course, she'd guard his secret; he was her son." Nicole said bitterly.

"I suppose that's possible, but you said yourself, everything she told us was a clue."

"Well then, explain how my father's name is on Brenda's birth certificate—only a year before I was born."

"Was it by chance before your parents were married?"

"They were married over ten years by the time I was born. Mom told me herself she couldn't have—" Nicole sucked in a heavy breath of air and held it.

"Nicole? What is it?"

"Mom had a surgery so she could get pregnant. That's why they were married so long before they had me."

"When did she have the surgery?"

Nicole shrugged her shoulders. "I don't know. Obviously, before I was born." When she looked at Hunter, he was quiet and frowning. She recognized that look. He was compiling data. Nicole tried to think, tried to think of a way to believe in her father again. To believe Gram was right, and he didn't have an on-going affair with Yvonne DeCarlo Casey. She finally gave up and watched Hunter think instead. She knew the instant something registered with him.

"If they thought they couldn't have children," he said, "maybe they got involved in a surrogate mother program with Yvonne."

"Then why didn't they raise Brenda?"

"Maybe Yvonne changed her mind and wouldn't give the child up, and that's when your mother had the surgery and got pregnant with you."

Nicole felt relief flood through her like a dam bursting. "I suppose that could explain it. Is there anyway we can verify the surrogate mother idea?"

"Probably. I'll call my brother and my secretary tomorrow and get them on it. There should be some records. What we don't know is where it might have been done. It could have been in New York or here in Minneapolis—or even somewhere in between. There's also the possibility that it was handled privately, and then we'd have a hard time tracing it. At least that would fit in with what your grandmother said, as well as your certainty that your father loved your mother and wouldn't have had an affair."

"Thank you, Hunter," Nicole said, smiling wanly. "Even if it turns out that you're wrong. Thank you. I think I'm starting to like you, just a little."

"Just a little? Well that's certainly a start."

"Don't let it go to your head. It's actually your brain I like."

Hunter chuckled. "Let's finish up here." He turned back to the diminishing pile of papers and started sorting again. "Do we have any coffee left?"

"I think so." She got up to get the coffee, filled both their cups, and sat back down to look at the pictures again.

As he worked, Hunter found more and passed them to her, none were of Kyle. She started putting the loose ones back in the album. "This other baby picture of Brenda is a different pose. She was a beautiful baby."

"I'm not surprised," Hunter murmured without taking his eyes off his work. "She resembles you a lot."

Nicole snorted. "That's a stretch. You said she was stunningly beautiful."

"So?" This time he did glance up at her.

"So, I'm not beautiful."

Shrugging, Hunter turned his attention back to the papers. "I guess I would have a different opinion on that."

While Nicole searched for a comeback, she realized

Hunter had suddenly become motionless. He was frowning, staring at a document in his hand. Reaching in the pile of papers he'd set aside, he quickly fished through them, pulled one out, and held it up next to the one in his hand. He was making her uneasy again.

"What did you find, Hunter?"

He didn't answer.

"Hunter?" She started to get up to go around the counter when he let his hands drop and stared at her.

"This is a death certificate," he said.

"Brenda's?"

"Yes. It says she died three weeks after she was born."

Chapter Six

That night Nicole slept fitfully. Too many emotions rattled around in her head, like ghosts dragging chains, tormenting her. The one consolation, they were not the usual ghosts that pursued her. These were of Brenda waving a birth certificate in one hand and a death certificate in the other.

At five a.m., she finally gave up trying to sleep. She got up and took a shower—a long hot shower. The soothing spray cleansed her body and cleared her mind, so by the time she'd finished, she was ready to go to work. Work always chased away her nightmares.

She dried her hair, pulled on a mint green sweater, and slipped into her work worn jeans. As usual, she did no further fussing with her appearance. She walked through the quiet house, illuminated with predawn light, to her studio. This was her element, the setting where she could forget everything else and concentrate on her project at hand.

She finished matching the pattern pieces before setting to work on the fabrics and colors. She bought all her fabric in bolts, most of them special ordered, many from as far away as Italy and Japan. Each bolt had an identification number attached to it.

Several books of sample pieces helped her to match the numbers with the designs. Of the twenty-five costumes needed for the upcoming play, she could pull at least six from their inventory. After a production was over, she often bought back any costumes in good condition and reused them. Every costume in her shop was of her own design and each one was unique.

Men's outfits were the most difficult. She often had to take small liberties in her designs; because, if she were to conform to actual colors and clothes in history, most of them would be laughed off the stage, even in a serious production. It was difficult to portray a hero with a character wearing pink tights.

Dawn peeked through the windows when she became aware of the aroma of coffee. The thought of Hunter being an early riser made her smile. Five minutes later, he came into the studio carrying two mugs of steaming brew.

"Don't you believe in sleep?" he asked, handing her a mug.

She took the coffee with an appreciative smile. "It interferes with work."

He glanced over the materials and sketches on her drawing table. "So what are you working on?"

He listened attentively while she explained some of the details of her work. When he didn't understand something, he asked questions. She took her coffee mug with her and walked him through the shop, explaining as she went. He made a soft whistling sound when he saw the full racks of costumes, and again, when she took him through the storeroom brimming with colorful bolts of fabric and neatly organized supplies.

"Are the kids still sleeping?" she asked when they returned to the studio.

He smiled. "Yes, and would you believe, Mr. Komodo is sleeping between them. It's the first time I've seen them sleep without clutching on to each other." Hunter drained his coffee cup. "This place has done wonders for them, and so have you," he added. "I think you have a lot more maternal instinct than you give yourself credit for."

"It's not difficult with them. They are so needy."

"Yes, there's no doubt about that. You want more coffee?"

She handed him her empty cup. "Please, yes—you'd make somebody a great wife."

"You mean like Chuck?"

Nicole looked at him with surprise. "You knew he was gay?" At Hunter's nod, she asked, "how?"

"You let him hug you." He took her cup and headed back toward the kitchen, leaving her staring at his back.

"I want sugar this time," she called after him.

A minute later, he was back. He eyed the computer on a large, antique, walnut desk in front of yet, another fireplace "I need a place to work," he said. "Would it disturb you if I worked here?"

She shrugged. "It's more like you would be the one disturbed. It can get a little noisy with the machines and chatter in the shop."

"Not a problem for me. I can tune out anything."

Nicole smiled. She remembered the trances he went in when he was thinking. "The only phone in the room is here on my worktable."

"I'll use my cell phone. Are you connected to the Internet?"

"Sure, help yourself."

"Great, I'll get my things."

After he was gone, Nicole had a peculiarly warm feeling about his working in the same room with her. The fact that she knew what he would be doing put a damper on her thoughts, but she really did want the whole business of Brenda cleared up. If the woman posing as Brenda Casey wasn't really her sister, that would mean Shanna and Kyle weren't really her niece and nephew. Those kids had nested in a corner of her heart in less than twenty-four hours. The thought of them leaving was disconcerting. The thought of

Hunter leaving was equally disturbing.

She left the room to check the inventory on velvet fabrics. When she returned twenty minutes later, Hunter had settled at the desk and was talking on his cell phone.

"What the hell are you doing in bed, Virgil? You're an hour earlier than we are here."

"And where, pray tell, are you?" Virgil Douglas asked, with yawning disinterest.

"Minnesota."

"Is that still part of the United States?"

Hunter laughed. "Must be, I didn't need a passport to get in."

"So why are you calling me at this ungodly hour?"

"Don't let this go to your head, but I need you."

Virgil grunted. "What's up?"

"You'll need to take notes." Hunter said. He was relieved when Nicole left the room to let Chuck in the outside shop door.

"Yeah, hold on, not everybody has a computer for a brain like you do. What did we ever do before cordless phones? Go ahead, I'm all set."

"First check on surrogate mother programs in New York. We're talking thirty years ago, so there probably weren't that many. The name you're looking for is Yvonne DeCarlo Casey. She had a daughter named Brenda Marie Casey, and the father listed on the birth certificate is Robert C. Anderson. I'll fax you a copy of the birth certificate. A hooker, calling herself Brenda Casey, died of an overdose last Wednesday. See if you can find out who she really was. There's a file at the office on some research I did for her seven years ago."

"What makes you think she wasn't really Brenda Casey?" Virgil asked.

Hunter paused. "I have a death certificate that says Brenda Casey died when she was three weeks old. So either there's another Brenda Casey, or she was an imposter. See if you can find anything of interest concerning any of those names."

"Do you have any idea how many Robert C. Andersons there are?"

"I can narrow it down. He lived in Minneapolis and died seven years ago. You can find the address in Brenda's file."

"Is that it?"

"Until I think of something else. Oh, see if you can get a copy of the autopsy report on Brenda."

"How do you expect me to do that?"

"You're the lawyer, use that degree for something besides decorating your wall."

Vigil snorted. "I'm getting some odd vibes here. What exactly is your involvement in all this? I didn't even know you were planning a trip to Minnesota."

"It's confidential."

"Smells like a woman to me. Is she good looking?"

Hunter looked at Nicole through the shop door. She held notes in her hand and was explaining something to Chuck. She turned and started walking back toward the studio.

"Hunter? You still there?" Virgil asked.

"Yeah, what was your question again?"

"I asked if she was good looking."

Hunter grinned. "Stunningly."

"A word of advice, Hunter. Stay away from the party girls; the folks want grandkids."

"I'll enter that data, thanks."

"By the way, Mom's surprise party is tomorrow night. Will you be back?"

"Shit. I forgot about that. You'll have to give her my regards. Buy her some flowers from me."

"Great, she's turning sixty, and all she gets from her number two son is flowers from her number one son. What kind, or do I have to decide that for you too?"

"She'll have the rest of you there. If you're all as

obnoxious as you usually are, she might not even know I'm missing, me being one of the middle children and all."
Hunter watched Nicole bend over some sketches stacked on the floor. "Make it Sweet Peas," he said. "I'll call Ma from here during the party."
"Where is here?"
"Call me on my cell phone. You have the number."
Hunter ended the call as Nicole came in and returned to her work. He shifted uncomfortably in his chair. Trying to work with a king size erection was more than a little distracting.
"I'll go see if the kids are awake," he said.
"Do you need me for anything?" Nicole asked, straightening up.
Hell, yes, I need you for something, woman. Are you blind! "No, you look busy. I'll call you when breakfast is ready. Invite Chuck, if you like."
Nicole went back to her work, stopping only to let Carmen and Amanda in. Carmen was forty-three, divorced five years, and had two teenagers at home. She had a talent for reading Nicole's designs and needed to ask few questions. By her own admission, she was not nearly as talented at picking men. Amanda, on the other hand, was the same age as Nicole and a genius with needle and thread. She often added her own little touches to the costume details, enhancing both their authenticity and overall appearance. She did all the intricate finishing touches. Amanda had a live-in boy friend who adored her. Both women set up their workstations and wasted no time getting started and staying focused.
Until Hunter walked in.
Two pairs of wide-open eyes swiveled to Nicole.
"Well, are you going to introduce us to this incredible hunk of manhood or not?" Carmen asked.
Chuck chose this moment to walk in from the supply room, brandishing a medieval sword. "Down girls, he's taken."

Carmen's eyes narrowed on Chuck. "He's yours?"

Laughter rumbled in Hunter's chest. "Sorry ladies, I didn't mean to interrupt." He looked at Nicole. "I just came to tell you breakfast is ready."

Carmen chuckled wickedly. "If you're replacing Berta, I'm going to start taking my meals here."

Nicole finally found her voice. "This is Hunter Douglas. And no, he is not replacing Berta, he's here on business," she said, stressing the last word. "Hunter, that is Carmen Jansen at the sewing table and Amanda Tanner at the cutting board." She gestured to each woman in turn, giving Carmen a warning look, which the older woman ignored.

Hunter dipped his head. "Pleasure meeting you, ladies. I guess I better get back to the kitchen." He looked at Chuck. "Have you eaten?"

"Sure have. Thanks Hunter." Chuck grinned at Carmen and said, "Told you he was taken."

When Hunter left the room, Nicole rounded on Chuck. "Will you kindly set these two straight?"

"Aw-w, do I have to?" Chuck wheedled.

Nicole caught up with Hunter in the foyer. "I'm sorry," she said.

"For what? I haven't had so much fun since I convinced my little brother that hamburgers come from cows."

"You aren't angry?"

"Do I look angry?"

"Well—no."

"And what can we assume by that?"

"That you have a quirky sense of humor?"

Hunter laughed. "I think it's called small town survival. Let's go eat. Shanna and Kyle are asking about you."

When they walked into the kitchen, Shanna and Kyle chimed in unison "Good morning, Auntie Nicky."

Nicole eyed them both suspiciously. "He told you to

say that, didn't he?"

Shanna managed to keep a straight face, but Kyle started giggling. He looked at Hunter and giggled harder.

Nicole took her seat and whispered none too quietly to Kyle. "Would you tell Honeypot to feed me before I start chewing on his leg?"

Hunter reached around her and set a plate of scrambled eggs and ham in front of her. He whispered close to her ear. "Promises. Promises."

Hunter set plates in front of Shanna and Kyle, taking his own seat beside Nicole. He winked at each one of the kids in turn.

"How are the eggs, Nicky?" he asked.

She gave him a beguiling smile. "Just the way I like them, Honeypot."

"You best enjoy them today, because tomorrow morning we're going to have them in milk—raw." He held up his glass of milk. "See, you just crack them in a glass and swallow them whole." He downed the glass of milk in two gulps.

"I think I'm going to be sick." Nicole moaned.

Both Shanna and Kyle made sour faces. "I think I'll have orange juice tomorrow instead of milk," Shanna said.

Kyle giggled. "Me too."

* * * *

"Are we going fishing today?" Shanna asked when they'd finished eating.

"Maybe we can catch our fish back again," Kyle said eagerly.

Nicole smiled at his innocence. "I don't think Chuck has time to take you, but I have another idea. This house has lots of fun places to play. My brother, Billy, and I used to hide out for hours in little corners. We especially liked the attic, and if I'm not mistaken, there is still a large box of toys up there. You could play up there or ask someone really strong to carry some things downstairs for you."

"Where is the attic?" Shanna asked.

"On the third floor," Nicole said. "There's a stairway in the storeroom on Billy's wing."

"I have a better idea," Hunter interjected as he carried dishes to the sink. "Yesterday you mentioned giving some school kids a tour. Maybe you should give Shanna and Kyle a tour so they can get familiar with the whole house."

"That's a splendid idea," Nicole said. "Would you like to be included?" she asked Hunter.

Hunter gave her a heartwarming grin. "I wouldn't miss it for the world."

Connected to the kitchen by a swinging door was the dining room where Nicole started the tour. First, she pointed out the high, recessed, oak paneled ceiling, the cream-colored wallpaper simulating a damask pattern, and the large, burl-walnut veneer table dominating the center of the room. She named each piece of furniture and wall hanging just as she did when showing her home to adults.

"This was my grandfather's pride and joy," she said, running her hand over the cool, marble fireplace. Lovingly, she touched the life size figurines flanking the mantel. "He brought these marble cupids from Italy. They're called amorini; they represent Time and Love." She pointed to the painting hanging between them. "That's an oil replica of The Poppies, by Monet. It was his wedding gift to Gram."

"Do you ever use this room?" Hunter asked, lifting Kyle up to finger a scantily clad cupid.

"We used to when we were kids. Gram entertained a lot. Now the city council has monthly meetings here, and periodically, other groups use it for small dinner parties, Berta does the cooking, it supplements her income. Sometimes, they even rent costumes."

"Séances?"

"Not since Gram retired," Nicole said, giving Hunter a sly wink.

Beyond the dining room, along the inside wall, two wide pocket doors opened into the sitting room—or parlor, as it was once called. Modernized to some extent, the sitting room encompassed the backside of the house behind the staircase. Six floor-to-ceiling windows, half of them patio doors opening to the deck, provided cozy natural light.

Nicole pushed a button that slid the drapes open to a breathtaking view of Sunset Lake.

"It's so beautiful," Shanna gasped, looking out at the tree-hugged lake, "Like a fairy tale."

Beside her, Kyle whispered something to which Shanna replied, "I hope so."

Nicole and Hunter locked eyes for a scant second before Nicole continued. "The wildlife paintings were all done by my great-grandmother. The fireplace is made of native rock and is actually, the only wood burning one left in the house. This big lamb's wool rug came from New Zealand and was a twenty-fifth wedding anniversary gift from my parents to Gram and Gramps. Billy and I used to sneak down here at night and sleep nested in the thick furry softness," Nicole added, smiling, bending down to run a hand lovingly over the rug.

A cushy, butternut leather sofa, matching loveseat, and two reclining chairs, along with a television and video recorder, were the only things in the room that were added within the last thirty years. Her grandfather designed and made all the side tables and the glass top coffee table, carved from rough-cut cedar.

Several dozen candles and numerous magazines on costume design scattered about the room gave it a cozy, lived-in look. Her grandmother, she explained, made most of the candles.

On the far side of the sitting room, Nicole pointed out two more pocket doors that opened into the workshop, originally designed as a ballroom.

"We usually go from here, through the foyer, and end in the workshop," Nicole said, taking Kyle's hand. "But since you are special guests, you will get the deluxe tour upstairs."

Shanna rushed up to take Nicole's other hand. "You have a really wonderful house, Aunt Nicky."

Nicole squeezed her fingers. "Thank you, Shanna, I was hoping you wouldn't be bored."

"Oh, no. It's like a palace, where kings and queens stay. If I lived here, I would be like a princess."

"What would I be?" Kyle asked, looking around Nicole to Shanna.

"You would be a prince. Aunt Nicky would be the queen."

Kyle smiled at that. "But what about Hunter?"

"Hunter would be king," Shanna said brightly.

A heavy grunt came from behind them. "Yeah, and we'd all live happily ever after. Too bad life isn't like that."

"If Hunter doesn't believe in fairy tales," Nicole said, "I think we should make him the troll under the bridge."

Both kids turned and giggled at Hunter, who attempted to make a nasty troll face at them.

At the top of the stairs, Nicole pointed out the things of interest in the two-story foyer, in particular, the sky-toned, cloud-studded fresco ceiling, made, she explained, by painting it before the plaster dried so the colors become incorporated. The entire second floor, surrounded by the u-shaped banister, looked down on the foyer.

Nicole bypassed the room occupied by Hunter and the connecting one where Kyle and Shanna slept, the rooms she and Billy used when they were kids, and went straight to her wing.

Above the dining room, Nicole's bedroom with the seating area was an exact duplicate of Billy's, except for the end room above the kitchen. The one on Billy's wing, above the studio, and leading to the attic; the room connected to Nicole's bedroom, was originally intended for a nursery but now used for storage.

Nicole's bedroom had a king-size canopy bed. Mr. Komodo stretched lazily in the center of it. Shanna and Kyle immediately scrambled up on the patchwork quilt to give the cat some attention.

Hunter's gaze turned to her just as the phone beside the bed rang. Mr. Komodo leaped off and ran for the connecting lounge area. Kyle and Shanna scrambled after him.

Nicole answered, "Hello." She listened for a moment, glancing at Hunter when she said, "Yes, Barney, what is it?"

Nicole was aware that Hunter watched her face anxiously. She kept her expression stoic, saying only "uh huh" into the phone. Finally, she said, "Thanks, Barney, you've been very helpful. Hunter will be glad to know about that. Oh, I'll be sure to tell him. Call again if you remember anything else. Bye."

Taking a deep breath, she faced Hunter. He had a most annoying 'I told you he'd call' look on his face.

"What did he remember?" Hunter prodded.

"He said his friend Sam was at the One Stop Station having coffee Saturday night just when it started to rain. A car drove by three times, stopped, and asked directions to my house."

"Did you get a description of the man?"

"Yes, Barney said he was a good looking sort and quite tall."

"What kind of car was he driving?"

"A dark blue Mercedes." A burst of laughter escaped from her. It took Hunter less than ten seconds to compile that data, but by then, her laughter brought tears to her eyes.

Hunter stood at the foot of the bed, his eyes narrowing on her. He prowled toward her like a hungry cat stalking its prey.

Nicole grabbed a throw pillow and flung it at him, then scurried across the bed to the other side. Her taunting laughter hadn't stopped. "I sent you a map along with directions easy enough for a three year old to follow. Apparently, that huge brain of yours doesn't work for understanding directions."

He was now coming around the foot of the bed. "The problem with your directions," he said flatly, "was that they were lying at home on my table. I had to go by memory."

"But you never forget anything," she said jumping back on the bed.

"Except in this case, I barely glanced at the squiggly little scrawls you drew." He dodged another pillow. "If every Tom, Sam, and Barney within a twenty-mile radius hadn't known where you lived, I may still be looking." He paused for just a second as though forming a plan of action. "I think it's time I called in my marker."

When he lunged for her, Nicole threw herself face down on the bed. He landed on top of her, pinning her. Laughter was still shaking her body when she shrieked for Kyle and Shanna to help her. Seconds later, both kids were piling on top of Hunter, and he had to roll off Nicole to keep from squashing her. He ended up on his back with a child on each arm, holding him down, their little fingers tickling his ribs.

"I give up. Stop. I give. She's the nasty one. Go tickle, Auntie Nicky."

When Hunter finally gave up the fight, they both ended up on his chest with one of his arms around each of them.

Nicole looked up to see him press a kiss to the top of Shanna's head. The tender display, forced her to swallow a lump rising in her throat. Feeling left out, she moved to lean against Hunter and put her arm over Kyle. The four of them remained like that until Mr. Komodo jumped on the bed to investigate. Kyle and Shanna immediately wriggled free and turned their attention back to the cat. That left Hunter with his arms empty and Nicole's hand on his chest. His arm opened, and she wasted no time lifting her head and settling into it.

Lying in the warmth of Hunter's arm felt so right. The arm around her tightened ever so slightly, and he turned to press his face into her hair. He was breathing deeply, and Nicole held her own breath not wanting the moment to end. Without warning, he released her, sat up, and got off the bed. "We better finish the tour," he said gruffly, turning away from her. "So I can get back to work."

Nicole moved off the bed, wondering if he was as affected by their closeness as much as she was. "We only have the attic left."

The door to the attic, through the storage room, on Billy's wing, was at the top of a long, narrow flight of stairs. Both the kids and Hunter stared in awe at the wide-open expanse of the third floor. On one end, boxes of all sizes and shapes crowded the corners, on the other, abandoned furniture stood in piles of semi-organized clutter.

Nicole pointed out the large box of toys under a dust-covered window. With exclamations of delight, Shanna and Kyle hurried to examine the contents.

Hunter commented on the furniture. "Do you realize you have a fortune in antiques here?"

"It's mostly leftover stuff that didn't fit in anywhere. When I modernized the sitting room, I brought everything up here. Old settees are nice to look at, but they don't provide much in comfort. I prefer plush stuffed leather and more livable furniture for lounging around."

He gave her a teasing grin. "Does that mean you actually do something besides work once in a while?"

Nicole sighed. "Yeah, on the nights we have a blue moon."

"When is the last time you went out for a romantic dinner and dancing?" he asked.

Nicole stared at him, blinking. The question had caught her off guard. "I don't remember." She said quickly, turning her back on him, ending the discussion. Her nonexistent love life was a subject she avoided at all costs.

She walked toward the kids, her smile back in place. Kyle pushed one of Billy's old trucks over the dusty wood floor, and Shanna went through a stack of puzzles. Their enthusiasm warmed her heart. "Do you want to take some things downstairs? You can play in the sitting room, or your bedroom, or even in the workshop if you like."

"Can we take anything we want?" Kyle asked.

"Anything or everything. If you want it all, we'll make Hunter carry it. He looks strong enough to handle the job, don't you think?"

Kyle looked at Hunter who had walked up behind Nicole. "Hunter is maybe even as strong as Hercules," he said grinning.

A few minutes later, they had Hunter loaded down with trucks, games, and building blocks, cautioning him not to drop anything as they followed him down the narrow stairs.

Back in the storage room, he caught Nicole's eye. "Hercules, huh?"

Nicole smiled. "You have another flight to go, Big Boy. They want it in the sitting room. After they see how large the shop is, they might change their minds."

As it turned out, they did prefer to play in the shop where all the activity was, particularly, when they found Chuck there.

Nicole went back to matching fabrics, and Hunter went straight to his desk and his phone.

His assistant, Marla Hawkins, answered on the second ring.

"Hunter? This better be you."

Hunter laughed. "If the building's on fire, save the files and get out."

"Very funny," Marla said dryly. "Where the heck are you? I've been calling your apartment and your cell phone for two days."

"I'm in Minnesota."

"Minnesota? We don't have any cases going on there."

"It's personal. What's on fire, anyway?"

The Sinclair family we're researching. I can't find anything going back farther than 1775."

"Didn't they say their ancestors came from England?"

"Yes, but I can't find the name of the ship they came over on. I was hoping you had something stored in that monster brain of yours I could use."

Hunter laughed. "Was that a compliment, Marla?"

"Only if you give me some good data."

The Sinclair's weren't a poor family, so you might be able to narrow it down. Look at the Harbinger or Vintner. They were more like cruise ships and catered to the wealthy."

"I've been looking for this thing for eight hours, and you have the name of the ship in your head. Do you have a crystal ball in your back pocket?"

Hunter burst out laughing at her choice of words. "I could be wrong."

Marla snorted. "Now that would be a surprise."

"What else do you need?" he asked.

Marla went through a list of things. Hunter either gave her the answers she needed or told her where to get them. While he talked, his eyes followed Nicole as she worked on her samples. She gave him a genial smile as she walked into the shop carrying an armload of designs and fabric pieces. He had to lean forward to observe her explaining something to Carmen.

He suddenly realized the other end of the line was silent. "Marla, you still there?"

"Oh, I'm here," she said. "I was just waiting for you to get your mind off of whatever it is that's distracting you."

Hunter tore his eyes away from, Nicole. "Sorry. Was there anything else?"

"Nope, I think we covered it all. Now, what are you getting yourself into in Minnesota?"

"I'll fill you in later, but I do need you to do some digging for me. A dark man with a beard, probably Arabian or Israeli, rented a cheap car from a low budget rental place, most likely not a chain of any kind. Try the local places in Minneapolis, the twenty-bucks-a-day, type rentals. See if you can get a name or how long it's rented for, if he still has it, and where he's from."

"You want me to find out what kind of underwear he's wearing too?"

Hunter chuckled. "No, but he's wearing a jacket that looks kind of itchy."

"You're right there in the area. Why aren't you doing it?"

"They would be more likely to give that kind of info to a distraught wife from New York, looking for her husband."

"They might find it curious I don't know the name of my husband."

"Hell, use your charm, Marla. Give them a sob story. I hear the guy looks 'like a terrorist'. They'll be more than happy to accommodate you. See what you can find. Call me on my cell."

"Hunter?"

"Yeah."

"Stay away from the party girls."

Hunter hung up the phone, swearing. One bad marriage and the whole damn world remembered it. He was thirty-three years old. Didn't they think he was capable of choosing his own females? It wasn't exactly like he made a habit of dating the wrong women, at least, not in the last five years.

He glanced at his watch—almost lunchtime. He had just enough time to send the faxes to Virgil. In his room, he searched through the old suitcase for the papers he needed when he spotted a picture in one of the side pockets. It was a snapshot of a girl about six or seven years old, riding a horse on a merry go round. She had auburn curls and a smile as big as the sun. Pretty girl. Obviously, Brenda.

He saw Nicole sitting at a little table with Shanna and

Kyle on the far end of the shop. Rather than encounter Carmen and Amanda again, he laid the picture on the desk and sent off the faxes to his brother. That finished, he headed for the kitchen thinking about macaroni and cheese.

* * * *

A short while later, when Nicole came into the studio looking for Hunter, the pungent aroma of cheese told her where to find him. Passing the desk, she noticed the picture Hunter had left there. Curious, she walked over and picked it up.

She stared at the little girl in the picture, swallowing, trying to keep her hand from shaking, unaware that she was holding her breath until she was forced to release it in one gasping rush. Without taking her eyes off the photo, she walked in a daze toward the kitchen.

Hunter took one look at her stricken face and dropped what he was doing. "Nicole? What is it? What's wrong?"

She held up the picture. "Where did you get this?" she whispered.

"It was in a pocket of the suitcase."

"This is a picture of me. How did it get in Brenda's suitcase?"

Hunter put his hand under Nicole's chin, tipping it up to look at him. Tears swam in her eyes. "Because, it's Brenda."

Nicole held up the picture. "Hunter, this is me."

"Do you have one like it?"

"No. I've never seen it before."

"Then what makes you think it's you?"

"Because, I remember when it was taken. We were at the state fair. Mom was pregnant with Billy. He was born five weeks later. Please tell me this is a joke and you found it in a drawer upstairs." When she blinked, a tear slid down her cheek.

With his thumb, Hunter brushed the tear away. "You know I would never do that to you."

"Then help me understand this. Everything in my life

is suddenly turning upside down. I find a picture of Brenda in my family photo album. We find a picture of me in Brenda's suitcase. We have a death certificate saying Brenda died before I was even born. A strange man breaks into your trunk. Hunter, tell me what's happening."

Hunter pulled her into his arms. He smoothed his hand over her hair, letting her sob her frustration into his shoulder. "I promise you, we'll figure it all out. My brother is working on it, and so is my assistant in New York. I've tried to put it together, but there are too many missing pieces, and I need more information. But I promise; I won't leave until I have all the answers."

That last statement comforted her. She liked having him around to lean on, to rationalize things when they became too confusing. He dealt with facts. She had to believe, if anybody could put some normalcy back into her life, he could. If the leaving part made her uneasy, she chose to ignore it.

Hunter kissed the top of her head, before releasing her. He pulled a tissue from a box on the counter and handed it to her. "Dry your eyes now, before the kids come in and think you hate my macaroni and cheese."

Nicole blew her nose and managed a soggy smile. "I seem to be forever sobbing on your shoulder. Would you believe I haven't cried since my father's funeral?"

Hunter went back to the stove. "Until I came into your life and dumped all this chaos in your lap."

"I guess blaming you would make me feel a lot better," she said attempting a joke.

Hunter chucked her playfully under the chin. "That's the spirit. Now, go see who's brave enough to come and eat this gunk I made."

* * * *

In the studio later, Hunter stared at the computer screen. He had pulled up the Internet but he wasn't using it. It drove him crazy to have dots in front of him he couldn't connect, and these dots seemed to span all the way from

New York to Minnesota, but there were still too many missing. Some of those answers had to be right here, in Minnesota. Something was dangling, like a carrot, in front of him, close, but out of reach.

Nicole came in from the shop. She walked up behind him to see what he was looking at. He hadn't moved from the opening screen.

She dropped into the side chair. "Any luck?"

"No," he said. "We're missing something, and I can't figure out what it is. I'm not even sure where to look." He turned toward her, his elbows on the arms of the chair, his hands steepled in front of him. "I need your help."

Nicole raised her eyebrows. "I'll do whatever I can. Just tell me what you need."

Hunter hesitated, remembering her earlier reaction to the picture he'd found. The last thing he wanted was to put her through more turmoil, but he needed to fill in the missing pieces. She was the only one who could do it.

"You said you remember your mother being pregnant with Billy?"

Nicole nodded.

"Do you think you might have his birth certificate?"

"I know I do. There's a small lock box in the attic with Dad's things. It's in there, along with their marriage license, baptismal records, school diplomas, and stuff like that."

"Your birth certificate too?"

"Yes," she said slowly. "Mine too."

"Would it be possible for me to have a look in that box?"

"Of course, I'll get it for you."

"What other things do you have from your father? Any other personal papers? Documents? Canceled checks?"

"What exactly are you looking for?" Nicole asked warily.

Hunter ran a hand through his hair. "I wish I knew.

What I do know is that we have a lot of unanswered questions. I'm certain some of those answers will come from your father. If you're uneasy with me going through his things, I'll understand."

Nicole didn't flinch. "No, I'm not uneasy about it. I loved my father, and I'm going to trust in him until something proves otherwise. If you happen to be the one to find that proof—I'll deal with it. I suppose I should call Billy. Brenda would be his sister too." She looked past Hunter toward the window. "If Brenda even existed," she added ruefully. "Maybe I'll wait another day to see if you can come up with some answers first. I don't want to needlessly tarnish his image of Dad." She gave Hunter an imploring look. "Please don't keep anything from me. I don't want to be kept in the dark to have my feelings spared. The worst part of all this is imagining what might be."

"You have my word on that—for more than one reason. I can only see things from one point of view. Your thoughts and ideas could be the spark that ignites the flame."

"You mean the one in your brain?"

Hunter returned her half-smile. "That's one way to put it."

With that agreed upon, Nicole took Hunter up to the attic to show him where her father's things were stored. Besides the metal strong box, there were half a dozen legal size bankers' boxes.

She gave the stack of boxes a despairing look. "I didn't realize there were so many. I guess I just never got around to throwing anything away."

Hunter grunted. "In this case, that's a good thing. At least, I have something to work with."

"Is it all right with you if I go back down to the shop? I still have so much to do."

"Sure, you go ahead," he said, already busy dragging a table and chair over to the boxes. He would start with the lock box first.

After she left, he realized he didn't have the key for it. Rather than walk back down two flights of stairs, he started on the file boxes.

Three hours later, the only worthwhile thing he came up with was some interesting cancelled checks. He stood, stretched the kinks out of his back, tucked the checks and the lock box under his arm, and went back down to the studio. Chuck and the girls must have left for the day; because, both the studio and the shop were empty. Glancing out the window at the late afternoon sun, he saw Nicole down by the water's edge with Shanna and Kyle.

Hunter left his things on the desk in the studio and walked out onto the deck. He watched Nicole playing with the kids and wondered how she could ever have believed she had no maternal instincts. He didn't realize she'd noticed him until she called out.

"Come and join us, Hunter"

He took the steps leading to the lake, two at a time.

When he stepped beside her, she smiled, looking out over the still water. "Isn't it beautiful out here? I love this time of day, just before the sun sets. I usually keep working after the others go home, but I just wasn't in the mood today. Did you find anything?"

"Not much. I didn't have the key to the lock box. I hoped you knew where it was."

"Sorry, I should have thought of that. I can open it for you."

Kyle ran up to them with a stone in his hand, "Watch how far I can throw, Hunter." He threw the stone with as much power as his thin arm could muster.

Hunter walked down to the lakeshore, laughing. "Looks like you're just about ready for little league, son."

He looked up at Hunter with dark, anxious eyes. "Can we play ball sometime?"

Hunter smiled. "Of course, we can. Next time I go to town, I'll pick up a ball and a bat, and we'll see if we can break some windows. Here, let me show you how to skip rocks over the water."

Both Kyle and Shanna watched in amazement as the flat rock Hunter threw skipped five times before it stopped and sank. Kyle immediately started looking for more flat rocks.

"Look what I found," Shanna said quickly, showing off her bucket of shells. Hunter knelt to examine her treasures.

When Hunter came back up the bank, he was breathless, but laughing. "Those two have a lot more energy than I do," he said.

"They're both so beautiful," she said in a choked voice.

Hunter sent a curious glance in her direction. "Is something wrong?"

She nodded dismally. "What are we going to do about them? You want them, and so do I. They're starting to get attached to both of us. I don't want to break their hearts. I feel like I'm in a competition and no matter who wins, three people will lose."

Hunter shoved his hands in his pockets and looked across the lake. "I don't know what we'll do either, Nicole. I've lived in New York all my life. My business is there and so is most of my family."

A moment of silence hung between them.

"But it sure is peaceful here," Hunter said finally. "I'll bet the sunset will be spectacular tonight.

Chapter Seven

Back at the house, the kids raced up the stairs to find Mr. Komodo while Nicole went to open the strong box for Hunter. She positioned the box on the desk and rapped it sharply with her closed fist. It popped open.

Hunter grunted. "I guess I could have done that." He motioned to the side chair. "Why don't you sit down? I have something to show you." He sat down at the desk and handed her the stack of cancelled checks he'd found. "Take a look and tell me what you think."

She looked at the first couple on top. Her heartbeat increased with each check she flipped over. "These are all made out to Yvonne Casey. My God, they're for a thousand dollars each."

"Notice who signed them."

Nicole swallowed at the lump in her throat. "My father," she whispered.

"Keep looking. The ones on top were written the last year your father was alive."

Her eyes widened in shock. "The last few are all signed by Mom. She actually signed the checks to make support payments for an illegitimate child. I guess this answers the question of whether or not she knew about it. My parents lived quite comfortably, but they weren't wealthy. Why so much money?"

Hunter rubbed the back of his neck and sighed. "I wish I had an answer for you. I didn't find anything suggesting they owed child support, or anything else, to Yvonne Casey. The canceled checks are the only proof that money was sent, but they don't explain why. The checks I found were dated over a period of five years before your mother died. If they were for Brenda, there should have been earlier ones, but I didn't find any others."

Hunter started lifting papers out of the strongbox. "I found Billy's birth certificate. Everything checks out on that: the names, the date, and the seal. William Andrew Anderson. Mother, Dawn Marie Anderson, father, Robert Capulet Anderson. Nothing looks out of order." He handed it to Nicole, and then kept going through the box until he found Nicole's birth certificate.

He showed it to Nicole. Her parents were named exactly as on Billy's.

"This is obviously a photo copy, since there's no embossed seal," he said. "Do you have the original?"

Nicole shrugged. "Not unless it's in that box or in the other boxes upstairs."

"I went through those pretty thoroughly, and I don't see it in here."

"Is that important?" she asked.

"Do you have a passport?"

She shook her head. "I've never needed one."

"It may not be important, but you really should have an original. I believe you have to request it in writing. Let's do that tomorrow."

Nicole ran a hand through her thick hair with an exasperated sigh. "I swear," she declared, "I can work ten hours a day and not become as frustrated and exhausted as I get doing one hour of this stuff. Is this the kind of work you do every day?"

Hunter gave her an encouraging smile. "Yes, but there is a big difference, I'm rarely personally involved in what I do. Mostly, I research family histories, going back as far as there is available data. In some cases, I travel out of the country to dig through ancient archives in dusty old buildings, looking for missing pieces. I partner with my cousin, Quint, and we have an assistant, Marla Hawkins, who helps us. She puts all the loose ends together and prepares the final draft of the family tree. She's the nail buffer."

Nicole groaned. "I can't believe that I actually called her a nail-buffer."

Hunter laughed. "That's not all you said. What was it you called her, a short-skirted—"

"Please, don't remind me."

Hunter smiled. "Don't be too hard on yourself, you weren't that far off. Marla has her nails done every week, and I've never seen her wear a skirt below the knees." He stood up and stretched his shoulder muscles. "How about, we get out of here for a while. Let's take the kids and go up to that hamburger place to eat."

"I thought you didn't like to go out."

"Maybe, I just never liked the company before, and maybe, I'm in the mood for a little country atmosphere."

"You actually want to deal with the locals? You must be feeling especially brave tonight."

Hunter put an arm around her shoulders and drew her out of the studio. "You sure know how to put a man at ease. Let's get the kids rounded up before I change my mind."

* * * *

The Red Oak Inn was busy for a Monday night. A jukebox blared out a Reba McIntire tune while a ball game filled the large television screen above the bar. Several men hovered around the single pool table in the center of the room. Small booths, most of them occupied, surrounded the crowded space, more of a bar than a restaurant. A connecting room held several tables and more booths along the walls.

Hunter motioned Nicole into the adjoining, quieter

room and directed them to a corner booth by a window. Kyle and Shanna scooted into the U shaped booth while Hunter and Nicole sat on the outside across from each other.

Not surprisingly, two dozen pairs of eyes trained on them. More than one person called out a greeting to Nicole while Hunter received hostile glares from the men and lip-licking stares from the women.

"Do you come here often?" he asked after the waitress handed them the one-page menus.

"Only when Billy's in town. He comes over to mingle with his old friends and coerces me into going with him. He says I don't get out enough."

"I'd bet that's an understatement."

Hunter looked at Shanna and Kyle. "So, what are you guys having?"

"Can I have a hamburger?" Shanna asked.

Hunter tugged gently at one of her red curls. "You can have anything you want, Funny Face."

"Then can I have French fries too?"

"Certainly."

"And orange pop?"

"You got it." He turned to Kyle. "What about you, Champ?"

Kyle stared at the menu the same way he saw Hunter doing. "I want a hamburger and French fries—and orange pop." He gave Hunter a mischievous grin, adding, "And a cookie."

"What kind of cookie?"

"A big one."

Hunter gave Nicole a smile that slam-dunked straight to her heart. The raw physical attraction she felt for this man was a new and unfamiliar thing to her. She concentrated on the menu, hoping he didn't notice the heat that rose to her cheeks.

Nicole was grateful when the waitress came to take their order and thankful for the kids' chatter while they waited for their food. Hunter teased them until they giggled, and they teased him back. Their banter relaxed Nicole, and by the time the food arrived, she had joined in the fun.

To an outsider, they appeared to be a happy family having an enjoyable meal.

As the waitress cleared the dishes, the jukebox switched to Elvis singing *Love me Tender*. A postage-stamp dance floor in front of the Jukebox would have made four couples rub elbows. There were already three on it.

Hunter winked at Shanna. "What do you think, Shanna, should I ask Nicole to dance?"

Shanna looked at Nicole with twinkling eyes and nodded. Kyle ducked his head, giggling.

Hunter looked at Nicole with eyes the color of rich chocolate, rich melting chocolate. "I know this isn't exactly the Ritz Ballroom, but would you like to dance?"

The thought of being in his arms made her limp all over. She wanted nothing more at this moment than to dance with Hunter Douglas. She couldn't find her voice, so she nodded. The next instant, her hand was in his, and he led her to the dance floor.

Hunter swung Nicole into his arms and drew her against his chest. She pressed her body against his tall frame, thinking what a perfect fit they made.

Nicole wanted the dance to go on forever. Having his arms around her, holding her with firm gentleness was more arousing, more erotic than anything she'd ever imagined possible. When the music ended, she pressed her face into his shoulder and clung to him unmoving. She didn't care that every eye in the Red Oak Inn was trained at her, and the man who had broken down her defenses.

"The song is over," he whispered huskily.

Nicole nodded and forced herself to separate from him.

With a possessive hand on her waist, Hunter directed Nicole back to their booth. A startling scene awaited them.

Kyle had his face pressed into Shanna's chest, sobbing uncontrollably. Shanna's arms wrapped around Kyle's small, shaking shoulders, trying to comfort him.

Alarm brought Nicole out of her stupor like a dash of ice water. She slipped into the seat beside Kyle, encompassing both children with her arms. Hunter was on the other side by Shanna, doing the same.

Hunter put a hand on the boy's shoulder. "Kyle? Kyle, what happened? Are you hurt?"

Kyle continued to cling to his sister, his small body shaking.

Nicole touched Shanna's damp cheek. "What happened, honey?" she asked. "Why is Kyle crying?"

When Shanna didn't answer, Hunter repeated the question. "What happened, Shanna? Please talk to us."

Shanna finally lifted her head to stare at Hunter with moist eyes. "Kyle thinks he saw Asha outside the window. I told him we were in Minnesota and it's far, far away from Mama's house, but he doesn't believe me. Hunter, tell him Asha can't be here, it's too far away."

For the briefest second Hunter met Nicole's baffled gaze. His concern mirrored hers. They both glanced quickly out the window. It was dark except for a streetlight. Nobody was out there.

"Who is Asha?" he asked Shanna.

Shanna went back to soothing Kyle and didn't answer.

Hunter reached in his wallet and threw a fifty-dollar bill on the table. He spoke softly to Shanna. "Can I take Kyle so we can go home?" he asked.

She gave her brother a reassuring squeeze. "It's okay, Kyle, Hunter is here now. He's strong. He'll protect us."

Kyle finally reached for Hunter, and Hunter grabbed him almost fiercely to his chest. "Bring Shanna," he said to Nicole. "Let's go home."

They made the drive back to Nicole's house in tense silence. Nicole sat in the back of the Mercedes holding Kyle while Shanna took the seat in front beside Hunter. By the time they got home, Kyle had stopped shaking, but his round, dark eyes were still fearful.

"Let's go in the sitting room," Hunter said. "We need to talk about this."

They sat both kids on one of the plush leather sofas. Hunter got the lights while Nicole pushed a button, drawing thirty feet of hanging drapes across the glass wall. She received a nod of approval from Hunter. Hunter then took a seat beside Shanna, and Nicole sat down next to Kyle. Her heart went out to them. They sat quietly, pressed together with heads hanging as though waiting for some punishment. She put her arm across the back of the sofa in a gesture of protection. She wanted to spare them and she prayed Hunter wouldn't fire questions at them the way he normally did when he was after information.

Hunter leaned forward, closer to them both. "You don't need to be afraid," he said softly. "Shanna, do you understand why we need to know who Asha is?"

Shanna kept her head down and nodded silently.

"Do you know if Asha has another name, a first name or a last name?" he asked.

Shanna shook her head, keeping her eyes fixed on her hands clenched in her lap.

Hunter took a deep breath. The look he gave Nicole told her how much he hated doing this. It seemed his twenty-question drill tactic worked a whole lot better with adults then it did with frightened children.

This was not going to be easy.

She smoothed a hand over Kyle's dark curls. "Are you afraid of Asha?" she asked.

Kyle nodded.

His response told her they needed to start with simple yes and no questions. "Was Asha a friend of your mother's?"

Kyle nodded again, and Shanna's head came up. "He told us never to tell anyone about him," she said.

Hunter's jaw tightened. "Did he ever hurt you?" he

asked.

Shanna shook her head. "No." Before Hunter could form another question she added, "But he hurt Mama."

"What did he do to her?" Hunter asked.

Tears filled Shanna's blue-green eyes. "He stuck needles in her. He brought us videos, then turned the television up really loud, and closed the bedroom door so we couldn't hear, but sometimes we could hear anyway. I know he was hurting her because she made strange noises. I tried to tell Kyle everything would be okay, but he always cried anyway."

Kyle lifted his head. "He always made Mommy sick, and he said he'd hurt us if we told anyone he was there. We had to stay alone with him when he made Mama go out."

Hunter rubbed a hand on his temples "Do you know where she went when she went out?"

Shanna brushed a tear from her cheek. "She always left with a man that Asha brought with him. We told Mama we were afraid of Asha and we didn't like him."

"What did she say when you told her you were afraid of Asha?" Nicole asked.

"She said she was afraid of him too. Then she said she knew a place we could go where we would be happy and never have to see Asha again." A small hiccup escaped Shanna's trembling lips. "I thought she was going to come with us."

"When did she tell you that?" Hunter asked thickly.

"When she was really sick," Shanna said. "We were sitting on the bed with her. I tried to help her, but she was too sick. She told us some nice policemen were going to come and we should go with them."

Kyle curled his legs up and hid his face in Nicole's arm. "She told us not to be afraid and that she would always love us. But then she went to sleep, and she wouldn't wake up anymore." Warm tears spilled on her hand.

With his elbow braced on his knee, Hunter pressed his

face into his hand rubbing his eyes and forehead. Without lifting his head, he drew a ragged breath. "Was Asha there before your Mama got sick that night?"

"Yes," Shanna said in a small choked voice.

Blinking rapidly, Nicole held a firm arm around Kyle. "What does Asha look like?" Nicole asked with a catch in her breath, fearing what the answer would be.

"He had a black beard and dark hands," Shanna said, frowning.

"And mean eyes," Kyle added. "Like the bad man who tried to kill Hercules."

Hunter exchanged a look with Nicole, mouthing the word suitcase.

She nodded.

Hunter reached across Shanna to pull Kyle on his lap. "Tell me what happened when the bad guy tried to kill Hercules?"

Kyle managed a limp smile. "Hercules made the bad guy go away and everybody was saved."

Nicole slipped closer to Shanna and reached over to put a hand on Kyle's leg. "Remember when you said Hunter was as strong as Hercules?"

Kyle nodded.

She gave Hunter a glistening smile. "Well I think he is too. And I think Hunter can chase away any bad guys that come around here."

Kyle turned and gave Hunter a trusting smile before he threw his small arms around Hunter's neck. Hunter drew him close with one arm, the other he slipped around Nicole pulling both her and Shanna closer to his side.

Chapter Eight

Together, Nicole and Hunter put the kids to bed and sat with them until they fell asleep. Afterwards, walking down the stairway together, Hunter gave Nicole's shoulders a squeeze. "How about a cup of decaf?"

Nicole released a long weary sigh. "Add a double shot of brandy to it and you're on."

"That's all I'd need," Hunter said bitterly. "I'm one step away from hunting down this Asha and strangling him with my bare hands. It would only take one shot of brandy to make me take that step. How about a glass of wine instead?"

"I was thinking of taking that same step myself. Maybe we had better stick to the decaf. You want me to make it?"

Hunter grimaced. "No."

In the kitchen, Nicole sat at the counter, while Hunter made the coffee. Her gaze followed his movements but her mind was on Shanna and Kyle. What those two kids went through was almost incomprehensible, sitting on the bed with Brenda the night she died. Nicole remembered how quiet they were when they first came with Hunter and the progress they'd made since. The fact that they could even smile was a small miracle. She hoped this last encounter wouldn't make them regress.

"Penny for your thoughts," Hunter said sitting down across from her.

She gave him a weak smile. "Right now my brain can't come up with a thought worth a penny," she said.

"Pretty gruesome picture they painted."

"Do you think they really saw this Asha?" she asked.

Hunter took a deep breath, released it in a huff. "If it weren't for the suitcase, I'd say the chances were slim, but given that—"

"Do you think he might have killed her?" she asked.

He shook his head. "No, not directly. She knew she was going to die. Too many things add up to her taking her own life; the note on the table with instructions to call me to take the kids, the packed suitcase, the call to the police. There was nothing in that call to suggest anyone else had done anything to her."

"But what about the needles they said he stuck her with."

Hunter shrugged. "For all we know, she could have been diabetic."

Nicole's eyes widened. "Is that what you believe?"

"No, but I also don't believe she died of a heroin overdose. She was too lucid before she fell asleep. If she'd had a heroin overdose, her mind would have been on another planet. She wouldn't have been telling the kids she loved them or even have known they were there. My guess is she took some kind of pills."

"Because she couldn't bear living in fear of Asha any longer?"

Hunter got up to get the coffee. He pulled two mugs out of the cupboard, filled them, and came back to the counter, handing one to her. "Right now, we can only guess as to the method and the motive behind her actions. I hope by tomorrow my brother will have a copy of the autopsy report and that will at least explain the method."

Nicole took a cautious sip of the hot coffee. "Either

way, Asha, whoever he is, is not a man I would want in
my circle of friends."

The phone suddenly screeched to life and Nicole
jerked, spilling coffee on her hand. "Damn!" she swore,
grabbing a handful of napkins to dab at her burning fingers
as the phone kept ringing.

"You want me to answer that?" he offered.

"I can handle it," she said, getting up to lift the
receiver from the wall phone. "Can you get me a glass of
ice water?" She sat back at the counter before putting the
phone to her ear.

Before she could even say hello a voice barked at her.

"Who are you talking to, Nicole? Who the hell is there
with you?"

Nicole glanced at Hunter. She held the phone three
inches from her mouth. "Excuse me, sir," she said to
Hunter. "What did you say your name was again? My
brother Billy would like to know."

"Don't play games with me, Nicole," her brother
ordered. "I just got a call from Chris. He said you were at
the Red Oak tonight dancing skin-to-skin with some
stranger he never laid eyes on before."

"Thank God for small towns," she mumbled, sticking
her burning hand in the ice water Hunter set in front of her.

"Nicole. Quit toying with me."

"What if I tell you it's none of your business?"

A medley of hissed curses came over the line.

Nicole sighed. "Is it so impossible to believe I could
have a date?"

"I talked to you less then a week ago. You never
mentioned a man in your life. Okay, so I'm concerned
about you. Is that a crime?" Billy's voice softened. "Just
talk to me, Sis. Or, you can put him on the phone and let
me tear him apart."

Nicole let her amused gaze slide over Hunter. "Are
you sure you want to? He's sort of built like Hercules." She
held the phone away from her ear and toward Hunter so he

could hear Billy swearing. Hunter shook his head, smirking. When Billy finally stopped snarling, she waited quietly.

"Nicole? Nicole, are you still there?"

She hesitated another second or two. "I'm here. Are you finished with your little tirade?"

"I'm sorry." Billy said a bit more calmly. "Just tell me you're all right and deliriously happy and I'll go away."

"I wish I could," she said. "But it's not that simple. I really don't want to explain over the phone. I can assure you though; he's just a friend. Call Gram if you don't believe me."

Billy chuckled. "Like I could believe, or for that matter, understand, anything Gram said. Hell, last Christmas, she was still trying to read my palm. I haven't been suckered into that one since I was fourteen, but if you tell me he's just a friend, I believe you. You aren't in the habit of lying. Still, Chris said nobody knew who he was—and he had two kids with him."

"Tell Chris to stuff a sock in it."

"Sounds like you're fine, DeeDee. Just because you're being such a brat, I shouldn't tell you my news, but I can be just as big a brat. I'll see you this weekend, and I won't be alone. I'm getting married."

The phone clicked in her ear. Her eyes narrowed on the buzzing receiver. "Is that a man thing?" she asked Hunter.

Hunter looked at her, his expression blank. "Is what a man thing?"

Nicole got up to plunk the receiver, none too gently, into its cradle. She returned to her seat and put her stinging hand back in the water.

"To drop a bomb shell on a woman, then hang up before she can comment."

Hunter's quick grin showed an even row of gleaming white teeth. "I'm sure that would never happen unless the women in question took advantage of the fact that she could smart off to her heart's content since the man in question was too far away to get his hands on her."

Nicole pulled her hand out of the ice water and flicked icy droplets on his face. "You men stick together like fleas on a mangy dog."

Laughter shook Hunter's shoulders. He picked up one of her discarded napkins to dab at his face. "That's because women don't play fair." He got up from his chair and started to leave the room. "I'm going to find something to put on that burn."

"What do you mean, we don't play fair?" she called after him.

He was already out the door. "When men make bets, they don't look for loopholes to keep from paying off."

"I always pay my—" She stopped. Hunter was out of hearing range. They didn't even need a telephone to use that 'leave-you-hanging' tactic. She swore under her breath. Suddenly, her spine stiffened—the kiss. He was talking about the Dumpster bet. She was hoping he'd forgotten about it. Needless to say, that was wishful thinking. The human computer never forgot anything.

Hunter came back in the kitchen carrying a tube of ointment and a small roll of gauze bandaging. Except for the barest hint of a smile, he gave no indication that a conversation had even taken place before he'd left the room, but he didn't fool her for a minute. He had quite skillfully planted his little seed. Again, there was that little smile—or was it a smirk?

Nicole eyed him warily as he sat down on the stool next to her. He shifted enough to draw it in close to her, set his medical supplies on the counter, and hook his long legs on the rung of the stool, turning her to face him, he locked her legs between his knees.

"Dry your hand off and give it to me," he instructed.

"Do you mind if I leave it attached to my arm?" she quipped, drying her hand on the napkins.

He gave her one of his heart-stopping, slanted grins.

"Please do, I hate the sight of blood."

"Hercules can't stand the sight of blood?"

"Just goes to prove we all have our weaknesses. What did Billy say to get you all worked up?"

Nicole rolled her eyes. "He said he'd be home this weekend, and he wasn't coming alone. Then he added, 'I'm getting married', and hung up the phone."

Hunter chuckled. "He's getting married? Why is that such a shock? Doesn't he have a girlfriend?"

Nicole snorted. "Last year he had a half dozen. He's quite charming."

"Yeah, I could tell by your phone conversation."

Nicole flinched when Hunter started rubbing the ointment at the base of her red thumb and the back of her hand.

"Does this hurt?" he asked.

"Just a little. I appreciate what you're doing, but it really isn't that bad."

"Humor me. I like to play doctor. You were telling me about Billy."

His hands were gentle, clean, and well manicured; he could have been a doctor. His gentle touch was sending little shivers up her arm. Actually, it was more like heat than shivers. She tried to remember what they were talking about… *Oh yes, Billy.*

"This is his last year in school, and he's been so busy studying, he only came home once, and that was for Christmas. He didn't talk about girlfriends at all. He never even hinted that he was serious about anybody, much less, ready to get married. He's only twenty–two."

"What is he studying?"

"Zoology. He loves animals."

"Sounds like my sister. She wants to be a veterinarian. You're lucky you only have one sibling to contend with. I have three—and a cousin who's like a brother," he said, tying the last knot on her bandage. "There, how does that feel?"

"A lot better, actually. Thank you. Nice job," she said, examining his work.

"Just call me Dr. Douglas. Now, for the other part of our conversation."

A sudden pink heat started creeping up Nicole's body, stopping with a rosy tint on her cheeks. He was sitting much too close. His knees subtly trapped her legs. It was too late to play ignorant. Her face gave her away.

Hunter shrugged and started to back away. "Of course, if you're looking for loopholes—"

"No. Don't you move. I said I pay my bets. We might as well get it over with so I don't have to hear about it again." Rushing blood hammered in her ears, but she took a deep breath, pursed her lips, and closed her eyes. She waited, holding her breath.

Nothing happened.

Finally, she gasped and opened her eyes. He hadn't moved. In fact, he had his eyes closed and his lips pursed, calmly waiting.

"What are you doing?" she asked.

Without moving his lips or opening his eyes, he mumbled, "I'm waiting for you to kiss me."

She stared at him wide-eyed. He looked so ridiculous; she couldn't keep a straight face. It started with a small snort, then chuckles, then became full-blown laughter. When he started to grin, she laid her head on her arm on the counter and laughed until she was breathless.

When she finally caught her breath, she talked into her arm. "You are the craziest, most obnoxious, most ridiculous person I've ever met."

"Great, now you sound like my sister," he said. "You expect me to kiss you when you remind me of my sister?"

When he started to move away, she reached out and clamped her fingers on his leg just above the knee. At least, she was pretty sure that's where she had her hand since she still hadn't raised her head from the safety of her arm.

"You are not leaving this kitchen," she said into her

sleeve, "until we've finished with this damn kiss."

Her hand on his thigh brought Hunter to instant, full-blown, sexual alert. He took a couple of seconds to put a check on his self-control. If he grabbed her the way he wanted to, she'd flee like a scared rabbit. For his own sake, he knew it would be better to end this thing before it started. He sensed her fear, her hesitation, but it was obvious she wasn't going to give up until she'd fulfilled her end of the bet.

Before he could reach for her, she lifted her hand.

With her head still buried in her arm, she pointed to the light switch on the far wall. "Switch the light off," she said. "I can do this better in the dark."

"Look, Nicole, you don't have to—"

"Just do it, please, before I lose my nerve."

He wanted to ask "what nerve,", but he didn't. Instead, he got up, switched the light off, and came back to stand behind her. The outside security lights illuminated the room with a latent glow. She jumped when he touched her shoulder. If he'd thought for one minute she didn't want to do it, he would have stopped right there. As it was, he didn't want her to feel she had no choice because of some silly bet.

"The lights are off, Nicole. You can stand up and turn around now." He didn't believe she would, but, as much as he wanted to, he wouldn't touch her unless she made a move first.

She surprised him. She did stand, and she turned, but kept her eyes lowered. He placed a hand under her chin and lifted her head. Her long, dark lashes helped her avoid direct eye contact with him. She seemed to be watching his mouth instead. Unconsciously, she ran her tongue over her lips. Never in his life had he wanted to kiss a woman more.

He framed her face with his hands, touching the corners of her mouth with his thumbs. From there, he moved to her cheeks, to the smooth lines of her jaw. Her lips parted slightly, and she took a ragged breath.

"Nicole," he whispered in a husky voice. "I'm releasing you from your bet. If you still want me to kiss you, I want to hear you say it."

He was so close; Nicole felt the warmth of his breath on her cheek. She opened her mouth to speak but nothing came. She was dizzy, light headed. His fingers were moving over her face, touching her hair. His thumbs moved with a gentle caress over her lips. Sexual heat was literally swallowing her up, melting her senses. He was making love to her face.

"Nicole? You need to tell me you want this."

In another minute, he would have to pick her up off the floor. She couldn't think, much less talk. All her adult life, "desire" was just another word in the dictionary, and now she found herself consumed by it. She finally took a deep breath.

"Would you just get on with it," she managed to say.

Hunter chuckled. "And you call me crazy and obnoxious," he said. He bent down just enough to place his lips on hers, nibbling with the softest, lightest touch possible.

Nicole leaned into him trying to return the kiss with innocent eagerness. His hand went from her jaw to the back of her neck as he guided her mouth, directing her moves. His mouth was soft, yet firm, demanding, yet gentle. When his arm circled her waist, pulling her body against him, somewhere in the back of her throat she released a helpless moan. She pressed taut breasts against his chest, put her arms around his neck, and pulled his head down to deepen the contact. A husky groan escaped his mouth as it moved hungrily over hers, urging her lips apart with a gentle flick of his tongue. Sweet sensation flowed to every vital part of her body like delicious, hot honey. Every movement he made intensified the sensation.

Nicole's one experience with kissing had been with a

boy her freshman year of high school. It didn't take experience to realize Hunter Douglas was far removed from puberty. On the same note, his hand pressing against her lower back made her acutely aware of the rest of his adult body—the full, aroused length of it.

She didn't know how long it lasted but Hunter suddenly dropped his hands and backed away. He released a deep *whooshing* breath.

When he moved toward the light switch, she stopped him. "No, please, don't turn it on. I—I'm not ready for light just yet."

"Sounds like a good idea to me," he said with a catch in his voice. "What I am ready for is that glass of wine. How about you?"

"Yes."

"I'll get the wine. Why don't you light a candle so I can see what I'm doing."

Nicole lit a candle and sank down on a stool, staring at Hunter while he poured two glasses of white Merlot. He set one in front of her and sat across from her with the other.

When she picked it up, he held up his own glass for a toast.

"Here's to one hell of a kiss, lady."

Nicole's hand trembled when she touched her glass to his. "Thank you, Hunter. You couldn't possibly know what that kiss meant to me."

Hunter smiled. "I wouldn't take any bets on that, Ms. Anderson."

* * * *

Nicole awoke to the pale light of dawn. It was the first time in more nights than she cared to remember that something other than ghosts beckoned her from sleep. Memories of the night before washed over her like warm rain, bringing a smile to her face.

She snuggled under the covers trying to savor the feeling, to think about what went beyond a kiss, but habit won over. Work called. She had too much to do in the shop. Daniel, the theater director, expected her to do the fittings in ten days. They still had a long way to go before they were ready.

Forcing her mind on things she had to do downstairs, she got up and turned on the shower. A hot shower always did wonders for her in the morning. Afterwards, she quickly dried her hair, dressed in jeans and a burnt orange silk blouse, gave herself a skeptical once over in the mirror, and headed for the studio.

She smelled the coffee by the time she reached the bottom step into the foyer. For just a second, she considered heading for the kitchen but quickly abandoned the idea. She wasn't certain she was ready to face Hunter. Especially, since she couldn't be sure he wouldn't make some light banter about the kiss they'd shared. What was earthshaking to her was probably commonplace for him. Better to put it off as long as she could.

She flicked the studio lights on and went straight to her worktable and her drawings. Only five left to work on. If she stuck to them, she could be finished by the time Carmen and Amanda arrived. Then she'd be free to help out in the shop.

Normally she didn't have trouble concentrating, particularly early in the morning when she was alone, but the coffee aroma was a vivid reminder that she wasn't exactly alone. Hunter was only a few steps away. Orion, The Hunter, one of the most beautiful constellations in the universe. So beautiful that both Alexander the Great and Napoleon tried to get it renamed after them.

Pen poised in hand and staring out the window, Nicole sucked her lower lip into her mouth, recalling the taste of his tongue on her lips and the husky moaning sound he made deep in his throat. Warmth gushed over her like a wave of summer heat.

"I hope I'm not disturbing anything really important."

Nicole gasped. Heat rose to her cheeks.

"Sorry," he said softly, "I would have knocked, but

my hands were full." He indicated the two full coffee mugs he was carrying. He set one down on her table.

He wore a short-sleeved, royal blue knit shirt, which fit snuggly over his biceps and flat torso. His jeans fit equally snug from a narrow waist down to his...

"You can disturb me anytime with morning coffee," she said quickly, tearing her eyes away from him, hoping he hadn't noticed her perusal and wondering if every woman became unglued after one kiss.

"You were off in another world someplace."

"I was—thinking."

"About?"

"About how much work I have to do," she lied.

"Guess I better let you get back to your thinking then."

Hunter walked over to the desk that had become his own workspace. He hid a grin behind his coffee mug. He almost had to check if he was still wearing clothes after that once over she'd given him. For a man used to having women stare at him, she had a way of unnerving him far more than he cared to admit. And if he didn't stop thinking about the color of her eyes, he'd never get any work done. They were like the deep Caribbean Sea when she got that seductive look on her face.

Hunter glanced at his watch. Marla wouldn't be in the office yet, and Virgil would probably hang up on him if he got the morning grump out of bed two days in a row.

He took out his legal pad to make some notes, starting with Gypsy's riddle; 'Where flames burn and flowers bloom. A gift of love in another time. Resting. Waiting. Cappy's secret, not mine.' He drew a deep breath and expelled it in a frustrated rush. Without more information, he could stare at those words until his hair turned gray and not find the answers.

Hunter picked up his mug and went back to the kitchen for a refill before stepping out on the back deck. Sunset Lake was reverently still. The water winked like elusive diamonds when a gentle breeze disturbed the surface. A pair of loons floated out of the mist over the glassy ripples, their haunting calls echoing in the silence, speaking a language as foreign to him as Nicole's peaceful country life.

Looking out over the lake, hearing the loons, smelling the pines, he understood Nicole's love of this place, so far removed from New York, his apartment, and his life. More than distance separated the two. It was a state of mind. In the still air, he heard the faint rumble of a motorboat starting on the other side of the lake. That would be Chuck on his way to work.

He turned to the sound of the sliding glass door behind him. Nicole had his cell phone in her hand.

"Hunter, your phone was ringing. I hope you don't mind—I answered it. It's your brother."

Hunter glanced at his watch and made a soft whistling sound. He'd completely lost track of time. He thanked Nicole, took the phone, and followed her back into the house.

"Virgil, you're up before breakfast. Are you ill?"

"Smart ass. Who's the woman?"

"I'm surprised you didn't drill her."

Virgil chuckled. "Hell, don't think I didn't try. She's more close-mouthed than you are. What's going on, Hunter?"

"Bear with me just a little longer and I'll tell you. What did you find?"

"Everything on the birth certificate and death certificate for Brenda Casey looks legit. The baby had a heart defect and never left the hospital. If there was some kind of a surrogate program involved, I see no hint of it. On that subject, a man named Richard Levin started the first legal surrogate mother program in 1979. The key word there is 'legal', anything before 1979 is off the record. Hell, it could have been done by a veterinarian or cut rate doctor who didn't quite make the grade in medical school."

Hunter groaned. "What about birth certificates?"

"You'd have to go to the state and county where the baby was born. I checked Manhattan where the original Brenda Casey was born. Yvonne didn't have any more children there. Yet, here's the interesting part; Yvonne Casey spent two years at Johns Hopkins University in Maryland, studying to be an RN until her daddy was sent to prison for embezzlement, and she was left penniless. Apparently, she quit school and took a waitress job just to support herself."

Hunter rubbed a hand over his eyes. Nicole sat at her worktable watching him. Most likely, trying to grasp anything she could from the mostly one-sided conversation. There was a familiar *rat-a-tat-tat* at the shop door, and Nicole left the room to let Chuck in.

"So where do we go from here?" he asked Virgil.

Virgil released a huff of air. "It would help if I knew exactly what you were after."

"For starters, I want to know everything I can about the Brenda Casey who died last week. The father listed on the original birth certificate is Robert Anderson. I have reason to believe he did not have an affair with Yvonne Casey. That opens the possibility of surrogacy."

"What makes you believe he didn't have an affair?"

"A fortune teller told me. Hell, Virg, trust me on this. I don't believe he was screwing her. You tell me how else she could have gotten pregnant. I'm also convinced she had a second pregnancy the same way."

"All right, let's go with that assumption for the time being. My guess is if it was an illegal procedure, the people involved probably knew each other. Is there any way you can find out if Robert or his wife knew Yvonne before the first baby was born?"

Hunter's eyes trained on Nicole walking back in the room. A long shot struck him. He held his hand over the mouthpiece to speak to her. "Nicole, did either one of your parents ever go to a medical school?"

Nicole nodded. "My mother was an RN. She went to Johns Hopkins in Maryland. Why?"

Hunter held up his hand to stall her. Into the phone he said, "Dawn Anderson went to Johns Hopkins."

"Bingo! That's the connection I was looking for. What was her last name then?" Virgil asked.

Hunter looked back at Nicole. "Did your mother use her maiden name when she went to Johns Hopkins?"

"Yes, it was Baxter," Nicole answered, coming around his desk to sit in the side chair.

Hunter went back to the phone. "It was Dawn Marie Baxter before she married."

"At least that gives me something to go on. Let me do some more checking. Maybe I can come up with some information by the time you call to wish Mom Happy Birthday tonight."

"Thanks Virg, I appreciate your help on this."

"No problem. I owe you. Oh, one more thing. Just how close were you to Brenda Casey?"

Hunter hesitated. "Not very. I hadn't seen her in seven years. Why?"

"The autopsy report: she was HIV positive and she was dying. Her arms were full of scars, apparently, from taking heavy drugs. There hasn't been a final ruling yet on suicide but everything points to it. I'm guessing you know she had two kids."

Hunter drew a ragged breath. "Yeah."

"Well I found out something else by accident through a colleague of mine. There was a half a million-dollar life insurance policy taken out on her three years ago. She had a full physical then and there was no sign of illness. Unfortunately, the insurance doesn't pay off on a suicide. And here's where it gets really interesting. The beneficiary was her son, Kyle. No mention of the daughter, Shanna. Another odd thing, Brenda took both kids in for an AIDS test a week before she died—both came up negative."

Hunter was breathing heavily. He was trying to think,

but for one of the few times is his life, his brain was mush. He glanced at Nicole. Her sea green eyes anxiously glued to his face.

"Hunter? You okay?" Virgil asked.

"Yeah. Yeah. I was just thinking."

"Anything you care to share?"

"No. Yes. I have Shanna's birth certificate. I'm going to fax it to you. See if you can use the information to get a copy of Kyle's. I'm guessing they were born in the same county hospital."

"The laws for obtaining birth certificates have restrictions on them. I can get information, but I can't get a registered copy. If there are no parents, you need the custodian's written okay. I also need power of attorney, in writing, along with a copy of the custody papers. My information tells me one Nicole Anderson in Minnesota is that person. Anybody we know by chance?"

"Possibly. I'll send you what you need, and I'll talk to you tonight."

Hunter hung up and put his elbows on the desk, resting his head in his splayed fingers and rubbing them over his brow. He spoke to Nicole without lifting his head. "Brenda was dying. She had AIDS." He heard Nicole's gasp, along with a religious expletive.

"Was it suicide then?" she asked.

"It hasn't been ruled on yet, but that's what everything leads to. There's an insurance policy, but it won't pay if it was suicide." He dropped his hands to look at her. "The only beneficiary listed is Kyle."

Nicole sank into the chair at the side of his desk. "I don't understand. Why would she do that?"

"I wish I could answer that," Hunter said. "But I'm still waiting for a bolt of lightening to jump start my brain."

"Why did you ask about my mother's school?"

"It seems Yvonne Casey went to the same school."

Nicole's eyes widened. "What are you thinking?"

"I'm thinking that we found a link that could support

the surrogate mother theory, except no legal procedures were done before 1979. Virgil is looking into it."

Before he could expand on the conversation with his brother, Shanna and Kyle appeared in the doorway; both fully dressed, Kyle clutching Mr. Bear. Solemnly, they walked hand in hand toward the desk.

As if on cue, Hunter and Nicole rose to meet them with outstretched arms. Nicole hugged Shanna to her breast and Hunter raised Kyle in his arms.

Hunter put on a jaunty smile. "Is anyone ready for breakfast?"

Chapter Nine

They sat around the counter eating oatmeal when Chuck breezed in the open kitchen door. He took in the cozy little family scene with amused curiosity.

"Marge called on the shop phone. She wanted to know if tomorrow at two was a good time to bring her class over for a tour. I told her if it wasn't okay you'd call her back."

"Tomorrow's fine," Nicole said. "Did she tell you she wanted you to do it in your Robin Hood costume?"

Chuck grinned. "Yeah. The kids love it. Speaking of kids," he said, looking at Kyle and Shanna. "It sounds like we won't be doing any particular theme, how about we put you two in costumes for the tour? If that's okay with Auntie Nicky and Uncle Hunter."

Shanna's blue-green eyes twinkled. "Hunter's not our uncle."

"Yeah," Kyle said quickly. "Aunt Nicky is our aunt because she's Mama's sister."

Chuck sent a silent, raised eyebrow look at Nicole and received a warning glare in return.

Hunter cleared his throat. "Help yourself to some oatmeal, Chuck. There's more than enough. I got a little carried away."

"I'll take you up on that. I am a little hungry." Chuck

went to the stove to dish up oatmeal. "By the way, I caught some walleyes last night. I brought them along in a cooler." He glanced at the kids. "They're already cleaned. Anybody object if I make lunch today?"

"You have my vote," Hunter said quickly.

"Mine too." Nicole added. "And I also think having the kids in costume is a great idea." She smiled at Shanna. "How about it? We have a whole rack of things that would fit you. You can choose whatever you like."

Shanna nodded eagerly.

"Me too?" Kyle asked.

Nicole laughed. "You too."

Kyle looked at Chuck and back to Nicole. "Can I be Robin Hood, too?"

Nicole couldn't help smiling at his enthusiasm. "I don't see why not. If we don't have a costume your size, we will make it for you."

Chuck sat at the end of the counter scooping sugar on his oatmeal. He gave Hunter a cheeky wink. "We usually all dress up when a tour comes through."

"Yeah, Hunter," Kyle chirped. "You can be Hercules."

Shanna explained. "Kyle thinks Hunter looks like Hercules because he has big, strong muscles and stuff."

Chuck waggled a bushy, blonde eyebrow at Hunter. "Gee, I hope we have a costume big enough for your muscles and stuff."

Hunter stood up attempting to conceal a grin. "If you all will excuse me, I think this is my cue to leave. I have some phone calls to make." He took his empty bowl to the sink, stepped between the kids to give them each a peck on the cheek, and left the room.

Chuck met Nicole's narrow glare with a grin. "He doesn't rattle too easily, does he?"

Back at his desk, Hunter dialed the number to his office.

"Hello, Seek and Find Enterprise. This is Marla."

"Marla, it's Hunter. What do you have for me?"

"You're not going to like your phone bill. I called five different places on three different shifts until I reached someone willing to talk to me. A place called Cheap Car Rentals—real original isn't it—located in Bloomington, just off the strip by the big hotels. They rented a Ford Escort to a shady looking character last Saturday. He gave his name as Asha Jameel and had ID to verify it. He paid a whopping seventy bucks for two weeks rental with an option to rent longer. I hope that's what you were looking for."

"That's it exactly, Marla. Good work. Remind me to think about giving you a raise. Is Quint back from Puerto Rico yet?"

"He called to say he'd be in this afternoon, said his trip was very successful, and drilled me about why you were in Minnesota. What should I tell him?"

"Tell him to dig into Asha Jameel. Look under slimy rocks. He may have been into illegal drugs, pimping, and petty burglary. I'm certain his shady character image isn't just imagination, so I can't believe he wouldn't have a record. Have him start with his connections at the local police department. There must be a file on Jameel someplace."

"Virgil was here for the Brenda Casey file. Does Jameel have anything to do with that?"

"Yeah, same case. Tell Quint I'll talk to him when I call Mom tonight."

"This project must be awfully important if you're missing your Mom's birthday bash."

"It is."

"Hunter—"

"Yeah, yeah, I know, no party girls. You worry too much."

After Hunter hung up the phone, he sat back in his chair staring at his steepled fingers. There was no longer any doubt in his mind that Kyle had seen Asha Jameel at the Red Oak Inn. What he didn't understand, was why. Why did Jameel follow him all the way from New York to break into his trunk and steal an old suitcase? What would he have done if he hadn't found the suitcase in the car? If that was actually what he was after. And if it was, Hunter had no idea what Jameel had removed. All the current papers were in his briefcase. Brenda's death certificate, the custody papers, including the one he'd written up for Nicole to sign the kids over to him, a copy of the police report, and the letter to Nicole.

Hunter checked his briefcase to make sure nothing was missing. Everything was intact, including the letter tucked in the zippered, inside flap. Maybe there was something in the letter incriminating Jameel. Hunter squeezed his thumb and fingers over his throbbing temples. What if there was something in the letter pointing a finger at him. Damn! He should have leveled with Nicole right away about Shanna and given her the letter that was rightfully hers. He knew he had to work up the nerve to do it, and soon. He had to tell Nicole about Shanna before he gave her the letter. The last thing he wanted was for her to find out in any other way than from him.

Through the open shop doorway, he saw Nicole and the kids enter from the wide foyer doors. She was chatting with Amanda and Carmen, probably about costumes for Kyle and Shanna. He had to give Chuck credit for bringing them out of their slump. Funny thing with kids, they adapted to new surroundings a lot easier than adults seemed to.

Hunter found himself more interested in watching Nicole than his Internet screen. Each time she bent her head, her hair fell to the sides of her face. She was continually sweeping it back behind her ears where it never seemed to stay. Whenever she puzzled over something, she sucked in her lower lip and narrowed her eyes. Then she'd flip her hair back again. She wasn't doing anything out of the ordinary and yet, covertly watching her little gestures was highly arousing. It brought sweet memories of the kiss they shared in the kitchen. Her lips were trembling and hesitant, like a teenager experiencing a first kiss.

'Twelve years of pain,' Gypsy had said. Something terrible happened to her when she was sixteen, something traumatic enough to warrant four years of therapy.

She had settled the kids at their little table and walked toward him with flushed cheeks and an amiable smile. Her smile faded when she saw the look on his face.

"What is it?" She asked, dropping into the side chair. "Did you find something?"

Hunter drew a deep breath. "Asha's last name is Jameel. He took a two week rental on a car in Minneapolis the same day I flew in with the kids."

"But what does he want?"

"Hunter brought his chair forward. "I wish I knew. My cousin has some connections with the New York police department. I'm having him check for a record on Jameel. Maybe that will tell us something. In the meantime, and until we know what he's after, we need to be sure the kids never go outside alone."

Nicole pushed her hair out of her face in a nervous gesture. "Chuck wanted to take them fishing later this afternoon."

Hunter smiled. "I can't think of a safer place for them than in the middle of Sunset Lake, and besides, Chuck appears to be good for them. They've certainly taken a liking to him."

"He is a bit of a comedian," Nicole said laughing. "I'm glad you're able to take his humor with a grain of salt."

A thick lock of hair had fallen over her face again, and he really wanted to reach over and tuck it back for her. She beat him to it. "I have a cousin who's gay. He's the most gentle and bravest person I know. I owe him more than I can ever repay." He could have said he owed Grant Douglas his life but that would bring on questions he didn't care to answer; questions about Diana and a fiery car crash.

"You mean your partner in your business?"

"No, another cousin. His brother actually."

"My goodness, how large is your family?"

"I have enough aunts, uncles, and cousins to fill a stadium."

"All I have is Billy and Gram. It must be nice to have so many people to care about you."

Hunter laughed. "Sometimes it is and sometimes it isn't. Besides, Billy cares enough about you for ten people and what about the other five thousand people in this community? It seems to me they all have an interest in you and what you do."

Nicole grimaced. "Not quite the same," she said. "And Billy, well, he's just being a brother. I'll bet you're that way with your sister too."

Hunter didn't answer. He couldn't. If he had been that way with Diana, she might still be alive. Instead, he chose to end the subject.

"I need to type up a power of attorney paper for you to sign so my brother can get a copy of Kyle's birth certificate. "Is that okay with you?"

"Of course, I'm as anxious to get this all cleared up as anybody. I trust you to do the right thing."

A pang of guilt shot through Hunter. He glanced at the open briefcase sitting between them. The letter from Brenda was in the zippered pocket. He silently vowed to give it to Nicole, soon. Real soon.

He gestured to the other papers inside. "There's the copy of the custody papers and Brenda's death certificate, along with some other documents, you're welcome to take a look at them while I type this up. I'm also going to type a request for your original birth certificate. I called the Hennepin County Government Center. They said you can fax the inquiry, along with a credit card number, and they'll have a validated copy to you in a couple of days. It might speed things up if we send a copy of the one you have along with the request."

Nicole nodded. She was reading Brenda's death certificate. It put her death at approximately three o'clock the previous Wednesday—the day Hunter had called, changing the entire direction of her life. The next paper she lifted out of the briefcase was one waiting for her signature. She glanced at Hunter. When he said he was bringing custody papers for her to sign, he wasn't just making idle chatter. By his own admission, he had only known the kids a few hours at that point. It was hard to imagine a single man so willing to undertake the raising of two young children. She wasn't sure why that should bother her, but it did. Although, thinking about it, she was ready to accept them almost immediately. However, they were blood kin to her—at least they appeared to be. Then she realized she now had them in addition to Billy and Gram.

Hunter laid the forms in front of her to sign and handed her a pen.

"Write your full name on each one," he said, collecting the other documents he needed to fax. "Do you have a credit card number we can use? Since the request has to come from you, they may not accept mine. It's only fourteen dollars."

"There's a card we use for company purchases in the drawer in front of you." She reached over, opened the drawer and pulled out a small cardholder. When her arm brushed against his chest, he sucked in a breath of air. She gave him a curious glance then picked up the forms to look them over. She signed her name along with the card number and handed them back to Hunter. "Do you think we should call the sheriff about Asha?"

"I doubt it would do any good. What would we say? Other than Barney's statement, we have no proof he took the suitcase." Hunter walked over to the fax machine and started punching numbers. "When I finish here, I'm going to take a drive to some of the local motels, see if I can spot his car, maybe talk to some people. I'd sure like to know where he's holed up."

Alarm shot through Nicole. "What will you do if you find him?"

Hunter turned to her with a tight smile. "I won't kill him, if that's what you're worried about. Although, I think I'd enjoy it. If I'm not back for lunch, save me some fish."

* * * *

Hunter spent three hours driving to all the motels in the area. At each one, he stopped to question the proprietor; no one knew or heard of a man with Jameel's description. Even with summer resort visitors, a man like Jameel would have stood out. At each place, he left a card with his cell phone number and received a promise that they would call if they saw or heard anything. It should have annoyed him that six of the eight people he talked to asked about Nicole, but he was getting used to her popularity. Besides, they seemed more than willing to talk to him because of his association with their beloved Nicole. More and more, he was getting the feeling that if he ever did her wrong, in any way, he could face a small town lynch mob. She probably wasn't that far off when she said five thousand people would be expecting an invitation to her wedding.

The last stop he made was at the Moose Lake Drug Store. He sat in the car for five minutes before he worked up the courage to walk inside. Christ, he was acting like a teenager buying his first condom. Irritated with himself, he got out of the car and entered the store. A little bell announced his entrance. The young female clerk glanced up, gave him an appreciative once-over, smiled a warm hello, and went back to filling a gum rack at the counter.

He walked directly to the back of the store toward a pharmacy sign. The condoms hung on orderly little rows between the cough drops and feminine products. He was about to make his selection when a voice from behind called out his name. He quickly grabbed a bag of cough drops and turned to face the last person he wanted to see.

"Hunter Douglas, I was hoping to run into you again."

A sheriff's badge winked at him from the man's chest. "Nicole forgot to introduce us yesterday. John Martin's the name." He extended a beefy hand.

Hunter shifted his cough drops to his left hand and shook hands with Sheriff Martin. He stifled the urge to cough. Damned if he was going to behave like a guilty twelve-year-old. "What can I do for you, Sheriff?"

"Barney tells me somebody stole a suitcase from you."

"Yeah, broke into my car trunk. I got it back though."

John Martin scratched the back of his head making his sheriff's hat fall over his eyes. "Well, it seems we've had several break-ins the last couple of days." He straightened his hat. "They hit a liquor store Sunday night, took booze and money. Then last night, the drug store here, they got money and a variety of drugs. And at least two vacant lake cabins looked like somebody had slept in them. We get a lot of strangers up here in the summer but some kind of stand out more than others. Like men traveling alone, not camping or staying at any of the local resorts."

"Does that mean you consider me a suspect?" Hunter asked incredulously.

"Heck no. Not a guest of Nicole's. Besides, my brother, Chuck, would vouch for you in a minute."

Hunter groaned. The sheriff was Chuck's brother. Lord, save him. If he ever had the urge to buy condoms again, he'd drive the hundred and ten miles to Minneapolis.

"Anyway," the sheriff went on, "Barney gave a pretty good description of the man who got your suitcase; I've got my eye out for him. I'll let you know if I come up with anything. I know where to reach you."

Hunter, feeling like he'd just been gut kicked, watched the sheriff walk out of the store. Grabbing a couple of candy bars for the kids, he headed for the front of the store when he noticed a plastic bat and ball set in the toy section. It looked perfect for a four-year-old.

After one more stop at the supermarket for ice cream and frozen pizzas, he headed back to Sunset Lake, wondering if he should have told the sheriff about Jameel. Maybe Quint had come up with something that might tell him just how dangerous Asha Jameel was. He could always call John Martin then.

It was three o'clock by the time Hunter got home. He let himself in the garage with the opener Nicole had given him. She must have heard him drive up because she was waiting for him at the connecting kitchen door. He wondered what she'd do if he grabbed her and planted a huge kiss on her lips. Probably not a good idea. She had concern written all over her face.

He carried his bags in, giving her a smile instead. "You are a welcome sight," he said, placing his bags on the counter.

She smiled and looked genuinely glad to see him. "We saved you some fish." She said quickly. "Any sign of Asha?"

Hunter put the pizza and ice cream in the freezer. "No, but I suspect he's making a mark around town." He relayed everything the sheriff told him.

"Do you think it's him?" Nicole asked anxiously.

"I'm sure of it. I checked every motel within a ten-mile radius but with no luck. At least that explains where he's been staying. He probably ran out of money."

"What does he want?"

Hunter cupped a hand under her chin. "Don't worry, we'll find out."

Nicole threw her arms around him. "I'm glad you're home, Hunter. I was so worried about you."

Hunter held her close, enjoying the feel of her against his body. She was soft and her hair smelled of honeysuckle, but she was trembling. The fact that she was trembling because of concern for him sparked an unfamiliar emotion in him. He wasn't used to having anyone, outside of family, care about him. Rubbing his hand over her back, he tried to soothe away her fears. He was just thinking about kissing her when she pulled back.

"Oh, you must be starved. Chuck saved you some walleye."

He released her reluctantly. He wanted to tell her just how starved he was—and not for fish. "Where are the kids?" he asked. "I brought them some candy bars."

"You just missed them. They went fishing with Chuck."

Hunter's gaze settled on her mouth. "Does that mean we're alone in the house?"

He stood less than two feet from her, and the look on her face told him she wanted to be kissed again, but when he brought his hand up to touch her, she quickly moved past him to the refrigerator.

"No, Amanda and Carmen are still working in the shop. I'll get your fish for you. You can heat them up if you like, but they're good cold too."

"I'll eat them cold," Hunter said thickly. He sat down at the counter, watching her. When she set the plate in front of him, her hand clearly shook. Her nonchalant attitude didn't fool him. She wanted him as bad as he wanted her, but this wasn't the time or the place. She was still far too skittish. She set out a fork, a napkin, and the remains of a small salad. Then she poured milk for him. It was the most domestic he'd ever seen her. When she laid a half loaf of bread on the counter and asked if he wanted butter, he realized he better stop her before she emptied the entire refrigerator.

He pointed to the stool opposite him. "Sit."

She stopped and stared at him.

"Sit down," he repeated, breaking into a smile. "I can't eat with you fluttering around like a nervous butterfly."

She shrugged her shoulders and sat with her hands clasped in her lap. She took a deep breath. "I-I just—"

He waited for her to finish, but she seemed to have lost her tongue. "It's all right," he said gently. "I understand."

She stole a glance at him, and her cheeks turned pink.

He was afraid she would start crying if he didn't say something. He knew the subject that would bring her back to planet earth.

"When we were up in the attic yesterday, there were all those boxes belonging to your father, nothing specifically to your mother. Are you aware of anything of hers that dates back to before they were married?"

As he suspected, that captured her attention. Her head shot up.

"She had a trunk. It's in my room."

"Do you know what's in it?"

Nicole released a short huff of air. "Just her wedding dress and some childhood mementos she'd saved for her grandchildren," she added with a whisper. "Was there anything in particular you were looking for?"

Hunter shrugged. "I guess just anything that might lead to a clue about Brenda; college yearbooks, old letters, photographs, medical records, that sort of thing. Women are more inclined to hang on to that sort of thing than men are. We don't have to look if it will disturb you."

"No, of course not. I haven't looked in that old trunk since she died, so I really don't remember what's all in there. I can show you where it is."

Hunter smiled. "Sounds like a good plan." He swung his long legs from the stool and started clearing his dishes away. "I'll have to remember to thank Chuck for the fish. Even cold, it was good."

Nicole smiled. "It doesn't come any fresher than straight out of the lake."

"Maybe next time I'll join him when he takes the kids out. I've never fished."

Hunter followed her upstairs to her bedroom. She gave no outward sign that she was uncomfortable with him being there. From the center of the king-size bed, Mr. Komodo yawned and stretched.

Hunter stopped to scratch his ample belly. "When does he eat? By the looks of him, he doesn't miss many meals, yet I've never seen him downstairs."

"In the middle of the night," Nicole said laughing. "He likes to prowl around in the dark." She led the way into the adjoining sitting room and a large trunk in one corner. She pulled a small patchwork blanket, made of pastel blues, off the top of it. "Gram made this little quilt for my Dad when he was born." She ran a loving hand over the worn fabric. "Maybe tomorrow I'll take Shanna and Kyle in to see her."

"How are you coming with your costume order?" Hunter asked.

"Right on schedule," she said, unlatching the trunk. "The sewing goes faster than the designing. Chuck ran out of some materials, which is why he could take the afternoon off to spend with the kids."

"Did you find costumes for the kids?"

"Yes, they both look so adorable." She lifted the heavy lid on the trunk and knelt in front of it. "You may be in trouble though. Kyle is insisting you be Hercules."

Hunter groaned. "Maybe I could just disappear for a while." He sat down on the floor beside her.

Nicole gave him a slanted grin and made a chicken clucking sound. "Good luck." She pulled a garment bag out of the trunk and gently set it aside. "This is Mom's wedding dress." She looked at a picture hanging above her head. "That's their wedding photo."

"She was very beautiful," Hunter said, staring at the petite, dark haired, young woman smiling in the black and white photo. Her husband was a good head taller. "Since you're so comfortable wearing older clothes, I imagine you plan to wear her dress someday."

Nicole shook her head. "It wouldn't fit. Mom was really tiny. She always said I got my height from Dad."

"And your red hair?"

"From Dad, Mom was dark—and it's not red, it's auburn."

Hunter glanced at her auburn hair thinking he could judge the color a lot better if he could run his fingers through it.

Nicole reached into the trunk and pulled out a dime store jewelry box. She opened it to show him the contents. "This is just full of trinkets. She said she'd had it so many years it seemed a shame to throw it out. She told me to give it to my daughter someday—if I had one."

Hunter wanted to remind her that she'd once told him she never wanted children. He decided to let it pass. He, himself, had considered never having children after his disastrous marriage. Being around Shanna and Kyle had a decidedly paternal effect on him, he imagined maybe it did for Nicole too.

She set the jewelry box aside and pulled out some scrapbooks, and high school and college yearbooks. She handed them to him and reached in for an old shoebox. There was a rubber-banded packet of letters inside and another packet of pictures.

"These were all from Dad before they were married." She put the letters back in the box and handed the pictures to Hunter. "I think most of these were taken before she married Dad."

He took the pictures and shifted his body to get more comfortable on the floor. When he brushed against her leg, she jumped. Hunter stared hard at her. Her cheeks were a rosy pink, and she busied herself with the remaining contents of the trunk. If she felt the same jolt he did every time they touched, he could understand her skittishness. Moreover, it had nothing to do with fear, or maybe for her it did.

She had exceptionally smooth skin with a creamy-peach tint, the same color as the roses blooming in his mother's garden. Nicole had the kind of complexion that didn't need makeup; no powdery substance to come loose if a man nibbled on her face. Hunter suddenly realized if he didn't change the direction of his thoughts, he was going to become extremely uncomfortable.

Forcing his eyes away from her, he removed the band from the pictures and started flipping through them. They were all black and white and mostly of young people in 1950s clothing. Some had names or captions written on the back, most didn't. He found little of interest until he came across one obviously taken on a college campus. In spite of the poor condition, Hunter could make out two women with a tall man standing between them. He had an arm around each one, holding them both close to his sides. A sign behind them, partially hidden, appeared to say Johns Hopkins. He turned the photo over.

Dawn, Jon, and Von
The Renegades

Hunter quickly skipped through the rest of the pictures, hoping to find a similar one that was less faded. There were no others. He went back to it, his brows creased in thought.

"What is it? What did you find?" Nicole asked.

He handed her the picture. "Does this look familiar to you?"

She studied the old photograph before pointing to the smaller woman. "I'm sure this is Mom."

"Read the back."

Nicole turned it over and drew in a sharp gasp. She whirled the photo around and remained silent for a long moment. "Do you think it's Brenda's mother?" she finally asked.

"What do you think?"

She glanced up at him. "I think it is. This means they not only knew each other, they were friends." She stared back at the picture, holding it up to catch the light. "There is something vaguely familiar about the man. Then again, I've seen the contents of this trunk before. There's a good chance I saw the picture at one time or another. I wonder who he is."

"The name Jon doesn't ring any bells for you?" When

she shook her head, Hunter shrugged. "Another classmate? A friend? I don't know, but maybe we can find out. Did you find anything else?"

"No, I don't think so; just some old medals, badges, souvenirs, things probably important to Mom." She picked up the college yearbook that had Johns Hopkins printed across the front in gold lettering and began flipping through the pages. She stopped, frowning. "Mom's graduation picture is in here, but I don't see Yvonne Casey."

"If that was your mother's last year, I doubt you'll find Yvonne in there. Virgil said she only went two years. She had to drop out for financial reasons. See if you can find a man with the first name Jon: spelled J-O-N."

When Nicole started scanning the album, Hunter slid beside her to help. In a matter of minutes, they had gone through the whole book with no success.

Nicole closed the book, clearly disheartened. "I guess we might as well put everything back, unless you want to look at anything else."

"No. Not now. But let's keep this Renegades picture out; we might be able to use it." Hunter glanced at his wristwatch. "It's getting late, the kids might be back soon, and they'll probably be hungry." He got to his knees and started lifting the things back in the trunk.

Nicole did the same. "Well, at least it wasn't a total waste," she said. "You did find the picture with a name on it."

"Yeah, and that could be important. We won't know until Virg has a go at it."

While Nicole carefully replaced her mother's wedding dress, Hunter sat on the floor with his back against a heavy chair, his legs stretched out in front of him, arms folded across his chest. He watched her smooth the baby blanket over the top of the trunk with loving hands. Thoughts of putting an end to his celibacy weighed heavily on his mind, and his body. Her hair fell over her face and she pushed it back behind her ears. It didn't stay. He couldn't remember a time when he'd been at such a loss as to how to romance a woman. He wasn't used to having to work at it and didn't know how to battle her ghosts.

Finished, she sat down on the floor in front of him, staring at her hands in silence, her legs tucked under her. Twice she opened her mouth without saying anything. She fidgeted with the buttons on her blouse. Hunter sensed she was on the verge of wanting him as much as he wanted her, but he knew better than to rush her.

"You have something on your mind?" he asked finally.

Without looking up, she nodded.

He watched her closely and waited.

She took a deep breath and brought her head up to look at him. "Hunter, I—I want to know—" She dropped her gaze again. "I can't say it," she murmured, blinking rapidly.

Hunter unfolded his arms and held them out to her. "Would you like me to hold you while you tell me what it is you want?"

Nicole moved into his embrace, pressing her face into the softness of his knit shirt. He didn't try to kiss her, he just held her. She put one arm around his back, and the other, she placed on his chest. He pressed a kiss to the top of her head while threading his fingers through her hair.

For a long moment, he just held her. Enjoying the softness of her in his arms, trying to make himself believe she was really there, willingly.

"Tell me, DeeDee Sweet Pea, what it is you want," he said huskily into her hair.

She swallowed nervously, rubbing her hand over his chest as she'd done when she was pretending to measure him. "I want to know what it's like to be a whole woman," she whispered tightly. With her ear pressed against his chest, she could hear Hunter's heart increase its beat. "I feel so inadequate, so—so, I don't know, so undesirable, I guess. I understand if you don't want to—"

Hunter's arms tightened around her, his hand stilled its movement in her hair. "Nicole, you are, without a doubt, the most desirable woman I've ever known, but you are also so vulnerable, so innocent. I can't even kiss you without feeling like I'm taking advantage of you."

"That's just it," she said quickly. "I'm too—too damned naive."

Hunter laid a gentle hand on her face. "Are you telling me you've never been with a man?"

Nicole felt a familiar flush creep up her neck. This is the moment she had dreaded all her adult life. Now she had to make a choice. She could refuse to answer and run, or she could stay. If she ran, she might never again find a man she would allow this close to her. If she stayed, she would have to answer his question. But there were a very limited number of those questions she would allow.

"I'm not a virgin if that's what you mean."

"I guess that's what I mean." He wasn't exactly sure what he meant, but it had taken her too long to answer. He knew that something haunted her past and had been troubling her for twelve years. Whatever it was, she clearly didn't want to talk about it. Maybe she'd had an unpleasant experience with a boy when she was sixteen, but he was quite certain she'd never made love to a man. He wanted her all the more for it. He wanted to make slow, sweet love to her, to introduce her to the incredible pleasure she yearned for, and to make her whole.

Hunter moved his hand from her face to cup her chin. He brought her head up, bent forward, and brushed his lips over her eyelids, nose, and then, her waiting mouth. He was using all the willpower he possessed to go slowly with her, not to frighten her.

Her arm reached around his neck. She pressed against him, her lips parting slightly, an urgent hungry cry coming from somewhere deep inside her.

When she made that sound, Hunter forgot about moving slow. He pulled her over his body and rolled them both to the floor with her halfway beneath him. She literally melted in his arms. Her hands dug like talons in his back. His kiss intensified, slaking her eager mouth with his own hunger. Each moan, each cry she made, increased his need of her.

He moved a knee between her legs. She gave no resistance. He wanted to touch her, all over. Very slowly, he loosened her silk blouse from her jeans. When he laid his hand on the smooth flesh of her back, he hesitated. This was the moment in their first kiss, when she'd stiffened up and drew away from him. In spite of her panting eagerness and her apparent willingness, he wasn't going to take that chance again, even if stopping now would be difficult and painful for him.

He withdrew from her hungry mouth to raise his head and look at her. Her head rested on his arm in what appeared to be total surrender.

"Nicole?"

Her eyes were squeezed shut, and she continued to breathe heavily.

Hunter forced himself to keep from ravishing her. He did allow his hand to move around her ribs to her belly. She drew her breath in sharply but continued to cling to him.

"Nicole, open your eyes and look at me."

"I can't," she whispered.

"Yes, you can. You need to reassure me I'm not taking advantage of you. I want you to look at me and tell me what I'm doing is okay." He could tell she was struggling with herself.

She finally opened her eyes.

The pain he saw in those green depths griped him at his core.

Nicole stared back at him, unflinching and took a deep breath. "I don't think you realize how long I've waited and wanted this, or that I fully expected to go the rest of my life waiting and wanting. I don't want to fear the past any longer, and I believe this is the only way to bury it. Vanquish my ghosts. Hercules...make love to me."

Hunter took his hand from her belly and touched her face. At this moment, he wanted nothing more in life than to remove that haunted look from her eyes.

At this moment, it wasn't to be.

They heard the sounds from downstairs at the same time, first the outside door closing, then the excited voices of Shanna and Kyle as they moved from room to room calling and looking for them; their young voices joined by an older, masculine one. Chuck.

With a groan, Hunter pulled Nicole to a sitting position. He planted a firm kiss on her lips and another one on her fingertips.

"I'll go downstairs and give you time to pull yourself together."

The smile he gave her held a promise. They would finish what they'd started. Soon.

Chapter Ten

When Nicole came downstairs, she found Hunter popping a frozen pizza in the oven. The kids sat at the counter, relaying their fishing tales to him. They both greeted her with an exuberant, "Hi, Aunt Nicky." Hunter's quirky smile made her blush from the tips of her toes to the roots of her hair. Normally, it would have made her uncomfortable, but right now, it made her feel desirable. She returned his smile, hoping some natural, female instinct made it seductive.

Hunter dropped an empty pan on the floor.

Nicole eyed him dubiously as he retrieved the pan. "Is there anything I can do to help?" she asked, walking toward him.

Hunter shot her a curious look, his eyes on her swinging hip. She resisted the naughty urge to rub up against him, but the look in his eyes said he knew exactly what she wanted to do. He brought his hand around to give her a playful swat on the rump, but she anticipated his move and dodged him with a bubbly giggle.

"You can set the table before you get of us both into trouble," he said, giving her an X-rated grin.

Nicole glanced at Shanna and Kyle. They were staring out of curiosity, or amusement, or maybe both. It was as though they knew something had changed.

Nicole reached for the plates. "So, how many fish did you guys catch today?"

"Three," Kyle said quickly. "Shanna got four, but she's afraid of the worms."

Shanna made a face. "They're icky."

"I can put my own on," Kyle said, "because, Chuck showed me how. He said I'm a natural."

"What is a natural?" Shanna asked. "We don't know."

"Well," Nicole said, laying out napkins and silverware, glancing at Hunter. "A natural means you're very good at something."

Hunter came up close behind her and started pouring milk. He deliberately reached around her so his chest pressed against her back. "It's like knowing how to do something with very little training; because, you have a talent for it; a thing that comes naturally." His breath brushed her ear with his last words.

"Like knowing how to cook frozen pizza," Nicole said with a shaky laugh.

Hunter grinned. "I suppose knowing the difference between cooking and baking could be considered a talent."

The ringing phone gave Nicole an excuse to sidle away from him, before she really made an idiot of herself. She picked up the receiver and turned to send Hunter an impish smirk.

"Hello," she said into the phone.

"Hi, Nick. It's Chuck. I just remembered I ordered some supplies from the Feather and Leather Shop in New Mexico. I couldn't find the credit card, so I made it COD. It'll be a day or two, but I wanted to tell you before I forgot."

"Sure, thanks, Chuck. I used it today. I must have forgotten to put it back in the drawer."

"No problem. Is everything okay over there? You sound kind of strange."

Nicole had her eyes on Hunter bending over to look in

the oven. She wondered why she'd never noticed how good men looked in jeans, but maybe they didn't all look that good.

"Nicole? Are you okay?"

"Peachy. Just peachy. Thanks for asking."

She heard a loud groan before Chuck said goodbye and hung up.

* * * *

After pizza and ice cream, Nicole herded them all into the sitting room to play a game. She directed them to sit around the large coffee table with Hunter on the sofa and the kids pulling up little stools across from him. She sat down beside Hunter, shuffling a deck of cards.

For the next two hours, she taught them simple card games. Most of them took minimal skill, so Kyle was able to participate. Both kids took to the cards with surprising ease.

The playful laughter around the table was something Hunter hadn't known since he'd left home to go to college. Listening to the kids' giggles reminded him how much he missed it. He was even able to recall a couple of games he'd played with his siblings.

When Kyle started yawning. Hunter glanced at his watch, surprised at the time.

"Sorry, to break up the game," he said apologetically. "My mother is having a birthday party tonight, and I promised to call and wish her Happy Birthday."

"Go ahead." Nicole said. "Come on you two. Bedtime. Say goodnight to Hunter so he can go make his call."

Both Shanna and Kyle scooted around the table to throw their arms around Hunter.

"I love you," Shanna said to him.

"Me too," Kyle said quickly.

It took Hunter by surprise. It was the first time either one of them had initiated affection toward him.

Shanna sat back on her heels to explain. "Chuck said if you love someone you should tell them, because if you don't, they might never know."

Hunter felt an odd squeeze in his throat. "I love both of you, too," he said. "And Chuck is right. Unless people can read your mind, they might never know." He glanced at Nicole, noting the wistful look on her face before she turned away. That look weighed heavily on his mind as he headed toward the studio to get his cell phone.

Hunter walked back to the sitting room and the leather sofa, dialing the number to his parents' home.

His brother Stephen answered.

"Hey, little brother, how are you?" Hunter said over the noise in the background.

"Hey, big brother, I'm doing great. I'm not even going to ask how you are. I hear you're shacking up with some gal in Minnesota."

Hunter laughed. "You are an obnoxious little twerp, and when I get home, I'm going to pound you into the ground."

"Does that mean you're not shacking up or you're not talking about it?"

"Both."

"Oh, well, your loss on the first count, mine on the second. You're missing one hellova celebration here. Oh boy, and does your sister have news for you. Here's Virgil, he's chomping at the bit to talk to you. Take care of yourself."

"Hunter? That you?"

"Yeah."

"Before you say a word, don't blame me for anything the twerp said. He yaks strictly from imagination."

"Why did he say *my* sister has news for me? Anytime you guys call her *my* sister, it means bad news. What kind of trouble is she in now?"

"Trouble. That's the right word," Virgil said, laughing into the phone. "But she'll kill me if I tell you. Now, about your other little dilemma. I don't have anything new for you. Do you have anything for me?"

"We found an old picture."

"We?"

Hunter sighed. "Like you don't already know that I'm staying at Nicole Anderson's house. It's far more complicated than I want to get into right now. Anyway, we found an old college picture taken in front of Johns Hopkins. On the back, it says, 'Dawn, Jon, and Von, the Renegades.' Dawn is Nicole's mother and Von is obviously Brenda's mother. The fellow in the middle is the one I'd like to locate. If he was a medical graduate or even a dropout, he might have had the expertise to perform an insemination, using Robert Anderson's sperm and Yvonne Casey as a surrogate. After all, they called themselves The Renegades.

"Shit. That really sounds like a long shot."

"I know, Virg, but there are a lot of unanswered questions. I want to follow any possible leads. Just check the university records for his name. Go from the time Yvonne started to a year or so after Dawn graduated. Oh, and the spelling on the photo is J-O-N. It might be Jonathon. Sorry, but that's all I have. How about the autopsy report?"

"Nothing yet, but I'm on top of it."

"And I suppose nothing on Brenda's birth certificate?"

"I'm checking all the states bordering New York, but it's a slow process."

An insistent female voice interrupted Virgil. He came back on the line. "I guess you better talk to Corina now, before she bursts." Vigil laughed. "Literally, I mean."

"Hunter, sweetie, is that you?"

"Yeah, Corina, what's the big secret? You flunk out of puppy dog school?"

"No, you big, overgrown brat, it's a lot better than that. Are you sitting down?"

"Yeah, I'm lounging on a sofa with my feet up. What is it?"

"I'm pregnant."

Hunter came to a fast sitting position. "What!"

"Mom and Dad are finally getting a grandchild."

"The hell you say! When did this happen? Who's responsible?"

Corina's laughter ripped through him. "I guess you could say I'm partly responsible. We met in school and it happened almost five months ago. I'm barely showing."

"Who is he? And where is he?"

"As a matter of fact, he's right here."

"Let me talk to him?"

"Why? So you can grill him? I don't think so."

"Any marriage plans?"

"Gee, you sound just like Dad. I'll let you know. Heck, I might even invite you to the wedding. Well, gotta go. Love you, you big ape. Here's Quint."

"Hey cuz, what are you up to? Marla filled me in as much as she could."

"You can compare notes with Virg," Hunter said. "It's all the same project. Actually, it's the same project but a separate problem. This is a very large can of worms. Anything on Jameel?"

"Nope. Sorry. I got to the office too late to work on it today. I'll get to it first thing in the morning. If the guy has any kind of a record, you know I'll ferret it out."

Hunter grinned. "That's why I love you, Quint. Tell me about Corina's boyfriend."

"She knows you and I too well," Quint said, laughing. "She won't even give out a last name. Just calls him, Andy. I'm trying to work him over, but he's a tough cookie. Seems like a decent fellow though. Here's your mom."

Nicole walked in the room. She knelt down to the coffee table across from him and quietly started gathering the cards together.

"Hunter Orion, whatever you're up to, had better be important to miss my party."

Hunter pulled his attention from Nicole, who looked positively delicious, to his mother's voice.

"It's very important. Happy Birthday, Mom. God, you are looking good. You don't look a day over fifty."

"Flattery will not get you off the hook. Thanks for the flowers by the way. How did you know sweet peas were one of my favorites?"

Nicole had gotten up to close the drapes on the glass wall. His eyes followed her. "Lucky guess?" he said, smiling.

"Now that's a joke. You've never had to rely on luck. I'd be willing to venture a bet you can remember everything you've seen or heard since you were two."

"Not everything."

"Ah, what did you get for your birthday when you were three?"

"A red fire engine."

"See what I mean—I don't even remember that."

"Hunter burst out laughing. "I was counting on that."

"You always did have a sassy mouth. You got that from your father. The brains, you got from me; the sass, you got from him."

"How is he doing?" Hunter asked.

"He's in his glory right now. He's dragging Corina and her boyfriend into the den. I wouldn't be surprised if she comes out with a ring on her finger."

"I wouldn't either. He can be pretty persuasive. Say hello to everybody I didn't get a chance to talk to. I'll see you soon."

"You take care of yourself, Hunter."

Hunter glanced at Nicole, who had come back to sit across from him on the floor again. She smiled at him, her elbows on the table, her chin resting in her hand. "I will, you do the same...and Mom...I love you."

"Hunter? Are you feeling okay?"

"I've never felt better." Hunter said, grinning. "Bye."

He hung up before she could question him further.

Nicole smiled. "I take it that was your mother? She sounds really nice."

"Yeah, she is," Hunter said, chuckling. "She thinks I can remember back to my second birthday."

Nicole's eyes widened. "Can you?"

"Of course not."

"Just how good is your memory?"

Hunter shrugged. "I don't know, certainly not as good as she thinks. It's just that I'm observant. I pay close attention to things."

"Okay, what is the picture above the fireplace hanging in your room?"

"That's too easy. It's Di Vinci's *Virgin on the Rocks.*"

"I suppose that was too easy. What about the picture over the fireplace in the dining room? You only saw that once."

"Monet—The Poppies."

"How many chairs are in the dining room?"

"Twelve; ten around the table and two on the side."

Nicole's eyes narrowed. "How many steps up to the attic?"

"Thirteen, counting the top one."

"That's it! You're not human. Why would you remember something so ridiculously insignificant?"

Hunter gave a shout of laughter. "I don't. All I needed was for you not to know the answer."

"You really are a brat," she said.

"So I've been told."

He leaned back with his arms folded over his chest. "I could stand a glass of wine, how about you?"

Nicole felt a sudden heady warmth creep up her cheeks. She nodded. "Yes, wine would be good. Do you want me to get it?"

"No, I'll take care of it." He got up from the sofa in one smooth, lithe motion. "Light a candle or two if you like," he said as he left the room.

Nicole's hands shook as she lit the five-tiered candelabra on the mantle and a couple of single votive cups on the side tables. She picked up a fat, three-wick candle, lit it, and placed it on the coffee table in front of her. That finished, she sat back on the floor to wait for Hunter. She didn't realize he'd returned until the lights switched off. The candle's soft a glow illuminated the immediate area, leaving the rest of the room in flickering darkness.

Nicole's heart began a flutter dance.

Hunter returned to his place on the sofa across from her, set the glasses on the table, and filled them both.

Nicole took a sip of wine. She was aware that Hunter was watching her, studying her, with dark eyes. Fortunately, the muted glow in the room covered the rush of blood to her face. The heat didn't stop at her face; it warmed her clear to her toes, and everywhere in between. The promise of the kiss earlier that afternoon was in his dusky gaze. It brought both fear and anticipation. Only this time, she would not allow fear to rule her mind. She wanted Hunter. Even knowing that in the end, he would go back to New York, leaving her to face her ghosts alone in Minnesota. Yet maybe, just maybe, the ghosts would be gone and she could go on with a normal life. Life without Hunter was not something she cared to dwell on right now.

Hunter's voice penetrated her thoughts. "You seem a bit tense, Nicole. Why don't you relax, nothing is going to happen unless you are comfortable with it. You do understand that, don't you?"

Nicole didn't even realize she'd drained her wine glass until Hunter reached over to refill it. She kept her eyes fixed on the candle in front of her and murmured a small, "Yes."

Hunter smiled at her "You look as tense as a turkey at Thanksgiving. Relax."

"Right," she mumbled, willing her body to do exactly that. "So how are things with your family?" She asked, attempting to shake the sacrificial lamb look.

"My sister is pregnant," he said.

Nicole looked at him, surprised. "Would that be

Corina?"

"Yes, that would be Corina." he said slowly. "But I don't recall mentioning her name?"

Nicole grinned. She motioned to the candle flickering in front of her. "Maybe I can see things when I stare into candlelight."

Hunter snorted. "Don't expect me to fall for that again."

"You remember things; I see things. What's so hard to believe about that?"

"Not the same, at all," Hunter said. "Remembering things is fact. Seeing things in candles is fiction.

"Maybe I can convince you."

Hunter made no effort to hide his amusement. "Go ahead, give it your best shot. A little entertainment right now sounds like a good idea." He held out his hand. "Do you want to see my palm?"

"That won't be necessary. Gram does it that way. I can use the candle."

Nicole stared into the flames.

When she was motionless for several long moments, Hunter sat forward. "Are you going into a trance or something?"

"Hush, your ruining my concentration."

Clearly amused, Hunter settled back into the leather sofa, watching her, smirking.

"You have a brother, Virgil."

"The same one you talked to on the phone," he said easily.

Nicole held up her hand. "Shhh." She was frowning heavily, brows drawn. Without taking her eyes off the flame, she drained her wine glass. She was beginning to feel the warming effects of the liquid in her veins. She stifled an urge to giggle.

"Stephen," she said. "You have another brother named Stephen."

Hunter became very still, staring at her. Wordlessly,

he reached over and emptied the bottle into his glass.

"Who is, Delta?" she asked in a whisper.

Hunter became still again, the bottle poised in his hand. "Delta, is my mother," he said thickly. "How did you know that? I never told you Stephen's name—or hers'"

Nicole hushed him again. She waved a hand over the flames. They danced and flickered, casting eerie shadows on the walls. "Your father then, is Hank...no...Henry." Nicole glanced at his face. He was staring into the flames with wide, disbelieving eyes as though he hoped to see exactly where she was getting her information.

When he finally raised his eyes to hers, she winked at him, grinning. "So," Nicole said smiling, "tell me about Corina. Is she married?"

Hunter set his glass down, his eyes narrowing on her. "Why don't you just look in your little crystal candle and find the answer?"

"It doesn't work that way. I can't just call up information. It has to ah...sort of...come to me."

"Exactly how did my family's names come to you? And don't give me any bull about their names being stars."

"But they are all stars."

"Not my father."

"Well no, but—"

"Okay. So, I give. How did you know?"

Nicole stared into his eyes. They were like dark chocolate pools, waiting anxiously for her answer. The combined sensation of the wine and his eyes had a melting effect on her.

She licked her lips, savoring the last of the wine. "Maybe I did it the same way you knew there were thirteen steps to the attic."

When her pink tongue flicked over her lips, Hunter wanted to leap over the table and grab her. He was certain those teasing green eyes were sending an open invitation to do just that. For a woman who appeared to know so little about sex, she sure knew how to push his buttons. He wanted her—bad—and she already admitted to wanting him. Just thinking about that last kiss was more than enough to send him over the edge.

"I'm giving you fair warning," he said. "You have thirty seconds to tell me how you figured out those names or I'm coming around the table."

A fast grin appeared on her face. She reached into the pocket of her jeans and held up a small piece of paper. "Here's your answer, Honeypot." She held it within a fraction of an inch of the flame.

He grabbed for the slip of paper with lightening speed, but she was waiting for him. She literally snatched it out of his fingers and held it just out of his reach. Before she could react, he came around to her side of the table and tried to capture her with his arms. With a frantic squeal, she made a dash to avoid him, crumpling the paper in her fingers. They both collapsed on the floor with her on her stomach and him, halfway on top of her.

Except for the laughter shaking her body, Nicole went limp. His fingers circled her wrist below her clenched fist. His other hand he splayed across her ribs, threatening her.

"Hand it over, Nicole, or we're going to find out just how ticklish you are." He wiggled the fingers across her ribs to emphasize his point.

She gave a small shriek and opened her hand. "I give. You can have it."

Hunter snatched the small slip of paper, but when she made a move to get up, he swung a leg over the back of her knees. "Oh, no, you're not going anywhere until I read this."

Her shoulders were still shaking with laughter. "For someone as smart as you are, you should have been able to figure it out on your own."

Hunter moved his hand from her ribs to the roundness of her buttocks. "And for someone as smart as you are, you're behaving awfully frisky for being in a totally vulnerable position." He held her pinned.

Using one hand, he smoothed the paper and held it up to catch the light of the candle. It was a list of names and phone numbers of every member of his family. The last time he'd seen it, it was in his wallet.

"Where did you get this?" he demanded. His hand moved over her buttocks strongly suggesting that she answer quickly.

"From John Martin, the sheriff. You dropped it in the mercantile."

"And you were hoarding it? Why?"

"I thought it might come in handy," she said, not even trying to stifle a chuckle. "Besides, why do you have a phone list of names and phone numbers of your family when you can remember everything from the time you were conceived? I was waiting for you to miss it so I could actually believe you were human by not remembering something."

"Hah, you would have had a long wait. Actually, I did forget something—I forgot I had it. If you recognized my handwriting, you'd know I didn't write this. My secretary, Marla, did it as a joke, six months ago, when I went to London for two weeks. She thinks I don't communicate enough when I'm out of town."

Nicole was suddenly feeling a rush of heat from the pressure of his warm hand on her backside. He seemed in no hurry to move the hand or the long hard body pressed against her side. When he started nuzzling her neck, she squealed.

"All right, I give."

His hand moved slowly from her buttocks to her rib cage. "What exactly are you giving, Nicole?" His husky voice breathed warm against her ear.

She froze. Twice in the same day, she was faced with the decision to stay or run. Run to her lonely room and the ghosts that lived there or stay and bask in Hunter's radiating heat. She was confident he would release her in a second if he believed she was unwilling in any way. She wanted to stay. His fingers caressed her midsection. She knew it was a test.

He still had her pinned on her stomach, pressed against the woolly rug. She wasn't sure if he was still teasing when he ran his hand smoothly and slowly over her back. Whatever his intention, his touch was exotically arousing. She felt her body tremble and then tense. It took all her willpower to force herself to relax.

He pressed his rigid erection against her hip and whispered her name "Nicole?" His was husky and strained.

Drifting in mindless pleasure, she answered with a throaty moan.

"Nicole?" he persisted. "Sweetheart. Come to me." He moved his leg and turned so she faced him. She looked at him through dark feathery lashes. An instant later, she was in his arms. In the next second, she was halfway beneath him, moaning under the intensity of his kiss.

His hands slid behind her, drawing her closer as his lips took possession of her surrender. She was trembling, but she was returning the kiss with a fire of her own.

Nicole fitted her entire body against him, unable to get enough of the feel of his firm length. Her arms slipped around his neck, and she clung to him, moving her mouth beneath him, meeting him kiss for kiss.

Hunter drew back to look at her. His breath was coming in harshly drawn gasps. "Nicole, do you want to come upstairs with me?"

Nicole stared back at him through glazed eyes and whispered a muted, "Yes."

Hunter got to his feet, pulling her with him. He drew her toward the stairs, his arm tightening around her shoulders.

"Wait," she said. "We have to blow out the candles."

Keeping her pressed to his side, Hunter blew out all the candles but one. That one, he carried with them up the steps. At the top of the stairs, he hesitated until she drew him to the left toward her room.

Hunter set the candle on the nightstand beside the bed and turned to take her back in his arms. She went eagerly.

The instant his lips closed on her mouth, Nicole's knees turned to butter. Her arms circled his narrow waist, and she pressed her body against his hungrily. He made a husky sound deep in his throat. His hands slipped beneath her hair as he guided her head and her mouth to comply with his own hungry need. His tongue traced an exotic pattern over her lips, urging them apart.

Nicole, her body a raging furnace, could do little more than sag against him and follow his lead. Her hands moved over his back, clawing at him, silently cursing the fabric that kept her from feeling him completely.

He must have understood her need because he moved her away from him and began to unbutton her blouse. After each button, he stopped to kiss her, her ears, her eyes, and her chin, until every part of her face was covered.

Sometime between buttons, he managed to whisper. "Nicole, I want you. I want to see you and touch you all over. Tell me if I'm going too fast." With a catch in his throat, he murmured, "Tell me if you want me to stop."

Nicole's answer was to tug his shirt from his jeans and slip her hands to the warm flesh beneath it. Hunter gave a sharp gasp. He slipped her blouse off her shoulders; her bra followed. She took her hands from him long enough to shrug both to the floor behind her.

Nicole nearly screamed with pleasure when his hand cupped her breast. He teased the nub of her nipple with his thumb, bringing from her a soulful moan that came from somewhere deep within her.

When he bent down to take her nipple in his mouth, she cried out. Her hands dug into his dark hair, and she pressed her face into its softness. She breathed deeply of his clean smell, trying desperately to keep herself upright. He was doing things to her that turned every muscle in her body to mush.

Just when she thought she couldn't bear it any longer, he stood back to his full height. The only light in the room came from the candle glowing on the nightstand.

Hunter's breath seemed to have caught in his throat. He pushed back the hair from her face. "God, you are so beautiful. Would you like to undress me?"

She nodded, reaching for his shirt to pull it over his head. When she hesitated at his jeans, he helped her. Then, when he stood before her naked, he removed the rest of her clothes, picked her up, and placed her on the bed.

Hunter lay down beside her and gathered her quivering body in his arms. His mouth took possession of her breast again while his hand moved from her breast down the slim line of her ribs and waist to the gentle curve of her hip. He repeated this motion several times before allowing his hand to rove to the triangular mound of curling hair between her legs. She stopped panting long enough to stiffen and gasp.

Hunter brought his hand back to her hip and his lips back to her ear. "It's all right, love. I promise, I won't hurt you or do anything you don't want me to. It's just that you drive me wild, Nicole. But I can slow down."

Nicole had difficulty breathing. What did he mean by *she* was driving him wild? She was the one on fire. Every place his hands touched brought immense pleasure. He was being so gentle, so tender with her; it almost brought tears to her eyes.

"No," she gasped. "You don't need to slow down. You just surprised me. I feel so inadequate. You're doing everything; I'm not giving anything back. Please teach me what to do."

A soft, husky chuckle escaped Hunter. "Nicole, sweetheart. Your very innocence is doing unbelievable things to me. You're giving me more than you could imagine."

"But, I want to touch you, feel you."

Hunter was motionless for a moment. Finally, he bent over and kissed her, tightly closed eyelids, then lay back on the bed. "All right," he said softly. "I'm all yours."

At first, she moved her hand slowly, shyly. She brought it to his waist, then to his belly. His body was well muscled, firm and taut under her searching fingers. She followed the coarse curling hair from his navel, going lower until she couldn't bring herself to keep going. When his erection touched the back of her hand, she gasped and started to draw away.

"No, don't stop," he said quickly, holding her hand where it was.

"I can't do it," she said miserably.

"Do you still want to?"

"Yes."

Hunter picked up her hand and placed it over his throbbing organ. He made a ragged hissing sound when her fingers closed firmly around him. He instantly pulled her hand away and brought it to his lips. "I'm sorry, sweetheart. You'll have to do that later. There's only so much I can take."

"But—"

He silenced her with his mouth as he rolled her onto her back. "Just trust me on this." He said. "I'll explain later." Very slowly, his hand blazed a path back to her center triangle, and this time she didn't clench up. He moved his hand to her inner thigh, coaxing her legs apart. She complied.

When his finger slipped inside her, she gasped, arching her body and calling out his name. His thumb sought out the firm nub as his finger continued to move inside of her. He threw a leg over her to hold her still and captured her screams with his mouth.

Nicole sank into oblivion, mindless pleasure, and melting heat. Her entire body tingled and writhed with the explosion of her first orgasm. When she finally stilled, her heart was slamming into her chest like the violent beating of a war drum. He had given her selfless pleasure, and he hadn't even entered her yet.

He held her until her breathing slowed. "Nicole, I don't have a condom. If I have sex with you, I could make you pregnant. Make no mistake, I want you so bad it's painful but—"

"In the drawer, beside the bed."

Hunter rose to an elbow to stare at her. "You have condoms in your nightstand."

Nicole pressed her face into his chest so he couldn't see her eyes. "I raided Billy's room this afternoon," she mumbled sheepishly, blowing at the hair tickling her nose.

Hunter bent over and drilled his tongue in her ear. She squirmed, making a soft squealing noise.

"You are such a little minx," he said, laughing. "And just when I was beginning to think nothing you could do would surprise me." Taking her with him, he leaned over and dug his hand into the drawer. They were the first things he touched on. There was a whole pile of them. He looked back at her in wonder. "Have you ever put one of these on?" he asked.

She shook her head vigorously.

"I'm letting you off the hook this time," he said, "but the next one is yours." He slipped the condom on then gathered her back in his arms.

He was touching her again, using his fingers in the same way as before. Nicole's body leaped hungrily to respond. This time, however, he stopped short of climaxing her. She gave no objection when he parted her legs and hoisted himself between them.

Nicole held her breath. She knew what was coming, and she was ready, but it didn't stop the anxiety that she had been nursing for twelve years. Somehow, Hunter sensed her fear and hesitated. He halted his entry to talk to her.

"Nicole, are you okay?"

She nodded, eyes pressed tightly shut.

"Talk to me, sweetheart." He probed her gently with his erection. "Tell me you want me, Nicole."

She sucked in her breath, holding it, waiting.

"Nicole, tell me you want me," he repeated.

When she still refused to answer, he pushed in a little further. He moved slowly, giving her a little then drawing back. Her breath was becoming more ragged than his was. She pushed her body up to meet him, to take him deeper, but he denied her as well as himself. She clutched at his back, opening herself to him, begging with her body language.

"Tell me you want me," he said for the third time, withdrawing from her.

She made a strained groan before she all but shouted at him, "I want you, dammit."

When he plunged into her as deeply as he could, she said it again, then once more before she gave herself up to the exquisite pleasure. When she had climaxed earlier, she thought she had experienced the sheerest ecstasy possible, but that was mild compared to having him inside her, filling her with his male hunger. Every thrust seemed to go deeper and deeper, demanding her surrender, seeking her release. When she finally gave in to it, she cried out with a wild shudder that racked her body in waves of pure primal lust.

He said something in her ear she didn't comprehend. He gave a final thrust along with a deep male wailing sound before he sagged weakly on top of her, his breath coming in strained gasps, his body drenched in sweat.

He buried his face in her hair and rolled to his side, taking her with him, holding her so as not to lose the contact. The pleasure she had given him was insurmountable. He didn't know if it was because he had restrained himself so long or if it was just her. Either way, being sheathed inside her heat had driven him to a frenzy he'd never experienced before.

He didn't realize how tight he was holding her until she squirmed.

"Hunter, are you okay?" she asked.

He loosened his hold on her but only slightly. "No, I'm not okay," he murmured in her hair. "I think you've killed me. Check my pulse, would you?"

"You're definitely alive. Your heart is pounding like a freight train."

His chest moved with the racking of chuckles.

Nicole sighed loudly and smiled. "Wow. That was...wow."

Hunter kissed the rapidly beating pulse on her temple. "I'll second that. Honey, it was like soaring off Mount Everest."

She snuggled against him. "I never imagined it would be so—wonderful." Very quietly, she added, "I think after this, my ghosts will have to find somebody else to haunt."

Chapter Eleven

Sometime later, after they'd snuffed the candle and sought the warmth of the covers, Hunter spoke into the darkness.

"You want to tell me about your ghosts, Nicole?"

Not surprised by the question, Nicole nestled in the security of his arms. She knew he would ask. She also knew he wouldn't press her if she chose not to answer.

Years before, a counselor had told her the healing would not be complete until she could talk openly about what had happened to her. They all said the same thing; they couldn't help her unless she'd talk about it. After the initial police reports, she had refused to discuss it with anybody; not her parents, not Billy, not Gram, and especially not the strangers who insisted they only wanted to help her. She didn't want their help. She thought she could bury it herself. That worked during the day when she kept busy, but at night, when she closed her eyes and slept, the ghosts came to haunt her. Not every night but she never knew when it would happen. It was time to end it.

Hunter didn't ask again. If he hadn't been rubbing her arm, she might have thought he'd drifted off to sleep.

Nicole took a deep breath, releasing it slowly. "I had just turned sixteen. There was a rock concert downtown, and I really wanted to go. Most of my friends being allowed to go, but my parents were adamant about my not going. They stuck together on it. I had never defied my parents on something that big before, but I was upset. I felt they didn't trust me."

Nicole took another deep breath, dragging the painful memories to the surface. "After they went to sleep, I crawled out my bedroom window and took a bus downtown. I had no idea there would be so many people at the concert. Nearly two thousand, the paper reported the next day, and several streets blocked off to accommodate them all. It was a melee with kids drinking and doing drugs—not just kids, older people too. I couldn't find my friends, so I didn't have a ride back home. I pushed and shoved my way through the crowd for two hours, looking until I decided I'd better find the bus and get home. The police figured someone had spotted me alone and followed me."

Hunter didn't say anything, but his arm tightened around her. Nicole swallowed hard at the bitter taste in her throat. She knew if she didn't continue she might never have the courage to tell it again.

"Someone grabbed me from behind, slapped a hand over my mouth, and dragged me into an alley. I was in such a state of shock that I nearly passed out. The last thing I saw was a green van with white writing on the side. Someone pulled me inside, then blindfolded and gagged me. They held me down. I think there were three of them but I'm not even sure about that. I just know there were hands all over me. It was a girl's worst nightmare, in triplicate."

Hunter brushed a tear from her cheek with his thumb. "Were they caught?" he asked gently.

Nicole pressed closer to Hunter. A small sob shuddered through her. "No. I never saw their faces. They dumped me a few blocks away in a deserted alley, along with my clothes and my purse. They were so high they didn't even take the fifty dollars I had in my wallet. By the time I got the blindfold off, they were gone. Two thousand people downtown and nobody saw anything. A police car patrolling the area spotted me and picked me up within a few minutes. I don't remember much after that. I guess I was hysterical. I must have told them who I was; because, Mom and Dad showed up at the hospital to take me home. They were wonderful through it all. The fact that I had disobeyed them never came up."

Nicole glanced up at Hunter; there was just enough moonlight filtering through the lace curtains to see his face. She reached up to touch the frown lines furrowing his brow. "Thank you for listening, Hunter."

Hunter grabbed her hand and pressed her fingers to his lips. "I haven't done anything, sweetheart."

"Oh, but you have. That attack destroyed a part of me. I'm not sure I can explain it, but somehow, what just happened between us made me whole again."

"Thank God you didn't get pregnant."

Nicole suddenly became very still. He said something else she couldn't hear through the blood pounding in her ears.

Then he was hovering over her. "Nicole? What's wrong?"

When she didn't answer, he laid his hand tenderly on her cheek. "Please, talk to me, Nicole. You've gone this far. Don't shut me out now."

"I did get pregnant," she whispered raggedly.

"Sweet, Jesus." He tightened his hold on her and waited for her to go on.

"I was still so distraught over the whole ordeal; I was four months along before I realized it. If I'd known right away, I could have had an abortion. But by then..."

"Didn't they do a test on you at the hospital?"

"Yes, but the hospital was so busy that night with the concert in town. A new intern did the test, he messed something up."

All the while she talked, his hand moved up and down her arm in a gentle caress.

"What did you do?" he asked after a few moments of silence.

"I carried the baby to almost seven months, but it was born dead. I nearly suffocated on guilt because I had prayed for it to die. I never even asked if it was a boy or a girl. I thought not knowing would help make it seem less real. But it *was* real, and at times, I still hear a baby crying in my nightmares."

"No one could blame you for not wanting a baby conceived under those circumstances."

"I know. I've accepted that. Actually, my mom convinced me that I didn't do anything to bring on the baby's death and that sometimes things happen for no reason." Nicole looked at Hunter with a sad smile. "Now, I just want to put it all behind me"

"My dear, sweet, Nicole. In spite of all you went through, you flourished. You're a successful, well-respected businesswoman. You've accomplished more than a lot of people do in a lifetime. Thank you for trusting me enough to share your pain. How can I help you forget?"

"You can kiss me, Hunter."

"I'll do more than that," he said, leaning over and taking her fully in his arms. He kissed the salty tears from her eyes then brushed his lips over hers. Tenderly at first, until she returned the kiss, then he seized her mouth with raw, hungry emotion.

That was all it took to make her forget everything except making love with Hunter. His hands roamed over her body finding all the sensual spots that made her cry out with pleasure. He played with her and teased her until she surprised herself by begging him to go further. True to his word, he made her put the condom on. She was clumsy, and her hands shook until he finally had to help her. By that time, he was as ready for her as she was for him.

He entered her slowly, penetrating her with a desperate need that shocked him. Driven purely by instinct, he plunged into her, muffling her cries with his mouth. She wrapped her legs around him and drew him even deeper into her vibrant heat. He knew the moment she climaxed. She arched against him, releasing a sweet cry. Her pulsing center tightened around him bringing his own shuddering explosion almost instantly. With a low groan, he gave himself up to the wild wonderful release.

Resting on his elbows, he attempted to protect her from his weight but she would have none of it. She welded her arms around his back and pulled him down against her.

He gave up and rested on top of her until his breathing slowed enough to talk.

"Woman, you are going to be the death of me." He grabbed her face in his hands and kissed her firmly, then rolled to his side. With a small protest, she rolled with him, clamping her leg around his knee.

Nicole sighed with contentment. "You really are Hercules, aren't you? How many times can you do that?"

Hunter chuckled. "How many condoms do you have?"

"Not enough, at this rate. I thought—"

"You thought what?" Hunter asked, giving her a squeeze.

"Well, the way Carmen said, men could only do it once."

"Up until this last hour, I would have agreed with her."

"What do you mean?"

He leaned over and kissed her in the ear. "It means you are the sexiest woman I ever met."

Nicole wriggled away from his probing tongue. "Yeah, right," she snorted indelicately. "Feed that line to somebody who believes you."

Hunter blew out a long breath of air. "My dear, Ms. Anderson. It doesn't necessarily take experience to drive a man wild."

Nicole didn't believe him, but the fact that he said it made her feel special. She ran her hand over his arm, enjoying the feel of his firm, tight muscles, touching on a long, jagged scar that extended from his collarbone to his shoulder. She traced it gently with her fingers before continuing on to the dark, matted hair on his chest. When she advanced to his hard nipple, his hand shot out to stop her.

"You've already worn me out. If you keep that up neither one of us will be able to walk tomorrow."

"I just want to feel you all over."

"Later," he said, putting her hand behind him. "Right now, you can stick to rubbing my back; that relaxes me."

Nicole smiled. The thought that she could excite him was delicious. She went back to the scar. "How did you get this?"

When he didn't answer right away, she thought he wasn't going to.

"Car accident," he said finally.

"Was it long ago?" she prompted. Her hand slid from his shoulder to his forearm. She ran her fingers lightly over the crisp hair on his chest, enjoying the way it tickled her palm.

"Yes," he said softly. "I was nine. My aunt and uncle died—and so did my sister, Diana. We were going to stay at their house for a couple of days because my mother was in the hospital having Stephen."

Nicole's hand froze on his arm. She remembered the first night he came to her house, when she'd guessed his sister's name was Diana. It must have brought up very painful memories. She didn't know what to say.

Hunter's hand sifted through her hair. "The car burned. I would have died too if my cousin, Grant, hadn't pulled me out, along with his brother, Quinton. Grant was sixteen and Quint was five—the same age as Diana. That's when Quint came to live with us. Diana was in the front seat with Quint and Grant's parents. They died instantly as well as three teenagers in the other car. Two of them were seventeen, the other sixteen, and they'd all been drinking."

Tears stung Nicole's eyes. She put her arm around him and pressed her face to his chest. "How awful for you. And for your family."

"Yeah. Mom almost lost it. I really think the only thing that kept her sane was having Quint to nurse back to health, that and the new baby to take care of."

"And you," Nicole said. "You were apparently badly injured."

"Not as bad as Quint. When he finally recovered, he became a permanent part of our family."

"Where did Grant go?" she asked.

"To an older sister who was married. I almost think it was toughest for him. He went to school with the kids in the other car. They were on the way to pick him up. He had tremendous guilt because he never even got a scratch."

"But he was a hero."

"Quint and I sure thought so. But he didn't." Hunter sighed. "I have my own guilt to carry. The only reason Diana sat up front was because we didn't want her in back—because she was a girl."

"But you were just kids."

"Yeah, that should justify it. I try to tell myself that but it doesn't always work."

"I guess I, of all people, can relate to that.

"It seems we both have some unfriendly ghosts in our past."

Nicole reached up and touched his face, trying to erase the tension lines she saw there. He in turn, brushed a curl from her temple. She realized that baring their souls to each other was as intimate as their lovemaking had been.

* * * *

When Nicole woke up, bright sunlight streamed in through Gram's handmade, lace curtains. She couldn't remember the last time she had opened her eyes to the glare of the sun. By this time, she usually had an hour or two of work done.

Hunter no longer lay beside her, and the rich smell of coffee wafted from the kitchen below. She stretched lazily, remembering. In spite of the glow inside her, she had an uneasy feeling on the outside. How could she get up and face Hunter in the daylight after everything that had transpired between? Even after sharing their most intimate secrets, she still hardly knew him. She did know that she enjoyed his company immensely. His quick mind challenged her and brought out a playful side of her that she had shut out a long time ago.

When her thoughts drifted to the future, she jumped out of bed and switched the shower on. She wouldn't allow herself to think that far ahead. After all, she was a grown woman and understood that their relationship was temporary.

Normally, with a tour coming through that afternoon, she would have dressed in costume. However, she decided to wait since she planned to take the kids in to meet Gram this morning. After drying and brushing her thick, rust colored hair to a glossy sheen, she slipped into black jeans and a soft black and white, cotton blouse. Finished, she glanced in the mirror, and for the first time in her life, liked what she saw. A sensual woman smiled back at her with mischievous green eyes that twinkled as though they held the secrets of the universe. She topped the look off with a touch of apricot lipstick and literally bounced down the stairs.

Nicole had expected to find Hunter in the kitchen. It was empty. She poured herself a cup of coffee, thinking he must be in the studio. Then she caught a glimpse of him out on the deck, braced on one foot, half perched on the railing, staring out over the lake. A coffee mug rested on his thigh. For just a secret moment, she stared at him. His dark hair, not quite black but a deep mahogany, was damp, the unruly ends, curling down one side of his forehead. He wore faded jeans and a cream-colored tee shirt that hugged his broad shoulders and bulging biceps in a way that was downright indecent. The man fairly oozed sexuality. Something she would not have thought about before last night. The sight of him took her breath away.

Nicole's heart started thumping wildly against her chest. She took a deep breath, summoned her courage, and stepped outside, hoping he wouldn't notice how her hands shook. She needn't have worried. The smile that greeted her as she walked toward him reached clear to her toes.

He held out an arm to invite her into his embrace, and she went to it without a second's hesitation. From the position he was in, she equaled his height.

He captured her shoulders and drew her against his sturdy frame. "You look ravishing this morning," he said, placing a kiss in her hair, breathing deeply of her scent. "Mmm, I love that shampoo you use."

Nicole nestled against him and looked out over the water. He made her feel warm and secure and...sexy. She wanted to say something clever. "Beautiful morning, isn't it?"

Hunter's deep chuckle raced through her system like a jolt of electricity and stained her cheeks a bright pink. "Sure is. I just saw an eagle," he said, pointing to a tall Norway pine about eighty yards from the house. "I'm thirty-three years old, and I've traveled to eighteen different countries. This is the first time I've ever seen an eagle in the wild."

"They nest up there. That tree is over two hundred years old."

"Unbelievable," Hunter said, shaking his head.

"What? The fact that the tree is two hundred years old or that the eagles nest in it?"

Hunter turned to look at her. His mouth was only inches from her lips.

"The fact that some guy hadn't discovered you a long time ago, put a ring on your finger, and kept you barefoot and pregnant."

His words took Nicole completely by surprise.

"I'm not exactly a prize catch," she mumbled.

Hunter stared at her, finding it difficult to accept that she actually believed that. He wasn't sure if he should feel guilty for being the one to discover her, only to be the one to leave her when his mission in Minnesota was finished. He should be satisfied he'd been able to help her—bring her out of her shell—so she could eventually let some man into her life. Bloody hell! That thought didn't please him one damn bit. He didn't want some other man touching her. Just the idea of it rankled him.

For both their sakes, he would have to manage, somehow, to distance himself from her before he left. Maybe he would grow tired of her like he usually did after a relationship began to wear on him. He couldn't quite see that happening with Nicole.

Nicole absently settled her hand on his thigh. Her touch affected him as no other woman's ever had. He could already feel his jeans tightening. Shit. The last thing he wanted to do was distance himself. What he really wanted to do was take her back upstairs and—

A soft giggling overhead interrupted his thoughts. He looked up to see a pajama clad duo peering down from the balcony.

"Don't look now," he said in a loud voice, "but I think we're being invaded by the pajama monkeys. They must be looking for their bananas."

Another volley of giggles came from above them.

Kyle's dark face animated with mischief. "Were you kissing, Aunt Nicky?" he asked before Shanna was able to clamp a hand over his mouth.

"Shhh, Kyle, you weren't supposed to say it."

Kyle pulled her fingers away. "You said it first, Shanna."

Shanna quickly whispered something in his ear.

Hunter laughed up at them. "You guys better hurry and get dressed, or you'll miss breakfast. The last one at the table gets raw eggs. Remember?"

Shanna made a disgusted sound and ran for their room. Kyle made a similar noise and hurried after her.

After they had disappeared, Hunter grinned at Nicole. "I do believe those two are starting to act like normal kids."

Nicole's face, still turned toward the balcony, was too tempting. Hunter stood and brought his arm from her shoulders to the back of her neck and pressed his mouth to her lips. She responded with a breathless moan.

Hunter released her, laughing shakily. His breath caught in his throat when he looked down at her dreamy smile. "You look like the mouse that just ate the cat's cream."

She gave him a throaty, "Yum."

"Later," he said thickly, pushing her ahead of him toward the house so she wouldn't see what her playful 'yum' had done to him. "You just want me to be the one eating raw eggs."

* * * *

After breakfast, Hunter settled down to the computer to read the E-mail messages he'd ignored for three days. Four came from Marla asking for specific information and another ten were either answers or questions to projects he'd been working on before he left New York. The Internet could supply most of the answers he needed; the rest he could handle by phone.

The activity in the shop was a lot easier to ignore than Nicole's walking back and forth to her worktable. He liked the way her jeans hugged her slim figure. The same figure he'd had his hands all over just hours ago. The thought of her eager body responding to his touch made him ache to touch it again.

Hunter was more than relieved when she announced she was taking the kids in to see her grandmother. He declined her offer to go along in order to catch up on his work.

Nicole hummed as she pulled out of the driveway, relieved to get away from Chuck and Carmen. She wasn't sure how they knew she had slept with Hunter, but obviously, something had inspired their mischievous looks. The content-as-a-cat smile she wore, and being late getting down to the shop was unusual enough to make them suspicious.

At the assisted living home, Gram was sitting in her room watching a game show. Her face lit up when Nicole walked in with Shanna and Kyle. Nicole had explained to the kids in the car about Gram being their great-grandmother.

Nicole gave the older woman a delicate hug. "Hi, Gram. I want you to meet Shanna and Kyle, Brenda's children."

Gypsy's eyes were drawn immediately to Shanna. "Well, aren't you just about the prettiest little thing I ever saw?" She held out her arms to both of them. Shanna went right to her; Kyle followed a bit tentatively. "And you are a handsome young man," she said to Kyle, coaxing him closer.

Kyle finally gave her a shy smile. "Aunt Nicky said you are Mama's grandmother."

Nicole saw a shadow cross Gram's face before she quickly masked it. "That's right, my darling." She gave him a light squeeze. "And you are making this one of the happiest days of my life by coming to see me." When she turned to Shanna, moisture pooled in her eyes, "You look so much like your mother," she said. "Except your hair is a brighter shade of red and so curly. What a precious child you are. How old are you?"

"I'm six," Shanna said.

"And I'm four," Kyle said proudly holding up four fingers.

"Did you know our mama?" Shanna asked.

Nicole was gaping at her grandmother, about to ask the same question. She held her breath, waiting for the answer.

Gram shot a quick look at Nicole then turned her attention back to Shanna. "I knew her in my heart," Gypsy said. "And I saw pictures of her. She was very beautiful."

Nicole's heart slammed into her ribs. "When did you see pictures, Gram?"

"In my heart, Sweet Pea. The pictures are in my heart."

Nicole wanted to press her further, but Shanna and Kyle were hanging on every word. This wasn't the time. She sank into a chair, feeling suddenly weak.

"We have a great-grandfather too," Shanna told Gypsy.

Nicole's head came up with a start. Instant adrenaline pulsed through her veins. Before she could open her mouth, Kyle spoke.

"Yeah, but he did bad things so he has to live in a jail."

"It's a prison," Shanna corrected him.

"Yeah, a prison," Kyle said.

Nicole was speechless. Why hadn't they thought of asking the kids if they had relatives? She, at least, had assumed that if they'd had anywhere else to go, they wouldn't have been delivered to her.

She finally found her tongue. "Do you know your great grandfather's name?"

Shanna looked at Nicole and shrugged. "Mama called him Grandpa Willard. We only went to see him once. I didn't like him because he wasn't very nice to me. Mama said he only liked boys. Kyle was too little, he doesn't remember him."

"Yeah, I don't remember, but I don't like him either," Kyle said emphatically.

Shanna's face brightened. "We have a grandpa too," she said. "But we don't see him anymore."

"Yeah," Kyle added, "because he lives far away."

Nicole stared at them, stunned. "Where does he live?" Nicole asked.

Shanna shrugged. "I don't know. In a hospital, I think. Mama said he was hurt when our grandmother died."

"Yeah, in the 'splosion." Kyle said.

"Your grandmother died in an explosion?" Nicole asked, glancing at Gram. Gram's face was discerningly vacant.

"It was before we were born," Shanna said.

Nicole looked accusingly at her grandmother. "Did you already know all this, Gram?"

Gypsy reached out and touched Nicole's face with weathered fingers, her other hand, she put to her chest. She smiled a painfully sad smile. "I promise you, Dee Dee, the secrets will not die with me. I will leave you the key."

Chapter Twelve

By noon, Hunter finished all his business calls. Quint was out of the office, and he hadn't heard from Virg. Two seconds later, the cell phone rang.

It was Virg.

"I've got a few crumbs for you, Hunter."

"Hallelujah. I'm up against a blank wall here."

"This is really odd, but then it seems everything about this situation is odd. Jon's last name was Sanders until he married Yvonne, that's when it became Jonathon Casey. Apparently, *he* took *her* last name. I haven't figured that one out yet, but I have a lead I can follow up on."

"When did they get married?" Hunter asked, scribbling notes on a pad.

"Just before they started school together—a year before Dawn started."

Hunter digested that a moment. "What's your other lead?"

"Yvonne's father, Willard Casey, is still alive. He's been in and out of prison several times in the last thirty years. Right now, he's eighty-five years old and doing time in Adirondack for fraud."

"Shit. I wonder if he's lucid."

"Want me to pay him a visit?"

"I'd appreciate it."

"Already planned on it."

"I guess I don't have to tell you what to look for. What about the autopsy report?"

"I'm sure I'll have it by tomorrow."

"Anything else?"

"Yeah, Yvonne died in an explosion at her home."

"Christ! I knew she died, but I didn't know how. Should have been about seven years ago."

"Exactly, seven years ago. Here's the interesting part—she had a daughter, Megan, who died with her."

Hunter's mind suddenly went blank. He tried to put that bit of information into the equation but it just didn't fit.

"Hunter, you still with me?"

"Hell no! You lost me at Megan. I don't get it. Are you sure?"

The library has the newspaper write-up on microfiche."

"Did it say how old the girl was?"

"Around five."

"Five? God! Yvonne must have been...what—in her mid to late fifties. She had a five year old child?"

"Actually, Yvonne was only fifty-one."

"That would have made her forty-six when the girl was born."

"Not impossible by any means. Anyway, that's what the paper reported. Plus, Jonathon Casey was in the house too—he was injured, but he didn't die. I haven't had time to find out what happened to him after that. I'll look for a birth certificate on Megan but don't get your hopes up. Unless you're a family member, they're getting real sticky about giving out information. I'll do what I can, though."

"What caused the explosion?"

"Suspected gas leak, but unconfirmed at the time. I can get Quint on that."

"Shit. What a tangled, fucked-up mess. It seems the more we know, the more we find out we don't know. Let's hope the old duffer can shed some light."

Silence hung for a moment until Virgil spoke again, his voice edged with concern. "You ready to tell me why you're involved in this?"

Hunter grimaced and blew out a deep breath of air. "Nicole Anderson got custody of the kids. Somehow or other, she's Brenda's half-sister—at least, I think she is—I just haven't figured out how yet."

"So how did you get in the middle of it?"

"I was left in charge of delivering the kids to her."

"So why didn't you deliver them and come back home?"

Because one of them is mine, dammit!

Hunter thought it, but he wasn't ready to say it out loud—to anybody. He ignored the clenching in his gut. The sound of the garage door opening brought his attention back to Virgil. "It's a rather complicated story. I'll get back to you on that."

Virgil grunted. "Right. So, what is Nicole Anderson like?"

"Beautiful. Intelligent. Nice—too damn nice!" Sexy. Hot. On fire.

"Are you getting in over your head?"

"Only up to my chin," Hunter said, wishing he believed that. "Call me when you get out of prison."

Virgil chuckled. "Do you need rescuing? Remember, I have a wealth of experience when it comes to women."

"I'll yell when it gets too deep."

"Don't wait as long as I did."

"Hell, Virg, you never did yell for help."

Virgil gave a shout of laughter. "It's hard to yell when you're up to your ears in cow manure."

"No argument here."

Nicole peeked into the studio waving a large carryout bag. She pointed to the bag, then to the deck, mouthing the word picnic.

Hunter noted the serious expression on her face. Her

visit with Gram must have revealed something. Whatever it was, he had plenty to add to it. He nodded, finished his conversation with his brother, and hung up the phone.

With the kids at hand, Hunter didn't get a chance to talk to Nicole. The most he was able to do was give her a smiling wink before Chuck and Carmen joined them for lunch. He adored the way her cheeks flushed like a teenager and the way her lips always seemed ripe for kissing. The conversation around him centered on the tour that afternoon, so it left him free to concentrate on his own thoughts. Making love to Nicole again was at the top of the list.

Chuck was grinning at him, and he realized the man had asked him a question. "So are you going to dress up like Hercules for the tour?"

Hunter grimaced. "I don't think—"

"Pleeease," Kyle pleaded.

Hunter looked to Nicole for support—no help there.

"We're all going to dress up," Shanna said with a small pout.

Hunter smiled at her. "I'm sure they don't have a costume to fit me."

"Sure do." Chuck said quickly.

Hunter gave him a sour look. "Thanks a lot, pal."

Chuck's grin widened, "My pleasure, Herc."

Nicole looked at Hunter, smiling devilishly. "Well, I guess that settles it then. We better get ready; they'll be here by two."

Forty-five minutes later, Hunter stepped out of the dressing room feeling like a world-class clown. To make matters worse, they were all standing outside the door waiting to greet him with hoots and cheers. Both Chuck and Carmen whistled mercilessly. Amanda, who had shown up while he was dressing, had a look of utter disbelief on her face. Nicole was trying very unsuccessfully not to grin, but the admiring look on Kyle's face convinced him he'd done the right thing.

Shanna rushed up and threw her arms around him. "Hunter, you are the best Hercules there ever was." She turned to Nicole. "Auntie Nicky, isn't he just about the handsomest, most beautiful, mightiest, warrior you ever saw?"

Hunter watched Nicole scrutinize him from the knit leggings that hugged his legs to the sleeveless leather tunic that covered his broad shoulders and thighs but left the muscular expanse of his arms bare. A studded leather girdle draped his narrow waist and hips like a glove. He truly looked like he had just stepped out of a medieval scene.

"Yup," she said, "I guess that just about covers it."

Nicole wore a high-waist, pastel green silk gown with puffed sleeves and swooping neckline, cut low enough to offer a view of her neck and a hint of bosom. Green silk slippers peeked out beneath her flowing hem.

She squirmed a bit when Hunter made a point of staring at her with his dark chocolate eyes.

Carmen and Amanda appeared as wenches who might have just stepped off a pirate ship. Kyle was a miniature Chuck dressed in Robin Hood greens and browns. His face beamed while Shanna danced around like a fairy princess in pink silken chiffon. Pink matching ribbons fell to her waist from a tiara on her head. There wasn't a single article on any of them, from their headwear to their shoes, that didn't look remarkably authentic.

Hunter shook his head in admiration. "You all look fantastic." *If you can't lick 'em, join 'em,* he thought good-naturedly. He made an elaborate bow at the waist then, bending on one knee, took Shanna's hand and kissed the back of it. For his efforts, he received a round of applause. He got to his feet and turned to Nicole. With the smoothness of stately knight, he took her hand and pressed it to his lips.

"You, your royal loveliness, are a gifted genius and so are all your worthy subjects."

Carmen made a loud *swooning* noise and collapsed,

forcing Chuck to catch her. They were all laughing when Marge arrived with her first and second graders for the tour.

After Chuck explained the history of each costume, Hunter was more than glad to get back to his computer while they went on their tour. The irony of typing on a keyboard, dressed like an ancient Greek myth, did not escape him. Nicole, however, dispelled any qualms he had when she came up behind him and put her arms around his neck. She snuggled her chest warmly against his back.

"Thank you," she whispered in his ear. "Kyle and Shanna will never forget this and neither will I." Before he could respond, she stuck her tongue in his ear then dashed away when he made a grab for her, leaving him with her honeysuckle scent and an uncomfortable ache in his groin. He would have gone after her, but she was already engrossed in conversation with Carmen.

Moments later, the shop bell rang, and Nicole let three people in, one of them Sheriff Martin. The sheriff spotted Hunter and walked through the shop toward him.

His smile was down-home friendly as he extended a hand. "Mr. Douglas, good to see you again."

"Hunter shook the smaller man's hand. "Hello, Sheriff. Why don't you call me Hunter?"

"Hunter it is, and call me John. We aren't real formal around here. I brought my sister-in-law and her hubby over to pick out some costumes." He cast a furtive glance toward the shop. "Actually, I'm real glad you're still here. I worry about Nicole all alone in this big house; especially with that burglar still on the loose."

"Any leads yet?" Hunter asked.

"No, he seems to know just how to keep a step ahead of me." He glanced back at the shop and lowered his voice. "I don't want to alarm Nicole, but Simon down at the lumberyard was doing a job for one of the neighbors yesterday and he spotted a car parked up on the main road, watching the house."

"Nicole said a lot of people drive by to look at the house."

"Yeah, except this guy was using binoculars."

Hunter sucked in a sharp breath of air. "Did he say what make or color the car was?"

"That's just the thing. It was a white Ford Aspire. According to Barney, the guy we're after drives a dark car. Something else, the license plates were smeared with mud, so he couldn't read them."

The fact that Simon tried to read the plates impressed Hunter. It seemed these local people took pains to look out for each other. It wasn't nearly so annoying when their curiosity wasn't zeroed in on him. He especially liked the fact that they looked out for Nicole. At least she'd have them to support her when he left.

John Martin absently rubbed the back of his neck. "I have to tell you, Hunter. Your being here has raised a lot of eyebrows in the community. It's no secret that every single fella within forty miles has tried to date that little gal. She's turned them all down flat. More than once, I might add, not so much as a dinner date. Then you drop out of nowhere with two little kids and…well I guess you can see what I'm getting at."

Hunter could have just told him it was none of his business and left it at that but somehow, that didn't feel right. The sheriff's concern clearly went beyond curiosity.

"The reason I'm here is confidential, anything beyond that you'll have to take up with Nicole. It's actually more her business than mine. What I can tell you, though, is that I didn't come here to pursue Nicole. In fact, that was the last thing on my mind. I expect by the time I leave, she'll be ready to explain everything."

John Martin gave Hunter a long look. "I guess that means you do plan to leave then? I'm sorry to hear that. It's none of my business—and certainly no offense meant—but you're a fool if you do."

A week ago, he would have told the man to go to hell,

but a week ago, he didn't know Nicole Anderson. It was hard to fault a man for stating a truth. "I'll keep that in mind," he said.

Neither one of them heard Nicole walk in the room. The circumspect smile on her face told Hunter she'd heard at least some of their conversation.

"Millie said to tell you they're finished," she informed the sheriff.

He gave her a ready smile. "Okay, Hon, I guess we'll be going then." He turned back to Hunter. "Oh, by the way, nice outfit you have on. I give you credit; most men wouldn't have the guts—or the body," he added, smiling.

After John Martin left, Nicole walked over to stare out the window.

Hunter got up to stand behind her. "Nicole, how much of that did you hear?"

She turned to face him with liquid eyes. "It doesn't matter, Hunter. I'm not a naive teenager. I understand the practicalities of life. I've known all along that you would be leaving when you're finished here. The only question has been whether or not Shanna and Kyle would be leaving with you."

"Maybe I'm missing something here," Hunter said, balancing on the edge of irritation. "Most women in your position would be upset, even furious, to hear me talk about leaving. They'd be screaming that I seduced them, took advantage of them, pulling the 'love 'em and leave 'em' bit."

Nicole swallowed hard at the lump threatening to choke her. "I guess that just proves, one more time, I'm not like other women." She took a deep breath, fighting desperately to maintain control. "I learned a long time ago that there are some things you can change and some things you can't, and the only way you can survive is by knowing the difference. The fact is Hunter, you live in New York, and my life is in Minnesota. A temper tantrum is not going to erase fifteen hundred miles, nor is it going to make either one of us want to pull up our roots and move. Furthermore, it certainly wouldn't get rid of that paper in your brief case waiting for me to sign the kids over to you so you can take them with you when you leave. So what would the point be?"

Nicole turned her back on him again, before the tears could spill down her cheeks. "Besides," she said staring out the window, "you didn't seduce me; I seduced you. Maybe you don't realize it, but you gave me something last night that was long overdue. After you're gone, I may finally be able to allow a man into my life."

Hunter swore under his breath. "You sound like you can't wait to be rid of me so you can move on to your next conquest."

His outburst caught Nicole off guard. She stared at him, blinking at the tears stinging her eyes. She thought she was letting him off the hook. Instead, she'd somehow angered him. Wanting to get rid of him was the last thing she wanted, but she was certain that begging him to stay was the last thing he wanted.

"Don't be ridiculous," she whispered. "I want you just as much now as I did last night. I've never wanted anybody or anything as much as I want you right now. But I'm smart enough to know you don't always get what you want in life. If I had a choice—"

Hunter didn't give her a chance to finish. He took her face in his hands and captured her words with his mouth. She responded by wrapping her arms around his neck and pressing her body against him, moving her lips to comply hungrily with the demand of his kiss. His breathing became choppy, while a low groan rumbled from his throat.

He dragged his mouth from hers long enough to ask, "Where is the tour right now?"

"They're all out on the deck having milk and cookies."

"Shanna and Kyle too?"

"Yes."

He picked her up and carried her out of the studio toward the stairs before she could even think about objecting. In her bedroom, he stopped only long enough to turn and lock the door.

It took less than two minutes for him to have them both naked and a condom in place. She watched him wordlessly and maintained her silence when he picked her up again and placed her on the bed. In the same motion, he was on top of her, kissing away the salty tears from her cheeks. His need for her overpowered his reason. Wasting little time on foreplay, he thrust into her hot core and made love to her until she called out his name. Her sleek sheath tightened around him drawing the eager seed from his shuddering body and a turbulent shout from his throat.

He sagged against her, spent, cursing the lack of control that had driven him to take her more roughly then he'd intended.

Before he could voice an apology, she rubbed her soft hands over his back whispering huskily in his ear. "That was beyond words. It was—earthmoving. You make me feel so—so alive, so wanton, so wonderful. I just wish I had the experience to make you feel the same way."

Hunter found himself laughing. "Lord, help me, if you ever do. Sweetheart, that had nothing to do with experience. That was pure animal lust. You drove me over the edge downstairs when you said you wanted me. I'm beginning to believe you did seduce me."

Still laughing and working at catching his breath, Hunter rolled to his back, keeping her pressed to his side. He covered his eyes with his free arm.

Nicole threw a leg over his thighs. Her fingers played with the crisp hair covering his chest. "I might have if I'd known how."

"For some people, it comes naturally. I think you're one of those. You do it without even knowing it." He quickly clasped a hand over her roving fingers. "And if you keep touching me, we're going to spend the rest of the day in this bedroom."

"Oh, my God, Gram!" Nicole bolted to a sitting position. "I haven't had a chance to tell you about my visit with Gram."

Hunter sighed. "And I have some things to tell you that I learned from Virgil this morning. We better get dressed and go downstairs to compare notes. I don't think we want the kids, or anybody else for that matter, to come looking for us."

Nicole made a dash to crawl over him when his arms came around her waist and locked her in place.

"Before we go, there's one thing I need to clarify. Downstairs you mentioned that form I brought to have you sign the kids over to me. That form was based on our initial phone conversation. I fully believed you didn't want anything to do with Kyle and Shanna. I admit, I came here expecting you to sign it and send us on our way within twenty-four hours. In fact, I already had return airline tickets for the three of us to go back to New York the next day."

Nicole went limp against his chest. "But you never even asked me to sign it. Why?"

Hunter stroked her hair. "Because, I realized that first night that you were nothing like I had imagined over the phone, and I had overestimated my ability to deal with two troubled kids. It seemed to come naturally to you."

"But you're wonderful with them. You just needed more time." Nicole raised her head to smile at him. "After all, look what you did for me." She wriggled upward until she could place a quick kiss on his lips.

Hunter's hand shot around her neck, restraining her, pulling her deeper into the kiss. With a low groan, he rolled them both over until he was on top of her. Sighing throatily, he dragged his mouth away from her. "See what you do to me, woman. I'm going to get up now, and you'd be wise not to touch me again until you have your clothes back on."

Chapter Thirteen

Ten minutes later, Nicole, once again, looking like an Egyptian goddess, sat at the kitchen counter while Hunter made coffee. He had given up the Hercules attire for the comfort of his own clothes. They were soon to discover that their mornings had revealed a lot of the same information.

Hunter snapped the lid on the coffeepot then took a seat across the counter from Nicole. "Yvonne Casey's father is still alive. He's at the Adirondack Correctional Facility in upstate New York."

Nicole arched a brow at him. "That would be the great-grandfather Shanna talked about. She even said he was in a prison. What did he do?"

"Fraud, I think." Hunter said. "Virg is taking a drive up there tomorrow. Shanna told you about him?"

"Yeah, she told Gram she had a great-grandfather. He was in prison, and Shanna didn't like him because he wasn't nice to her."

Hunter shook his head. "Why didn't we think to ask the kids about relatives?"

"I assumed if they'd had any, they wouldn't have been left to me. But that's not all; they think they still have a grandfather too."

"That would be Jonathon Casey, Yvonne's husband."

Nicole shot him a quick, confused frown. "Her husband? I don't understand."

"His last name was Sanders. For some reason, he took Yvonne's name when they got married. Virg is checking into that too. They married just before they started school. A year before your mom did."

"The kids said he was hurt in an explosion that killed their grandmother, and they hadn't seen him in a long time because he lived far away. Do you think he's still alive?"

"It's certainly a possibility. I plan to do some hunting on my own on the Internet. Unfortunately, it's a lot easier to find out if and when somebody died then it is to locate him or her while they're still living. Virg is doing some research on him too. Maybe one of us will come up with something useful."

"Your brother sounds like a great guy to do all that for you."

Hunter grinned. "He is, but he's also the one with the brains in the family. Besides, he has a degree in criminal law and can find his way in and out of the legal system like a sewer rat. In addition—he owes me."

"For what?"

Hunter jumped up and rescued the coffee from boiling over. He pulled down two cups and set them on the counter. "A little over a year ago, he got involved with a woman. He had stars in his eyes, wedding bells, the whole bit. She was nothing but a gold digging hustler. The rest of us were wise to her, but he couldn't see beyond his idiot stick. Anyway, I ran an investigation on her and discovered she had a husband and three kids in New Mexico. She had cleaned out their bank account and made off with a two hundred thousand-dollar coin collection."

Nicole made a soft whistling sound. "Did he get over her?"

Hunter chuckled. "It took about two months; two months of hiding in a boozing, stinking hell hole, refusing to speak to me or anybody else."

"I guess he forgave you then."

"Forgave me? Hell, he was so grateful he promised me free legal services for the rest of my life. Anyway, that's the whole reason Corina wouldn't tell anybody her boyfriend's name, me in particular."

"One would think she'd be grateful for your concern," Nicole said.

Hunter grunted. "People can act damn strange when they think they're in love. By instinct, they come out swinging at the first person who tries to help, or interfere, as they see it."

"You sound like you're talking from experience."

Hunter got up and brought the coffeepot from the stove. "I am."

Nicole kept her eyes on the coffee he was pouring. "I guess that means you really loved your wife."

He returned the coffeepot, came back, and took his seat. He cradled the steaming cup in his hands for a moment before answering. "Like I said, people act strange when they think they're in love. I was more likely in lust. I have to believe love lasts longer than a year."

A peculiar knot tightened Nicole's chest. She tried to loosen it with a deep breath. It seemed that lust pretty well described their relationship. She let her breath out in a heavy gush. "At least you're smart enough to know the difference."

"One would think so," he said dryly.

Hunter watched Nicole stare into her coffee cup, furrows creasing her smooth, tawny brows. Since his marriage, he'd had a number of women in his life. Most of them claimed to be in love with him by the second or third date. That was always when he moved on, determined never again to confuse lust with love. Nicole Anderson just didn't fit the same mold as the other women he'd known.

Maybe it was time he told her about the envelope

Brenda mailed to him the same day she died. The envelope
containing the letter addressed to Nicole that was still in his
briefcase. He had no right to withhold it from her; he
should have given it to her right away. Now, he feared
she'd never forgive him if she learned the truth about
Shanna and knew he had concealed it from her. That
thought brought more pain to his chest than he cared to
admit.

She drew him from his thought when she looked at
him and said the last thing he'd expected hear from her.
"Well, Hercules, the way I see it, I'm definitely in lust with
you."

Having said that, Nicole reached across the counter,
she pushed back the curl on his forehead.

When her warm fingers touched his skin, Hunter
didn't move. For a moment, he just looked at her. If he had
thought she was toying with him, he might have reacted
with anger. However, he was damn sure she didn't even
know about all the little games men and women played;
silly, cruel little games. They usually had an agenda, they
usually worked, and they always worked best for the ones
who cared the least.

Nicole's face was too open, too exposed, and too
sincere to be playing any kind of game. Smiling, he reached
over and slid his hand along her sleek neck to the inviting
curve of breast that pushed upward from her silk gown. It
showed just enough skin to tempt a man's touch, yet hid
enough to drive him to madness. He was about to walk
around the counter and plant a very wet kiss on each one of
those delectable mounds when Shanna and Kyle rushed
into the room, followed closely by, Chuck.

Chuck took one look at the two of them and grinned.
"Want me to take the kids out fishing?"

Nicole blushed to the roots of her hair.

"Pour yourself some coffee," Hunter said. "Nicole was
just asking my advice on the benefits of doubling your
hours."

Chuck laughed. He took a cup from the rack and reached for the coffee. "At the same pay, I imagine."

"Of course."

"I'll take the coffee, but I'll drink it back in the shop while you convince my employer that having me around that much would put a tremendous damper on her personal life."

Shanna had already scrambled up on the stool beside Nicole. Hunter reached down and lifted Kyle up beside him.

Kyle's eyes sparkled. "I have a new friend named Jacob. He goes to school cause he's older. Can I go to school when I'm older, Hunter?"

"Mrs. Watson said I'm old enough to go now," Shanna said quickly. "Can I go to school, Aunt Nicky?"

Nicole exchanged a quick glance with Hunter before she turned back to Shanna. "Did you go to school in New York?"

Shanna shook her head. "No."

"Me not either," Kyle chimed.

"But…you can read," Nicole said, remembering the times she'd sat with the kids at the little table in the back of the shop. "How did you learn to read?"

"Mommy taught me," Shanna said proudly. "She said I was really smart. Kyle can read too, but I have to help him with the words."

"Do you know when Kyle's birthday is?" Hunter asked.

Shanna nodded. "Its March sixth, a week before me. He was four. My birthday is March fourteenth and I'm six."

Hunter gave Nicole a surprised look.

She gave him one back that said, easy boy, they're just kids.

"Mommy gave me a really big box of crayons for my birthday," Kyle said, "And coloring books too." He looked at Shanna with sad eyes. "Do you know where my crayons are?" he asked.

"I think they're still at Mama's house. Maybe we can get them later," Shanna said in a low, sad voice. She looked at Hunter with eyes much older than six years. "Are we going to go back to New York like you said on the airplane?"

Hunter exchanged a look with Nicole.

"Do you want to go back to New York?" he asked Shanna.

Shanna shook her head vigorously. "No, I want to stay here. I like it here." She looked at Nicole. "Can we stay, Aunt Nicky? I promise we'll be good."

Nicole tore her eyes away from Hunter and looked at Kyle. "How about you, Kyle, do you want to stay here too?"

Kyle looked up at Nicole. Tears clung to his long lashes. When he blinked a wet path traced down his cheeks. "If we stay here, Mama won't know where to find us."

"Mama's dead!" Shanna shouted. "Can't you understand? She's not coming back. When people die, they put them in the ground and throw dirt on them. We're orphans. Nobody wants orphans unless they're rich. They'll separate us because they'll only want you."

Kyle began sobbing under Shanna's onslaught. When Hunter pulled Kyle on his lap, Shanna leaped from her chair and ran from the kitchen.

Nicole raced after her.

Shanna took the stairs two at a time. She didn't stop at her own room but ran to Nicole's, instead. By the time Nicole caught up to her, she was lying on Nicole's bed clinging to Mr. Komodo, sobs racking her small body.

Nicole pulled Shanna into her arms right along with the big cat. "Shanna, sweetheart, listen to me. You're not an orphan. You have me and you have Hunter. We love you both, and nobody's going to separate you from Kyle. Why do you think people only want orphans if they're rich?"

Shanna rubbed at her nose. "I saw it in a story on television."

Nicole placed a kiss on top of Shanna's head. "Honey, stories on television aren't always true. Sometimes they're just make-believe."

Hunter walked into the room carrying Kyle. Kyle had stopped crying but still clung to Hunter. Hunter sat on the bed with Kyle on his lap, his hip pressed against Nicole's back.

He reached across Nicole to smooth the red curls from Shanna's damp face. "Everything Aunt Nicky said is true Shanna, and you can trust me when I say nobody is going to separate you."

Shanna quieted down but pressed her face into Mr. Komodo's yellow fur. "Mama said when people find out about Kyle's money they'll take him away."

Nicole stroked Shanna's arm. "Why do you think Kyle has money?" she asked quietly.

Shanna pulled the squirming cat tighter and didn't answer.

Hunter leaned over, closer to Shanna. "Shanna, do you remember the first thing I told you when I picked you up at the police station after your mama died?"

Shanna nodded but said nothing.

"What did I tell you?" he prompted.

Shanna sniffled and rubbed her eyes. "You said that Mama asked you to pick us up because she trusted you."

"And did you believe me?"

"Yes."

"Have I done anything to make you stop believing me?"

Shanna hesitated as though contemplating the answer. "No," she finally said.

Hunter smiled. "Good. Then you really don't have a reason to squash Mr. Komodo, do you?"

Shanna giggled brokenly and released her grip on the cat. Mr. Komodo scrambled to freedom.

Seeing that Kyle had brought up his head at Shanna's laughter, Hunter lifted him over Nicole and sat him on the bed beside his sister.

Kyle patted Shanna's shoulder. "It's okay, Shanna, Hunter will take care of us, just like he promised."

Shanna turned to hug Kyle. "I know, I'm sorry I yelled at you."

"Are we really orphans?" Kyle asked.

"No, you're not," Nicole said quickly. "You are going to live here with me." She glanced at Hunter. He thought she was expecting him to challenge her.

He didn't.

"Now, if Hunter is going to protect you," she went on, "he needs to know about this money you're talking about, Shanna. You need to trust us."

Shanna sat up on the bed and looked at Hunter. "Mama said that her grandpa Willard had money for Kyle."

"Why just for Kyle?" Hunter asked.

"Because he didn't like girls."

Nicole's back straightened. "That's obscene," she said, looking at Hunter.

"How much money?" Hunter asked.

Shanna shrugged her small shoulders. "I don't know. Lots, I guess, but he doesn't get it until Great Grandpa dies."

"That would be your Great-Grandpa who's in prison?" Nicole said.

Shanna nodded. "Yeah."

"Do you have any other family you haven't told us about?" Nicole asked.

"We had an aunt but she died before we were born."

Nicole's gaze shot to Hunter, then back to Shanna. "Do you know what her name was?"

"Megan," Shanna said. "But she died when she was little."

"Yvonne had another child late in life," Hunter explained. "I didn't get a chance to tell you about her. She was killed in the explosion with Yvonne."

Nicole pressed a hand to her brow and drew in a deep breath. "Shanna, will you be upset if I ask a couple more questions?"

Shanna shook her head. "No."

"Do you know who your father is?"

Hunter was sure Shanna didn't know the answer, yet he held his breath until Shanna shook her head negatively.

"What about Kyle?" Nicole pressed.

Shanna glanced at Kyle and down at her hands; again, she shook her head. Kyle's closed expression cast doubt on her denial.

Hunter got back downstairs to his phone after five o'clock, and New York was an hour ahead of Minnesota. Thinking Marla had probably left the office by now, he dialed the number anyway. Marla answered on the sixth ring.

"Seek and Find Enterprise, this is Marla, can I help you?"

"Marla, it's Hunter."

"Christ, Hunter, where have you been, and why aren't you answering your cell phone? Quint finally gave up and went home. I had already locked up when I heard the phone ringing."

"I've had a busy day. Did Quint find anything on Jameel?"

"I believe so, but he had to leave. He said he'd call you first thing in the morning."

"Shit. I guess that means he's out of touch tonight."

"Yeah, that's what he implied."

Frustrated, Hunter pulled a hand through his hair. "Listen, Marla, I need you to make another call to the car rental agency. Find out if Jameel changed cars."

"Sure, but the person with the info works the morning shift. I won't be able to call until tomorrow."

"Good enough, I was hoping you'd remember who

you talked to."

Marla chuckled. "Not to worry, boss, those of us with small brains keep good notes. We can even read our own hand writing."

"That kind of sarcasm will not get you a raise."

"Gee, I guess I'll have to try another kind. I'll talk to you tomorrow. I'm late for my nail appointment. Ciao."

Hunter hung up, then reconnected, and dialed Virgil at home. He got an answering machine. He hated answering machines. He cursed silently through the message.

"You've reached Virgil Douglas. If you're selling something, speak quick before the beep. You have three seconds. Anyone else…leave a message, but remember, anything you say can and will be held against you."

He waited impatiently for the beep. "Virg, its Hunter. It sounds like Willard Casey put some money somewhere in his great-grandson's name, Kyle Casey. See if you can find out anything on that score. The old geezer sounds like a prize jerk, so you might have to use some finesse when dealing with him, and be warned—he's a woman hater. See if he knows what happened to Jonathon Casey."

Hunter pushed the disconnect button. Both his stomach and his watch told him it was time to head for the kitchen and surfing the Net would have to wait. The shop lights were out and the house quiet. He walked through the sitting room and stepped out on the deck where he caught sight of Nicole and the kids down by the water's edge. Kyle chased a frog and Shanna gathered shells in a pail. They appeared to have bounced back to their cheerful selves and Nicole had changed into tight fitting black jeans. Watching the three of them sent a warm ripple through his veins. Seeing Nicole bend over in those jeans set his mind on something besides dinner. He watched her for a moment, trying to convince himself it was only sex.

After they'd eaten, the four of them went for a hike. Nicole led them on a path that followed the lake through the woods. They got back to the house in time to watch the sunset. A vivid blush of red and gold draped the horizon, promising a clear and cloudless sky the next day. In a matter of minutes, darkness swept over the lake, bringing with it the chill of a mid May evening.

When Kyle and Shanna ran up the steps in front of them, Hunter reached for Nicole's hand.

"You really know how to entertain those two," he said, rubbing her cold fingers. She gave him a smile that competed with the sunset.

"I can't imagine a kid not enjoying a jaunt in the woods," she said. "Did you do this sort of thing when you were a kid?"

Hunter laughed. "Not exactly. Our woods had paved trails and ended in a shopping mall. My aunt and uncle lived on an orchard, though, in upstate New York. Virg and I spent a lot of time there in the summer with Grant and Quint. They had a lot of trees but they all grew in neat rows. We had fun times…while it lasted."

Shanna called down from the deck with Hunter's cellular in her hand. "Your phone is ringing, Hunter."

"Why don't you push the talk button and answer it," he said. A second later, he heard her talking. Hunter grinned at Nicole. "I'm just beginning to realize how bright those two kids are. It's a possibility I misjudged their mother."

"It's Virgil," Shanna announced as Hunter stepped up on the deck. "He wants to talk to you."

"Thanks." Hunter tousled her red curls and took the phone. "Virg, you got my message?"

"Nice kid." Virgil said. "One of Brenda's?"

"Yeah, the oldest, Shanna. She's six."

"Must be tough on them. I got your message. I'll see what the old man knows tomorrow. I also got the autopsy report."

Hunter dropped down in one of the cushioned lounge chairs. "I'm getting really bad vibes from the tone of your voice, Virg. You might as well let me have it."

Virgil blew out a gush of air. "Well, she was HIV positive alright, but it wasn't active, and she was far from dying. There was also heroin in her blood, but not enough to kill her."

"I'm not sure I understand."

"They suspect she was being poisoned, either self injected or helped along by somebody else, but they haven't been able to identify the substance yet. If you want my opinion, I think somebody was trying to kill her slowly and make her believe she was sicker than she really was."

"Is that what killed her?"

"No, she took a major dose of over-the-counter sleeping pills."

Hunter absorbed that for a moment. Then he swore into phone. "So you think she might have killed herself because she believed she was dying of AIDS?"

"That's my guess. Whoever was set to collect on her insurance would be mighty pissed off with a ruling of suicide."

"But the money would have gone to her kids?"

"Yeah and if their father showed up to claim them…think about it."

Hunter was thinking fast and furiously, anger settling in his gut like a raw ulcer. "But Nicole Anderson has custody. Could that be contested?" He was sure he already knew the answer but he wanted to hear Virgil's opinion.

"I handled a case six months ago where an unmarried mother died leaving a two year old son. Her parents took the kid until some guy showed up claiming to be the father. A DNA test proved he was in fact the father, and he was awarded custody."

"Which side were you representing?" Hunter asked feeling sick.

"The grandparents."

"Jesus."

"Right. To make matters worse, the guy was a jerk. The woman died in a work accident so there was undisputed insurance money involved. Are you getting the picture here?"

Hunter heard the haunting call of a loon across the dark lake. The picture he saw was ugly as sin. He rubbed a hand over suddenly throbbing temples. "So, if Brenda thought she was dying and she didn't want the kids to be raised by a despicable father, she thought all she had to do was leave them to Nicole and commit suicide to negate the insurance."

"And now we have this new wrinkle to deal with, money from great-grandpa sentencing Kyle Casey to a possible life of hell. Let's hope it's a negligible amount and not worth Daddy's time or money to go after. Speaking of Daddy—do you have any clues?"

Hunter hesitated. He knew that Shanna's life was not in jeopardy, but Kyle? He'd kill that bastard before he let him take Kyle. "The kids know who was giving the shots to their mother; they're scared to death of him. I don't know if he's Kyle's father, but I have a strong suspicion he thinks he is. His name is Asha Jameel. Quint is trying to get a rap sheet on him. I missed Quint tonight so I don't know what he found. I do know Jameel rented a car in Minnesota and has been watching the house. Somebody broke into some cabins nearby so the local law is suspicious of him too. Unfortunately, even if they catch him, they'd still have to prove it was him. What do you think we're up against if he turns out to be the boy's father?"

"Well, there are a couple of things that could happen. He could find out about the suicide and just go away rather than expose himself. He could show up there and try to extort money out of Nicole. That's illegal by the way. Let me know if he tries that, we'll nail his ass to the wall. Or, the worst case scenario is he knows about Grand Pappy's endowment and will go after the kid for that."

"What are chances of pinning him with Brenda's death?"

"Slim to none, and my bet is on none. She called the

authorities herself to pick up the kids. She had a perfect opportunity to ask for help if she wanted it."

Just then, Nicole, having settled the kids in bed, walked out on the deck. She was smiling. One look at Hunter's expression and her smile faded.

Hunter sat up and moved his legs, spreading them to the sides of the lounge and motioned her to sit in front of him. The last thing he wanted to do was end her evening with Virg's news, but he had no right to keep any of it from her. Nor did he want to.

When she sat down, he put out his arm and drew her against his chest with her back to him. His sturdy arm circled her shoulders. She laid the side of her face on his wrist and he rested his cheek in her hair. When he heard Virgil's voice, he realized he still had the phone pressed to his ear.

"Hunter? You still with me buddy?"

"Yeah, yeah, I'm here. I guess we'll just have to wait until tomorrow and see if you can get anything out of the old man. I can check his criminal record on the Net but it takes a couple of days to get the results."

"Okay, I guess that's it then. Take care of yourself."

"Wait, one more thing. Does your information give Brenda's birth date?"

"I believe so. Hold on a second."

While he waited, Hunter rubbed his hand up and down Nicole's arm. She was shivering. He turned and pressed his lips to the top of her head.

"Yeah, here it is. She was twenty-nine, January fifteenth."

Hunter sat bolt upright swearing into the phone. "Son of a bitch, Virg! That's the date on the birth certificate of the Brenda who died when she was three weeks old."

"Are you sure?"

"Damn right, I am. I sent you a copy. Take a look."

There was a brief pause then Virgil was back on the line. "You're absolutely right, Hunter. That means they used the first Brenda's birth certificate. No wonder I couldn't find another one. How the hell did they manage that, and why?"

Hunter's brain kicked into overdrive. "When you checked the school records at Johns Hopkins, did you happen to see what field of medicine Jonathon Casey specialized in?"

"Just a sec, I had the information right here." There was a moment of paper shuffling. "I'll be damned. Looks like obstetrics."

"That explains the how. He must have delivered her at home, but why, why would they do that unless they were trying to hide something?"

"When we find him, that can be the first question you ask," Virgil said blandly. "Hell, maybe Anderson was paying blackmail money. Maybe they never had a baby; maybe they stole a kid and passed it off as their own."

"I doubt that. Brenda resembled Nicole too much. Somehow, they have to be related." Hunter sighed. "Whatever. I'm giving up on it tonight. My mind is turning to mush. Call me as soon as you grill the buzzard."

"Roger. Talk to you then. Oh, give my regards to the little woman."

Before Hunter could comment, the phone buzzed in his ear. He clicked the off button and collapsed back in the lounge, his arm, now free, slipped below Nicole's breasts. He could feel her heart racing through the soft fabric of her blouse.

"Tell me what's happening, Hunter," was all she said.

Chapter Fourteen

After Hunter relayed all Virgil's information to Nicole and answered most of her questions, they moved into the sitting room. Hunter lit the fire in the fireplace and sat down facing her cross-legged on the thick pile rug in front of the fire.

"Do you really think Asha is Kyle's father?" Nicole asked.

Hunter jabbed the poker into the fire to stir the wood. "I don't know. I sure as hell hope not. Unfortunately, that would explain why he followed me here and why he's hanging around. Then, there's the matter of the suitcase."

"And the fact that there were no pictures of Kyle or papers relating to him," Nicole replied somberly. Fear, for Kyle and Shanna if Asha turned up on her doorstep, made her stomach clench. In the silence that followed, she flexed her neck, trying to work the ache and worry out of it. "I don't know about you," she said finally, "but I'm ready to table this subject for tonight."

"I'll second that," Hunter agreed. "Scoot over here and turn around. I'll do that for you."

The thought of Hunter's hands on her put delicious ideas in her head. She quickly swiveled around and backed up to his waiting ministration.

His long fingers expertly began to knead the muscles in her neck and shoulders. Nicole went limp. When his hands moved to her scalp under her hair, she sagged against him, purring like a kitten.

Hunter chuckled. "Are you enjoying this too much?"

His voice was so close to her ear she could feel his warm breath. It sent tingling splinters straight to the core of her most sensitive spot. In a state of euphoria, she wasn't aware that his hands had moved from her scalp to her breasts until her body responded to his stroking caress.

When he turned her face toward him and lowered his mouth to hers, she opened up like an eager flower, offering its nectar to a honey-seeking bee. His tongue flicked over her lower lip, sending tantalizing shivers of heat to her brain. Desire raced through her system like white lightening. She turned her body fully to press her breasts against the firmness of his chest. With an effortless twist he turned, taking her with him. Her back touched the thick rug. With one arm, he cradled her neck, while his free hand tugged her blouse from her jeans, and warm searching fingers found her ribcage. All the while, his searing mouth never broke the kiss.

Nicole gave a small gasp when his hand covered her naked breast. At the same time, he put his leg over her thigh and pressed his lower body against her hip. A week ago, two days ago, his aroused male hunger touching her so intimately, even between two layers of denim, would have put Nicole in shock. Now, she knew what waited beneath those layers. She squirmed, arching her body, seeking the closeness of bare flesh.

Hunter lifted his mouth to look at her face "Sweetheart," he whispered. "We have too damned many clothes on."

"Yes," she managed to gasp, "Definitely, too many clothes."

"Not a good idea to get naked here. I'm going to carry you upstairs."

"No...I...can walk."

Hunter chuckled. His arm was already under her knees, lifting her. "In your state, it would take you too long to get to the room. I'd end up taking you on the stairs. You just hang on."

Her arms locked around him like steel bands, and she buried her face in his neck, chewing and licking at the corded muscles she found there.

Hunter sucked in his breath with a hiss. "Damn, woman, slow down before I go off in my jeans like a teenager."

Nicole nuzzled his neck smiling, surprised, and delighted that she could excite him. "But, Honeypot," she said. "You taste so good. I could eat you for dessert."

"Just hold that naughty little thought, Tiger. You'll get your chance for dessert." He made it to the room where he none too gently kicked the door shut behind him.

When he set her on her feet and started unbuttoning her blouse, she reached past his hands and grasped the bottom of his pullover. He stopped with the buttons long enough to allow her to pull it over his head. He hadn't finished with the blouse yet when she started tugging at the snap on his jeans.

She had a sudden urge to clamp her lips on one of his hard nipples. When she acted on her impulse, she heard him suck in his breath in a shuddering hiss. The sound excited her beyond anything she'd imagined. He made a wild cry and took her head between his hands to pull her away from him. "Damn," he gasped, "is this some kind of torture treatment? Help me get these clothes off us and you can chew and lick on anything you want."

He yanked the rest of her blouse and bra off while she discarded her jeans and shoes. She made a leap for the bed, and he was one step behind her, naked, with condom in hand. For a few brief moments, they were a tangle of arms and legs and lips, with no direction, no agenda, just hungry, touching need.

Nicole knew what was coming, and yet she gave a sharp, breathless gasp when he filled her, stretching her with his size, and giving her such intense pleasure that she could do little more than concentrate on drawing one ragged breath after the other. Each thrust increased the tremors, building to a wild crescendo that had her arching to him and calling out his name.

Whether his name actually came from her lips or was merely screamed in her mind, she didn't know. What she did know was that she was having an out-of-the-body experience that words could never describe. When she finally found the release she was storming toward, a long soulful sigh, like that of a strange prehistoric bird, escaped her. It drew the life out of her leaving her body limp.

Hunter collapsed on top of her, equally spent. If not for his laborious breathing, she would have shaken him to make certain he was alive. She knew he must have found his own release but she didn't have a clue as to when it happened. He rolled over, taking her with him until she lay like a rag doll on top of him. His arms remained firm but gentle around her holding her against his chest as though she might have somehow had the energy to move.

She didn't.

Several minutes went by before he did.

Nicole knew the instant Hunter drifted into slumber. His erratic breathing slowed, and his hands, though they didn't drop away from her, relaxed. Very slowly, she started to ease her weight from him. His arms tightened immediately, and he bent his head to nuzzle her neck.

"Sorry," she said. "I was trying not to wake you."

Hunter chuckled sleepily. "I thought you were trying to escape." He rolled over so their bodies were side by side, his arms kept them in close contact, but he was already relaxing. He mumbled something incoherent in her ear.

Nicole wriggled to get closer to him. "Why would I want to escape the most wonderful experience of my life?"

"Because you're afraid it will happen again?"

Nicole smiled. She ran her fingers through the thick, damp curls on his head, kissing his equally damp cheek. "My poor, Hercules, you're exhausted. Go to sleep. You couldn't repeat that performance again tonight if your life depended on it."

He moved only enough to raise his hand to cup her breast, before his breathing became shallow again. For some time, the only sound in the room was that of their mingled breathing. Nicole was just about asleep when his hand squeezed very subtly on her breast.

"Wanna bet?"

* * * *

The first pink blush of dawn graced the skyline when Virgil Douglas left for the long drive up to the Adirondack State Correctional facility. Located midway between Saranac Lake and Lake Placid, it incarcerated 700 men who were not there to enjoy the scenery. One of those men was, Willard Casey. Even though only a medium-security prison, it was still a depressing place with gray granite walls and razor-wire fences. It certainly seemed out of place in a popular tourist area.

Virgil had called ahead to make sure he would get an audience with Casey. Apparently, the man, hungry for attention, didn't hesitate when given a chance to talk to a stranger. Virgil had assured Casey that, even though he was a lawyer, his mission was of a personal nature rather than business—and that he'd bring him a carton of straight Camels.

After five hours on the road, a guard showed Virgil into a room lined with tables and told him to wait. Ten minutes later, Vigil got his first look and impression of Casey. His face, hard and time-ravaged with bitterness, his stooped body emaciated to the point of being skeletal. He appeared pretty much as Vigil had expected for a man who'd spent more than half his eighty-five years behind bars. Only his eyes, cold and alert, sharp enough to pierce a man's soul, belied his age. Virgil remembered Hunter saying Casey hated women. This man looked like he hated all mankind. His drab, gray uniform and shaggy hair suited him perfectly. Not for the first time, Virgil wondered why Casey so readily agreed to see him.

Casey took a seat across from Virgil, eyeing him warily.

"You bring the cigarettes?" Casey asked in a gravely voice.

Virgil handed him a paper sack.

Casey glanced in the bag then pulled a crumpled half-pack of Camels from his shirt pocket and lit up. For twenty seconds, the man tried to cough up his guts before he glared at Virgil through watery eyes.

"So what do you want?"

"I'm here on behalf of your great-grandson, Kyle."

The old man's eyes narrowed. "Yeah, how is the kid?"

"Kyle is okay. I imagine you know his mother, Brenda, died."

"So they told me. Too bad, she was the only one of all them bitches in my life able to produce a boy."

"That was important to you?" Virgil asked neutrally.

"Damn right. I wanted a son, but my wife, the frigid bitch, had one kid, a girl, and then refused to have any more. I warned her, either she has a son or I leave her ass."

"I guess you left her then?"

"God damned right, I did. Actually, she left me, but it's the same damn thing."

Smart woman, Virgil thought sourly. He was more than a little surprised by the old man's willingness to talk, having expected to have to pry information out of him. He waited, letting the silence close in, certain Casey had more to say on the subject. He was right.

Casey shifted in his chair, clearly agitated.

"Then I had some hope, maybe I'd get a grandson from Yvonne—that was my daughter. She had a half-assed decent boyfriend, but she had highfalutin' ideas of going to school. So, I told her I ain't paying for no school unless she gets married—I had a few bucks back then. She knew it too, so she agreed, but said I'd have to put them both through school. I told her the only way I'd pay for both of them was if he took her name. I decided if I couldn't have a son, maybe I could still get a grandson to carry on my name."

Casey stomped out his cigarette on the scarred surface of the table and reached for a second one. After another coughing jag, he continued. "They were in school two years, and still no kid—and I'm paying. Hell, I was beginning to think the bastard was sterile."

Virgil would have liked to point out that having a baby while they were both in school wouldn't have been too smart, but he kept that thought to himself.

"So did they ever have a son?" Vigil asked even though he already knew the answer.

"Shit no! I got sent up here for five years, because they said I borrowed some money from that crackerjack place I worked for; those bastards. Anyway, Yvonne was pissed because they had to quit school. She swore she'd never have a son, just to get even with me. She got that bitchy shit from her mother. So she had girls; first Brenda, and then that other one, Megan." A craggy half smile appeared on his face. "Turns out old Jonathon had sperm after all. Too bad the worthless bastard could only make females. Shit, I even promised them my granddad's inheritance if they could produce a boy."

"Your granddad's inheritance?" Virgil prompted cautiously.

"Yeah, it went from my dad to me, but it couldn't be sold, and it had to be passed on to a male heir. Without an heir, it would go to the fucking state. Drove me fucking nuts, they did, with all their girls. I hired a lawyer to break the trust but they decided it was ironclad. Then I got sent up here again, and the state took all the lease money—for payback."

"The lease money?"

"Yeah, it's five hundred acres up north of here that granddad homesteaded. It pays over a hundred thousand a year in lease money. As long as I'm alive, it goes to the state. When I die it should go to Brenda's kid."

"She has two kids," Virgil reminded him.

"Only one is a boy."

"Kyle?"

"Yeah." Casey got a look on his face that could have passed as a smile. "She brought him up here once, when he was about two. Cute little guy. Dark hair. Kind of looked like me at that age. Anyway, I told her about the land. Would you believe she got pissed because I told her only the boy could have it? Typical woman, all cunt and no brains, wouldn't come back again."

Virgil couldn't think of anything to say that the old reprobate would appreciate hearing, so he gritted his teeth and waited.

"So, you said you were a lawyer?" Casey finally said.

"Yeah, I'm a lawyer."

"What would it take for you to look up my great-grandson and see that he gets that land?"

"I could look into it. Who all knows about it?" Virgil asked.

"Brenda did. So did Yvonne. I guess the only one left who knows is Yvonne's husband, Jonathon."

"And where is he?"

Casey shrugged. "Not sure. He got hurt in that fire they had. I guess he went to a nursing home—somewhere in the Midwest. He had a sister there." Casey started coughing again and quickly lit up another Camel. When he caught his breath, he said, "The doc said these fucking things would kill me before the year is out, so I'd really like to see the kid get that land before the state grabs it. Do you know were the kid is?"

"Yes, I know," Virgil answered.

"Good, then get on it if you can. I'll sign papers if you need me to, so you can get whatever pay you need. If I don't do something, the God damned state will get their greedy, fucking fingers on it."

At least now, Virgil knew why Willard Casey had agreed to see him.

* * * *

Hunter had spent the entire morning either on his cellular phone or on the Internet. He spoke with Marla, who indeed confirmed that Asha Jameel had switched cars. The engine blew on the black Esquire, so he now drove a white Ford Aspire.

The report from Quint was not what he'd hoped to hear. Jameel was Iranian. He had been a US citizen for ten years. The man had no criminal record to speak of, ten arrests but no convictions. His arrests ranged all the way from breaking and entering to prostitution and drug dealing. Quint believed he had to have a connection in the police department to get off that many times. Perhaps it was just coincidental that the chief of police in that particular precinct was of Iranian decent.

At least one case was still open. A woman he'd been married to six years earlier had died of suspected poisoning. Unfortunately, they cremated her before the final autopsy report came in. Another suspicious glitch as far as Quint was concerned. Jameel was set to take possession of her estate when a number of creditors showed up, leaving him with nothing.

Hunter was searching the Internet for further information on Jameel when his phone rang. It was Virgil calling from his car as he left the Adirondack Correctional Facility.

"Willard Casey is one hard boiled egg," Virg told him. "And he's trying to sentence his great grandson into a life of hell. Do you know who Kyle's father is? If you don't, you better find out."

By the time Virgil relayed the entire story, Hunter was in full agreement, and, unfortunately, certain he already knew the answer to Kyle's paternity. Kyle's olive complexion and the fact that Jameel was Iranian made the possibility that Jameel was his father too great to ignore. Also, if Brenda knew about old man Casey's inheritance there was a good chance Jameel knew. If Jameel had a criminal record, they would have a much easier fight to keep Kyle in Nicole's custody.

Hunter swore into the phone.

Virgil agreed. "Let's try to locate the son-in-law, Jonathon Casey, see if he knows anything. That's about the only good lead we have right now. If he's somewhere in the Midwest, you might have a better chance of finding him than I do. In the meantime, I'm going to do some major digging into Kyle's birth certificate."

After he hung up, Hunter sat staring at the bookcase on the far wall. The top four shelves contained books on costume design, assorted in chronological order from a variety of different centuries, the bottom was scrapbooks, sketchpads, and photo albums.

For a moment, he stared at the photo album. Something was gnawing at him. When Nicole left the activity of the shop and walked into the studio a few minutes later, he gave her a tense smile. She walked up behind him and massaged his taut shoulders.

"Was that your brother on the phone?" she asked.

Hunter leaned back, enjoying the feel of Nicole's fingers. "Yeah, and not with any good news. Apparently, the old man is leaving some valuable land to Kyle. Kyle will inherit that land when Willard Casey dies, and, in his own words, Great gramps is on a short clock."

Nicole sighed. "Good news, bad news, for Kyle." She sat down in the chair beside the desk. "What else did he have to say?"

Nicole listened silently while Hunter relayed his conversation with Virgil, until he came to the part of Kyle's heritage.

"Do you think Asha is Kyle's father?" she asked.

"I don't want to believe it, but the signs are all there."

"So if he doesn't have a record, why isn't he showing himself? Why is he sneaking around? What do you think he's planning to do?"

"My guess is, he'll show up before long to demand custody."

Nicole stared at Hunter with suddenly wide eyes. "Is there a chance he could get it?"

Hunter ran a hand through his hair. Tired lines of frustration etched his features. "According to Virgil, if he really is the father, yes. Without a birth certificate, he would have to request a DNA test. Legally you couldn't refuse to give it. If there was one in the suitcase, he probably has his hands on it. The only thing I feel good about is if he was named as the father on the birth certificate he would probably have made his move by now."

"We can't let him take Kyle! Kyle is terrified of him!"

Hunter gave her a smile that felt less reassuring than it looked. "I promise you, I will do everything in my power to prevent that, even if it comes down to paying him off."

"Do you think he'd take a payoff?"

"Not if he's smart. There's a little matter of extortion being illegal. On the other hand, that doesn't seem to have stopped him in the past. However, a custody fight could cost him money I don't think he has. He's renting junker cars and staying in break-and-enter hotels. I assumed he was hiding out from the law, but that doesn't seem to be the case. More likely, he's short on cash."

"Can we just tell him he can have the inheritance if he leaves Kyle alone?"

"I doubt it. The land can't be sold and can only be transferred to a male heir."

"That is preposterous."

Hunter agreed wholeheartedly. "Unfortunately, that document was probably written up around the turn of the century when carrying on the family name was more important than being fair. Comes from old England rules when the oldest son inherited everything and the others were left out in the cold, literally."

Nicole took a deep sighing breath. "I suppose we should be glad we don't have to fight for Shanna too."

Her words hit Hunter like a sucker punch to the stomach. He should have told her about Shanna right away. At this point, he was damned either way. Knowing he would be deserting his daughter when he went back to New York, even if it was for her own good, didn't help matters, either. He glanced through the shop to where Shanna and Kyle sat at the far end of the room, working over coloring books. Leaving his daughter and Kyle behind was going to be like tearing out a piece of his heart.

He looked from the kids to Nicole. Hair framed her face as she stared at her hands clenched in her lap. He would leave a sizable chunk of his heart in Minnesota, and when Nicole found out that he had deceived her about Shanna being his daughter, the choice of how long he stayed may no longer be up to him.

Suddenly, he remembered what had been gnawing at him earlier.

"Where is that photo taken at Johns Hopkins of your mother and the Caseys?"

"Right there, on my work table, with Brenda's album. I've been trying to match their faces with the others from the suitcase."

"Any luck?"

"No, the picture is just too scarred and faded. Did you want to see it?"

"Yes, old man Casey thinks Jonathon is in the Midwest and something is jogging my memory."

Nicole managed a smile for him. "Imagine that," she said sardonically. She got up, crossed the room to her worktable, and came back to hand the photo to Hunter. She stood behind him to help study the picture. One hand automatically rested on his shoulder as she looked over it. As he stared at the picture, his hand came up absently to touch her fingers. He concentrated for a moment on the photo, holding it first at a distance then squinting at it close up.

"Do you have a magnifying glass?" he asked.

"I think Chuck has one in the shop. I'll get it."

She disappeared into the shop, returning a moment later with a three-inch magnifying glass. She handed it to him then moved to look over his shoulder.

"What are you looking for?" she asked.

Hunter studied the picture through the magnifying glass. After a few moments, he leaned to the side so she could get a good view of the photo through the glass. "Take a look at Jonathon's cap. There's a sports logo on it. Do you recognize it? I'm not much of a sports enthusiast, but it looks to me like the same one that Chuck wears."

Nicole leaned in close, holding her hand over his to get the right angle and narrowed her eyes for a clearer focus.

"Oh, my God. You're right. It's a Green Bay Packer's hat. That's Wisconsin."

"Bingo. Midwest. Right next door. Nice work, Watson."

Hunter set the glass and photo aside and started pushing keys on the computer. "Let's see if we can find one Jonathon Casey. Willard thought he went to a nursing home, close to his sister, because of his injuries."

Carmen called from the shop with a question. Nicole gave Hunter an affectionate squeeze on the upper arm. "Good luck, I'll be back as quick as I can."

Hunter pulled his eyes from the computer screen long enough to watch her little derriere disappear into the shop. He went into public records, then to Wisconsin, searching for Jonathon Casey. From there, he went to death records and punched in the surname 'Sanders.'

When Nicole returned a few minutes later, Hunter was scrolling through a list of names.

"What did you find?" she asked anxiously, looking at

the screen.

"I brought up all the people in Wisconsin with the last name of Sanders, hoping to isolate a location where many lived or died. Unfortunately, Sanders is a common name. I found seventy-two matches on death records alone. The good news is, none of them has a first name of Jonathan. More often then not, relatives migrated together, and the older generation usually stayed in the same community. Many of them couldn't even speak English, so they stuck close together."

Nicole watched closely as he scrolled down the list.

"What about Casey. Wouldn't his last name be Casey?"

"I already checked for Jonathon Casey—no death record in that name either. Besides, even if he kept the name Casey, his male relatives would still be Sanders."

"There seem to be a lot from Milwaukee," she said.

"Yeah. I'm thinking it's too big; too many people who don't know each other. Maybe it's wishful thinking, but I'd like to start with something smaller. There is twelve Sanders' listed in Ashland. How big is Ashland?"

"About sixteen thousand, maybe. They had a historical pageant there about a year ago. I supplied the costumes."

"How far from here?"

"It's in a popular skiing area on the south shore of Lake Superior, probably three or four hours away."

He reached for his phone and dialed information for Ashland. When he got the operator, he asked for the names of all the nursing homes in town. He listened intently, writing quickly on a note pad. He hung up smiling.

"We're in luck. There are only three."

The first one was Court Manor. He dialed the number, while Nicole stepped around him to sit in the side chair facing him. He ignored her skeptical stare. The phone rang four times before a woman answered.

"Court Manor. Can I help you?'"

"I hope so. I'm trying to locate Jonathon Sanders."

"Who is this, please?" The woman asked.

"Hunter Douglas, it's regarding his grandchildren."

"Just a moment," A few moments later, she came back on the line, "No sir, nobody here by that name."

"What about Jonathon Casey?" Hunter asked quickly.

There was a sort pause. "You're looking for someone and you aren't even sure what his last name is?"

Hunter drew an impatient breath. "It's kind of complicated. Do you have a Jonathon Casey?"

"No. Try Ashland Convalescent or Forest Haven."

"Thanks, I will." Hunter hung up. He glanced at his note pad and dialed the Ashland Convalescent Home. The results were the same. They suggested Court Manor or Forest Haven.

He started to dial the number to Forest Haven when the look on Nicole's face stopped him. He had seen that look before.

Hunter hung up the phone. "What?"

"Hunter, do you know how many nursing homes there are in Wisconsin?"

"Probably several thousand—why?"

"Do you plan to call every one?"

"No, just as many as it takes to find Jonathon Sanders Casey."

She stared at him in disbelief. "That's insane."

Hunter grunted. "That's what you said about Dumpster diving." He started dialing again. "If I can't locate him in one of the homes, I'll start calling all the Sanders in the area. There must be nieces and nephews or cousins who—"

"Forest Haven, Jane speaking."

"Jane, Hunter Douglas here. I wonder if you could help me. I'm looking for Jonathon Sanders Casey. Is he by chance a resident at your facility?"

"I don't know about the Casey part, but there is a Jonathon Sanders here."

Hunter passed Nicole a smiling wink. "Is it possible

for me to talk to him?"

"You could talk to him but I doubt you'd get any response—not today."

"What do you mean, 'not today'?"

"Well some days he's with us and some days he's off in another world. Today seems to be one of his other world days."

"Can I visit him?"

"Sure, but unless he knows you, he probably won't talk to you. You're welcome to try though. Heaven knows, most of these people don't get enough visitors."

"Does he know about the death of his daughter?" Hunter asked.

There was a short pause and a long sigh. "Yeah, he knows, and he hasn't spoken a word since. Just sits and stares off into space."

Hunter thanked her for her help and hung up. He explained the situation to Nicole. "We have to go see him. Can you get away tomorrow?"

"Of course, we're putting the finishing touches on the costumes today. Chuck is done as far as he can go, and the girls can easily work without me for a day. I don't have to deliver them until Monday. My next assignment isn't due for another two weeks. It's only for twelve costumes and at least half of them can be filled from the shop floor."

Admiration showed in Hunter's smile. "This business of yours seems to be quite successful."

"Yes, very. When we don't have commissions, we make costumes to fill the racks in the shop. If not for the fact that I buy back a lot of my own costumes, we'd never be able to keep up." Chewing on her lower lip, Nicole gave Hunter an expectant look. "Do you think we should take Shanna and Kyle along?"

"Definitely! The receptionist said he's more likely to talk to someone he knows. Even if he wasn't Brenda's biological father, he raised her as his own, and it appears he has slipped since hearing about her death. Maybe seeing his grandchildren will bring him out of it. It might be good for them too."

Chapter Fifteen

The next morning, just before noon, Hunter turned his Mercedes into the parking lot of the Forest Haven Rest Home. The sky had clouded over, and a distant rumble of thunder in the west promised rain before the day was out. The air was thick with humidity, giving the trees a rich, green hue beneath an overcast sky.

He parked the car in front of a neatly trimmed hedge then turned to look at Kyle and Shanna sitting quietly in the back seat. They had explained to the kids where they were going and were surprised that Shanna remembered seeing her grandfather one time.

"Are you ready?" Hunter asked.

Both kids nodded cheerfully. They were still talking about the dairy cows dotting the rolling green hills of Wisconsin. Nicole had entertained them by pointing out the different breeds, and they prided themselves in now knowing the difference between a Guernsey and a Holstein. Even Hunter admitted that was something he hadn't known.

He reached over and gave Nicole's hand a squeeze.

"How about you?" he asked. "You ready for this?"

Nicole gave him a tremulous smile. "I'm as ready as I'll ever be." She rubbed her upper arms, feeling the need to warm up even though she wasn't actually cold "Do you really think he knows the truth about Brenda?"

"Yes, there's no doubt in my mind. The trick will be getting him to talk about it."

Directed to a room just off the nurse's station, Nicole lead the way holding Shanna's hand, Hunter followed with Kyle. A lone figure occupied the room. He sat in a wheelchair facing the window. A number of pictures covered the top of the bureau; one of them, to Nicole's surprise, was a recent shot of Shanna and Kyle.

Nicole turned to see if Hunter had noticed.

He nodded, motioning her forward.

Not wanting to startle the frail-looking Jonathon Sanders, Nicole called out his name.

There was no response so she moved around to the window where he could see her. Nicole's fingers tightened on Shanna's small hand at the sight of him. A grotesque scar, extending from jaw to eyebrow, distorted the right side of his face. Wisps of white hair hung from his head in thin strands. His waxen, disfigured hands, rested on the arms of the wheelchair.

He glanced at Nicole with ashen blue eyes, eyes that weren't nearly as old as Nicole had expected. It took only a fraction of a second for those eyes to light up.

"Brenda! Brenda, you came. They told me you died." He raised a scarred hand toward her.

Nicole took his hand in hers and sat down on a stool in front of him. Tears stung her eyes. "I'm sorry. I'm not Brenda. I'm Nicole. Nicole Anderson."

With shaking fingers, he touched her face then her hair. "I knew you weren't dead, Brenda. I just knew it."

Nicole glanced at Hunter standing behind the wheelchair. "It's okay," he said softly.

Nicole took a deep breath and gave Jonathon Sanders a weak smile. She put her arm around Shanna and drew her to her side. "Don't be afraid," she whispered.

"I'm not afraid," Shanna whispered back. She looked

at her grandfather and smiled. "Hello, Grandpa."

Jonathon's smile, made crooked by the distortion on his right side, glistened with silver fillings. "Meggie. My dear, sweet, Meggie." He reached out to give Shanna a hug.

"I'm not Meggie," she corrected. "I'm Shanna."

Shanna looked at Nicole. "Last time I saw him, he thought I was Meggie too."

"This is your granddaughter, Shanna," Nicole explained gently. "Brenda's daughter, do you remember Shanna?"

Understanding registered in his watery eyes. He turned to look up at the picture on his bureau. "Oh yes, of course, I remember you, Shanna. You have your grandmother's beautiful green eyes, and you have a brother, Kyle. Where is your brother?"

Hunter urged a reluctant Kyle forward.

Shanna pulled Kyle toward her. "It's okay, Kyle. It's just our Grandpa. You were too little when we saw him. So you don't remember." She pulled Kyle into the circle of her arm.

Kyle gave his grandfather a timid smile.

Jonathon put a trembling hand on Kyle's head. "You are certainly a handsome lad; the last time I saw you, you were just a toddler. How old are you now?"

Standing very straight and tall, Kyle displayed four fingers. "When I'm older, I can go to school like my friend Jacob. He can read, but I can draw really nice pictures. When I come to see you again, I'll make you a picture."

Jonathon's eyes twinkled with laughter. "I would like that. Your grandmother could paint nice pictures too. We hung them in our house."

He reached out beckoning both children into his arms. Shanna went to him, drawing Kyle with her. "I'm so happy you came to see me," he said, placing a kiss on the top of each head. When he released them, he brushed the back of his hand over his eyes.

Glancing up at Hunter, Nicole took a deep breath,

blinked rapidly several times, and swallowed the lump in her throat.

Speaking to Shanna, Jonathon pointed to his dresser. "In the bottom drawer there is an old cigar box. Would you get it for me, please? There's something in there I want you to have."

Shanna glanced at Hunter.

Hunter smiled and nodded. "Go ahead."

She walked to the dresser, opened the drawer, and pulled out the box, which she carried back to her grandfather.

Jonathon's hands shook as he opened the battered box with his clumsy fingers. He pulled out a heart shaped locket and handed it to Shanna.

"This belonged to your grandmother; she would want you to have it. It was a wedding gift from me and she wore it all the time. The picture inside was taken the day we got married." He then pulled out a pocket watch and handed it to Kyle. "This watch has the same picture. It was my wedding gift from your grandmother."

Both children examined their gifts, thanking him simultaneously. Hunter showed Kyle how to open the watch and set the time for him.

"Kyle doesn't know how to tell time," Shanna said. "But I could teach him."

Jonathon touched her cheek. "You're a very bright girl, just like your mother." His gaze lifted to Nicole. He handed her the cigar box. "This is the only thing that wasn't destroyed in the fire. You take it. It belonged to your mother—except for the war medal. That belonged to my father. You can give it to Kyle someday, when he's old enough to understand what it is."

Nicole took the box, not knowing what else to do. She really wanted him to understand that she wasn't Brenda, but she didn't have the heart to pursue it. He had obviously loved his family very much, and he wanted his box of treasures to stay with them. She could always give it to

Shanna later. Nurturing that thought, she accepted the gift with a stricken thank you.

Tears pooled in his pale blue eyes. "Thank you for bringing the children, Pumpkin. I can't begin to tell you what it means to me. The rest of my family is gone except for a couple of nieces. I don't even know where they live anymore. You know, I enjoy your letters and pictures more than I can say. My eyes are failing, so I can't read them anymore. The volunteers read them to me."

"But enough about me," he said, looking at Hunter. "Who is this handsome young fellow you brought with you?"

"This is a friend, Hunter Douglas. He's visiting from New York. He would like to ask you a few questions. Would that be all right?"

"Of course, honey. You know I always enjoy talking to your friends."

Hunter dug in his pocket for a handful of coins. He gave them to Shanna. "I saw a soda machine out in the lobby. Why don't you take Kyle and get yourself each a soda. There might be a candy machine too. Ask the lady at the front desk if you need help."

Shanna grinned. "Thank you. I know how to do it. Come on, Kyle, I'll show you how to do yours." She handed the necklace to Nicole. "Would you put this on me?" After Nicole fastened the necklace in place, Shanna took Kyle's hand and skipped out the door. "Don't worry, I'll take care of Kyle," she called over her shoulder.

A smile tugged at Hunter's mouth as he watched them leave. When they were out of earshot, he pulled up a chair behind Nicole and extended a hand. "Hello, Mr. Sanders."

Jonathon Sanders offered his disfigured hand. "Pleased to meet you," he said. "Any friend of Brenda's is always welcome."

Hunter gave Jonathan's hand a gentle shake then glanced sideways at Nicole to see how she was faring. She offered him an encouraging smile.

Hunter turned back to Jonathon, watching him closely. "Did you know Robert and Dawn Anderson?" he asked. Quickly diverted eyes told him that Sanders knew exactly who they were. "I'm sorry if my questions are hard, but you're the only one who can clear up the confusion surrounding Brenda. Can you please tell us what your association was with the Andersons?"

"We met Dawn at school. Dawn was Yvonne's best friend," Jonathon said speaking in a clear, but subdued voice. His gaze turned back to the window where he seemed to be concentrating on a populated bird feeder in the courtyard. The threatening sky carried its somber darkness into the room.

Hunter remained silent, hoping Sanders would say more if given time.

After a few moments, Sanders brought his gaze back to Nicole. "I'm so sorry, honey. I know your mother told you some of the truth, and I understand you had to know. I just hope you don't hate me."

"Why on earth would I hate you?" Nicole asked incredulously.

"Because, what we did was wrong, but we wanted a child and so did they. By some quirk of nature, I couldn't have children and neither could Dawn. At the time, it seemed like such a perfect solution. Yvonne would have two babies. Robert and Dawn would take the first baby, and we would keep the second one. With what I'd learned in school, I was able to do the procedure at home. It only took three tries for Yvonne to get pregnant the first time, but the baby was born with a heart defect. She never left the hospital, and she died when she was only three weeks old." Jonathon shuddered. He placed his head in his trembling hand. His elbow rested on the arm of the chair. He shook his head back and forth. "All four of us were devastated when that baby died, but we were also determined. When Yvonne got pregnant the second time..."

When it became apparent, he wasn't going to continue, Hunter prodded gently. "Why is there no birth record of the second baby?"

Sanders took a deep breath. "Yvonne went into labor early. I handled the delivery myself at home. We—we used the birth certificate for Brenda, from the first baby."

"Why?" Hunter implored. When Sanders didn't answer, Hunter had the distinct feeling the old man was guarding and choosing his words very carefully. There was something he wasn't telling them. "Was there an argument over who would get the second baby?" he asked.

Jonathon brought his head up to stare at Hunter. "No, of course not. The first baby was theirs; the second was to be ours. We did what we did, because, it was the only fair way." He turned his sullen gaze back to Nicole. "It was the only fair way," he repeated as though it explained everything.

Nicole turned questioning eyes up to Hunter.

Hunter gave her an impotent shrug. Frustrated, he turned back to Jonathon.

"So you kept the second baby and Anderson paid a thousand bucks a month child support? I'm sorry, but that just doesn't make a hell of a lot of sense."

Jonathon sucked in a frail breath. "He wasn't paying child support for Brenda. You don't understand."

"Now that's the understatement of the year. So if not child support, what was the money for?"

Jonathon suddenly had the look of a cornered mouse. He glanced around the room as though searching for an answer. He didn't find one he was willing to share. His gaunt shoulders finally fell. He looked up at Nicole beseechingly. "I thought your mother told you about the money."

Since Sanders believed he was talking to Brenda, Hunter didn't wait for Nicole to answer. "If you couldn't have children, how did you get Megan?" he asked.

Jonathon put his head back in his hands. His shoulders

began to shake. "Megan was a gift from God," he said through broken sobs. "Such a precious little angel. I killed her...and my beautiful Yvonne. I killed both of them...an accident. I didn't mean to...the fire...my fault. I couldn't save them."

Hunter saw the tears in Nicole's eyes as she took one of Jonathon's crippled hands and kissed it tenderly. "You can't blame yourself for something that was an accident."

Without lifting his head, Jonathon said, "I will blame myself until death brings me peace. That's the only thing that will silence their screams." His fingers closed around Nicole's hand in an astonishingly tight grip. "You know Megan's secret, Brenda. You tell him."

Nicole gripped his hand. "I don't know Megan's secret," she whispered. "I don't know the secret because I'm not Brenda, Mr. Sanders; I'm Nicole Anderson, Dawn and Robert Anderson's daughter."

He looked up and stared at her for a long time. Hunter knew the instant understanding came to him. He opened his mouth to speak, but no words came out. His breath began to come in shallow gasps and Hunter thought for a moment he would hyperventilate. All the while he didn't blink and his eyes never left her face.

Nicole leaned forward and gripped his arms. "Mr. Sanders, are you all right?"

When he did finally blink, it seemed to clear his mind. "Yes," he said in a soft shaky whisper. He reached toward her and pulled her into his arms.

"Nicole." he said. "It's really you, isn't it? God took one angel from me and brought another one." He set her back to arms length so he could look into her eyes. "Do you know how much you look like Brenda? You are just as lovely, just as beautiful."

"So can you tell me Megan's secret?" Nicole asked when he released her. "And why Brenda didn't have her own birth certificate or why my father was sending money every month."

Sanders looked away, avoiding her questioning gaze. "I can't tell you...I took an oath... we all took an oath. Gypsy is the only one who can answer your questions...Gypsy knows everything. Go to her. Make her talk to you. Tell her I said it was time for the truth. I can't...please forgive me, forgive us...please...I'm sorry..." When he stopped talking, silence hung like winter ice inside the room. The birds outside made chattering noises at the feeder, the oak trees waved leafy arms, protesting the approaching storm, and Jonathon Sanders slipped back into his other world, the place that gave him peace from the screaming ghosts of guilt in his conscious world.

By the time they got to the car, quarter-size raindrops pelted the hood. Hunter quickly ushered the kids into the back seat, cautioning them to buckle their seat belts. He then eased behind the wheel and put the keys in the ignition. He glanced at Nicole and froze. She was staring out the window, her face pale as chalk. She had a white-knuckle grip on the cigar box in her lap. He reached over and gently turned her face toward him. Her green eyes seemed to look right through him.

"Nicole? What is it?" he asked.

Nicole forced her eyes to focus on his face. "When I was twelve years old, I went to a birthday party. We played this game. Somebody puts a bag over your head, spins you around three times, and you have to feel around until you find somebody you can identify. That's how I feel now, except I'm still spinning."

"How can I help you stop spinning?" he asked.

"Explain to me what that was all about. Who is Megan, what is her secret, and why doesn't Brenda have a birth certificate? Most importantly, why am I shivering when I'm not cold?"

Hunter tucked a stray curl behind her ear then moved his hand to rub up and down her arm. "You *are* cold, Nicole. You have goose bumps on your arms." He reached over, turned on the ignition, and started the car. "I'll get the heater going." He pushed a couple of buttons and moved a lever on the dash.

Nicole grasped his arm. "Hunter, something is terribly wrong here and the odd prickly sensation under my skin is telling me that I'm mixed up in it all. What is this oath they took?"

"I think it's time we paid another visit to your grandmother. If anyone can clear it all up, she can. Somehow, we have to convince her it's time to let go. Maybe telling her you have Jonathon's blessing will do it."

Nicole chewed on her lower lip. Her tawny brows drew together in a deeply furrowed, thoughtful frown. "I hope so," she said. "I've never been clairvoyant, but I have a disturbing feeling I'm not going to like what she has to say."

Relentless rain hammered the top of the Mercedes. A sound from the back seat reminded Hunter they weren't alone in the car.

Nicole must have realized it too; because, she turned back smiling. "Are you guys ready to go home?" she asked

Simultaneously, Shanna and Kyle gave a resounding, "Yes."

"Does anyone want to stop for ice cream?" Hunter asked.

Another duel "yes" came from the backseat.

"Can I have vanilla?" Shanna asked.

"I want chocolate," Kyle said quickly.

Their enthusiasm brought a laugh from both Nicole and Hunter.

Still smiling, Nicole turned to Hunter. "I never realized what medicinal power kids had. Their grins are more effective than Prozac."

Hunter winked at Nicole. "Do you realize," he said, speaking as softly as he could but still heard over the drumming above his head, "that Kyle made a request that didn't echo Shanna's?"

Nicole returned the wink, smiling. "Yes, I noticed."

Hunter put the wipers on full force. Their fast *swishing* had minimal effect. Hunter stared glumly at the blurred windshield. "Too bad they don't have the power to make this rain let up."

"This is a typical downpour in the Midwest," Nicole said.

"Yeah, I still haven't recovered from the last one."

That brought a chuckle from Nicole. "I remember seeing a Dairy Bar about two blocks away. Maybe we could make it to there. This can't keep up very long."

"Is that observation based on fact or opinion?"

Nicole laughed. "Opinion based on facts."

Hunter put the car in reverse. "I hope they have a drive up window."

* * * *

They ate their ice cream entombed in the Mercedes while pea-size hail hammered the car. The kids thought it sounded like a freight train going over them. Nicole dispelled their fears by telling a story about two little bears lost in the woods. They were able to find their mother by following her tracks in the hailstones covering the ground. Hunter rolled his eyes and laughed when she mentioned that the bear's names were Boshanna and Mckyle, but both kids broke out in giggles.

Hunter had been amazed that she was able to keep the story going until the rain let up. He was still thinking about that story after they were back on the road. He glanced first at the kids sleeping in the backseat, then at Nicole. She had her eyes fixed on the windshield, staring out at the monotonously persistent rain.

"I'm curious about something," he said finally.

Nicole gave him her full attention. "What would that be?" she asked.

"The first time I talked to you on the phone you said you had zero maternal instincts. I've watched you with the kids. You couldn't be more nurturing if you had a degree in motherhood. That story you made up to distract Kyle and Shanna came straight from the heart. So explain why you thought you didn't want children."

She turned her head to look back out at the rain. "For a long time, I believed my baby died because I prayed it would. I believed I was to blame and that, one way or another, I was responsible for its death. My parents and therapy finally convinced me that wasn't true, yet, even now, I can't always shake the feeling that I killed my baby. I was sure I would make a terrible mother and decided never to have children. It just seemed safer never to put myself to the test."

Hunter reached over and covered her hand with his. "I think you've been put to the test more than once in the last week, and if my opinion counts for anything—you belong at the head of the class. Where did you learn to make up stories like that?"

Nicole smiled. "My mother used to entertain us whenever we got restless on road trips or had to wait in the car for any length of time. She was a wonderful story teller."

"So are you," Hunter said. He glanced toward the sleeping duo in the backseat, slowly edged the car to the side of the road and stopped.

Nicole frowned. "Is something wrong with the car?" she asked quietly.

"No."

"Then what are you doing?"

Hunter unbuckled his seat belt and moved toward her. "Something I've wanted to do ever since those two little bears got lost in the woods."

The minute he reached for her, Nicole unbuckled her own belt and slid into his arms. She felt so damn good Hunter wanted to savor every second of her. She tasted of chocolate malt, and all he could think of was pouring chocolate all over her and licking her like a cone. His jeans were getting tight, yet he continued, knowing there wasn't a damn thing he could do about it.

"Maybe this wasn't such a good idea," he said huskily. He touched her lips with the pad of his thumb. She pressed his hand to her lips and kissed the palm. He groaned and drew his hand back.

"I just remembered," he said, "we need to stop at a drugstore."

When he moved back under the steering wheel, Nicole settled in her seat, sighing dreamily. "Do they sell those things by the case?" she asked.

Hunter eased the car back onto the road thinking about all the delicious things he was going to do to her when they got home.

"I hope so," he said.

A short while later, Hunter glanced at the cigar box she'd set on the floor by her feet. Nicole was lying with her head back. The look on her face told him she was not sleeping.

"Aren't you going to look in the box Sanders gave you?" he asked.

Nicole brought her head up with a start. "I forgot about it." She reached down and quickly pulled the worn box onto her lap. With a quick look at Hunter, followed by a deep breath, she lifted the paperboard lid. "Do they still even make cigar boxes anymore?" she asked fishing through the contents.

Hunter laughed. "I'm sure they do, but that particular box looks old enough to have seen both world wars." He adjusted the wipers to accommodate a sudden burst of rain pounding at the windshield. "What are you finding?'

She held up a handful of trinkets. "Rings, mostly cheap plastic, the kind found in Cracker Jack boxes years ago. Why would he even keep this stuff?" She picked yet another ring from the tangle of things. "This one looks like a high school graduation ring. It has Yvonne's initials on it. And look at this." She held up a tiny empty bottle of Evening in Paris perfume. The label was faded and discolored.

Hunter stared at the little blue bottle. "Good God, my grandmother used that stuff. It must have had some kind of sentimental value for Yvonne. That was the kind of inexpensive thing kids bought their mother's for gifts back then."

Nicole nodded. She set the bottle on her lap with the rest of the collection and lifted out a child's necklace. It had an aluminum wheel-type pendent hanging from it. "Billy has one of these," she said, holding it up. "He got it from a machine at a carnival. You dial in what you want stamped on it."

"Yeah, I've seen those," Hunter said. "What does it say on it?"

"It's too dark in here. I can't read it."

Hunter flicked a light on over her head. "How's that?"

Nicole stared at the wheel under the light. She read the inscription. "Happy Birthday, Megan, four years old," Nicole gave Hunter a frustrated look. "Where did Megan come from? Did they steal a baby?"

Hunter shook his head. "Damned if I can figure it out. I find it hard to believe they'd do something like that, but then they've done a few other things that are even harder to believe. What else is in the box?"

"The war medal Jonathon mentioned, beads, a brass bracelet, old valentines and...pictures..." Nicole's voice trailed off.

"Nicole? What is it?"

"This one is a family Christmas card picture we had taken when Billy was about six years old. I was thirteen."

"It makes sense that they would have exchanged Christmas cards." Hunter said neutrally. She held three pictures. "What are the other two?"

"One is a family picture of the Caseys, with both Brenda and Megan. At least, I'm guessing that's who they are. I recognize Jonathon. The woman beside him is likely Yvonne. Brenda is holding Megan in front of her so her face is partially hidden but I'd say Brenda is about eighteen or so; Megan, maybe two."

Without looking up, she handed it to him as she stared at the last photo. "This is a close-up shot of a little girl with brilliant red, Shirley Temple curls." Nicole turned the photo over to read the inscription on the back.

"Oh, my Gosh. This is Megan. Jonathon was right. She is beautiful."

Except for a brief glance at Nicole, Hunter kept his eyes on the road. "Let me see."

She held the photo up in front of him.

Hunter nodded. "And that rules out baby theft. She looks far too much like Shanna not to be a member of the same family."

Putting the things back in the box, Nicole agreed. "I'm going to take this box along when we go see Gram. Maybe I can convince her I already know enough to hear the rest of it."

For a moment, she rested her head back against the seat trying to sort out the events of the day. Nothing made sense to her; like a giant jigsaw puzzle, where the picture, instead of becoming clearer with each new piece, just got bigger. She mused over the fact that she and Billy had no idea all this was going on while they lived their Leave-it-to-Beaver life with warm, loving parents. Billy. She suddenly drew in her breath and sat up straight.

Hunter caught the startled movement. "Did you remember something?"

"Yes, tomorrow's Saturday. Billy will be home."

Hunter grimaced. "Oops. Will he be hunting for bear? Do I need to stay out of your room while he's there?"

Nicole laughed. "Not on your life, Honeypot. I'm a big girl. Besides, the brat said he was going to be married and hung the phone up on me. I owe him. By the way," she added, "Berta and Hank will be back tomorrow too. You might as well know she'll boot you out of the kitchen."

"Aw, shucks."

Chapter Sixteen

It continued to drizzle when they pulled in front of the garage, four hours later. Though it was only seven o'clock, low hanging clouds brought on an early darkness. Nicole couldn't remember leaving lights on in the house, and yet every window facing the drive was lit.

The kids had gone through the puzzles Nicole had purchased for them when they'd stopped to eat an hour earlier, and they were now anxious to get out of the car.

Nicole pushed the garage door opener only to find the spot Hunter had been using for his Mercedes occupied by a relic Ford Thunderbird convertible.

"Billy's home!"

Hunter made an appreciative whistling sound. "That's his car?"

"It belonged to Gramps. Gram gave it to Billy as a high school graduation gift. He keeps it at the house in Minneapolis—his house. When I inherited this place, he got Mom and Dad's residence in town. An elderly couple lives there in exchange for house sitting. When he flies in from school, he picks up his car and drives up here."

Nicole's voice animated with excitement.

"Why don't you go in?" Hunter said. "I'll pull the car over to the side and bring the...kids."

The kids were already racing out the door and through the garage in search of Mr. Komodo. Nicole shook her head, laughing and hurried after them.

Shanna and Kyle both came to a jarring stop inside the kitchen door. They gaped open-mouthed at the tall blonde stranger getting up from the counter.

He stared back at them with equal surprise.

William Andrew Anderson came to his full height on a muscular six-foot frame. His biceps gave evidence of regular trips to the gym. He wore a maize and navy colored T-shirt bearing a University of Michigan logo and cutoff shorts that might have been hacked from an old pair of jeans with a dull knife.

When Nicole appeared behind the two vigilant kids, his exuberant face broke into an enormous smile. He rounded the counter in two seconds, grabbed and lifted her feet off the floor with a gigantic brotherly hug.

When he set her back down, his gaze shifted immediately to the two kids cowering wide-eyed in the doorway. The girl was clutching the boy. The boy was clutching a stuffed bear.

"Who do we have here?" he asked, "Goldilocks and one of the three bears?"

Four wary eyes shot to Nicole's face. She quickly knelt down and put out an arm that reached around both of them. Speaking to the kids, she said. "You don't need to be afraid of this big, overgrown ape. He's your Uncle Billy."

"Uncle?" Billy quipped, pinning a skeptical gaze on his sister. "Would you care to expand on that?"

"Certainly," Nicole said, still looking at the kids. "Billy is your uncle because he's my brother."

Billy rolled dusky blue eyes. "Oh, that explains everything, thank you very much."

"Why don't you guys run upstairs and find Mr. Komodo." Nicole said, ignoring her brother.

Shanna drew Kyle around the counter giving Billy a wide birth. Her suspicious glare never left Billy's face until they reached the door to the foyer. There, she pushed Kyle ahead of her, and they both made a dash for the stairs.

"He's in my room," Billy called after them before turning back to Nicole. "Man, that little girl acted like I was the big bad wolf intent on gobbling up her brother...and I thought I was protective."

"You are," Nicole snapped, coming to her feet. "What's this about you getting married?"

"Oh, no. You're not going to change the subject on me. Who are those kids and who do they belong to?"

"They're hers," Hunter said from the doorway. He really wanted to shock Billy by planting a lusty kiss on Nicole's lips, but decided instead, to let her handle her brother in her own way. Hunter was at least two inches taller than the younger man was and equally muscled. Billy could hardly intimidate Hunter.

He stepped around Nicole, heading for the coffee he'd smelled from the garage. "Well, Uncle Billy, I hope you make better coffee than your sister does," he said, reaching for a cup. Ignoring Billy's narrowed eyes, Hunter filled his cup, carried it to the counter, and straddled a stool. From there, he gave Billy a look that said he was quite at home sitting at Nicole's counter sipping coffee.

Billy rounded on Nicole in a flash. "What's going on, Nicole. Where did those kids come from?"

"Good coffee," Hunter said, raising his cup to Billy.

Nicole gave Hunter a warning look. "You're not helping matters any."

Hunter shrugged, grinning.

"You better get yourself another cup of coffee," she said to Billy, "and sit down. It's a long story. Pour me a cup too," she added, taking a seat beside Hunter.

Hunter slung his arm over the back of Nicole's chair, smiling to himself when Billy grimaced.

Billy took his place across the counter and glared at Hunter before he turned to Nicole. "Okay, I'm calm and ready to hear this little saga.

Nicole cradled the warm cup in her fingers. "It seems I—we had a sister—"

"What?" Billy's accusing gaze shot straight to Hunter.

"Don't bother looking at Hunter," Nicole snapped. "He's just the messenger."

"Hunter? Huh. What kind of a name is that?"

"Will you just shut up and listen, Billy?"

Billy shrugged sheepishly. "Sorry. Go ahead. We have a sister. Explain please. Who screwed around?"

"You really are exasperating," Nicole, quipped.

"So I've been told. Sorry, again. So, we have a sister—"

"I said we had a sister. Her name was Brenda Casey, and she died a little over a week ago. Shanna and Kyle are her children."

"And yours?" Billy said to Hunter.

"Billy!"

"Yeah, yeah, sorry, go ahead."

In spite of Billy's repeated interruptions, Nicole was finally able to get the whole story told.

Hunter remained silent, except to offer clarification on some of the things his brother and cousin had uncovered. Billy seemed to take the news fairly well until Nicole told him about Asha Jameel

"You think this nut is watching the house?" he asked, alarmed.

Hunter nodded. "Simon, from the lumberyard, saw him parked out on the road at the end of the drive. He had binoculars trained on the house. We haven't actually seen him."

"Oh shit," Billy said grimacing. "Don't tell me he drives a white Ford Aspire?"

Nicole shot a quick glance at Hunter. "Yes. Why?"

"There was one parked on the road when we got here."

"Did you get a look at the driver?" Hunter asked

quickly.

"Nobody was in it."

Hunter hissed in a sharp breath of air. "That son of a bitch!"

"Does that mean he's outside walking around the house?" Nicole asked, glancing at the window as though she might see him lurking out in the dark.

"The car was gone when we got home," Hunter reassured her. "He must have left. What time did you get here?" Hunter asked Billy.

Billy shrugged. "About two and a half hours ago."

"You said we, was someone with you?" Hunter asked.

Billy gave Hunter a sardonic look. "You don't miss much, do you?"

Nicole snorted. "Wait until you're on the receiving end of twenty questions. However, I actually caught that we business too. Who was with you?"

Billy gave Nicole a crafty grin. "My wife."

Nicole stared at her brother, her jaw hanging open.

Billy snickered. "You should see the look on your face, Sis."

"That's not funny," she said bluntly. "Where is she? Who is she?"

"She's up in my room, taking a nap. I met her at school."

"You're already married? When?"

"Yesterday."

"What was the all-fired hurry? You haven't even graduated yet."

"Talk about twenty questions—you're pretty good at that yourself," Billy said, laughing. "You sound like a mother. Besides, graduation is next week." He gave her a boyish wink. "Her father seemed real keen on a quick wedding."

"But—"

Billy held up his hand. "Why don't I go up and get her. You can give her the motherly degree. She was disappointed that you weren't home when we got here. She's real anxious to meet you. I'll be back in a flash but it might take her a few minutes to get presentable. I promise, you'll love her on sight." He got up and strolled out of the room, calling over his shoulder, "By the way, she loves the house."

After Billy left the room, Nicole turned to Hunter. Her face showed every emotion associated with sibling anxiety. Hunter swiveled his chair toward her and held out his arms.

"You want a moment of distraction?" he asked softly.

Nicole nodded, stood up, and went between his knees to his waiting embrace. It seemed only natural for their lips to meet. The kiss intensified on contact. Her hands, and then her arms, slipped to the back of his neck

At that moment, Billy walked in, leading his new wife by the hand.

Billy cleared his throat, loudly. "Are we interrupting something?"

Nicole tried to pull away from Hunter, but his arm snaked possessively around her waist, holding her in place as he turned to greet Billy's bride.

His words froze in his throat.

The woman with the bright red curls at Billy's side gaped back at Hunter with wide disbelieving eyes.

"Hunter?"

Hunter found his voice. "Corina, what the hell—"

Billy stared at his wife. "You know him?" he asked.

Corina smiled impishly at Billy. "Remember the brother I told you about? The one, not at the party? The big, overbearing, in-my-face protective one?" She turned to Hunter with a smile that turned instantly to an accusatory frown. "What are you doing here, Hunter? If you came to spy on me, you're too late. I'm married—with Dad's blessing," she added quickly.

Hunter was already on his feet, coming toward her with outstretched arms. She met him halfway, throwing her arms around his neck. She squirmed when he squeezed her.

"Take it easy, bruiser—remember my delicate condition."

Hunter set her back, to stare at her. "You're what?"

Corina gestured to her slightly rounded belly.

"You're pregnant? Of course, you told me on the phone." Hunter's gaze narrowed and went straight to Billy. "You did this to her?"

Billy's expression went from confusion to amazement in the space it took him to realize the absurdity of his wife being Hunter's sister. Confronted by Hunter's accusation, it leaped to hilarity. His grin turned into wild laughter.

"Of course, he did it, you big baboon. Can't you see how proud he is," she added with a touch of sarcasm. Her husband had collapsed onto a stool, tears of laughter building in his eyes.

Nicole was staring dumbstruck from one to the other.

"Ain't it a small world, Uncle Hunter," Billy said with another round of laughter.

Corina rolled green eyes and ignored her husband. "Why don't we all sit down and sort this out." She took a stool beside Billy and motioned Hunter to sit across from her, beside Nicole.

"I'm so happy to finally meet you," she said smiling at Nicole, while giving Billy a hard pinch under the counter.

Billy winced. "Be careful," he said to Nicole. "The woman is vicious."

Nicole smiled at her brother. "I would have thought she was smart too, but that doesn't explain why she'd marry you." She held out her hand to Corina. "Welcome to the family, to Minnesota, and to my home."

Corina's eyes sparkled. She gave Nicole's hand a squeeze. "Thank you, thank you, and thank you. I'm so glad to see somebody in your family has manners."

Billy winked at Nicole. "She can be so testy."

Ignoring Billy, Corina turned to Hunter. "Quint said you were in Minnesota working on a case; however, I find it hard to believe your being here is a coincidence. If you tell me you're here investigating Andy, you're going to get the same pinch he did, and worse!"

Hunter's brows lifted in question. "Andy?"

"Everybody at school calls me Andy," Billy explained.

Hunter turned to his sister with a grim smile. "Well, I hate to disappoint you, squirt, but it happens my being here is purely coincidental."

Corina looked unconvinced.

"It's true," Nicole said quickly. "My half sister died, and he brought her children to me."

"That would be the two darling kids I met upstairs?" Corina said.

Nicole nodded. "Yes. Shanna and Kyle."

Corina's skeptical glance settled back on Hunter. "Since when have you been in the child delivery business, or are they yours?"

Hunter flinched. Ironically, Billy spared him from answering.

"Oh boy, here we go again," Billy said chuckling. "It's a long story, honey."

Hunter and Nicole, with numerous interruptions from Billy, took turns explaining the details to Corina.

When they finished, Billy rubbed his palm over the day's growth of beard on his chin. "I take it then," he said to Nicole, "you're actually thinking of taking on the care of those two kids."

Nicole slanted a look at Hunter before answering. "Yes. Their being here has meant more to me than I can explain. Wait until you get to know them, they're darling kids."

"They are," Corina agreed. "I could tell that in just the few minutes I spent with them upstairs. I can't believe how well adjusted they are with their mother only being gone— when was it, ten days ago. How long have they been here?"

"A week," Nicole said.

Billy's eyes widened. "Berta was gone all week,

who's been doing the cooking?"

"Hunter," Nicole said, proudly.

"So...how long are you planning to stay?" he asked Hunter.

Hunter didn't answer right away. There was no sense getting angry with Billy when Billy's only concern was for his sister.

"I have no intention of leaving," he said finally, "until we've cleared up this thing with Jameel. I think the man could be dangerous, if not to Nicole and Shanna, certainly to Kyle."

"And then?" Billy persisted.

Hunter was becoming unceasingly annoyed with Billy for putting him on the spot, but it wasn't in his nature to squirm, and damned if he was going to start now. Well aware of Nicole's eyes on him, Hunter looked straight at Billy and said, "As my father used to say...we'll cross that bridge when we come to it."

If that didn't stop the inquisition, Shanna and Kyle entering the kitchen did.

An hour later, Billy and Corina announced they were going to their room. Corina asked the kids to come along; she wanted to show them some animal photos she had taken at the zoo in Michigan.

"By the way," Billy said as they were leaving, "a peculiar fax came this afternoon."

"What fax?" Nicole and Hunter said simultaneously.

Billy gave Nicole a coy smile. "The one that says you don't exist?"

Hunter and Nicole both stared at Billy.

"Where is it?" Hunter asked quickly.

"Still on the fax machine, I read it...and left it." Before Billy even finished speaking, Hunter was halfway out the door. Nicole was one step behind him.

"We're going to bed," Billy called after them. "Goodnight."

Hunter went straight to the fax machine.

Nicole flicked the light switch.

Hunter picked up the one page fax, holding it so Nicole could read at the same time.

It was from the Hennepin County Government Center.

Ms. Nicole Anderson:

We are unable to fulfill your request for an original birth certificate. While we did find six Nicole Andersons, there was no match for the copy of the birth certificate you supplied. Please confirm the information regarding parents' names and location of birth and we will continue the search.

Nicole felt the blood drain from her face.

Hunter quickly drew her to a chair, sat down, and pulled her on his lap.

"Nicole? Sweetheart? Are you okay?"

Nicole managed a nod that said she was anything but okay.

"Try breathing slow and deep for a minute. Through your mouth."

Nicole did as instructed. The even breathing took away the dizziness but not the anxiety.

"What does it mean, Hunter?"

"It might all be a mistake. It wouldn't be the first time records were lost. Give me a chance to check it out," Hunter said, rubbing his hands over her arms. "You're cold and shaking. Come here, I'll warm you up."

Nicole buried her face in his shoulder, welcoming the sturdy arms that surrounded her.

"Am I overreacting?" she mumbled into his neck.

"In view of everything that's taken place in the last week, I don't think so. What we need to do now is widen our search to neighboring states and find out when your mother had her surgery."

Nicole stiffened. "Why? What are you suggesting?"

"I'm not suggesting anything except what the next step should be."

"Fine. Check in other states."

"And your mother's surgery?"

"No."

"But—"

"No." Nicole jumped off his lap. She whirled to face him. "I had a mother and a father. If you're trying to suggest otherwise, I don't want to hear it. Nothing you find out about me could possibly make a difference in Shanna and Kyle's life. Thanks to Jonathon, we already know the truth about Brenda. There's nothing more to be gained."

"What about—" Hunter stopped talking when Nicole started backing toward the door. He stood up and threw his hands in the air. "All right. Fine. After all, it's your life. If you're satisfied, who am I to question it?"

"I'm going to check on the kids," Nicole said quickly. She turned and left the room before he could finish saying what she didn't want to hear. His last words echoed in her ears as she hurried up the steps. It's your life. If you're satisfied.

Tears stung her eyes. Satisfied? How could she be satisfied now that he had planted the seeds of doubt in her mind? Silently, she cursed him. She knew it wasn't his fault, but she had to lash out at somebody.

Shanna and Kyle were already in their pajamas, sitting on their bed, entertaining Mr. Komodo. Apparently, the cat had decided that the newcomers were the answer to his boredom.

Nicole swallowed the thick lump in her throat and gave them each a good night kiss.

"Tell us a story," Shanna said, ducking under the covers.

Kyle followed her with Mr. Bear in tow. "Yeah, tell us a story. Sometimes Mama told us stories when she wasn't too sick. Once she told us about when she was a little girl and she went to the zoo."

"Can we go to the zoo with Uncle Billy and Aunt Cory?" Shanna asked.

"Where did you get an idea like that?" Nicole asked.

"Uncle Billy said they were going to the zoo tomorrow," Shanna said.

Nicole smiled. "I guess we'll have to wait until tomorrow and see. Now close your eyes while I tell you a story."

"About going to the zoo?" Kyle asked.

Laughing, Nicole moved to the head of the bed by Kyle and tucked him in.

"I think I know a story about two little monkeys who lived in the zoo. They always dreamed about escaping. One was named Shanna Banana and the other one, Coconut Kyle…"

Twenty minutes later, Nicole quietly left their room. She hesitated at the balustrade by the top of the stairs. The only light below came from her study. Hunter was undoubtedly still there, probably working, probably at the computer. She couldn't help wondering what he was working on. She had, after all, given him permission to search the surrounding states for her errant birth certificate. Maybe it would turn out to be something that simple. The Wisconsin border wasn't far away. Her parents could have been visiting there when her mother went into labor, or maybe she was seeing a specialist in another state. There were numerous possibilities.

The only one of the possibilities that really made sense, however, was the hope that the records department had made a mistake. Any other scenario, no matter how she looked at it, resulted in her parents falsifying her birth certificate. The certificate she had, stated that she was born in Hennepin County, which was the Minneapolis area, where they lived at the time.

Nicole drew in a deep breath, releasing it with a melancholy sigh. She moved to sit down on the top step. She wasn't fooling anyone, not Hunter and not herself.

Hunter was right—she wouldn't be satisfied not investigating further, but what if they discovered her mother had the surgery after she was born? Jonathon had said Yvonne only had two pregnancies. He'd already admitted one of the babies died. Why would he bother with a lie at that point? Of course, he was clearly hiding something where Megan was concerned. Maybe he was hiding something else.

Gram. Tomorrow she would pay a visit to Gram.

She stared at the lighted doorway below until the light went out. The rain had stopped, and there was just enough light in the large foyer to see Hunter step out of the studio and walk toward the stairs.

Hunter stopped at the bottom of the stairs when he saw Nicole sitting there. She looked so forlorn, so lost, and so very, very beautiful. Her obvious pain gave him an empty feeling. He wanted nothing more than to comfort her.

He mounted the stairs and sat down next to her, not touching her, not talking.

"You were right," she whispered at length. "I won't be satisfied until I know the truth. I just needed some time to think about it."

Hunter put his hand on her back and began rubbing the tension from her tight muscles.

"I'll proceed any way you want me to," he said softly. "The last thing I want to do, Nicole, is to see you hurt in any way."

Nicole nodded. "Tomorrow, I'm going to see Gram. I plan to tell her everything I already know. Maybe then, I can convince her to fill in the gaps."

"Sounds like a good plan."

After a moment of silence, Nicole looked up at Hunter, frowning. "I also think we should call John Martin and tell him what we know about Asha."

"I already did," Hunter said, "The minute you left the studio. I can't believe Jameel is as clever as he appears to be—I think it's more likely he's just been lucky to avoid anyone who'd question him. I bloody hell wish I could catch him parked out there. It almost seems like he knows when my car is gone."

Nicole leaned into his chest, seeking the comfort of his arms.

"I'm so glad you're here," she said.

Hunter kissed the top of her head. His arms tightened around her and he murmured something incoherent in her hair.

Nicole turned her face up to meet his lips. Somehow, their brief estrangement had intensified their need for closeness.

"We better move to the bedroom," he said. "I don't think I want to try to explain to Billy why I'm making love to his sister on the stairs, even if he made my sister pregnant."

"I seriously doubt he did it alone."

Hunter took her by the hands and lifted her to her feet. They walked toward the bedroom with her in the protective circle of his arm.

He swung the door to Nicole's room open, chuckling. "You don't know Corina. If she'd had a choice in the matter, Billy would be the one pregnant."

"Now, that's an interesting concept."

Without bothering to switch the lights on, Hunter heeled the door shut behind him and drew her to the side of the bed. Their lips came together in mutual hunger.

"Too many clothes," she mumbled into his mouth, her hands pulling his shirt from the waist of his jeans. When she freed it, her hands slid beneath it up his rib cage.

Somewhere deep in his throat Hunter made a hungry animal sound as he fumbled with the buttons on her blouse. His hands shook like a teenager on his first date.

He was still working on the buttons, when her nimble fingers slid down his body to his belt and the snap on his jeans. Her hands moved inside his jeans to cup his firm buttocks and pull him against her. She rubbed against his rigid erection.

"Damn," Hunter swore softly. "You're going to make me cum in my jeans if you don't help me out here."

She stepped back and pushed his hands aside. "The last one naked and in bed has to put the condom on." Her laughter poured over him like liquid silk.

Hunter had his clothes off in four seconds. He made a dive for the bed, turning on his side to gloat at her. She hadn't even started undressing. Instead, she surprised him by lighting a small scented candle on the dresser. The flame reflected against the mirror, setting the room aglow in soft amber light. A sweet musky scent filled the air.

She stood in front of him and very slowly started removing her clothes. Hunter became extremely still. His hungry gaze followed her movements, his blood hammering with need. She finished undoing the button on her blouse then slipped it off to reveal shoulders that gleamed like creamy gold in the soft light. Next, she undid the snap on her jeans and slowly stepped out of them, revealing lace underwear the color of a ripe plum. It matched her bra.

Hunter's eyes came to rest on her face. "You are so beautiful," he whispered, his voice husky with emotion. He held out a hand. "Come to me."

Nicole went to him. She sat down on the bed holding the condom she had taken from the nightstand. She took a deep breath and clumsily slipped it on him. When she finished, Hunter drew her into his arms and pulled her over him, rolling with her until he could look down at her.

With extreme tenderness, he brushed silken strands of hair away from her face. His hand came to rest on her flushed cheek, his thumb caressing the corner of her full lips. Very lightly, he brushed her lips with his mouth. His hand moved to circle her ear then the slender column of her throat. He could feel her throbbing pulse in the palm of his hand.

He removed the last of her clothing, parted her thighs, and sank into her moist sheath. Moving slowly, he murmured sweet, incoherent words, kissing her eyelid, her nose, and the soft pulsing spot at the base of her neck, always returning to her mouth to drink in the essence of her.

He knew the moment she soared off the mountain. She dug her hands into his sweat-slickened back and cried out his name.

Hunter lay beside her exhausted, mentally and physically. The very scent of her stole his power to think. Never had he allowed a woman to become so much a part of him. Separating himself from her would be like ripping his heart out. The thought was disturbing.

It scared the hell out him.

Chapter Seventeen

The early morning sun filtered through the lace curtains in lustrous ribbons spreading bright streamers across the bed.

Nicole awoke snuggled in the security of Hunter's warmth. She was lying on her back, held in a sensual prison by his long limbs. One of his arms cradled her neck, the other her bosom. His leg slung over her with a knee resting intimately between her thighs. His lower body pressed against her hip.

When she blew playfully at the dark curly hair on his chest, his limbs all tightened in one movement.

Hunter nuzzled his face in her hair. "Are you trying to start something?" he mumbled.

Nicole smiled. "Who, me?"

Groaning, Hunter lifted his arm to look at his wristwatch. "It's barely six o'clock. We've only been sleeping for three hours. Woman, you are insatiable."

"And you, Mr. Douglas, have a one-track mind."

"Who, me?"

Laughing, Nicole wriggled out from under him. She gave him an affectionate slap on his bare bottom, before heading for the bathroom.

The sound of the shower lulled Hunter back to sleep.

Twenty minutes later Nicole tiptoed out of the bathroom fully dressed in a pair of tan slacks and lime green silk blouse with three-quarter length sleeves. Lime was Gram's favorite color.

Nicole hesitated, looking down at Hunter asleep in the center of her big bed, one hand stretched toward the bathroom, as though he had been reaching for her. She resisted the urge to brush the unruly curl off his forehead.

A bittersweet smile touched her lips. "Hunter Orion Douglas," she whispered softly. "Do you have any idea how much I love you?"

Nicole turned and quietly left the room. She went straight to her studio, having decided to wait for Hunter or Billy to make coffee. She really did need to learn how to be a bit more domestic. After all, she no longer had just herself to think of.

She pushed that thought aside and dug into the notes the workers had left her the day before. Carmen and Amanda were almost finished with the theater costumes. Chuck still waited for a shipment from Arizona that had somehow managed to go astray in the world of rapid service. He'd had it traced and expected delivery by noon. She was to call him when it arrived. He promised to have everything ready by Monday if the delivery showed up.

Nicole went out to the shop to do the final inspection. After making a few notes on changes, she went back to the studio to start on the drawings for her next project—a play for a local small town celebrating their centennial.

She was able to keep her mind on her work until she smelled the aroma of coffee from the kitchen. Five minutes later, Billy brought her a steaming mug of the dark liquid.

Billy plunked a brotherly kiss on her cheek. "I see you still don't waste any time sleeping," he said. "I had hoped having a man in your life might have changed that."

Nicole laid her drawing pen down to accept the coffee. She gave her brother a wan smile. "You might as well know that Hunter is going back to New York when everything here is settled."

Billy raised bushy blonde eyebrows at her. "I guessed as much. He's going to dump you—just like that?"

"I wouldn't call it dumping me. We both went into this thing with our eyes wide open." Nicole looked out the window, concentrating on her coffee and avoiding Billy's frown. "There was never any question that he would stay here."

Billy stared at her long and hard for a moment. "Maybe you should have kept that in mind before you fell for him," he said sardonically. "There must be twenty guys around here who would go to the ends of the earth for you. You give your heart to an out-of-towner who will forget you in a week."

"That's not true."

"What is not true? That you lost your heart or that he'll forget you in a week?"

"It's not that simple. His life and his work are in New York."

"So is Cory's," Billy said, "and she's moving here."

"That's different—you're married."

When Nicole turned her face away from Billy, his voice softened.

"Sorry," he said. "I seem to have a habit of sticking my nose in where it doesn't belong. Hell, Nick, I just want you to be happy. I should be grateful to Hunter. He appears to have done something for you that's been long overdue. I hope you were smart enough to use protection."

Nicole gave him a misty smile. "Yes, thanks to you."

Billy laughed. So, that's where they went. I was hoping it wasn't the kids. Well, I guess I won't be needing birth control for a while anyway."

"When is your baby due?" Nicole asked more than glad for a chance to change the subject.

"Halloween. How's that for planning?"

"You're telling me you actually planned to have a baby."

Billy shrugged. "Well, not exactly. You know how it goes."

Nicole gave him an understanding smile. "You said Corina was moving here. What are your plans?"

"We've applied for summer jobs at the Duluth Zoo. We're going up this morning for personal interviews. This fall we'll be back in school, or at least, I will. We haven't worked out the details yet."

Nicole brightened. "That's only forty miles away. You can stay here for the summer."

"I was hoping you'd suggest that. I promise we won't be any kind of a burden."

"Are you kidding? Between the two of you, and Shanna and Kyle, Berta's going to be in caretaker heaven."

"You will be keeping the kids then."

"I certainly hope so. We just have to get this thing with Asha Jameel resolved. There is no way he can have custody of Kyle. The child is scared to death of him."

"What about Shanna?"

Nicole gave Billy a grim smile. "At least she is safe from that monster. We have no idea who her father is, and with any luck, it will stay that way."

Billy nodded. "So, what would happen to them if...say, you didn't want to take on the responsibility of two preschoolers?"

Without thinking Nicole said, "Hunter would take them."

Billy nearly spewed up a swallow of coffee. He gave Nicole a decidedly suspicious glare. "For God's sake, why? Why would a single man want to take on two little kids that aren't his? Am I missing something here?"

"No, you're not missing anything," Nicole retorted. "He was the one who had to pick them up at the police station after Brenda died. He had specific instructions, spelled out by Brenda, to deliver them to me along with a falsified document stating that I agreed to accept custody." Nicole stopped for a moment to swallow a gulp of coffee.

"You wouldn't have recognized them as the same kids a week ago. Hunter cared for them for three days before he brought them here. They adore him and they'll both be devastated when he leaves."

Nicole jerked her eyes from Billy's stare.

She gripped her coffee mug to still her shaking hands and took a deep breath, facing Billy with a shallow smile. "Speaking of the kids, they said you asked them to go along to the zoo."

When he took his time answering, Nicole expected him to pursue the subject of Hunter. Instead, he gave her the little brother smile that had always turned her heart to butter.

"Yeah. I think they'd enjoy it and it would give us a chance to get to know them a little better. Our interviews won't take that long, and Cory wants to see the whole zoo anyway. That woman loves animals almost as much as she loves me. Maybe more."

Nicole laughed. "Oh, I think you have enough animal in you to sway her to your side."

Billy's grin widened. "So is it okay with you—and Hunter, of course."

"Is what okay?" Hunter asked from the doorway, coffee in hand. He glanced quickly from Billy to Nicole. "Morning. I trust you slept well."

A pink blush colored Nicole's cheeks. "I slept very well, thank you."

"Shit," Billy said. "You two are pathetic."

Hunter quirked a dark eyebrow at Billy. "You wanted to ask me something?"

"They want to take Shanna and Kyle with them to the zoo in Duluth," Nicole said quickly. "He and Corina are both interviewing for positions up there. They've agreed to stay here at Sunset Lake for the summer. Isn't that wonderful?"

"Corina always did have a thing about animals," Hunter said, giving Billy a wry grin. "Her biggest weakness was stray dogs."

Nicole glanced at Billy, relieved to see him smiling. Those two were like a couple of backyard tomcats defending their turf. Now, through some crazy quirk of fate, they each had a sister to hover over.

"So, what do you think?" she asked Hunter. "Is it safe for the kids to go to the zoo with them?"

Hunter shrugged. "If they want to go, I don't see why not." He turned to Billy. "Just keep an eye out for that white Aspire and call me immediately if you do see it."

"You can count on it," Billy said. "I better see about rousing Cory. We have to leave in a couple of hours. She really isn't much of a morning person."

"Oh, by the way," Hunter said. "One of you better head to the kitchen and revive that poor woman I found in there. She nearly fainted when I walked in, then when I told her I was Billy's-wife's-brother she started fanning herself with a dish towel."

"Berta!" Nicole and Billy said simultaneously.

"I'll go," Billy said quickly. "I probably have the most explaining to do. She'll come around quickly when I tell her there'll be six for breakfast, including two kids and a mama-to-be. That woman thrives on feeding people."

Walking out of the room, Billy stopped at the doorway and looked back at Nicole. "I think I'll let you explain about sleeping with my wife's brother. If seeing Cory pregnant doesn't put her into shock—that sure as hell will."

Nicole shook her head at his departing back. "That boy can be so exasperating."

Hunter burst out laughing. "That, my dear, is an understatement. The worst of it is that he's my brother-in-law."

"I guess that means we're related?"

He tipped her chin and placed a quick kiss on her lips. "Just don't make me call you Sis."

Nicole laughed. "Not to worry. One brother in my life is all I can handle. Now, I better go see Berta and get the kids up."

Nicole deliberately swung her hips as she left the room. She didn't have to turn around to know Hunter was watching her. Instead, she concentrated on facing her housekeeper. Billy was right about one thing. Berta would need a king-size fan when she learned that Nicole had a man in her life. Heaven knows, though, Berta's been pushing that issue for years.

* * * *

Two hours later, Hunter and Nicole stood on the front steps waving goodbye to an excited Shanna and Kyle. Not only were they going to the zoo, they would be riding in Billy's convertible.

Nicole glanced at the cloudless sky. She sighed pensively. "Well, at least it looks like the rain is finished. They should have a wonderful time being outdoors all day."

"Sounds like you would have liked to go with them," Hunter said. "Maybe you should have accepted Billy's invitation."

"You're right, I would have loved to go but I need to see Gram. I'm not putting it off any longer."

"Do you want me to go with you?"

Nicole shook her head. "She's probably more likely to open up if I'm alone." She looked at him with a smile. "But thanks for the offer."

"I guess then, I'll go hunting."

"Hunting?"

"Yeah...for a white Aspire."

Nicole's face fell. "You'll be careful, won't you?"

Hunter draped his arm around her shoulders, giving her a light squeeze. "Don't worry, my sweet. Remember, I can't stand the sight of blood—my own in particular."

"Do you think he's dangerous?"

Hunter studied the woods in front of the house, noting the distance to the main road. He estimated it to be about two hundred yards. The brush was almost heavy enough to hide the house from the highway; almost, but not quite. He released a thoughtful sigh. "I hope not. I do know that until he's caught we need to be extra careful, especially with the kids."

Hunter was more concerned about Jameel than he cared to admit to Nicole, not for himself, but for her and the kids. Besides, he damn well didn't like being stalked by an elusive ghost. He wondered just how much of the house you are able to see from the road.

"I think I'll take a little walk up to the road. Maybe I can see some tire tracks or something."

"And I guess I'll go see Gram."

Hunter gave her a reassuring smile. "Good luck. Maybe you should let her read your palm."

When she snorted, he planted a quick kiss on her cheek and headed down the steps toward the road.

Hunter had walked about halfway when an RPS truck turned into the drive. The driver, a husky looking female, passed him an energetic smile and waved. He was no longer amazed at the friendly gesture. He waved back and kept walking.

When Nicole heard the bell ring at the shop door, she glanced out a front window. She breathed a sigh of relief when she saw the truck. Chuck's supplies. Recognizing Brandy Nelson, the usual driver, Nicole unlocked the door and swung it open with a smile.

"Hi, Brandy. You're a welcome sight today. I hope you have a large package—we are in dire need of those supplies."

Brandy gave her an affable grin. "Yeah, sorry about that. Somebody screwed up. Hey, I just saw the man of my dreams walking up your drive. Tall as an oak, looks like dessert with a designer body, do you know him?"

Laughing at Brandy's description, Nicole was happy to know there was at least one person living within ten miles who didn't know she had ended her fast. "As a matter of fact, I do. He happens to be Billy's-wife's-brother. He's—visiting from New York."

"Billy got married!"

"I'm afraid so."

"Well, shit, another hunk out of the game. Oh, well. I'll get your packages. Actually, there are three of them and they're all pretty big. I hope you know they're COD—the bill is over five hundred dollars."

"That's all right. You bring them in, I don't have that much cash, but I have a credit card."

"That works for me. I have a card swiper in the truck. I'll bring it in."

Brandy left to unload and Nicole went to get her card. When she didn't find it in the drawer, she remembered Chuck telling her the card was missing. At that time, she'd guessed it ended up in Hunter's briefcase. She hesitated a moment then decided she wouldn't be invading his privacy; since, he'd already given her permission to look at all the papers in it.

She located the card at the bottom of the case. As she rearranged the papers to fit them all back inside, she noticed a small, bulky envelope in the top pocket. Mildly curious, she pulled it out.

'Nicole Anderson' scrawled in large letters across the front of it.

For a second she stared at the hand written lettering, frowning. Before she could react, Brandy was calling from the other room. She quickly stuck the letter back in the briefcase and took her credit card to Brandy, thinking she'd have to call Chuck right away to let him know his supplies came.

After Brandy left, Nicole went back to the studio and called Chuck. He wasn't there so she left a message on his answering machine.

Nicole hung up the phone and looked at the briefcase, setting just as she'd left it, open, filled with papers. Even as she sat there, staring at it, her heartbeat kicked up and her breathing shortened. Why was there an envelope in Hunter's briefcase with her name on it, hand written?

She walked over to his desk and plucked the envelope out of the half-open, zippered pocket. Turning it over in her hands, she felt the thickness of it, and looked up to see Hunter staring at her from the doorway.

Chapter Eighteen

Hunter kept his eyes on her face as he entered the room and walked toward her. When he got to within five feet of her, Nicole took a quick step backwards.

"What is this?" she demanded, holding the envelope away from him as though she expected him to rip it out of her hand.

When she took another step back, Hunter stopped. "It's a letter."

"I can see that," Nicole interrupted acidly. "I can also see it has my name on it. Who is it from and what is it doing in your briefcase?"

"I can explain—"

"Please do, and quickly."

"It's from Brenda."

Nicole stared at him as the floor threatened to reach up and swallow her.

Hunter made a move toward her but she quickly regained her equilibrium and put her hand, palm up, in front of her. "No, don't come any closer. Explain from there. Explain why you have a letter addressed to me, obviously written almost two weeks ago, and why you haven't given it to me."

Hunter brushed an agitated hand through his hair. "It

came in the mail the day after I called you."

"It has no stamp or address on it."

"That's because it came in a larger envelope with a letter to me. She asked me not to give it to you unless you agreed to keep the kids."

A flash of anger and betrayal sent a wave of dizziness over Nicole so intense she couldn't breathe. She swallowed hard and gritted her teeth. "Does that mean you still don't believe I want them, and that you're expecting me to sign that paper to give you custody? Has this all been some kind of a game to you?"

Hunter swore under his breath. "Dammit, you know better than that!"

"Do I? Well, why don't you pretend I'm an ignorant country hick and tell me real slowly why you kept Brenda's letter from me and don't use any big city words I might not understand."

"It means," he said tightly, "that I wanted to explain some things before you opened it."

A hot wave of blood stormed Nicole's brain. "Have you read it?"

"Of course, not. What kind of a jerk do you think I am?"

"I haven't decided yet."

"Nicole—?"

Nicole brushed passed him toward the door. When he reached for her arm, she wrenched free of him. She didn't say anything. She just looked at him with eyes that could have burned holes in steel.

She knew Hunter watched as she stormed up the stairs to her room, but, at the moment, she was beyond caring. She slammed her door shut and turned the lock.

Nicole collapsed on the bed, the letter still gripped tightly in her hand. It took several deep breaths to get her emotions under control enough to slide her index finger under the flap and break the seal.

There were three hand-written pages on lined pink

stationary. Her hands shook when she unfolded them. A snapshot fell on her lap. She nearly stopped breathing as she picked up the photo and stared at it. She recognized the little redheaded girl from the picture in Jonathon's cigar box—Megan.

Slowly, Nicole unfolded the crisp pink pages and started reading.

My Dear Nicole,

If you're reading this letter, it means you are accepting responsibility for Shanna and Kyle. First of all, I thank you from the bottom of my heart. I can't tell you how sorry I am to put this on you, but my choices are limited. They are good kids and they don't deserve what life has dealt them, especially a mother like me. I really love them and wanted to do right, but things just got too messed up when I let Asha Jameel into my life.

Please don't misunderstand. I have no one to blame but myself. I allowed Asha to control me because at the time, I was desperate. Little did I know how horrible life could really be. For that, I do blame Asha. When I wanted out, he threatened not only me, but Shanna and Kyle as well.

By then, I was too sick to fight him, and too afraid for the children. It's for them I'm doing what I have to do. I messed up. It's not their fault.

On my mother's deathbed, she told me Robert Anderson was my father. Because of some kind of vow she took, she refused to tell me any more. After she died, my father (Jonathon Casey will always be my father) was mentally destroyed. I couldn't bear to tell him I knew about Robert Anderson. Instead, I hired an investigator to locate my birth father. That's when I found out about you and your brother, Billy. You don't know how badly I wanted to contact you, but since I doubted that you knew about me, I didn't think it was fair to drag you and your brother into it. I'm doing so now because I love my kids. Please forgive me and love them as I do.

I hope when I explain, you can understand. I am sick. Very sick. I'm dying. It seems I'm getting sicker every day, and I need to do this while I'm still able to control my mind. A couple of years, after Kyle was born, Asha encouraged me to take out a life insurance policy with Kyle and Shanna as beneficiaries. He even agreed to pay the premiums. He convinced me it was a good idea not to leave them penniless if something should happen to me.

I no longer believe it a coincidence that I started feeling sick shortly thereafter. Then Asha started giving me the shots. He told me it would make me feel better, and it did but only for a day or so. Soon, I needed the shots to keep from shaking. I still don't know what was in them, but I'm sure they were addictive, mind-altering drugs. I finally went to the doctor and found out I was HIV positive—likely from his dirty needles.

I know I should seek help, but I'm concerned about what will happen to Shanna and Kyle if I end up in a hospital for any length of time. They would be at Asha's mercy.

Anyway, Asha's shots made me feel better, so I allowed him to keep giving them to me, though I'm not sure I could have quit them if I'd really wanted to. Then a month or two ago, the shots seemed to be making me sicker instead of better. I have a suspicion that I'm being poisoned through the shots. I may be hallucinating, but when I met Asha, he was involved in a court case involving his deceased wife. She supposedly died of some type of poisoning but it was never proven exactly what it was, or how she was exposed to it.

Now I'm faced with a horrible reality. Asha is Kyle's father. When I die, Asha could get custody of him. I can't even imagine what would happen to Shanna. He has no love for the kids, but he will fight for custody because of the insurance money. It won't pay on a suicide. He won't want Kyle without the money. I'm dying regardless, at least choosing my time gives me a chance to try to protect Kyle and find a home for him and Shanna. I pray that home will be with you.

There is one other problem to deal with.

When my grandfather, Willard Casey, dies, his inheritance property will go to Kyle. He is in the Adirondack Correctional Facility. I don't think Asha knows about it, but I can't be sure. I don't care if he gets the money—just so he doesn't get my sweet baby Kyle.

Please, I beg you; do whatever you can to keep my children away from Asha. He is a horrible, evil man. He will destroy them as he has me.

Before Nicole turned to the last page, she stopped reading to wipe the tears from her eyes. Shocked by Brenda's painful story, and if only half of what she said about Asha was true, the man was dangerous. He shouldn't be out walking the streets. She already knew she would do anything to keep him away from Kyle. The thing she couldn't understand was Hunter withholding the letter from her. She continued reading.

A couple more things you should know about: One is regarding Shanna; I feel like a tramp telling you I'm not sure who her father is, but someday, if she asks, I want you to at least know the possibilities. I always hoped Hunter Douglas was her father, but she didn't look anything like him, and our relationship, if you can even call it that, lasted only a couple weeks, after he finished the investigation on Robert Anderson for me. There was nothing more to it than that, and I had a boyfriend at the time, so I assumed Shanna was my boyfriend's child. His name is Barry Brighton. He since married and never had children, so my hopes that Hunter is Shanna's father may be realized yet, especially since she looks nothing like Barry either. Since I assumed Barry was her father, I never contacted Hunter.

You can do what you feel is necessary with that information when the time comes. Since Hunter knows about you, and is the one person in the world I trust, I chose him to bring the children to you. He has probably already given you the details.

The last item, I'm afraid, will be painful for you. Mama shared this with me on her deathbed. I promised her that someday I would find you and tell you the truth. Since I won't have anymore 'somedays', it will have to be now.

The picture enclosed is of a little girl named Megan. She was so beautiful. Daddy always called her an angel sent from heaven. She was born premature and he delivered her. Nicole, there is just no gentle way to tell you that Megan was your child. I don't know what your state of mind was when she was born, but I suspect, since they allowed you to believe she had died, you were desolate. Believe me, Nicole, if anyone can understand desolation, I can. My heart goes out to you. She died in the same accidental fire that took my mother. Just know, that for her short life, she was very loved. If you can offer my children even half as much love, it will be enough.

I can't explain the bond I feel with you, but know, that besides leaving my children behind, my biggest regret is that we will never get to meet.

All my love, Brenda Casey

By the time Nicole finished reading the last page, a freight train of emotions raced through her. Fear. Sorrow. Pain. Anger. All were fighting for control.

Fear for Kyle and what Asha Jameel could do, and sorrow, for a sister she never knew. She sensed Brenda's turmoil as though it were her own.

Then, the pain rushed in—Megan. Tears clouded Nicole's vision. She quietly wept for the beautiful child she never held. How could she blame her parents, or the Caseys who took in, and loved the unwanted baby?

Her own words came back to haunt her. I wish it would die. I hate it. No, I don't want to see it. Then there was a prick in her arm followed by peaceful darkness. When she woke up, she never even asked about the baby that she believed was delivered stillborn, in this very house. The pain of labor was horrific, but minuscule compared to the pain she felt now. Yet, somewhere in that pain filled memory, a doctor's gentle face loomed over her. Jonathon Casey.

Fresh tears came when she picked up the picture and stared at the little face that looked so much like Shanna's. Shanna.

Nicole brushed away her tears and lifted the letter from her lap, rereading the top half of the last page. "I always hoped it was Hunter Douglas." Whether Shanna was his daughter or not—he had had an affair with Brenda, a fact he avoided mentioning. Small wonder he didn't want her to read the letter. He must have suspected Brenda would reveal his name.

Now that she thought of it, he never actually had to lie, thanks to her.

When Billy confronted Hunter about being the kids' father, Nicole had chastised Billy before Hunter had to answer. Furthermore, the first night she met Hunter, she had asked if he was Kyle's father. She now remembered the amused look on his face when he said there was no chance. He must have had a good laugh on that. She never asked about Shanna. Only, as Brenda said, she looked nothing like him. He probably would have sidestepped the question anyway. Now she knew what had haunted her this morning when Shanna and Kyle left for the zoo with her brother and his new wife. It was the striking resemblance between Shanna and Corina, same hair, same skin coloring, and even the same turned up pixie nose.

If she recognized the likeness between his sister and his daughter, surely Hunter would have noticed it the first time he laid eyes on Shanna. That explained Hunter's eagerness to accept custody of two little orphans.

Suddenly, she realized he probably never intended to leave without Shanna. If Nicole had refused to give them up, he would have undoubtedly pulled a DNA test out of his briefcase—and to hell with his noble statement about not separating them.

Damn him! Damn him to hell—the conniving bastard. Why did he have to bring them to Minnesota and wait until she attached herself to them? If he had told her over the phone that he was Shanna's father, she may not have insisted on seeing them. Somehow, that thought didn't sit well with her. Plus, she would never have found out about Megan.

Nicole massaged trembling fingers over her temples. She could finally forgive herself for wishing her baby dead. She never admitted to anyone, not her parents nor the string of counselors she had seen, that she always wondered whether the baby was a boy or a girl and what it looked like. Now, knowing that her little girl was loved might allow her to lay those nightmares to rest.

She took a deep steadying breath. It was time to put the past behind her and face the present. She wanted to march downstairs and tell Hunter to get out of her house and out of her life. But if she did that what would happen to Shanna? And there was still Asha to deal with. She needed

Hunter for the kids' sake.

Except, when he left, he'd leave alone. She would not give either one of those kids up without a fight.

She folded the letter, tucked it back in the envelope with Megan's picture, and put it in her nightstand.

It was time to visit Gram.

There was still the matter of her birth certificate to clear up. If she left through the kitchen, she probably wouldn't have to see Hunter right now. That was fine with her. Let him wonder about what was in the letter. The only good thing about this whole mess was at least she wouldn't have to waste any tears on Hunter when he left.

Nicole splashed cold water on her face and ran a comb through her hair. There wasn't anything she could do about her red eyes, except avoid Hunter until the swelling went down. That plan fell through the second she opened her bedroom door.

Hunter stood right there, waiting for her, leaning against the banister, arms folded across his chest. His expression gave no clue as to his thoughts, but his eyes locked instantly on her face.

Hunter could tell she'd been crying. He wanted to gather her in his arms, but the setline of her jaw told him that wouldn't be happening anytime soon. When she tried to brush past him, he stepped in her path.

She backed off evading his touch. "Get out of my way, Hunter."

"What was in the letter, Nicole?"

Her eyes flashed. "What do you think was in it?"

"Don't play emotional games with me," Hunter said sardonically.

"I have no intention of playing any kind of games with you, emotional or otherwise. Get out of my way. I have things to do."

"Like what?"

"I'm going to see Gram!"

"I'll go with you."

"You're not invited," she snapped. This time when she attempted to step around him he let her pass.

He followed her. "You shouldn't be going out alone. It's not safe."

"I don't need a body guard."

When she reached the bottom of the stairs, he put a hand on her arm to stop her.

She yanked her arm free, turning on him with icy fury. "Don't touch me."

Hunter threw his hands in the air. "For Gods sake, are we back to that again?"

"Not exactly," she said smoothly. "This time, it's not because I'm afraid of you, just disgusted." She turned her back to him and headed for the kitchen.

He was on her heels. "Will you just stop this nonsense and talk to me, dammit. You're being unreasonable. The contents of that letter could be important."

Nicole snatched her car keys from a peg on the wall. "You should have thought of that a week ago." She went out the back way into the garage, snapping the door shut behind her.

Hunter stared at the closed door that ended their conversation, if you could call it that. He really wished his anger could be justified, but he knew better. She was one hundred percent right. Now she wouldn't even talk to him long enough to let him explain. Explain what, though? Truth was truth. No amount of explaining would change the fact that he'd had an affair with Brenda, Shanna was his daughter, and, worst of all, he'd concealed it from Nicole. She had a right to be furious with him. He could only hope that by the time she got back from visiting her grandmother, she would have a chance to think things over and cool off. In the meantime, if he didn't get that look of betrayal on Nicole's face off his mind, he'd drive himself crazy.

He walked back to the studio, trying to think about

work. His phone was ringing. He was in no mood to talk to anybody right now, but snapped his cell phone open and growled into the receiver.

"Yeah!"

"Jesus, Hunter, who twisted your tail? Sounds like woman trouble to me."

"Stuff it, Virgil."

"Anything I can do?"

"Yeah, tell me what an asshole I am."

"My pleasure."

"On second thought, forget it. I can take care of that myself. What's up?"

"Thought you might be interested in knowing there's an APB out for your friend Jameel."

Hunter's back straightened. "For what?"

"The coroner found a foreign substance in Brenda's blood. They ran a computer match on it and guess whose name came up with the identical substance in her blood?"

"Jameel's dead wife?"

"Bingo."

"Holy shit!"

"Not quite. It seems he brewed his own type of poison using a mold he created in a test tube. When the match showed up, they got a search warrant for Jameel's townhouse and found all sorts of interesting things in his basement lab. Apparently, this stuff kills very slowly when injected in small amounts, so small in fact, that it's impossible to identify."

"But Brenda died of an overdose."

"Yeah, he didn't off Brenda only because she cheated him out of the time to do it, but the good news is, they have enough to stick him with murder one for his wife. It would give me great pleasure to tell the local authorities where to find him. Most likely, they'll call in the Feds if he's in Minnesota. Okay with you?"

"Hell, yes. In fact, they can contact the local sheriff, John Martin. He's out looking for the bastard as we speak."

"You might want to tell him to be wary. I don't think Jameel knows they have enough to pick him up, but if he finds out, the man could be dangerous." Virgil paused. "So how's everything else?"

"Dandy. Just dandy. I can tell you all about Corina's husband."

"She's married? I'll be damned."

"Oh yeah, and there's more to it than that. She married Nicole's brother."

"You gotta be shitting me."

Hunter laughed. "That's exactly what I said." He shared what he knew about Billy Anderson, then hung up and dialed John Martin's number.

Chapter Nineteen

Nicole didn't realize she'd forgotten her purse until she got out of the Blazer at the assisted living home. It really didn't matter. All she intended to do was see her grandmother.

She found Gypsy, as she usually did, sitting at her little table playing solitaire. Her eyes sparked with pleasure at the sight of her granddaughter.

"Dee Dee my Sweet Pea," she crooned. She patted the chair beside her. "Come sit with me."

Nicole took the suggested seat, put an arm around Gypsy's shoulders, and planted a kiss on her wrinkled face. "Hello, Gram, how's my favorite fortune teller?"

Gypsy's deep-set eyes studied Nicole. "You need your fortune told, Sweet Pea?"

Nicole laughed softly. "No, Gram, actually, it's my past I want told, but first I want to know if you've seen Billy?"

Gram chuckled. "Oh, yes, the big rascal. He stopped by this morning, said he had a surprise for me, and surely he did. It gave my poor old heart a jolt when he introduced that curly haired redhead as his wife. She's the cutest little gal, looks a lot like your sweet Shanna. They brought them both along, Shanna and the boy, Kyle. Those two are so quiet, too quiet, and too sad. Somebody needs to teach them how to be children, how to play and laugh."

Nicole swallowed hard. "Yes, I know. Maybe they just need a little more time." She forced a smile. "Did Billy and Corina tell you they were going to have a baby?"

Gypsy nodded mischievously. "I offered to read her palm, to tell them what it would be, but Billy wouldn't even let me get close enough to shake hands with her. He did tell me if it's a girl they were going to name her Gypsy Rose. How about that?"

"That's wonderful, Gram."

"Won't matter," Gypsy said shrugging. "It's a boy. Maybe the next one."

Nicole shook her head laughing. "Why do I believe you?"

Gypsy's smile suddenly faded. "Your laughter isn't reaching your eyes. Why are you sad, my Sweet Pea?"

Nicole took a deep breath—and then another. She laid her hand on the table. "I want you to read my palm, Gram."

Gypsy stared at the hand but didn't touch it.

"Let me help you." Nicole said. She reached over, taking one wrinkled hand and placing it over her own. "I met Jonathon Casey, Gram. I know how they got Brenda."

Gypsy's face remained impassive, her hand lifelessly still.

"I also know about Megan."

The fingers, so still in Nicole's hand, jerked. Tears filled Gram's eyes.

"I'm sorry," she whispered. "I begged them to tell you the truth. You had strength they didn't know about."

Nicole squeezed her shoulders. "It's okay, Gram. I'm not so sure how I would have handled it at the time. Only now, I need to know the other secrets. I need to know why my birth certificate is not real? It's time to release the secrets from your heart, Gram. Jonathon Casey told me to come to you."

Gypsy was silent for a long time. Just as Nicole

decided her wily grandmother was going into one of her self-imposed trances, Gram's fingers began to move over Nicole's palm.

Gram spread Nicole's hand and gently traced the exposed lines, slowly and carefully studying them. Her voice took on a monotone quality.

"The answer you seek rests between time and love," she said softly, quietly, just above a whisper. "It sleeps in a marble tomb. I can give you the key, but you must find Cappy's heart on your own."

Nicole wasn't sure she dared to breathe. Her heart pounded in her ears. "The key, Gram, where is the key?"

Releasing Nicole's hand, Gypsy reached up to her neck. She lifted a chain over her head; on the end hung a small brass key. She laid the chain in Nicole's hand and closed her fingers over it.

"Go now, Dee Dee Sweet Pea, but go only with thoughts of love. Remember, without the secrets of the heart, you would not be."

* * * *

Grappling with her thoughts, Nicole stood in the parking lot beside her car. She stared at the tiny, chained key in her hand. If she understood Gram correctly, she had all the clues she needed. In a marble tomb—between time and love. Where the flame burns and the flowers bloom. Poppies. It all fit together. She knew exactly where to look. With shaking fingers, she stuck her key in the car door and unlocked it.

Nicole heard a rustling in the tall bushes behind her. Before she could react, a rag pressed to her face. A sharp stinging odor permeated her nose, her lungs, and her brain. She fought to keep from falling, but her knees buckled under her, and she sank into a pit of darkness.

* * * *

Hunter paced the studio, growing more impatient with each passing minute. It was nearly four o'clock and Nicole still hadn't returned. Even though she'd been angry when she left, Nicole was a rational person. She wouldn't do anything foolish or stupid. He doubted she went shopping; her purse was on her desk in the studio. She would probably be royally pissed if he hunted her down.

Let her be pissed, he decided. He was going to call the assisted living home to see if she'd left yet. Earlier he'd heard Berta bustling around in the kitchen; she would have the number. He grabbed his cell phone and headed through the foyer.

Good smells were coming from the oven, but Berta wasn't in the kitchen. Before he could consider another plan, he heard the overhead garage door opening. Breathing an enormous sigh of relief, he yanked the door to the garage open, hoping to find her in better spirits.

Instead of Nicole's Blazer, he saw Billy's convertible pulling into the garage. Shanna and Kyle stepped out of the car, excitedly talking about giraffes and tigers and monkeys. Hunter squatted to gather them in his arms. When he stood, they both came with him. Each had an arm slung around his neck.

"Look what Uncle Billy bought for me," Shanna said holding up a stuffed animal with an orange face and a long tail. "It's an orangutan," she pronounced proudly. "We saw a mama orangutan at the zoo."

"Yeah, and she had a baby named Luna," Kyle chimed in. "But I liked the tigers better. I got a white tiger. He had to ride in the trunk because he was too big. Hunter, did you know tigers have stripes and leopards have spots?"

Hunter laughed. "Well, If I didn't, I do now," he said. "It sounds like you both had a good time."

Kyle threw his arms around Hunter's neck in a fierce hug. "We really had fun. Will you come with us next time?"

Hunter rubbed his chin on Kyle's soft dark hair. He blinked rapidly and swallowed. Before he could answer, Shanna smothered him with a hug that encompassed Kyle.

She placed a soft kiss on his cheek, adding, "And Aunt

Nicky too. Uncle Billy and Aunt Cory are going to work there. They said we could come while they're working if you bring us."

Hunter buried his face in Shanna's hair. It smelled like Nicole's honeysuckle shampoo, with a hint of barnyard. Out of the corner of his eye, he saw Corina come in the door carrying a stuffed tiger twice the size of Nicole's cat. She was watching him with tawny raised eyebrows. Hunter gently lowered the kids back to their feet.

"I'm sure you can go to the zoo again," he said.

With an animated cheer, Kyle took his tiger from Corina and started for the foyer. "Come on Shanna. Let's go see if Mr. Komodo likes my tiger. I'm going to call him Mr. Stripes."

Shanna hurried after him. "Okay, then I'm going to call my orangutan, Mrs. Banana."

Corina shook her head, laughing. "Those two are a stitch." She slanted Hunter a sideways look. "They seem to have you wrapped around their little fingers," she said with a bit of mischief in her tone.

"Where's Nicole?" Billy asked Hunter from the doorway.

"She went to visit your grandmother," Hunter said. "She should have been back by now. I was going to call the assisted living home, but maybe I'll just drive over there instead. You mind keeping an eye on the kids?" he asked Corina.

"Of course, not." She stood on her tiptoes to press a kiss to his cheek. "You'll make a wonderful uncle," she said. The look she gave him said that uncle was not the word she really meant. She turned to give Billy a quick nibble on the lips. "I'm going to go take a shower. I smell like buffalo dung."

Billy kissed her back, allowing his hand to linger on her behind. "Might as well get used to it, Babe, at least until you start smelling baby poop."

She made a face at him and wriggled away. "Don't

worry; you'll smell your share of it too."

Hunter observed the exchange between his sister and her husband. They seemed to have a comfortable, loving relationship, something he suddenly wanted. It was nearly five o'clock. He had to find Nicole.

"I'm taking a drive over to the assisted living home," he said, heading for the front door. "Call me on my cell phone if Nicole gets home before I do. The number is on a pad on the desk in the studio."

Billy was two steps behind him. "I'm going with you. Cory, you okay with the kids?"

Corina waved them both on. "Yeah, yeah, we'll be fine. Go."

Hunter welcomed Billy's company, thinking Nicole would be civil with her brother along. What he didn't count on was Billy's questions the minute they got in the car.

"You seem overly concerned. Just how long has Nicole been gone?" he asked before they even cleared the driveway.

"About one o'clock."

"I can't believe she'd still be at Gram's. She must have gone into town for something."

"She didn't take her purse."

Billy gave Hunter a skeptical glance. "Women never go anywhere without their damned purses. She must have left in a hurry. What kind of mood was she in?"

Hunter flinched. His hand tightened on the steering wheel in a white-knuckle grip. He wanted to tell Billy to mind his own business, but Nicole was Billy's sister. She was his business. He was in no frame of mind to start explaining what had gone on between him and Nicole before she stormed out of the house. But he also didn't want to lie to Billy.

Before Hunter could answer, his phone rang. He flipped it open with a quick snap of his wrist and put the phone to his ear. He muttered a curt "yeah" into the receiver.

"Hunter, it's Sheriff Martin. A girl at Nicole's house gave me your number. She said you were looking for Nicole."

Hunter's heart quickened. "She went to see her grandmother four hours ago and hasn't returned. I'm on the way there now."

"I'm ten minutes from there. I'll meet you."

Hunter snapped his phone shut and a few minutes later, pulled into the Golden Sunset parking lot.

"That's her Blazer. Over there in the corner." Billy said, pointing to one of five vehicles in the lot. "She always parks in the shade of that tree by the lilac bushes."

Hunter didn't know that, but then there were a lot of things about her he didn't know. He did remember her parking there before, though. He pulled up next to the Blazer on the passenger side and opened his door to get out. "Why don't you go in and see if she's with your grandmother," he suggested to Billy.

Billy disappeared through the front door about the time John Martin pulled up behind Nicole's car. He got out and came around his squad car to look into the back of Blazer.

Hunter walked around the front of it. He stopped short, staring at the door on the driver's side. The keys were hanging in it.

Coming around the other side, John Martin saw the keys at the same time. "What the hell…"

Both men looked up when Billy burst out of the assisted living home. "Gram said Nicole left three hours ago!"

"Her keys are here in the door," Hunter said. He was already feeling a squeeze of panic in his chest when his eyes happened on something shiny in the recently graveled blacktop at his feet. He bent down and picked up a chain with a small brass key attached to it. He wound the chain around his fingers and looked at Billy.

"Do you know if this is hers?" he asked.

Billy was breathing deeply. "No, but Gram was murmuring something about a key."

Blue eyes met brown eyes in mutual concern.

"Did she say anything else?" Hunter asked.

Billy shook his head. "Nothing that made sense. She was mumbling something about looking for snow in green trees; who knows what the hell that means."

Hunter ran a hand through his hair, swearing savagely. His words ended with Asha Jameel. "If he harms one hair on her head, I'll tear him apart one limb at a time. We have to find her. Check on the ground around the car. Watch for anything that might be a clue. Look for tire marks. Asha's car has three bald tires and one new one. There have probably been a dozen cars in and out of here in the last three hours, but we don't have a hell of a lot else to go on."

John Martin stared at Hunter with raised brows and something akin to admiration. "I'll go inside and ask around. Maybe somebody saw something."

Hunter nodded mutely. Knowing this town, if anybody seen anything suspicious concerning Nicole, they would notify the sheriff immediately. His gaze was already scanning the parameter of the parking lot and beyond. It came to rest on the wall of lilac bushes a few feet beyond the grass behind him.

He walked toward it, the chain still gripped tightly between his fingers. He shouldn't have let her go off alone. Even while he cursed her stubbornness, he knew he was at fault. It all boiled down to one thing. He shouldn't have concealed that letter from her.

On the other side of the bushes, he found a vacant lot. What he saw in the soft damp earth made a chill spiral up his spine and knots of fury tighten in his gut: footprints getting in and out of a car with three threadbare tires. On closer examination, he saw far more prints than it took to simply get in and out of the vehicle, but the prints where all made by the same shoes. Some were just deeper than others were. A combination of anger and fear closed in on him as he followed the tracks to where they backed up and took off to the left. From there, the tracks disappeared onto the paved street. He didn't hear Billy come up behind him until he heard the younger man swear under his breath.

* * * *

Nicole was climbing out of a dark pit, a noxious odor hung in the air, burning her lungs and stinging her eyes. She tried to lift her head but it hurt too much. She tried to think but even that hurt. Her limbs felt like lead weights. The only energy she had came out in a moan. It seemed like a long time later that she was able to open her eyes.

Without moving, she focused on her surroundings. The drapes drawn, allowing only a small glow of light into what seemed to be a large room. She could make out a table with six chairs about six feet in front of her. One of the chairs held a tattered, olive green knapsack. There was a kitchen on the far side of the table. The kitchen reminded her she was thirsty.

Very thirsty.

She closed her eyes and swallowed. She tried to call for water but wasn't sure if she actually formed the word or not. When she opened her eyes, again there was a blurred form in one of the chairs. A man. A dark face. She finally managed to focus on his face. Eyes as black as sin stared back at her. An adrenaline rush clutched at her heart, closing her throat.

The man got up and walked to the kitchen. Then she heard water running. Her heartbeat accelerated as he came back, walking toward her. He sat her up, braced her head, and held a glass to her lips.

She drank greedily, bringing her own hand up to tilt the glass and empty it. When she finished, he allowed her to sag back on the cushions in a half sitting position. He moved back to his chair where he sat quietly, watching her, and waiting.

There was little doubt in her mind who he was. Shivers of fear crawled over every inch of her skin. She opened her eyes just enough to look at Asha Jameel through covertly thin slivers. She wasn't sure what she had expected him to look like, but it certainly wasn't the handsome stranger staring back at her with piercing dark eyes. His deep olive face partially concealed by a short clipped beard and mustache, both as coal black as his hair. She judged him to be about five-foot-nine, only slightly taller than she was herself. He wore a black t-shirt that hugged sturdy arms and shoulders. His age was difficult to determine beneath all the facial hair, but probably somewhere between thirty-five and forty-five.

The fog in Nicole's head was beginning to clear and with that clearing, came confusion. For the moment, curiosity overrode her fear. What could he possibly hope to accomplish by abducting her? No matter how much she puzzled over her situation, she knew the only way she would learn anything was to open her eyes and talk to him. As much as she dreaded facing him, there was little else she could do. She had already decided not to let him see how truly frightened she was. Taking a deep breath, she opened her eyes and met his unwavering gaze with one of her own.

His slow smile was anything but comforting.

"Welcome back to the living," he said.

Her eyes were alert enough to acknowledge she heard him but she kept silent, determined to let him do the talking. She hadn't noticed the highball glass on the table until he lifted it to take a sip of the amber liquid in it.

When he lowered the glass, the smile vanished.

"That was quite a little stunt you pulled, my love. I'll have to admit you had me fooled, with your red hair and all, until I saw you driving around with that new boyfriend of yours. That had me stumped for a couple of days. I suppose he's the one who orchestrated the whole stupid charade. You sure as hell aren't that clever. I wouldn't even have caught on if I hadn't caught that bastard making off with my kid."

Nicole blinked, trying to comprehend what he was

saying. Either her mind remained fogged or she had missed something in his conversation, or both. He seemed to be satisfied doing the talking, so for the time being, until he said something that made sense to her, she would listen in silence.

She wasn't prepared for the crashing sound of his glass slamming down in front of him. Her body reacted with a spastic jump as liquor splattered, and ice cubes skittered across the surface of the table.

His ferret-like gaze settled on her face. "I could almost forgive you for trying to cheat me out of your insurance money with that little suicide act, but going so far as to cut me out of everything by taking off with my kid? I have to tell you, Brenda—that really makes my blood boil."

Brenda. He thought she was Brenda. Good God, she couldn't look that much like her half sister.

Nicole opened her mouth to tell him she wasn't Brenda, but the words stuck in her parched throat. He wasn't listening anyway. He was still talking, in that bone-chilling, slurring voice.

"I see you're managing without your shots, or is your new lover giving them to you? To bad, I didn't bring any of my equipment with me. We could take care of that right now. But then I didn't expect to find you here." Asha stopped talking long enough to take the last swallow of his spilled drink. "Just how in the hell long have you been planning this thing? You must have been wearing a fucking wig at home to hide your long hair."

Nicole's heart hammered when he got up from his chair and came toward her. Much to her relief, he walked past her to a liquor cabinet. He plucked out a bottle of Scotch, carried it back to the table, and refilled his glass.

Nicole used his distraction to look around the room hoping to identify where she was. The woodwork was solid oak and the furnishings expensive, obviously, not just a weekend getaway, unless it belonged to somebody very wealthy. She had been in many of the homes on nearby lakes, but she didn't recognize this one, probably because everything looked new. With all the blinds and curtains drawn, she couldn't see outside, but she was certain they were on a lake; she could hear boating activity outside. She wasn't restrained; apparently, he was confident that she couldn't escape. Maybe he believed Brenda too weak to resist him. That thought alone was enough to convince her to keep her identity to herself. It was unlikely he'd believe her anyway if she told him her name was Nicole Anderson.

Asha came toward her and snatched the water glass out of her hand. She didn't even realize she'd been holding it. He tossed the remaining water on the carpet, poured a splash of Scotch in the glass, and stuck it back in her hand.

"Drink," he commanded when she didn't move.

Since she was in no position to defy him, she put the glass to her mouth, intending to satisfy him by wetting her lips. He quickly grabbed the back her neck and upended the glass, forcing her to empty it. The liquid scorched a firry path down her throat. She came up choking when he released her, grabbed her glass, and took his seat back at the table. He looked at her and smiled the same evil smile that had her cringing before.

He watched her wipe spilled liquor off her chin and laughed. "What's the matter, sweetheart? Nothing to say for yourself?"

"What do you want from me?" she asked finally. Her voice was barely more than a croaking whisper.

His laughter was as ugly as his smile. "Oh, now that is the question of the hour. I'll tell you what I want." He moved his chair to within three feet of her then leaned forward in it, bracing his elbows on his knees. He rolled his highball glass between his fingers. "You and I are going to get married."

Surprise made Nicole snort before she could stop herself. "Why would I marry you?"

His dark eyes narrowed. "Don't get snippy with me, Brenda. You know how far that will get you. I don't care if you want to marry me or not. You will. Only first, we'll pick up my son, and just for kicks, we'll take Shanna along too. You wouldn't want anything awful to happen to that sweet little angel, now would you?"

Nicole could only stare at him. The thought of what he was insinuating both frightened, and enraged her. Using the kids to manipulate Brenda was obviously something he was accustomed to doing. Small wonder they all feared him as she already had an overwhelming hatred for the man. The thought of him touching either one of those two innocent children sickened her.

Wondering how, exactly, he planned to get his hands on them, she realized the more information she had the better.

"Just how do you expect to get Shanna and Kyle?" she asked, not really believing he'd answer.

He surprised her.

He didn't even hesitate. "I'm not going to get them. You are."

He chuckled when he saw the defiance in her eyes. "When the time comes, you'll pick up the phone and arrange to have them delivered right to us. Honestly, who will deny you? After all, they're your kids. Plus, we both know you'll do whatever I tell you to do."

Nicole held her tongue. She wanted to tell him how wrong he was. Nothing on this earth could make her turn those kids over to him. Only, this wasn't the time to tell him that. Right now, her best defense was to behave and react like Brenda. At least if he believed she was Brenda, he wouldn't do anything rash. He needed her, and she needed to buy time to escape, or be rescued.

She glanced at a clock on the wall. It was half past six. Billy and Corina would be home by now. Surely, Billy and Hunter would be wondering where she was.

Hunter. Tears stung her eyes. He had betrayed her but right now, she'd forgive him anything to have his arms around her.

"I need to use the bathroom," she said.

Asha nodded toward a hall behind her. "Fine. It's over there. Just leave the door open. Just don't go getting any ideas to run. No screaming either. There's no one near enough to hear you, but you make one move or sound I don't like and I'll tie you up and duct tape your mouth. Is that understood?"

Nicole shuddered. "Yes."

"Good, then go do your business, get your ass back out here, and fix me something to eat."

Chapter Twenty

A wave of dizziness rushed up to meet Nicole when she stood up. If not for Asha grabbing her, she would have collapsed at his feet. Her reaction to having his hands on her was potent. With a startled cry, she shoved him away from her and hurried toward the bathroom. Using the wall for balance, she managed to make her way down the hall without toppling over.

Asha's laughter followed her. The horrid man took sadistic pleasure in her weakness, in Brenda's weakness. God, how she must have despised him.

By the time Nicole reached the bathroom, she was able to stand on her own. She left the door open and ran cold water in the sink to splash on her face; it helped to clear her head. She noticed a window inside the tub enclosure. With a furtive glance over her shoulder, she stepped into the tub. Disappointment nearly took her to her knees. The window was far too small to think about squeezing through.

She looked out the tiny window, hoping to at least identify where she was—which lake. From what she could tell, it wasn't more than eight hundred acres, at the most. Several cabins hugged the shoreline, most partially hidden by trees; none of them looked familiar. If there were homes directly next door, she couldn't see them from the view she had. There were probably six or seven lakes near this size within a ten-mile radius of her house, but she had no idea which one this was. Whatever Asha used to make her black out had worked all too well; she had no concept of direction or any idea how long it had taken him to drive to where they were.

A movement in the oak tree, directly outside the window, caught her eye. An albino squirrel scurried to the top branches. A sob caught in her throat when she realized the irony of seeing the rare squirrel. When she and Billy were kids, she told him white squirrels became knights in shining armor when kissed. He laughed at her and said she'd have a lot better luck catching a frog to kiss. But the animal lover side of Billy was fascinated by oddities of nature, especially anything albino.

Asha's voice threatening to come and get her if she didn't hurry, brought her out of her childhood memories. She stepped out of the tub and quickly used the toilet, flushed it, washed her hands, and headed back toward the kitchen. As before, she used the wall for support if only to keep Asha believing her condition had not improved.

He was glaring at her. "Are you going to be able to cook?"

If she dared, she'd have laughed in his face. Her wobbly legs had nothing to do with her being able to cook. Obviously, Brenda had some skill in the kitchen.

"No," she croaked, dropping heavily to the sofa. "I can't even stand. I'd probably end up poisoning you."

The look he gave her was lethal. She thought he was going to strike her. Instead, he went to the kitchen and started banging pans around, swearing profusely.

Nicole laid her head back and closed her eyes. It's too bad she hadn't thought of really poisoning him. Right now, that seemed like a first class idea. She drifted off to the growl of a can opener and metal scrapping metal.

It seemed like only a few minutes had passed when

Asha's voice woke her up.

"You better get over here if you intend to eat. I want to get those kids before dark."

She opened her eyes to the sight of Asha sitting at the table, shoveling what looked and smelled like chili, into his mouth. Even if she had been hungry, the mention of Shanna and Kyle and what he intended to do would have made her stomach rebel.

"I'm not hungry," she replied.

He shrugged. "Suit yourself, but get over here and sit anyway. You have some notes to take."

Nicole didn't have the energy to resist him. She got up and slowly made her way to the kitchen. She found a glass, poured it full of water, and took a seat across from Asha, where he'd laid out a pen and paper. He hadn't even paid any attention to her when she walked behind his back to go to the kitchen. Nicole doubted he'd be as relaxed if he knew she wasn't Brenda. She'd noticed a butcher-block holder full of knives on the counter and wished she had the courage or strength to use one. Maybe she wasn't so unlike Brenda after all. Two years of self-defense courses wasted. Tossing a harmless man, who didn't toss back, on a mat wasn't even remotely related to real life.

Wearily, she picked up the pen.

"Here's what you're going to do," Asha ordered. "You're going to call that Anderson house and tell your boyfriend, or whoever is in charge over there, that you want your kids to be dropped off at the Catholic Church outside of Willow River. They should sit on the steps and wait for us."

Nicole stared at him as though he'd lost his mind.

"Write!" he hollered, slamming his fist on the table.

Nicole's whole body jerked. A startled scream tore from her throat before she could even think about stifling it. Fear pumped like frozen blood through her veins, immobilizing her. When she didn't move, he got up, stomped to the kitchen, and yanked a meat cleaver from the knife block. He came back to the table and with a quick snap, imbedded one corner of it into the beautiful oak less then six inches from her right hand.

She wrenched her hands back, gasping convulsively.

Apparently, this time her face had the appropriate amount of fear on it because he smiled.

"Now, do you write, or do I start taking your fingers off, one knuckle at a time?"

Nicole picked up the pen. She put it to the paper and held it ready to write. In spite of the fact that her hand shook so violently nothing she wrote could possibly be legible, he appeared to be satisfied and sat back down.

"You're going to call, say you've decided to go back to New York and take your kids with you. If anybody questions you, just remind them that they are, in fact, your kids, and you can do whatever the hell you please with them."

Cold anger started to build in Nicole. She gripped the pen so tight her fingers hurt. "Nobody will believe that," she said adamantly.

He gave her a malevolent glare. "Convince them. Talk to your lover boy. Tell him you finally realized how much you still love me. Shit, you're contagious, he'll be glad to be rid of you. Oh, and tell him no cops."

He had no concept of how ludicrous his proposal was. Nicole was writing, but her mind had started to work again. She tried to imagine Hunter's reaction when she called to say she was Brenda and wanted him to drop her kids at a church. She had already decided to make the call. At least, Hunter would know what had happened to her and could somehow set a trap for Asha. She certainly didn't have to worry about Hunter taking her seriously and actually bring Shanna and Kyle to the church. Her main concern: that he catch on quickly, and play along before he started calling her Nicole. That meant she had to talk to Hunter. He was the only one who knew how much she resembled Brenda, and if Billy was there and on his toes, she might be able to throw in a clue as to where she was.

* * * *

John and Chuck Martin sat at Nicole's kitchen counter brainstorming, while Hunter and Billy paced like caged animals. Corina alternated between keeping the kids entertained upstairs and stepping between Hunter and Billy. The two of them had spent the three hours driving around and looking for a white Ford Aspire. The only thing they both agreed on was that Berta needed two aspirin and handed over to the care of her husband. The paper towels she'd been wringing and sobbing into lay on the counter in wet shreds.

"We should all be driving around looking," Billy said.

Hunter ran a frustrated hand though his hair. "I want to be here if she calls. Besides, there must be five hundred lakes in this vicinity with fifty thousand cabins on them."

"Actually," John Martin said, "there are only about seventy-five lakes and maybe fifteen hundred cabins. Of course, that doesn't include the houses that aren't on lakes."

"That's if he stayed in the area," Billy said. "Who knows where he might have taken her?"

Hunter grunted. "He's not far. It's Kyle he wants, not Nicole. He just grabbed Nicole because she was the only one he could get his hands on."

"That means he'll be calling," Chuck said.

His brother nodded. "So long as he doesn't know he's wanted for murdering his wife, I don't think he'll dig himself in any deeper by harming Nicole."

Hunter gave John Martin a hard stare. "You do know I'm going to kill him if he hurts her. I might kill him anyway, just for the hell of it."

Before the sheriff could point out the folly of Hunter taking the law into his own hands, Corina walked in.

She gave her brother a suspicious smile. "It sounds to me, Hunter, like you're in love with that girl."

Billy stopped pacing long enough to gage Hunter's

reaction to Corina's words. Hunter's expression revealed nothing. "He's the one who got her into this whole mess in the first place," Billy snapped.

Hunter rounded on Billy angrily. "What the hell do you think I should have done, let Brenda's kids become wards of the state? In the first place, I had no idea Nicole didn't know about them, I was only following instructions from Brenda."

"Did those instructions include seducing my sister?"

This time, Chuck cut in.

"Whoa, Billy, you're way off the wall. You know better than anybody, there isn't a man within fifty miles who hasn't tried to seduce your sister, and that includes each and every one of your friends."

Billy grunted. "They didn't get anywhere. She hasn't even been out on a date in twelve years."

"Exactly, my point," Chuck said. "Nicole needed seducing."

For all of five seconds every eye trained on Chuck.

Finally, Hunter turned away swearing. "God dammit, I didn't set out to seduce her. It wasn't like that at all."

"Then how was it?" Billy asked.

"It was…hell, it just happened, and just for the record, what happened between us was by mutual consent," Hunter said.

Billy looked at his wife beseechingly. "He knew all along he would be leaving to go back to New York. She was so damn…vulnerable." Sudden tears sprang up in Billy's eyes. He turned his back on everyone to stare out a window. "Where in the hell is she?" he whispered.

Corina stood behind Billy, rubbing her hand over his back. She looked at Hunter with extreme tenderness. "Why don't you tell Billy about the call you made after Nicole left today?"

Hunter froze.

"What call?" Billy asked, turning to stare at Hunter through narrow, watery eyes.

Corina, too, was watching Hunter. "I never did get my shower this afternoon," she said, "What with the phone ringing off the hook and all; first the sheriff, then Quint, and then Virgil. Quint wanted to know how serious you were about expanding your business to Minnesota. Virgil congratulated me on my marriage then wanted to know if you were in over your head and should he run some interference."

"Interference?" Billy said numbly.

Ignoring Billy, Hunter gave Corina a heavyhearted look. "It doesn't matter. She despises me."

"I knew it," Billy said angrily. "Something happened after we left today. Nicole went out alone, obviously distraught. She never goes anywhere without her purse, or the can of mace inside it. What did you do to her?"

The phone rang.

Hunter grabbed for it.

"Wait," John Martin snapped. He quickly activated the speakerphone recorder he'd hooked up. At the second ring, he gave Hunter a nod. "Everybody else listen carefully and be quiet," he ordered.

Hunter's chest tightened when he picked up the receiver.

"Hello, Nico—"

"No, it's Brenda."

Behind Hunter, there was an audible gasp. It took him less than two seconds to grasp Nicole's situation. He turned quickly to face his dumbfounded audience and held up a hand indicating silence.

"Brenda." he said exuberantly. "Where are you?"

There was a click on the phone indicating someone picking up another line.

"I—I'm safe and...fine. Listen, I need a favor from you. I—I've decided to take the kids and go back to New York. I need you to take them to the Catholic Church, just outside of Willow River. Just leave them sitting on the steps, and I'll pick them up shortly."

Hunter had to pause a moment to get control of his breathing. He ignored the horrified stares of the people around him. "Fine!" he snapped, "and good riddance. I'm sick of those brats, and I'm sick of you. I suppose you're going back to your beloved Asha."

"Yes, yes. I've finally found my knight in shining armor."

John Martin held up a hastily written note.

TRY TO BUY SOME TIME

Hunter nodded. "There's just one problem," he said into the phone, keeping his tone even. "They went to the zoo with my sister, and they aren't back yet. Give me your number and I'll call you as soon as they get here. The quicker I'm rid of those two, and you, the better."

Some angry muffled whispers came over the speakerphone. Then Nicole was back on.

"I—I don't know the number here. I'll have to call you. When do you expect them home?"

John Martin held up another sign.

TOMORROW MORNING

Hunter gritted his teeth. He shook his head vehemently.

Billy grabbed the sheriff's notebook and started scribbling.

TWO HOURS. I KNOW WHERE SHE IS

Hunter gave Billy a doubtful frown, but he liked that answer better than John Martin's. He checked the time. It was eight fifteen.

"They'll be back at ten-thirty," he said.

"All right, I'll call back then."

Hunter squeezed the phone with a death grip. He didn't want to break the contact. He just wanted to hear her breathe. He wanted to ask if she was really okay. He wanted to tell her he loved her.

A click followed by a monotone buzz, came over the speakerphone. It took Hunter a few more seconds before he hung up.

He looked at John Martin hopefully.

Martin shook his head. "The number has a block on it."

"I can find her," Billy said confidently.

Hunter turned on him with duel emotions, one of doubt, the other hope. "If you're thinking of using the kids as bait, that's not an option."

Billy shook his head. "No, unless I'm mistaken, she gave a clue."

"I didn't hear any clues in that conversation," Hunter said.

"That's because you didn't spend summers at the lake with Gram, the clue master. Nicole said she found her knight in shining armor—"

"Yeah," Hunter interrupted. "She meant that for Asha."

"No, she meant it for me. When we were kids, Nicole pretended white squirrels turned into knights if you kissed them…like frogs turn into princes."

"Damn," Chuck said. "You're right. I remember that. I dressed up as a white squirrel one Halloween." Chuck received several surprised looks to which he shrugged, smiling sheepishly. "Hell, she had a king-size crush on me."

Hunter let that pass. "So, how is that going to help us find her?"

"Albino squirrels are rare," Corina explained quickly. "Billy actually took a course in school on animal oddities. We both did."

Hunter squeezed his index finger and thumb to the bridge of his nose. "So what you're saying is we have two hours to call every number in the phone book to research which residents have albino squirrels in their back yard?"

"Not hardly," Billy said. "I know of only three around here. One is in the woods behind Carmen's place, one hangs around the park at Denham, eight miles east of here, the third lives in a huge oak tree, behind the old Peterson shack, on Johnson Lake."

"That was sold and torn down last fall," Chuck said.

"Yeah," John agreed. "A doctor from the research center in Duluth bought it along with ten acres surrounding it. He built a six bedroom party house on the land."

John Martin looked as though a light went on in his head. "Shit. He's been in Europe for the last month. He asked me to drive by periodically to check on it. I went past three days ago. I didn't notice anything unusual, but hell, if someone is hiding out, they don't exactly put up signs."

"How far is it?" Hunter asked.

Billy answered. "Five miles by road, three by foot though the woods."

"What about the squirrel by Carmen?" John asked.

"I talked to Carmen this afternoon. She didn't mention anything unusual going on over there," Chuck said. "Besides, there aren't any other homes around her. The park in Denham is in the middle of town. A stranger couldn't get by with anything there."

Hunter was already digging in his pocket for his keys. He looked at Billy with candid respect. "If you're right about this," he said. "I'll kiss your feet."

"I'll be happy just finding Nicole," Billy said. "But as long as you're offering something, you can name your firstborn after me."

His firstborn? A twinge of conscience stabbed Hunter.

Corina misinterpreted the look Hunter gave her.

"Don't worry, I'll stay with Shanna and Kyle," she said. "You do what you have to do and don't worry about us. They were both so exhausted they fell asleep on Nicole's bed with that monster cat. I'll go up and move them to their own room."

"Thanks," Hunter said softly. "I appreciate it."

Corina gave him a tearful hug. "What are sisters for? Just find Nicole and bring her back safely."

"We have two hours," John Martin said. "We need a plan before we go rushing off."

The four of them quickly mapped out a strategy that included the possibility of Asha having a weapon. The house in question was thirty yards from the main road. If there was a back door, the sheriff knew how to jimmy the lock. Hunter got a skeptical frown when he said he could do it too. If they were able to see in a window, they'd first assess Nicole's proximity to Asha and determine if Asha had a weapon. They worked up a viable plan for each possibility.

Neither Hunter nor Billy was receptive to anything that included waiting. Both vehemently shot down the sheriff when he suggested they wait for more law enforcement.

The sheriff and Chuck had already walked out the door when Corina rushed into the kitchen, her face pale and anxious.

"Shanna and Kyle are gone. I can't find them upstairs anywhere."

Hunter reacted with disbelief. "What do you mean *gone?*"

Corina gave him a hapless look. "I looked in all the bedrooms. I can't find them, and the phone is off the hook in Nicole's room."

Hunter closed his eyes. His knees went weak and his stomach lurched. "My God," he whispered. "That's the click we heard. Shanna must have answered the phone. She was listening in when I told Nicole I was sick of them and would be glad to be free of them. She thinks I'm sending them back to Asha."

Hunter dropped to a chair, breathing deeply, remembering his exact words, and trying to quell the nausea churning in his stomach.

Billy put a hand on Hunter's shoulder. "Take it easy, Hunter. We'll find them. They couldn't have gone very far. Maybe they're in the attic. That's where Nicole and I used to hide out."

"They trusted me," Hunter said raggedly.

"You didn't betray their trust," Corina said. "They'll forgive you. Go find Nicole. I'll find Shanna and Kyle."

"Cory's right." Billy said, "Nicole's in danger, the kids aren't."

Hunter stood up, nodding. "We do need to go. Please find them," he said to Corina. "I love those kids more than life." He looked at Corina through moist eyes. "Shanna is my daughter," he said. "Nicole found out before I could tell her. That's why she left all upset today. This whole thing is my fault."

Billy grabbed Hunter firmly, but gently, by the back of the neck. "We'll worry about that later. I'll beat the crap out of you if it'll make you feel better. Right now, get your ass in the car." He drew Hunter with him out to his convertible, having obviously decided his brother-in-law was in no shape to drive. The Martin brothers were already in the squad car when Billy asked if Chuck would stay and help Corina look for Shanna and Kyle.

* * * *

Nicole sat in a large, overstuffed chair that left no room on either side of her in case Asha suddenly got the inclination to get cozy. She eyed him warily. He sat at the table where the bottle of Scotch had lost another inch since the phone call a half hour ago. Until ten-thirty came around, she had one fear and one hope. The fear was that Asha would get drunk enough to forget she was supposed to be HIV positive; the hope was he'd get drunk enough to pass out, allowing her to escape. Though he'd made no further threats since the writing incident, she found it impossible to forget the cleaver still stuck in the table.

Recalling her conversation with Hunter, she thought escape a better possibility than a rescue. Hunter's quick mind truly amazed her. He didn't even flinch when she told him she was Brenda. His harsh words had been so convincing she'd cringed in spite of knowing the performance was for Asha's sake. He was so convincing, in fact, that she didn't know if telling her the kids were still at the zoo was part of the act or if they truly hadn't returned yet.

If Billy wasn't there, her albino squirrel clue was for naught. As smart as Hunter was, he couldn't know about her childhood fantasy. He wouldn't catch on that it was a clue; therefore not relaying it to Billy; unless, of course, the conversation was recorded, which she doubted. That would take action from John Martin, and time. God only knows how long Hunter waited before he thought of her as missing. He probably expected her to be off sulking somewhere. Throw into the mix, Hunter's cynical view of small town law enforcement; he may not even have called the sheriff. The possibility of rescue before she had to make the ten-thirty call didn't look good.

She was certain Hunter wouldn't even consider using the kids for bait. To top it all off, she didn't even know how Asha planned to pick them up, so she was wasting time even thinking about it. Wasting time. She marveled at the irony of her own thoughts. What else did she have to do, other than watch Asha stare at her, while he continued drinking.

The man had eyes that could inhibit the devil, and those eyes were focused on her, studying her. Other then being unfocused from alcohol, she didn't like the intensity of his gaze. Maybe it would be best to engage him in conversation after all. Maybe she could get information at the same time.

"Why did you take the suitcase from Hunter's car?" she asked.

"Because I knew it was yours," he answered matter-of-factly.

"But how did you know it was in Hunter's trunk?"

Asha smiled. "He had it with him at the airport, and he didn't take it in the house with the other luggage."

Nicole's heart slammed into her chest. "You were following him even then?"

"Following him, shit, I was outside that house before

he got there. He left the fucking directions on his kitchen table."

Asha laughed at his own ingenuity. "Hell, I came on the same plane as they did. The dumb bastard didn't have a clue; it was those kids I had to watch out for. This whole thing has been a piece of cake. These local assholes are so fucking stupid they wouldn't know a bombshell if it dropped in their lap."

Anger flashed in Nicole's brain. She dragged a deep breath into her lungs and let it out slowly. Challenging him would only call his attention to her, serving no purpose. Besides, he was back to staring at her with those soul-piercing eyes. His smile suddenly turned upside down.

"There's something different about you," he said.

Nicole held her breath before replying, "What…what do you mean…different?"

"I'm not sure…your attitude maybe." He got up and walked toward her. He bent down and pinched her jaw in his hand. When she tried to draw back, he jerked her face toward him, squeezing her flesh and studying her eyes.

"Where are your contact lenses?" he asked.

Nicole tried to pull away, but he held her firm, squeezing hard enough to draw tears from her eyes. Fear closed her throat. She could barely breathe, much less talk.

"I—I lost one yesterday," she managed to say through clenched teeth.

He grabbed her from the chair and body slammed her against the wall, six feet away. She hit the wall with breath stealing force and slid to the floor, gasping for air. He towered over her, clenching his fist.

"Brenda had twenty-twenty vision," he said in an outrage. "She didn't wear contacts. Who the fuck are you, bitch, one of those look-alike undercover cops?"

Before she could answer, he went to the table and grabbed his knapsack, zipped it open, and pulled out a stub-nosed pistol. He loomed over her with the barrel pointed straight at her head.

Nicole couldn't talk. She couldn't think. She couldn't even scream. She had survived a triple rape, tied and gagged, but had never known fear like she did at this moment, staring into the small black hole in the front of his gun.

He kicked her in the leg. "Talk! And if I even suspect you of lying...let's just say it'll be the last time you dupe me. Now who are you? A cop?"

Nicole somehow managed to find her voice. "No. I'm Nicole Anderson, Brenda's sister."

He kicked her in the thigh. "Brenda didn't have a sister!"

Nicole grimaced with pain. "Half-sister...my father had an affair with her mother." The lie was far more believable than the truth.

He digested that a moment, then reached down, grasped her wrist, and picked her up from the floor. From there, he flung her back in the chair. He poured himself a drink and took a swallow. The point of the gun never wavered from her head.

"Your friend, Hunter, didn't hesitate when you told him you were Brenda. Why?"

"I—we—"

He reached forward and slapped her hard across the face. "Stop trying to think up lies. From now on, when I ask you a question, I want an answer immediately. Understand?"

Nicole nodded. She put a hand up to rub her stinging face. Tears burned in her eyes.

"Now, I'll ask one more time. Why didn't he hesitate when you told him you were Brenda?"

Nicole saw his hand flinch and answered quickly. "I can only guess he assumed you had me, and since I look like Brenda, he probably figured that you believed I was her." She stumbled over the words so fast she wasn't even sure if she made sense.

He seemed to accept her answer.

"Why the little charade?"

Again, she looked at his hand. He was already raising it. "Because, we were afraid for the kids, afraid you'd hurt them."

"So did they really go to the zoo?"

"Yes."

"Who took them?"

"My brother and his wife."

"What kind of car did he drive?"

"A red convertible."

He stared at her face, obviously, digesting whether or not she was telling the truth. Nicole didn't have time to think about her answers. So far, she hadn't told him anything he could use. At least, she hoped she hadn't.

After a moment, he smiled. That really evil, ugly smile she'd come to fear.

"Well, I guess then we'll just have to have a little change of plans, won't we? Get up."

Nicole pulled her throbbing lower lip into her mouth. She tasted blood. "What are you going to do?" she asked as she stood up. Her sore leg nearly buckled under her, but she managed to maintain her balance.

He smiled. "We're going to take a little drive, park on the road by your house, and wait for your brother to come home from the zoo. I always wanted a red convertible."

Anger, and panic, for Billy and Corina, suddenly overrode Nicole's fear. She had no idea if they really were back from the zoo or not. Charging past the gun, she clawed at his face. He sidestepped her attack, grabbed her arm and yanked it behind her back. She couldn't move without excruciating pain.

Broken sobs tore from her throat. "Don't hurt them…please. I'll do anything you ask. Just don't hurt them."

He chuckled. He was so close she could smell the Scotch on his breath. She tasted bile in her throat.

"Anything?" he said, sticking his tongue in her ear.

Nausea vaulted from her stomach. She swallowed hard. "Yes."

He rubbed the gun along her cheek. "I should have known all along you weren't Brenda. She was much thinner, too thin—skinny actually—and she walked around looking like a paste-white zombie all the time."

Thanks to you, Nicole thought. She didn't know, until this day, just how intense hatred could be. She wept silently, praying. Praying that Hunter had made up the story about Billy and Corina returning at ten-thirty.

The sound of Asha dropping his gun on the table sliced into her thoughts.

"This is going to be a test, of your little 'I'll do anything' promise," he said. With her arm still twisted behind her back, he brought his free hand up and shoved it inside her blouse.

Nicole bit down on her bleeding lip and froze. It was nine-thirty already. She would endure anything to buy time for Billy and Corina.

Unfortunately, he read her mind. He gave her breast a cruel squeeze and withdrew his hand. He picked up his gun, released her arm, and shoved her toward a door in the kitchen.

"Move. There'll be time for dick-licking later."

Tears trailed down Nicole's face. She didn't know how she would manage it but she knew she would die before she let him hurt any of her loved ones. A stark realization suddenly hit her. She understood why Brenda took her own life.

Asha opened the door that led to the garage and gripped her by the back of the neck to push her through it toward white ford Aspire parked inside. He hit a button with the side of his gun hand. The big double door started to grind its way up.

Before Asha could open the door on the passenger side of the car, Hunter appeared in the still-opening door. Asha saw him at the same time Nicole did. He swung the gun around, aimed at Hunter, and fired.

Nicole screamed even before the gun blast cracked in her ear. The spot where Hunter had stood a split second earlier was vacant. She had no idea if he'd been hit. Panic rose in her chest in the form of a gut, clenching vise. She was breathing so hard and loud she couldn't hear herself think. She could only react.

Asha's gun was still aimed at the place he'd seen Hunter. Nicole only half-faced Asha since he'd pushed her aside to open the car door. Somehow, somewhere, deep down in her memory, a Chuck Norris defense video flashed before her eyes. Before she could think about what she was doing, she brought her hand up and slammed the heel of it under Asha's nose. He stumbled backwards, screaming in pain, his hands on his blood-spurting nose.

The next thing she knew, Hunter was on top of Asha, pinning him to the cement floor, Asha's gun was in Sheriff Martin's hand, and Billy was pulling her into his arms and out of harm's way.

She didn't realize she was fighting Billy's grip and sobbing Hunter's name until Hunter stood up and came toward her. Asha was writhing on the floor. Blood poured freely from his nose, and he was clutching his ribs and stomach where Hunter's fists had made brutal contact.

He was still screaming profanities at Nicole, when Sheriff Martin yanked his wrists around and snapped handcuffs on them.

Billy released her, and she literally flew into Hunter's embrace. He was touching her hair and her back, saying words she couldn't hear over her sobs. Finally exhausted, she clung to him, weak and lightheaded from crying.

Hunter reached in his pocket, pulled out his cell phone, and tossed it to Billy. "Call the house and see if they found the kids."

Nicole fainted in Hunter's arms.

Chapter Twenty-One

Hunter sat on the step cradling Nicole's limp body. Billy ran into the house, coming back seconds later with a cold washcloth. Nicole moaned when Hunter pressed the cool compress to her face. The sight of the bruise on her cheek tightened his chest. Asha could count his blessing that he was being led away still walking.

"Dial," he said to Billy.

Billy quickly punched in the numbers to Nicole's house. He waited with the phone to his ear, listening. He looked down at Hunter, swallowing hard.

"There's no answer."

Sheriff Martin, having secured Asha in the back of the squad car, walked up behind Billy. "Want me to follow you home and help look?"

Hunter answered. "First, get that bastard locked up. Then call us."

Nicole opened her eyes.

John Martin squatted in front of her. "You okay, honey?"

She nodded. "What happened?"

Hunter stood up with her in his arms. "We'll tell you on the way home. Come on, Billy."

Billy jumped to open the door of the convertible,

allowing Hunter to sit in the front seat with Nicole on his lap. Dashing around to the driver's side Billy, started the engine, shifted into gear, and pressed the gas pedal to the floor. The car spun forward, fishtailing, spewing two streaks of gravel behind it.

Nicole was sickened to learn that Shanna had heard the conversation between her and Hunter. At the same time, she agreed with Billy that Hunter was not at fault. He couldn't have known Shanna was listening in. The important thing now was to find them and explain.

All the lights were on in the house when Billy pulled into his usual spot in the garage. Nicole raced inside with Hunter and Billy close at her heels.

No one answered Nicole's call.

"The patio door to the deck is open," Nicole said, hurrying toward the living room. Outside on the deck she called again.

Hunter pointed to the woods. "I see a flashlight on the trail to Chuck's cabin."

All three ran down the steps and toward the path. They met Corina coming out of the woods, carrying Kyle's white tiger. She was frantic.

When she saw Billy, she threw herself into his arms crying. "We can't find them."

The white tiger glowed like a beacon in the fast approaching darkness.

"Where did you get that?" Nicole asked.

Corina answered through broken sobs. "It's Kyle's. We bought it for him at the zoo. Chuck found it on the path in the woods. He said the kids knew it led to his house."

"Jesus." Hunter said running a hand through his hair. "They're in the woods. Where's Chuck?"

"He took a flashlight and followed the path," Corina said. "He said it was only a mile and still light when they left. He thought there was a chance they might have made it. Or he was hoping to find them along the way."

"Did you check the attic?" Billy asked.

"Corina nodded. "Yes, but there's a lot of stuff up there and we couldn't find all the lights. We called, but if they were afraid to come out...they could be hiding anywhere. Then we noticed the patio door open."

"I'll double check inside," Billy said quickly. "There isn't a hiding spot in that house I haven't used." He was already taking the steps three at a time.

Nicole tried desperately to stay calm. "Did you check with Berta and Hank?"

Again, Corina nodded. "Berta is a basket case. Hank is searching the garden area and woods in front of the house. "But it's getting dark..."

"We'll find them," Hunter said. "Go in the house and stay by the phone in case Chuck calls from his house. Nicole and I will keep looking out here."

Halfway up the steps Corina stopped. "Mr. Komodo is gone," she said. "He was there earlier when I first noticed the kids missing, then he disappeared too."

Nicole and Hunter were left standing alone in the dark. Hunter drew her into his arms. "How are you holding up, honey? You've been though hell today already, and I'd send you in the house, too, but I don't know my way around out here."

She rested her head on his shoulder, fighting tears. "I need to be out here with you. We've got to find them, Hunter."

"Yeah, let's keep looking. We can talk later." Hunter took her hand and drew her toward the lake, away from the path to Chuck's place. "Where do the woods go over this way?"

"Just around the lake, but there's too much brush and no path."

"Do you know how to drive Chuck's boat?" Hunter asked, looking at the dock where the red Lund was bobbing in the waves, tied up. "We could follow the shoreline."

Nicole nodded. "Yes, I know how to run it. We need a

flashlight, but I think he keeps one in the boat."

Together they hurried to the end of the dock. Nicole drew the boat against the protective buoys, preparing to step inside when Hunter gripped her arm.

"Shhh, listen," he whispered. "What's that humming sound?"

Nicole turned her ear toward the barely audible drone. Her heart leaped. "That's Mr. Komodo purring. It's coming from the boat."

While Hunter held the rocking boat steady, Nicole scrambled into it. She quickly groped under the console where she knew Chuck kept his flashlight. Her hands were shaking when she switched it on and aimed it toward the back of the boat. The canvas, protecting Chuck's fishing gear from the weather, was moving. Mr. Komodo poked his head out from underneath, yawning sleepily.

The sixteen-foot, fishing boat dipped only slightly when Hunter leaped into it.

They found Kyle sleeping, nestled on a bed of life jackets with Shanna curled protectively around him. Hunter and Nicole passed a look of unmitigated relief between them.

Emotion closing Nicole's throat, she sank to the bottom of the boat beside them, tears streaming down her face. She touched each one lovingly assuring herself they were really there.

Hunter dropped to his knees, knowing for certain that all three of them had become a part of his life that was as necessary as the air he breathed. Right now, he was breathing a lot of it.

He had to squeeze his way between the seats to get to Nicole. When he reached for her, she came into his arms so eagerly it stole his breath away. He kissed her damp cheeks, tasting the salt of her tears.

"I love you, Nicole Anderson," he said, his voice gruff with emotion. "I love you, and I love these kids more than I can even begin to tell you."

"We've only known each other a short time. How can you be so sure?"

Hunter's arms tightened around her and he simply said, "I'm sure."

"But—"

"My parents claim they loved each other from the moment they met. It made a good story, but I never believed that was possible until you turned around and looked at me in your studio with the lamp in your hand."

Nicole looked up at him, smiling. "I'm not sure I fell in love with you at that same moment, but I do know, I experienced feelings I'd never had before. After all the years I spent avoiding the touch of any man, I had an instant desire to reach up and push that curl from your forehead." She put her hand up to his face and touched the curl. "I have known for some time now that I loved you, but since I knew you would be leaving..."

Hunter grabbed her hand, kissed her fingers, and smiled. "I'm not leaving, but we'll talk about that later. Let's get our kids inside before these mosquitoes chew us all up. I have some major explaining to do to Shanna and Kyle."

"Did Shanna hear you call me, Brenda?" Nicole whispered.

"Thank God, no. I heard the click just after that."

"Are you sure? I heard the click too, but I can't remember exactly when."

"It's on tape. But yes, I'm sure."

"You take your daughter," Nicole said. "I'll carry Kyle."

Her face was so close to his, Hunter could see the moisture shining in her eyes. "I'm sorry, I didn't tell you," he whispered. "But I'm not sorry she's my daughter."

Nicole smiled through her tears. "I'm not either."

* * * *

Fortunately, Shanna was easily convinced when they

told her the truth about the phone conversation. Tears streaked down her small cheeks when she hugged both Nicole and Hunter, expressing her love for them. They were all thankful she'd had the foresight not to tell Kyle why she was whisking him out of the house. She said she didn't want him to be scared.

Shanna admitted they had started to go to Chuck's house, but got scared in the woods and turned back, deciding, instead, to wait in his boat. Mr. Komodo must have followed them because he crawled into the boat later.

Chuck came back to the house in time to hear her story. Everyone agreed when Chuck, praised Shanna for her courage in fleeing what she believed to be a dangerous situation, and her insightfulness in protecting Kyle. Chuck was especially touched that she was coming to him for protection.

After tucking Shanna into bed beside her sleeping brother, Nicole and Hunter walked down the stairs, arm in arm. They would wait to tell Shanna that Hunter was her father. She'd had enough trauma for one night.

Chuck went home after Sheriff Martin called to tell them Asha Jameel was safely behind bars in the jail after his broken nose and ribs were treated.

Billy and Corina waited in the kitchen with a bottle of wine to celebrate. Nicole and Hunter took seats at the counter while Billy filled three glasses with wine and one with sparkling water for Corina.

Billy held up his glass. "Here's to my brave and wonderful sister."

Hunter looked at Nicole with admiration. "How did you know that little trick with the heel of the hand to the nose?"

Billy laughed. "Yeah, I was watching through the window. He went down like a deflated balloon. I think I heard his nose crack from outside. Where did you pick that up? That's not one you learned from me—or practiced on me, thank goodness."

Nicole shrugged. "I bought a Chuck Norris, self defense tape at a yard sale. Actually, I can't even believe I had the nerve to do it."

"Oh, you did it all right," Hunter said, grinning. "And you probably saved my life in the bargain."

"Billy told me Hunter would have gone in and taken a bullet to rescue you," Corina said.

Billy shook his head. "I tried to stop him from charging in like an angry bull but, hell, he's bigger than I am. I couldn't hold him back, at least not without making a lot of noise."

Nicole looked at Hunter and shuddered. "I thought for a moment he did shoot you, and he was going to fire again. I know that was the only reason I remembered that tape. I had to do something to stop him."

Hunter put an arm around her shoulders, pulling her close. "Thank God, Billy recognized that thing about the white squirrel. We never would have found you otherwise."

Billy lifted his glass to empty it. "Actually, thanks go to Gram on that score. Spending summers with her was like living a real live clue game."

At that, Nicole laughed. "Billy's right, she—" Nicole's face suddenly went pale. "Oh my Lord, I forgot about the key Gram gave me—the key to the heart. What happened to it?"

Hunter reached into his pocket and pulled out a chain. "You mean this?" he asked, dangling it from his fingers.

Nicole's hand shook as she reached for the chain. "I know where the heart is," she whispered."

"The heart?" Billy said. "What heart?"

"Where Daddy's secrets are hidden. It's in the dining room." Nicole stood up and headed for the dining room, explaining as she went. The other three fell in close behind her.

"I don't understand," Corina said.

Nicole was already feeling the edges of the marble mantle, talking over her shoulder. "Don't feel too left out,

Corina. I'm not sure what I'm looking for either. Gram was being too evasive."

"Oh, now that's hard to believe," Billy cut in sardonically. "Not our, Gram."

Nicole smiled. "Billy, they don't know Gram like we do."

"I'm beginning to," Hunter said chuckling.

Nicole stepped back. "I'm not finding any opening, but I'm sure it's here. She said it's in a marble tomb between Time and Love."

"Time and Love?" Corina asked.

Billy pointed to the white statues flanking the mantle. "Those two infant cupids are called amorini. They're sixteenth century Italian replicas. They represent Time and Love. Gramps brought them from Italy himself."

Hunter looked at the Monet painting, "Where flames burn and flowers bloom. A gift of love in another time. Nicole mentioned the Monet was a wedding gift from your grandfather."

Nicole glanced at Hunter in wonder. His memory never ceased to amaze her.

"All the clues fit," she said emphatically. "The marble tomb has to be the mantle. It's deep enough, but how can it open, the statues are mounted on top of it." She was back examining seams this time, with Billy's assistance.

"Maybe they lift off," Hunter suggested.

Billy moved his head slowly from side to side. "They're solid plaster or whatever they're made out of. They must weight sixty pounds apiece. I can't imagine anyone designing a hiding spot that would require that kind of work to get at it." Still, he attempted to lift one off. It wouldn't budge.

Hunter put his hands on the other one. "What if you try to slide them?"

"You can't," Nicole said. "They're mounted from the back—"

Nicole gasped.

The statue in Hunter's grasp moved. A grating sound came from beneath it.

"It's turning," Nicole whispered.

"I think it's mounted on hinges," Hunter said.

Billy was already turning the one on the other side. "This one's giving too," he said excitedly.

Nicole and Corina stared in wide-eyed awe as both statues swung free of the mantle. Almost as one, Hunter and Billy put their hands on the heavy marble mantle and lifted. It opened easily on leveraged hinges.

Nicole raced between them. The fireplace was as high as her chin, and she had to stand on tiptoes to see inside the exposed cavity.

"There's a strongbox."

Hunter lifted it out. About a foot wide and eighteen inches long, the box was heavy enough to be fireproof.

"Where do you want it?" he asked.

"Let's take it to the kitchen, on the counter."

"This is like something out of a gothic novel," Corina murmured, following the others to the kitchen.

Billy laughed.

Hunter snorted. "Try walking into this place for the first time in the middle of the night when there's a lightning storm outside and no electricity."

"I don't remember it being that bad," Nicole said.

Hunter set the box on the counter. "Yeah, well, you didn't see yourself walking around in those spooky clothes, carrying a lantern in front of you. Then that monster cat nearly scared the be-Jesus out of me."

Nicole fit the key in the lock with shaking fingers. It gave easily. She took a deep breath and lifted the lid. Inside were several loose papers she took out and handed to Billy. The cardboard box, underneath the papers, was what held her interest. With trembling hands, she lifted out an old valentine heart, the kind that probably held candy at one time.

She laid her hands, almost reverently, on top of it and

hesitated.

Hunter smiled encouragingly. "Go ahead, honey, open it."

She lifted the heart shaped cover and set it aside. There were some pictures, letters, and a small notebook. She reached past the letters for the pictures.

Her heart was beating so loud and so hard, she felt dizzy. "Hunter," she whispered. "These are the same baby pictures that were in Brenda's photo album. I thought they were two different poses of Brenda." She handed the picture to Hunter. "Those were cut apart. Here, the babies are lying side by side."

Hunter stared at the photo. "They look like identical twins."

"What does it mean?" Billy asked.

Hunter handed the photo to Billy, took Nicole in his arms, and placed a kiss on her temple.

"It means," Hunter said. "Nicole and Brenda were identical twins. The Caseys kept Brenda; Nicole went to your parents."

"But who was the mother?" Billy asked. The last word faded off when realization hit him. He looked from the picture to Nicole. "Oh, my God."

With a hand on either side of her face, Hunter lifted Nicole's head to look in her eyes, forcing her to look in his. "It doesn't matter, sweetheart. You are who you are. It doesn't change what your mother was to you."

"But, what about me?" Billy said woodenly.

Nicole answered him through her tears. "Mother had an operation to get pregnant with you. Obviously, she had it after I was born. You're my half brother."

Billy just stared at her, saying nothing, until Corina put an arm around him.

"Honey, are you okay?" Corina asked.

Billy took a deep breath. He shook his head as though trying to clear his mind.

"Yeah, yeah, I'm—fine." Then he looked at Hunter.

"Maybe we should start at the beginning. I seem to be missing some pieces here."

Nicole nodded to Hunter. "You tell it," she said wearily, picking through the other items in the box.

"It seems," Hunter said, looking at Billy, "that both your mother, before her surgery, and Jonathon Casey were sterile. Jonathon had enough medical skills to artificially inseminate Yvonne with your father's sperm. Their plan was to do it twice, with the first baby going to your parents, and the second one to the Caseys. Sadly, the first baby, also named Brenda, died. The second pregnancy resulted in twins—Brenda and Nicole."

Billy sagged into a chair, staring at Nicole. "Jesus, they split you up, so they could each have a baby."

Corina held a hand over her rounded midsection. "I can't even imagine doing that. That must have been horribly traumatic for both couples."

"Without a doubt," Hunter said softly. "To make matters worse, what they did was illegal. They had to cover their tracks. They used the birth certificate from the first Brenda, making her appear a year older than she really was. For Nicole, and I'm guessing here, they created a false birth certificate, claiming she was born in Minnesota. I wouldn't be surprised to find she had a real one issued in New York."

"It's right here," Nicole replied, holding up a piece of paper.

"But how did they manage that in the hospital?" Billy asked.

Hunter explained. "Jonathon delivered the babies at home."

Nicole looked up from the notebook she was reading. "It's all spelled out in here," she said. "They made a pact never to talk about it and never to bring us together. It seems the only contact they had was to send pictures periodically. They're all right here, except for one or two that made it into our family album, easily passed off as me." She dropped the pictures on the counter for the others to see.

Billy picked the photos up and started flipping through them. "This is uncanny," he said, looking up at Nicole. "Except for the hairstyle, they all look exactly like you."

Nicole sighed. "Now you know how I felt when I discovered some of the photos in our family album were actually of Brenda. I didn't see any when she was an adult so I didn't realize the full extent of our likeness. Actually, Kyle noticed it first."

"Yeah," Hunter said. "The first time Kyle saw you he thought you were his mother. I recognized the resemblance, but Brenda was blonde, and she wore her hair short and curly. I hadn't seen her for—" he looked at Nicole apologetically, "—seven years."

Corina looked from the pictures to Nicole. "I've heard stories about identical twins having simultaneous thoughts and feelings. Did you ever experience anything like that?"

"How would I even know?" Nicole said. "It probably doesn't apply when you're separated at birth."

Corina nodded. "That could be true, but remember that girl in class, Billy, the one who fainted right out of her desk for no reason at all. It turned out her twin sister had a car accident two hundred miles away at the exact moment."

Nicole's gaze shot toward Hunter, who in turn was staring at her.

"What?" Billy asked, noticing their alarm.

"Nicole fainted the same day Brenda died," Hunter said.

Nicole shook her head in disbelief. "But I fainted at three o'clock, didn't you say Brenda died at four?"

"Yes," Hunter said slowly. "But...that was Eastern Standard Time."

Billy drew in a soft whistle. "Well, I'll be damned."

Corina released a big sigh. "I guess that just about clears up everything."

"Not quite," Hunter said, looking at Nicole. "Does that

notebook explain who Megan was or why your father was sending Yvonne a thousand dollars a month?"

Billy's wide gaze darted to Nicole. "What thousand dollars a month?"

"Who's Megan?" Corina asked.

Nicole had suddenly become very still. All three were staring at her, waiting. She drew a ragged breath then looked at Billy. "Our father was sending Yvonne the money for Megan's care." Her eyes, filled with tears, turned to Hunter. "According to Brenda's letter, Megan was my daughter."

"They gave your baby to the Caseys?" Billy cried, shaking his head. "I thought they were from the adoption agency."

Nicole stared at her brother. "What are you talking about, Billy?"

"I knew your baby didn't die," he whispered. "They thought I was in bed, but I could hear you screaming and crying, so I sneaked out of my room and sat at the end of the balcony to watch and wait. I heard a baby cry then it got very quiet. I was so scared; I thought you'd died. Then the doctor came out of your room carrying the baby. He handed it to a woman with long red hair. She was crying, so I thought the baby was dead. Only, I had a clear frontal view of the woman when she walked down the stairs. The baby's arms were flailing above the blanket."

"You knew all this time?" Nicole said with a catch in her throat.

Billy nodded. "Yes." He looked up at her. "I suppose I should have told you, but I was only nine years old, Nicole. Nobody ever talked to me. I imagine, because, they didn't know I'd seen the baby. I'm sorry, but I really didn't think you wanted to know."

Nicole reached out and took his hand. "What a terrible burden for you to have carried all these years. Don't be sorry. In truth, I was far too young and unstable to deal with a baby, and though it was short, Megan had a good life. She died when she was five years old in a fire with Yvonne."

"My God," Nicole added. "Yvonne was my mother, Megan's grandmother."

Billy reached across the counter and gave Nicole's hand a squeeze. "Yvonne was the redheaded lady."

"And Jonathan was the doctor," Nicole supplied.

Billy gave a short laugh. "You want to hear something funny? That was the reason I never wanted Gram reading my palm. I was afraid of what she'd see." Billy blew out a huff of air. "She knew everything all along, didn't she?"

Nicole smiled. "Yes, she knew. And if I think back on all the things she's said over the years, she probably gave lots of clues."

Billy shook his head. "Gram—the clue master, we called her. Why did I ever think she could actually see things?"

"Because maybe she can," Hunter said.

Billy snorted.

Hunter gave Billy an odd look. "She told you this afternoon where Nicole was."

Billy was thoughtful for a moment. "She told me to look for snow in green trees." His eyes suddenly became very wide. "The white squirrel. Damn, that woman is scary."

* * * *

After Billy and Corina had gone to bed, Nicole and Hunter walked arm in arm up the stairs to her bedroom.

As soon as they closed the door, Nicole turned to Hunter. "What exactly did you mean tonight, when you said you weren't leaving?"

Hunter took her hands, drew her to the bed, sat her on it, and knelt on one knee in front of her. "It means, sweetheart, that I've made steps to extend my business to Minnesota. I know this is somewhat sudden, but I have feelings for you and those kids that I never knew existed. I love you, and I love them. I want to legally claim Shanna and start proceedings to adopt Kyle. I want us to be a family. All you have to do is say you'll marry me, and we can make this fairy tale come true together."

Nicole blinked rapidly at the tears stinging her eyes. She threw her arms around Hunter. "It's been a long time since I believed in kings and queens and knights on white stallions rescuing ladies in distress. However, you coming here, bringing Shanna and Kyle, have made every dream I've ever had come true. Since I already know I'll love you for the rest of my natural life, yes, I'll marry you, Sir Hunter Orion Douglas."

Read on for a preview of Jannifer Hoffman's *Secret Sacrifices*
Coming November 2008 to Resplendence Publishing

Chapter One

Keeping a wary eye on her rear view mirror, Jamie eased off the accelerator, hoping the flashing red lights would pass her. The merciless patrol car stuck to her bumper like a pain-in-the butt hemorrhoid. When the siren howled, she muttered a curse and pulled over. Jamie's fingers did an impatient tap dance on the steering wheel as the officer got out of his car and ambled toward her, his no-nonsense expression anything but cozy. When she pushed the lever to slide her window open, the sweet scent of fresh mown hay awakened her senses. At any other time, she'd have paused to take pleasure in the earthy country smell.

"Good afternoon, ma'am, I'm Officer Gentry." His voice wasn't any too cozy either as he eyed her bright pink BMW like a pretty bug that needed squashing. "Do you know how fast you were going, young lady?"

"Yeah. A hundred and ten. Just give me my ticket and let me be on my way."

Officer Gentry's bushy brows rose. "Would you remove your sunglasses, please?"

She glared at his reflective glasses. "I will, if you will."

His brows went up another notch. "Fair enough." He took off his glasses and tucked them into his breast pocket.

His compliance surprised her, but didn't lighten her sour mood. She took off her Stussys and flipped them onto the padded dash.

The officer leaned down to allow his gaze to sweep the inside of her car, from the suitcase in the back seat, to the plastic covered medieval costume hanging over the far window, to the crutches and oversized purse laying on the seat beside her.

With a quick glance at her bandaged left knee, he straightened back up. "Actually, you were only going ninety-five."

"Whatever. The sooner you write my ticket, the sooner you'll be rid of me."

He gave her a curious frown. "Lady, if you have an ax to grind, the Wisconsin Interstate is not the place to do it."

Jamie looked away and stared through the windshield into the low hanging August sun. At the most, it had forty-five minutes of life remaining, and she was already two hours late. This stop was just another bad card in the miserable deck of her life.

"May I see your license, please?"

Jamie reached into her purse, dug out her license, and handed it to him.

Officer Gentry grunted, took a few steps toward his patrol car, stopped, and came back. For an uncomfortable moment, he studied her face and short-cropped, blonde curls. Then he looked straight into her amber eyes.

"You're Jamie LeCorre, the NASCAR driver."

"And I suppose you're a dedicated fan," Jamie shot back.

Gentry glanced at her bandaged knee. "As a matter of fact, I am. I happen to be one of the few people who think you got a bum rap when given the blame for that pileup in Indianapolis. I've watched you drive for the last eighteen months—you've placed in the top ten in all but thirteen races. No way you'd make a mistake like that in the last lap. I, for one, believe you would have won that race."

Jamie looked at Gentry with an appreciative shrug. She was impressed he knew her statistics. "Thanks for the vote, but as you said, you're in the minority. Unless I can prove it wasn't my fault, the association will expect an apology." Jamie stared back into the sun. Her hands gripped the steering wheel, her jaw clenching. "They're not going to get it."

Gentry grinned. "Good for you. Hang tough. Tell those good old boys to stuff it."

That forced a laugh from Jamie. "I guess I could use a few more fans like you. Sorry for coming off like such a smart ass."

Gentry handed back her license. "No problem. It sounds to me like you're into a little male-bashing right now, and maybe you're entitled, but try to keep your aggressions on the speedways and off the freeways. Trust me—Wisconsin is not the state you want to be caught speeding in."

Jamie tucked her license away, giving him a genuine smile. "Thanks for the warning. I guess I'd better hold it down for another sixty miles, until I get to the Minnesota border."

Gentry's grin broadened into a belly laugh. "Heck no, don't be giving them any money. Where you headed anyway?"

"Sunset Bay, a small town in rural Minnesota. I'm singing in a wedding for my college roommate. The ceremony is tomorrow, and I was supposed to be there for a five o'clock rehearsal."

Gentry glanced at his watch. "It's past seven. I'd say you're going to be a little late. Pretty tough to make up that kind of time by speeding."

"That's not why I was—" She really didn't want to admit that she was speeding because she was bitter at the world. "I called her earlier, and I already have my costume, so I didn't need to be there."

"Costume? Sounds like an interesting wedding."

Jamie laughed. "Very interesting. The whole wedding party, and most of the guests, will be wearing Renaissance attire. The bride is a costume designer."

Gentry whistled through his teeth. "Sounds like men in tights. Her future hubby must be one brave man."

"I haven't met him yet, but according to her, he's a regular knight in shining armor, so he should feel right at home in tights."

Laughing heartily, Gentry gave her a two-finger salute. "You take care now and keep your wings tucked in." For a brief moment, he gave her a hesitant look. "Sorry about your brother," he said. "I was one of T-Roy's fans too."

For three miles, Jamie managed to concentrate on the rolling green hills dotted with dairy cows, and avoid thinking about T-Roy. A year and a half and the memories still hurt. T-Roy had been the light of her existence, her beacon. One slip, one mistake, and his life snuffed out forever.

She was left with an abrasive father who'd virtually ignored her from the time she was dumped on his doorstep after her mother's death.

It wasn't Jamie's fault Katherine deserted Buster LeCorre and four-year-old T-Roy, without telling Buster she was pregnant. At five years old, Jamie not only had to deal with her mother's death but with a father who flew into a rage anytime he heard Katherine's name.

Jamie recalled vividly the day Buster came home with the results of the paternity tests he had done on both her and T-Roy. They must have proven she was his daughter because, though he swore so loud the windows rattled, he kept her with him. Unfortunately, all his love and dreams were reserved for T-Roy, leaving Jamie to feel like excess baggage. If T-Roy had not taken her under his wing, loving her and caring for her, protecting her from her father's lack of sensitivity, she didn't know how she would have survived.

The two of them grew up in the NASCAR pits where their father graduated to crew chief. It was a dream come true for Buster LeCorre when T-Roy joined the racing crew. T-Roy killed on a qualifying run at Bristol after four years on the track, shattered those dreams of Thomas Leroy LeCorre. He had never won a race.

Jamie was suddenly, against her father's wishes, shoved into a car and told to race, while her brother lay dying in the hospital. Up to that, point Buster LeCorre had ignored her while she secured a license, driving under T-Roy's tutelage in the Busch races. Since she went in as a substitute driver, she had to start in the twenty-sixth position. She surprised herself by finishing eighth. At the end of the four hour race, T-Roy was dead, the crew chief detested her, and their sponsor threatened to drop them if Jamie didn't continue to drive.

Pink Mink International, the sponsor, published notorious men's magazines, sold risqué outfits for women, and reportedly was involved in a number of other illicit activities that kept them regular visitors in court. They insisted on supplying her with a BMW in the Pink Mink signature color, along with a full line of outrageous clothing and magnetic decals to display on her car. Jamie flatly refused to wear anything they made while in public, and the decals found a permanent home in her trunk.

* * * *

Saturday morning dawned to a cloudless perfect-wedding-day sky. The guests who weren't staying at the bride's home were put up in a local motel three miles away. There were only twelve units. The groom's brother and cousin shared one of them.

When the phone rang between the queen-sized beds, Virgil Douglas answered it. "Yeah, hello."

"Hi, sweetie, it's Cynthia."

"Sorry, this isn't sweetie, it's Virgil."

"Oh—well, you sure do sound a lot like your cousin. Is Quinton there?"

"Just a minute," Virgil yelled toward the bathroom, "Quint, Cindy's on the phone."

Quint Douglas appeared in the bathroom doorway, stripped to the waist, shaving cream half covering his face. He'd heard his ex-girlfriend's grating voice all the way across the room. "What the hell does she want?"

Grinning, Virgil put the phone back to his ear, obviously, intending to ask just that. Quint was there in an instant, snatching the phone out of Virgil's hand. He took a deep breath before putting the receiver to his ear.

"This is Quint. What's on your mind?

He didn't have to ask how she found him in a rural Minnesota town. The woman had an IQ that was off the charts and more connections than the New York City subway system. As a talk show host, she made three times the money he did, had the personality of a pit bull, and was possessive as hell.

"Sounds like you have a little attitude problem," she said.

"If you called to check on my attitude, it hasn't changed since the last time I talked to you."

"What is your problem, Quinton? We were doing just fine. I don't see why you didn't want me to come to your cousin's wedding, and I don't understand why you want to break off a good thing."

Quint grunted; *a good thing for you, not for* me. He was nothing more to the infamous Cynthia Harman than a dog on a leash—a short leash. "I thought we settled all this before I left New York."

"You can't just dump me. Nobody dumps Cynthia Harman."

"Well I guess that makes me nobody." Quint dropped the receiver in its cradle with a satisfactory *thunk*. He turned hostile blue eyes on his grinning cousin. "The next woman I date is going to be blonde, stupid, and docile with a face that's not recognized all over the frigging country. If I forget, remind me, will you?"

Virgil gave an unsympathetic bark of laughter. "I can

just hear Harman's next topic to air, *Foolish Men Who Dump Powerful Women.*"

Quint snorted. "It wouldn't surprise me at all. Where does she find those goons anyway?"

"You mean foolish men who dump powerful women?"

In spite of his anger, a grin kicked up on Quint's face. "You met her first. Why didn't you keep her?"

"She was a client. Lawyers don't date their clients. Besides, she goes for wide-shouldered, blue-eyed, athletic types. Plus, I'm five years older than you, and five years wiser."

"Maybe I'll quit going to the gym," Quint mumbled, heading back to the bathroom. He glanced at the fifteenth century, leather smock and tights they'd be wearing for the wedding that afternoon. "We can all be glad she didn't come along. She'd have a field day, gathering information for her next show, *Men Who Wear Tights.*"

"To be honest, I'd rather wear these getups than a monkey suit. Look on it as a once-in-a-lifetime experience." Virgil sighed. "Our brother is one lucky man to find a woman like Nicole."

Quint stepped out of the bathroom, drying his face. "I'll second that, but you seem to forget, I'm just a cousin."

Virgil laughed. "You've been a member of the family for—let's see—I was ten when you came to live with us— you've been around twenty-eight years. You're grandfathered in."

"Sounds like lawyer mumble-jumble to me," Quint said, chuckling. He pulled a New York Yankees T-shirt over his head and sat on the bed to slip into his sneakers. "How about we hunt up some breakfast. I saw a Ma-and-Pa café across the street."

Before Virgil could answer, the phone rang again.

Quint swore. "Tell her I'm not here. I'll wait outside for you." Shoving his T-shirt into his jeans, he stepped into the early morning, August sunlight before his cousin could object.

His eyes fell on a brilliant pink BMW with Illinois plates parked in front of the unit next door. The thing stuck out like a flamingo in a chicken yard. It had a flat front tire on the passenger side, and the trunk was open. A curvy blonde displayed a delightful view of her jean-clad tush while she ran her hands around the tire. It was the nicest tush he'd seen in a long while. What did she think she was doing, trying to caress it to life? She looked like a damsel in extreme distress to him. After Cynthia, a blonde bimbo looked pretty good.

"You're not going to get that thing changed by feeling it up," he said, thinking he wouldn't mind at all being felt up by her.

She straightened up to a full five-feet-four inches and turned to face him. Her trim, little, cropped knit shirt matched the color of her car and hugged her softly curving breasts, leaving a slim waist, including belly button, exposed. Her jean cut-offs were short to the point of being sinful. She had a sensually pouty mouth and hostile amber eyes.

"Who the hell asked you?"

So much for the damsel-in-distress theory. An ill-concealed grin played on his lips. "Just thought you might need a man's help about now."

"Shove it."

Quint leaned back against his own car, folded his arms over his chest, and settled back to watch her. "I seriously doubt you'll find a AAA service within fifty miles…but suit yourself."

She ignored him.

He didn't notice her bandaged knee until she grabbed a crutch leaning against the car and used it to hobble to the trunk. A small pang of guilt shot through him—a pitifully small pang. He could have been a little more tactful when he'd offered to help, but damned, if he'd make another offer just to give her the opportunity to shoot him down again.

She pulled a small jack out of the trunk and positioned it under the car with amazing, nonchalant ease. Next, she lifted the dummy tire out, rolled it over, and let it drop beside the jack. He waited for her to ask for help, but she seemed determined to manage on her own. Too stubborn to be sensible, he decided—no skin off his back. With a car and body like that, she probably had a sugar daddy lurking about somewhere. He didn't know they even made cars that color, much less in a BMW. It had to be a special order.

She was loosening the lug nuts when Virgil stepped out of the motel. Virgil looked from the girl to Quint with a curious frown. Quint thought about warning him, but decided, instead, to stand back and watch the fun.

"Would you like some help with that?" Virgil asked.

"I'd appreciate it," she said in a sweet voice, handing him the tire tool.

She limped to the trunk and brought out a rag to wipe her hands. By the time she came back, Virgil had lifted the spare into place. Nursing his bruised vanity, Quint watched. When she glanced up at him with penetrating amber eyes, he expected her gaze to be antagonistic or smug but it was neither. In fact, if he didn't know better, he could have sworn it was sensual. He shook that thought off in a hurry. Obviously, his imagination worked overtime.

Virgil interrupted his thoughts. "Put that in the trunk for me, would you, Quint." Virgil nodded toward the flat as he lowered the jack.

Her wide gaze darted from Virgil to Quint as though just realizing they were together. Quint's first instinct was to refuse Virgil's request, but that seemed a bit juvenile. He bent down, picked up the tire, and carried it to the trunk. She looked like she wanted to object, but there was little she could do short of wrestling the tire out of his hands. She hopped ahead of him on one foot to re-arrange things in the trunk. Quint got a glimpse of two large Pink Mink decals before she was able to cover them. What in the devil was a Chicago Pink Mink doing in small-town Minnesota?

She waited for Virgil to put the jack in the trunk, slammed it shut, and got in her car, mumbling a curt "thank you" over her shoulder.

Quint and Virgil stood on the curb watching her drive away.

"Did you recognize her?" Virgil asked.

Quint stared at his cousin. "No. Should I have?"

"She was the Pink Mink centerfold about a year ago."

"Hot damn!" Quint said. "I've heard that magazine is nothing more than a front for high class hookers. No wonder she can afford a fifty-thousand-dollar car. I wouldn't mind seeing that body nude."

"She wasn't nude. If I remember right, she was wearing some kind of a racing get-up and was sprawled across the top of a race car."

"That's odd. Centerfolds are always nude. What did the article say about her?"

Virgil chuckled. "Those pictures come with articles?"

About the Author

Born and raised on a North Dakota farm, Jannifer started writing at the age of twelve, creating novels by memory while walking home from a one-room schoolhouse. After moving to Minnesota she began serious writing in 1974 while working full time. She has since retired and spends summers in Minnesota and migrates with the birds to Yuma, Arizona for the winter.

When she's not writing, she's sewing for craft shows, painting rocks, and pursuing her favorite pastime—traveling the world on a cruise ship. And, last but not least, spending valuable time with her incredibly awesome family.

She is currently working on her sixth novel, Blood Crystal.

Learn more at: www.janniferhoffman.com

Also Available from Resplendence Publishing:

A Perfect Escape by Maddie James

A changed identity. A secluded beach. A sniper…

Megan Thomas is running for her life. From Chicago, from the mob, from her husband. She runs to the only place she feels safe—a secluded cottage on an east coast barrier island.

Smyth Parker is running from life. From work, from society, from a jealous ex-wife—his only consolation the solitude of Newport Island. He doesn't need to anyone to screw up that plan. And he sure as hell doesn't need to complicate it with Megan Thomas.

But when Megan fears she's been found, she runs to the only safe place she knows, and straight into the arms of the one person who might be able to help, Smyth. Her escape might yet still be perfect.

Or is it?

$6.50 e-book
$15.99 print

Brilliant Disguise by JL Wilson

An undercover FBI agent in a tiny Iowa town finds you can't hide anything from a woman who's determined to find out the truth...

Nick Baxter, an undercover FBI agent, thinks his brilliant disguise will fool the hicks in New Providence, Iowa. They won't suspect he's there investigating widow Shannon Delgardie, under suspicion of treason. What Nick doesn't know is that everybody in town is conspiring to protect her and investigate him in return.

Shannon needs help. The men her late husband blackmailed are closing in and the FBI might be involved. When Nick approaches her, can she trust him? With the aid of computer hackers and hair stylists, she uncovers the truth, finding a love she never expected in a tiny Iowa town.

$6.50 e-book
$15.99 print

Project Seduction by **Tatiana March**

Project Manager: Georgina Coleman, VP at Pacific Bank, 28 years old. Brilliant and determined, but lacking in social skills.

Project background: Transfer from London to San Diego allows Georgina to shed her dowdy image and get a life.

Project objective: Seduce a man and lose her virginity.

Timeline: Seven weeks, starting from the completion of Project Flowchart.

Target: Georgina's downstairs neighbor, a surly cop named Rick Matisse.

Complication: Rick's 12-year-old daughter Angelina, who thinks Georgina would be the perfect girlfriend to keep Dad on his toes.

Distraction: Money laundering investigation which requires Georgina to mingle with a bunch of Colombian thugs who believe that every woman should be owned by a man.

Project evaluation: A project can go wrong despite successful completion, if Project Manager fails to plan for how to deal with the Target after project closure.

$6.50 e-book
$14.99 print

Find Resplendence Titles at the following retailers:

Resplendence Publishing:

www.resplendencepublishing.com

Amazon.com:

www.amazon.com

Target.com:

www.target.com

Fictionwise:

www.fictionwise.com

Mobipocket:

www.mobipocket.com